# A Butterfly in Winter

### A Love Story

# Alene Roberts

This is a work of fiction. All characters are fictional and any resemblance to persons living or dead is purely coincidental.

This book is not an official publication of The Church of Jesus Christ of Latter-day Saints. All opinions expressed herein are the author's and are not necessarily those of the publisher or of The Church of Jesus Christ of Latter-day Saints.

Published and Distributed by:

Granite Publishing and Distribution, L.L.C.
868 North 1430 West • Orem, UT 84057
(801) 229-9023 • Toll Free (800) 574-5779
FAX (801) 229-1924

First Printing;    February 2000
Second Printing;   March 2000
Third Printing;    June 2000

Cover Art and Design by: Tamara Ingram
Page Layout and Design by: www.SunriseBooks.com

ISBN: 1-890558-87-7
Library of Congress Catalog Card Number: 00-100953

# Other Titles

## by

## Alene Roberts

### A Rescued Heart; A Modern Old-fashioned Love Story

Delightful, humorous and romantic. Dilladora Dobson, the lonely, twenty-seven-year-old heroine, is convinced she will never find a man with the qualities of her beloved Uncle Obadiah who helped raise her. This strong-willed young woman, like a golden sunflower reaching for the sun, has planned an active, full life for herself, unencumbered by the complications of inferior members of the male sex.

Unfortunately, this same willfulness and tendency to act and speak her mind any time, any place for the cause of right, has landed her in several scrapes, including the scare of a threatened kidnapping.

A witty, clever, battle of the sexes, an up and down adventure which deftly inserts its message of "manners and morals" along with the laughs.

This novel should be read and enjoyed by both men and women—a page turner for both.

### Fragrance of Lilacs; A Love Story

This is the story of Torry Anderson, a grieving, deeply religious LDS widow, whose husbands leaves behind a heart wrenching mystery.

Feeling compelled to leave her home in Denver, she relocates to a small rural community in Utah. There, Torry meets temporary resident David Mayer, a Jewish man from Dallas, Texas, when she enters his bank to apply for a business loan.

David is immediately drawn to this beautiful woman, who looks far too young to have two returned missionary sons in college.

Torry who is in turn, feisty and confident, wary and vulnerable; and David, a wealthy and successful man of both principle and compassion, seem an unlikely match.

Alternately laughing and crying, women of all ages will find themselves drawn into the highly charged drama of Torry and David; both hiding their own emotional wounds in a story that moves to a gripping climax.

# Acknowledgments

My thanks and appreciation to the following:

Shirley Redd and Rayma Atkinson for their unknowing inspiration for parts of this book.

The office of the Attorney General of Texas. The State of Texas Law Library. The employees of the George L. Allen Sr. Courts Building in Dallas. Hal Turley, Attorney at Law. And, once again, to all of those who are a part of and work for Granite Publishing.

# *Dedication*

To the memory of my gentle mother,
who never saw my faults, and always
thought I was perfect.

# Chapter One

Monday morning, May 10th, in a Dallas district courtroom, Judge Wicken rendered her verdict with a harsh coldness that sent chills through the lone spectator on the last row.

Triumphant squeals from the defendant's table and the row of women behind her were a strident contrast to the man who had initiated the petition. Slumped over, elbows on the table, fists pressing into his forehead, he groaned.

As the celebrating crowd gathered around the defendant and slowly began moving down the aisle toward the now open courtroom doors, the back row spectator, dressed in a T shirt and jeans, pulled the canvas hat down further covering more of her short dark hair. Instinctively adjusting the dark glasses, worn to hide her identity, she watched the attorney for the defendant snap shut her briefcase and with a smile of triumph turn to follow the departing group. Ducking her head, pretending to look for something in her purse, the spectator waited for the courtroom to clear.

Relieved that she hadn't been recognized, the woman glanced up as the man who had filed the petition slowly rose from his chair and moved unsteadily in her direction. Grief etched deeply into his face, neither he nor his attorney gave her so much as a glance.

With the last of the stragglers ushered out, the bailiff turned toward the woman. "Ma'am, we need to clear the court room."

The young woman took off her glasses and nodded. "Give me five minutes, Larry, will you?"

The look of surprised recognition on his face was soon replaced by one of rancor. "Okay...five...ten, have it your way Ms McBride, you usually do anyway."

Before she could reply he was out, closing the doors, leaving her alone, the wake of his antagonism hanging heavily in the air.

A strange feeling came over her—a feeling she hadn't felt for years, but often had as a child. She felt as ugly as her name—Agnes. Suddenly, a flash of memory took her back in time.

*"Agnes Bagnes, baggy pants Agnes!" came the taunt. Then the taunt would change, "Baggy, baggy, saggy pants Aggie!"*

*Aggie whirled around and started chasing her tormentors as fast as she could. The oversized hand-me-down jeans, rolled up to fit her short legs and tied at the waist with an old grosgrain ribbon, almost tripped her as one pant leg came unrolled. Tears of frustration blinded her as the other pant leg unrolled, sending her flying face down into the hot Texas dirt, choking her. She could hear the laughter of the girls... "Baggy, baggy, saggy pants Aggie!" Kneeling, she rocked back on her heels and coughed out the dust, fiercely wiping away tears, making muddy smudges across her face. She watched the prissy little cowards, dressed in their fancy jeans, run around the corner and out of sight. Her heart banged against ribs that Mama said poked out too much.*

AGNES McBride shook her head. How odd. Why had she remembered *that*—now—at this particular moment? For whatever reason, it added to the feeling of depression produced by the events in the courtroom.

Putting the dark glasses back on, she scooted to the aisle and stepped quickly to the closed doors. Opening one slightly, she saw Sybil Martin, the attorney from her law firm, who had just won the case. She was surrounded by reporters. Shutting the door quickly, Agnes McBride walked to an exit near the judge's chamber, and on out through a maze of halls to the underground parking of the George Allen Courts Building. Today—unlike her usual routine—she had driven directly from her home to the hearing.

Stepping up into her slightly battered, secondhand van, she pulled out her cell phone and dialed. A slow, somewhat gravely, Texas drawl came over the line. "Barry Slocum Detective Agency."

"Barry, Aggie."

"You're back in town?"

"I am. I just came from the courtroom. I need to talk to you as soon as possible."

"I'm free if you can come over to the office now, Aggie."

"I'll be there in ten minutes."

She started the motor and drove out onto Commerce street, then turned left on Lamar. The downtown traffic today was more congested than usual, exacerbating Aggie's mood. She arrived at the parking lot both she and Barry used since their offices were in the same old red brick building just off Pacific Avenue. Near the area known as the old warehouse district, it, too, was simply a renovated old warehouse. From one of Aggie's windows, she could see the light rail line which brought passengers into the popular West End Market District. Aggie had chosen this building because the rent was cheaper and because it was just a few blocks from the district courthouse—within easy walking distance.

She ran up the steps of the well-kept old building and strode quickly under the overhang to the door on the right. Stepping inside, her footsteps muffled by the worn gray carpet, she reached a door that said: SLOCUM DETECTIVE AGENCY. She opened it and saw Barry sitting at his cluttered old oak desk, the phone to his ear. He smiled, motioning her in.

Aggie stepped in and sat down on one of the two padded chairs which had faded to an indeterminate hue. She let out a sigh of relief. Barry's office always felt comfortable and safe. The carpet was the same gray as the hall. The book case, a solid relic of the late 1800's, was filled with out of print history books, FBI cases, famous criminal cases and a few recent law books. The pictures on the wall were of Abraham Lincoln, Barry's deceased wife and his grown children. An old Norman Rockwell calendar, dated 1984, hung next to the window behind him. Pictures of his grandchildren held the place of honor on his desk.

The only up-to-date things in his office were a computer, a laser printer and a fax machine. The small kitchenette in the next room contained an old microwave, a small refrigerator, a sink and a small table with two chairs where she and Barry discussed cases while drinking a hot or cold drink, depending on the weather. A door from the kitchenette led to a small room full of case files.

As always, Barry's office smelled like old books, eliciting memories of many happy childhood hours in the library; escaping into other worlds, happy places, exciting places, a world different than that in which she lived.

Four years ago, she walked into this office and hired Barry for one of her cases. Up until then, she had never really trusted a man. Even though Barry was hired and well respected by many lawyers whose offices were in the new high-rise downtown buildings, it was with trepidation that she first interviewed him.

She soon found out that Barry Slocum not only had many friends in high places, but friends in all walks of life as well. People trusted him. Often he could get information out of them before they knew they were giving it. Because of this, he had helped her with many cases, ferreting out dark secrets which frequently attended the kinds of cases that came to her as a lawyer for women's causes.

Aggie studied Barry's face as he talked on the phone. Middle-aged, there were only a few strands of brown hair to comb straight back over his balding head. Heavy folds of flesh accented the deep lines on each side of his mouth. His thick lips, upturned in perpetual optimism, his green eyes, always twinkling and warm, were set into a long oval face—a lovable face, Aggie thought.

Hanging up the phone, he raised his scraggly brows, leaned back in his chair and smiled as he studied the young woman before him. "What's up, Aggie?"

"It's Sybil. She took a case I told her not to touch. I've only been gone two weeks as you know, so she had to have pulled some important and powerful strings to get the hearing into court so quickly. I was totally unaware that she had those kinds of connections. It ended today with Judge Wicken presiding."

Barry leaned forward in his chair. "Uh-oh, tell me about it."

~~~~~~~~~

Lucas Barnes stepped up into his Ford Ranger and turned the key. The motor and the radio came to life.

*"...Sybil Martin of this law firm, told reporters that winning this unusual case of custody/abortion is a victory for women everywhere. The father of the unborn child had petitioned the court for a ruling preventing his wife, the mother, from having the abortion, asking instead that the court rule the baby be carried to full term and that he be*

*granted custody of the infant at birth. Judge Wicken, after hearing and reviewing the evidence of possible harm to the mother if she were to carry the baby to full term, ruled in favor of the defendant, the mother. The abortion will be performed..."*

Luke angrily flipped off the radio. "What the hell?!" Shoving the gear-shift into first, he rammed the gas pedal, spinning the wheels, throwing a spray of grass and soil into the air. The truck lurched forward for a short distance, then he roughly shoved it into second, bouncing over the range grass onto the graveled road.

"The poor loser who married that unfeeling, selfish..." Through practiced discipline, ingrained in him by his mother, he refrained from the name he felt would best describe her. "We're all losers...and I'm the biggest one of all! I married Lila," he muttered. The gall of bitterness welled up in his throat so palpable he could almost taste it. Grinding his teeth he fought back angry tears. Whenever he heard anything about abortion, he reacted violently, but today he felt emotional. Why? he wondered. Probably because he was back at the ranch.

He screeched to a stop in front of the house. Stepping out of the truck, his tall rangy figure strode quickly to the wrap-around porch of the rambling house. He stood on the threshold of this place, once known as the King Barnes' ranch house, thinking how transient life was. And how rotten!

As he stepped inside, a deep loneliness engulfed him. Shoving his hands into the pockets of his jeans, his shoulders slumped. Aimlessly moving around the room, he ended up in front of the big stone fireplace staring at the center picture on the mantle, his parents, King and Ann Barnes. Abruptly turning away, he went over to the piano where his mother used to sit and play, filling the house with more than beautiful notes. She filled everyone's life with the music of her selfless love. He sat down on the piano bench. Leaning his elbows on the closed key board, he groaned.

"Mother, why did you have to go? I need to talk to you."

It seemed like only yesterday that his father, the invincible King Barnes, took his mother up in their light plane, a Cessna 150, and crashed, killing them both. It happened five years ago and he still had bouts of grief over it. Today was one of them.

"You and Dad were too young to die!"

Restlessness took him back to the mantle of the fireplace where he studied the other pictures. On the far right was a picture of his grandparents, Isaac McHulloh Barnes and Mae Downing Barnes. Isaac Barnes passed away when his father was only three, leaving his huge ranch east of Austin, Texas to his wife, Mae Barnes, who continued to run the ranch—and her only son, King Barnes. Mae Barnes, the powerful and dominating matriarch of the Barnes family, was living and still a force to be reckoned with.

In between his parents and grandparents was a family picture of his father, mother, himself and Amy, his younger and only sibling. He missed Amy. She lived in Pennsylvania with her husband, Ron, and their four children.

On the far left of the mantle, were pictures of his mother's parents, one of his mother and her only sister Edie, and near the center, one of himself, Amy and Doris. Doris was Aunt Edie's only daughter and his first cousin. Grandmother Barnes allowed Edie's husband Jim Russell and their two sons to work on the ranch when Jim lost his job.

Luke remembered how close he and his cousin, Doris, became, especially when he, Amy and Doris were teenagers. They attended dances and parties together, gathering groups around them and soon everyone group-dated.

Doris—he knew he could talk to Doris. He sat down on the big leather couch, stretched out his long legs and leaned his head back against his hands, thinking. He knew his sister, Amy, had worried about him ever since their parents were killed. He'd learned that she had asked Doris to look after him. Luke smiled. Though Doris and Amy were a year younger, they both mothered him. However, Doris could do it a little easier since she lived in Dallas.

Immediately after his divorce three months ago, Luke confided in Amy *why* he divorced Lila after only one year of marriage. He then told Doris about the divorce, but didn't tell her why. Luke asked Amy not to tell Doris, explaining that he wanted to tell her himself. He hadn't as yet. He couldn't bring himself to talk about it anymore—but he owed it to Doris. Soon, he promised himself, he'd go see her and Bob and tell them face to face.

# Chapter Two

Black clouds were gathering as Aggie left Barry's office at 3:00 P.M., making it almost dark as night. She quickly walked down the hall to the door and stepped outside to look. The muggy May air was heavy and still—tornado weather. Aggie weighed her options. She needed to check in with Sally and get some things done at the office just on the other side of this building, but Sybil would probably be there. Not trusting herself to meet with her just yet, she decided to go on home and try to get her head together—and her emotions under control.

She ran out through the parking lot to her van, unlocked it and got in, studying the black sky again. Starting the van, she drove out of the lot, turned onto Griffen and wove her way north to Cedar Springs Road. Flipping on the radio to check the weather, she heard the newscaster announce a tornado *watch* for Dallas County and a tornado *warning* for Tarrant County. Aggie loved Texas thunderstorms, but tornado weather frightened her. The announcer broke in on her thoughts...

*"The law firm of Agnes McBride has just won another case, perhaps its most controversial case yet. Sybil Martin, of that firm, was the attorney for the defendant who was seeking an abortion. The husband was petitioning the court to rule that the abortion be denied, claiming his wife was healthy and just didn't want the baby. He was asking for full custody of the baby at birth. Judge Wicken, after hearing testimony and reviewing the medical records, ruled in favor of the wife. Names are being withheld at the request of the heartbroken husband who left the courthouse today in tears, covering his face as he pushed through the reporters. Sybil Martin, all smiles, told the reporters that this was a victory for all women and..."*

Aggie flipped off the radio her mouth tightening in anger, painfully aware that the policy of the firm—the kinds of cases they would or would not take—should have been tightened up long ago.

Since the day she decided, as a freshman at SMU in Dallas, to become a lawyer, she had never wavered—her goals, her direction had remained clear. At least they had until about two years ago. Gradually, she began to see things in a different light. This change in herself was unsettling—she began to reevaluate some of her deepest feelings. Uncertainty had replaced conviction. The immediate reaction had been to throw herself more completely into her work—keeping herself too exhausted to think, to analyze—to make any painful decisions.

Her health had begun to deteriorate. Emotional turmoil combined with exhaustion diminished her zest for life—for 'the cause.' Thus, she had put off making the necessary changes in her firm—until it was too late.

Aggie McBride, one who never darkened a doctor's door did so three months ago. The doctor pronounced her in good health. She went to another one, who also reiterated that she was in good shape physically.

She began haunting the health food stores for vitamins and strange concoctions the clerks claimed would give one energy. Only a slight improvement came. Finally, her friend, Doris, insisted she try Dr. Davis, an internal specialist. Out of desperation she made an appointment. Soon, she found herself sitting in the doctor's office answering question after question while he jotted down notes.

He mused for a while as he considered all her answers, then announced, "Miss McBride, you are suffering from depression."

She stared at him in shock. "And what makes you a psychiatrist, Dr. Davis?"

"I'm not on the stand Ms. McBride, so save your courtroom interrogation."

"You aren't going to give me any tests? You're going to make a diagnosis just like that?"

"I can give all the tests you want. I can put you in the hospital and give you more tests, but the diagnosis will be the same."

"And what do you propose I do about this alleged depression?"

"My prescription is: walk for thirty minutes each day."

Aggie scoffed, "I run every morning for forty minutes, so now what is your prescription, Dr. Davis, anti-depressants?"

Dr. Davis stood up; his smile held no warmth. "Find yourself another doctor."

A blaring horn from behind broke into her thoughts, bringing an abrupt awareness that she was going too slow. Easing into the right lane, she realized Cedar Springs had already become Turtle Creek Blvd. and that she was almost home. About four years ago, she had, at last, saved enough to put a down payment on a small condominium in this beautiful area of Turtle Creek. It was also fairly close to her office downtown.

As she drove into the underground parking of the condominium complex, she remained in the car remembering her great relief at finally being able to move out of the small, shabby apartment downtown on Leonard street. It wasn't a safe neighborhood, but then she was used to that. Her mother rented a small house in that general area when they moved from McKinney, at the beginning of her second year of junior high.

Aggie felt her good luck began when at the beginning of the first year of law practice, a friend—a motherly law professor, who expressed confidence in her ability—offered to lend her enough money to pay the first four months rent for the office. She continued working part-time as an assistant chef at a restaurant to pay it back and to help with other expenses. Though her office didn't smack of a highly successful lawyer, it was respectable. By haunting garage sales and second hand stores, she eventually found enough furniture to furnish it.

By the time her third year of practice rolled around, she found that most of the clients who came to her still couldn't pay very much, some not at all, a few she was able to put on a payment plan. But that same year her luck held. The father of one of her clients who also happened to be wealthy, paid her well and in addition gave her valuable financial advice. He suggested that she use some of the fee he'd paid her to invest in stock of a new high tech company that he, too, had invested in. She took his advice and as it turned out, it was sound advice. The stock went up and split several times. The profit from the stock made it possible to save toward a new place to live and eventually quit the restaurant.

Still in the car, she realized the last thing she wanted to do was go up to her empty condo. She needed to talk to Doris! Picking up the cellular, she dialed the office first.

"Agnes McBride and Associates," the receptionist stated in a professional manner.

"Sally, this is Aggie. I told you this morning that I would be in this afternoon, but I've changed my mind. I won't be in for the rest of the day. Don't answer any questions from reporters. Hold all calls connected to Sybil's case and give them to me in the morning. You might suggest to everyone that they listen to the weather station and go home early if necessary, and that means you too, Sally."

"All right, I'll do that Aggie, thanks."

Next, she dialed Doris.

"Hello," came the cheery voice of her friend.

"Doris, this is Aggie. Can I come over and talk to you?"

"Of course. I kind of expected your call. I've been listening to the news."

"Thanks Dor, I'll see you shortly." Driving out of the parking area and back onto Turtle Creek Blvd., she turned north. She didn't know whether she was running from the tornado or from the storm she had created in her law firm.

The clouds seemed less black as she approached the area known as Highland Park. Swerving to the right slightly, she drove onto Preston road which soon brought her to Versailles Ave. where she turned left. Driving through the neighborhood of beautiful homes for a few blocks Aggie pulled into a circular driveway, feeling more at peace here at the lovely genteel home of Doris and Robert Biederman.

Getting out of the van, she walked to the wide porch, turned and stood for a minute, admiring the majestic oak trees that looked like sentinels, guarding the house on both sides. Their limbs, trimmed high, angled here and there in graceful beauty. Flower beds surrounded the bases of two impeccably trimmed live oak in the center of the yard.

A loud clap of thunder startled her. She smiled as she breathed in deeply the fragrant, humid air. Suddenly the sky opened up and rain came down in blinding sheets. Grateful to be under the eve of her friend's home, she felt safe from more than rain and tornadoes. The front door opened.

"Aggie! I saw you drive up and I've been waiting for the doorbell."

"Oh, hi Doris." She smiled and stepped inside. "I was admiring your front yard as usual."

"Come on into the kitchen, I have some of your favorite sherbet in the freezer."

Aggie's face lit up. "Thank you," she said, following Doris into the kitchen, "that's just what I need to cool me off—in more ways than one."

Aggie sat down at the table in Doris' cheery kitchen. "I feel better just being here, Dor, thanks. Where are the boys?"

"All three are visiting their grandfather and grandmother Biederman in Fort Worth for a day and then over to visit my parents for a day," Doris said, dishing out a bowl of sherbet for both of them.

"How nice for them."

"Yes, it is. I'm glad they're away today—because I have an idea I've been wanting to pass by you." Doris placed a bowl of sherbet in front of Aggie.

Aggie took a bite. "Mmm, this tastes good. Thank you. What idea?"

"First, tell me how you feel about Sybil getting a favorable ruling?"

"Angry, scared."

"What are you going to do about it?" Doris sat down at the table with her.

"I've already talked with Barry. I'm going to have him check on that so-called evidence Sybil came up with indicating health problems for the wife. They may be legitimate health concerns, but Sybil had to have access to powerful friends to get it in court before I returned. It makes me wonder where she got those kinds of connections."

"What if the evidence is on the level?"

"Regardless, I'm going to ask Sybil to leave the firm."

"Then you're going to make it a policy—no abortion cases?"

"It has always been my policy, in my own mind, that is. It's my fault for not making it clear before I hired each of the lawyers. Nevertheless, Sybil knew my feelings."

"Does the decision to investigate the health issue and fire Sybil make you feel better?" Doris watched her friend closely.

Aggie was silent, thinking. "It will ease my conscience, but only if I can find evidence that there is no medical reason for the abortion— and then if I can stop it. But feel better? Oh Doris..." She shoved the half eaten sherbet back, and placing her elbows on the table, she covered her face. Doris waited patiently, and finally Aggie removed her hands, cupped them under her chin and stared into space. "I don't know what I feel—I'm so tired."

"How many years have you been practicing law and fighting women's and children's abuse?"

"Eight, and I shouldn't feel this way—I'm only thirty-one."

"But, Aggie, stop and think; many of the cases you took the first four years were cases very few attorneys would accept, no win types, and women who were destitute and couldn't pay. Those years took their toll on you emotionally and financially. And don't forget that to survive during that time you wrote children's books in every spare minute as well as working at the restaurant."

"But Doris..."

"Oh, I know that the last four years, you've begun attracting cases from women all over the Metroplex, and even a few from Oklahoma, who could pay your fees and that you've made a little more money. But now that you're doing a little better financially, how are you doing emotionally?"

Aggie's curiosity was piqued. "Where is this all leading, Dor?"

"Well..." Doris knew she had to tread very carefully, "Bob and I have been concerned about you, Aggie, and we've bounced a couple of ideas around...uh...we...uh..."

"Doris, get to the point, I promise I won't bite."

"All right, you remember that promise. Bob and I were wondering if you would consider a leave of absence from your practice for—say six months."

Aggie was shocked. "And what would I do, pace the floor in my little condo?"

"You could spend the time writing."

"You can't be serious, Dor. I would go stir crazy there by myself. And besides, I couldn't afford to do just that."

"Well," Doris began, deciding ahead of time to purposely veer off the path a few times, "we've thought of several things. Bob and I have a cottage in Hawaii that you could use. You could lie out on the beach, relax, regroup—write."

Aggie laughed. "You and Bob have been busy, but you know me better than that, Dor, even in Hawaii I would go crazy being by myself. I need interaction with people now and then—and I still couldn't afford to do that. But thanks, I appreciate your offer and your concern."

Doris was pleased. She had expected all these objections. She had discussed the idea thoroughly with Bob who said to her one evening, "It probably won't work, Doris Ann, but you might as well give it a try. You won't rest until you do—just make sure the moment is right."

Doris felt this was the right moment. Aggie was so darn clever and bright, she had to be cautious. Taking another wrong path she asked, "You've thought of opening a restaurant on the side, remember?"

"That was quite a while ago when I wasn't feeling so exhausted."

"Maybe your exhaustion would disappear if you did something else for a while?"

I love to cook, as you know, but just cooking a plain meal for myself right now is almost too much."

"Why do you think that is, Aggie?"

"According to your Dr. Davis, I'm an emotional wreck."

"Could he be right about you suffering from depression?"

"I didn't want to even consider it at first, it seemed like such a ridiculous diagnosis, but I've been going to the library and reading up on depression. Apparently it manifests itself in many ways—ways that don't even seem like depression. I suppose I could be."

"Does it make sense to take a small leave of absence at this time?"

Aggie sighed. "It makes sense, but I can't leave my practice and even if I could, what would I do with myself and where would I get the funds?"

Doris held her breath. This was the moment to lead Aggie in the right direction—to *the* idea.

"Let me think a minute..." Doris began, pretending to come up with the idea spontaneously. After a moment or two, she said slowly, "This probably won't work, but—Bob and I have a friend, a slightly older man, who lives in Austin. Some time ago, he asked me if I knew of a cook he could hire to prepare only one meal a day—dinner at night. I told him I would like to find one for myself, but if I heard of anyone who wouldn't mind moving there, I would let him know. He divorced his wife and he can't cook."

"The poor man," Aggie said with sarcasm.

"Aggie, don't judge this man," Doris stated defensively.

"Don't get your ire up, Dor, I didn't know he was that close a friend...sorry."

"Do you want me to go on?"

"Is there more?"

"Just a few details. Behind his home, there's a small cottage, where, he said, the cook could live. He'll pay two thousand a month plus board and room. He could hire some one for less, but he likes gourmet cooking and he likes to entertain some. A Mexican woman, who has lived with his family for years, oversees the cleaning and has an apartment in the main house."

"Well, I wish him luck."

Doris sighed. "I guess that wasn't such a hot idea."

"Nope."

"Well, you come up with one, Aggie."

"I'm too tired."

They sat in silence for several moments, then Doris added the final touches. "Wait a minute, Aggie, maybe it isn't such a dumb idea."

"Why?"

"If this friend—his name is Lucas Barnes. If Lucas would go along with the idea of letting you take a breather there for only six months, you could cook, and still have time to write *and* be with people." There—it was all out. Doris knew if Aggie were to go for it, the seed would have to germinate a while.

Aggie was silent, thinking.

Doris knew the only way she could get Aggie to even consider it, was to mislead her about Luke's age and hide the fact that he was her first cousin. She had told Bob that these weren't lies—after all Luke *was* older than Aggie. He was thirty two—and, even though he was her cousin, she and Luke were close *friends*. When Bob shook his head over this, she had protested, "But, Bob, I love Luke like a brother and I love Aggie. It can't do any harm. Nothing may come of it but an employer/employee relationship, but Aggie will have had a rest and Luke will have enjoyed some wonderful cooking for a while."

Aggie broke into her thoughts. "Actually, that is not a bad idea, Dor, in fact it's a pretty good one, I'll have to admit, but no thanks. I'm going to have to get hold of myself without running away."

"What is that advice you give the women who are being abused by their husbands? I think you said something like, 'Putting your own physical and emotional welfare first is the only way you'll be able to serve those you love. It is an intelligent and responsible act and should never be called—running away.'"

"I don't have a husband who is abusing me," Aggie grinned, hedging.

"All right, Aggie, I'm out of ideas. It's up to you now. If you change your mind about cooking for Lucas Barnes, let me know. He may have hired someone by now anyway. Would you like me to call him and check?"

Aggie smiled affectionately at Doris. "My friend, you never give up."

"Yes I do. I'm giving up right after I say one more thing. You're burned out, Aggie. You've given so much of yourself, you need to replenish. If you don't like my idea, consider something else. Now, that's all I'm going to say on the subject."

"Well..." came a deep voice from the doorway of the kitchen. "If it isn't the odd couple—the rabid feminist and the rabid anti-feminist."

"Bob, you're home early." Doris went over to him and put her arms around him.

He kissed his wife. "Hi, Sweetheart."

Aggie watched her friends, and, as always, she was impressed with the love they felt for each other. Bob was tall and lean, with light brown hair. His clean-cut features were sharp, but pleasant and lit up when he smiled—which was often. Doris was also slim and tall. Her blonde hair, short and stylish, enhanced her warm blue eyes. To Aggie, Doris was beautiful both inside and out.

Looking over at their guest, Bob said, "Hi, Aggie, how are you?"

"Today I *am* rabid, Bob, I may bite."

"I heard the news on the radio. I take it congratulations are not in order."

"No, they are not!"

"Bob, I tried our idea out on Aggie about taking a leave of absence from her practice for a few months," interjected Doris.

"Oh?" His eyes met Doris', then riveted on Aggie. "And..?" he questioned, "how did the stubborn little lady react?"

"Stubbornly," stated Aggie, with a small defiant grin on her face.

"Ah, that's a good non-committal answer. Didn't I tell you, Doris Ann, that she wouldn't go for it? Didn't I tell you she's a workaholic and wouldn't take time out to be—a woman?"

"A woman?" Aggie raised her eyebrows innocently.

"Yeah," he said grinning, "you know, one of those feminine, nurturing creatures, rather than a hard biting, tough attorney, working in a man's world."

"Hmm, whose rabid around here anyway?" Aggie asked, throwing her wadded up napkin at him. "Bob Biederman, you are a rabid sexist."

Putting his arm up in mock protection, he edged to the door, "I'm getting out of here while I still have my head."

Doris winced inside. Bob and Aggie always went at it like this, each serious about the things they said in a kidding manner. A dangerous habit for friends to indulge in, she felt. The sincere affection between the two seemed to keep them from hurting each other—but still, there was always a first.

Upstairs in the bedroom, Bob Biederman wrenched off his tie, threw it on the bed and heaved a sigh, grateful to get his suit and tie off on this muggy day.

As he undressed and put on casual clothes, he thought of Aggie and the outcome of the case. He felt more concern over it than he let on. The Metroplex was part of the Bible belt. Some of the journalists, not to mention the letters to the editor, would make mincemeat of Aggie.

His mind went back to the first day he met Agnes McBride. Two-and-a-half years ago a family friend asked him to take her spouse abuse case. He had explained to her that he would be out of his depth since he was only a corporate lawyer. She told him she wouldn't take it to court then because she didn't trust anyone else. Knowing the seriousness of her situation, he finally agreed to do it, but only on the condition he could counsel with an attorney who specialized in these kinds of cases. She gratefully agreed.

The first attorney who came to mind was Agnes McBride, better known throughout the Metroplex as "The Iron Butterfly." He had read about her cases in the newspaper through the years and felt mixed emotions. His heart went out to abused women and children and was glad that someone like Agnes McBride was fighting their battles. However, the feminists seemed to gather at court once in a while during certain of her cases, leaving him feeling slightly suspicious. Nevertheless, her success rate spoke well for her ability, so he called her.

He remembered his shock when she stepped into his office that first day. She looked like a teenager, no more than eighteen! She was only five feet three inches tall, very slender with eyes almost too large for her face. He had read in the paper that unlike her female peers, tailored business clothes were far from her style. Seeing her in person, he understood why the press had nicknamed her "The Iron Butterfly" Her look of femininity, glamour and youthful innocence was deceptive. She was brilliant, tough and an avowed feminist.

He was prepared to dislike Agnes McBride, but to his surprise, he found her disarmingly sincere and straightforward.

The feminists he'd known were hostile and defensive. Aggie McBride was neither. However, one thing she did have in common with the other women was that she distrusted men in general. She helped him with the case and they won it. To Bob's surprise, she refused any kind of remuneration because he was doing it for a friend.

When he went home and told Doris, she insisted on inviting Aggie to dinner to show her their appreciation. The minute Doris and Aggie met, they hit if off and soon became close friends. Bob found this odd. They were so different in every way—even physically. Aggie was short and dark haired; his lovely Doris was tall and blonde. Also Doris was the epitome of womanhood and a rather vocal anti-feminist—yet, as Doris put it, she and Aggie were 'kindred spirits.'

When Bob walked back into the kitchen, he saw his wife preparing dinner and Aggie padding around in stocking feet, helping her.

"I see you're staying for dinner, Aggie."

"Yes and you may have me all night if this weather keeps up."

Bob stepped over to the window and saw the fierce, shearing wind blowing torrents of rain in onto the covered patio.

~~~~~~~~~

Doris stood on the front porch after an early dinner and waved goodbye to Aggie, who had taken advantage of a lull in the weather.

Lightning lit up the sky and loud thunderclaps followed. Doris studied her flowers, sighing over the beating they'd already taken.

Looking at her watch, she saw that it was only 5:15. Maybe she could catch Luke. He said he was going to the ranch for several days. She sat down at the kitchen table and dialed.

"Luke Barnes speaking," came the voice low and abrupt.

Doris frowned. He was in one of those snarly moods that began shortly after his marriage to Lila, and had become worse since the divorce.

"What's the matter, Luke?" Doris asked without a greeting.

"Doris!" He sounded relieved. "I've been thinking about you."

"Oh? What have you been thinking?"

"That I need to get to Dallas and visit you and Bob and see the boys."

"Good. When are you coming?"

"Oh, maybe in a month or so."

"When are you returning to Austin?"

"Tonight, but I may not survive another week of beans and tamales. Where's that cook you promised me?"

"Now, Luke, you know I didn't promise. But I need to find out if you would be amenable to the idea of hiring her for only six months?"

"Why?"

"Well, I think it would be a good idea if you both try a short term arrangement just in case you aren't happy with her and in case she isn't happy cooking for you."

Luke was silent a moment. "I believe you may be right. I've been toying with the idea of selling the house in Austin. As you know I built it for Lila. Actually, Doris, I feel restless and at loose ends. I don't know what I want to do, so it's probably best to give it a try for just six months."

"Good. I talked to Agnes McBride this afternoon and she's thinking about it. If she decides to take the job, it will take some time for her to wind things up here. But I do promise—if she decides to take your offer, she's worth waiting for."

# Chapter Three

Aggie woke up promptly at 5:00 A.M., a habit acquired from years of training herself to do so. A night person by nature, she learned, through hard knocks, that the world runs on a morning schedule.

Her early routine consisted of getting out of bed immediately, dressing in running gear, then, as she had informed Dr. Davis, jogging for forty minutes. However, this morning, as usual, she felt almost as tired as she did when she went to bed the night before.

"What's the use of jogging, it's not helping me," she muttered aloud. So giving into her weariness, she lay there thinking.

She made one firm decision while driving home last night. The right perspective always seemed to come into sharp focus whenever she visited Doris. She decided to fire Sybil today and give her the small severance pay as stipulated in the contract.

Suddenly the realization that she should have taken care of something last night, drove Aggie out of bed. She should have gone over Sybil's file the minute Sybil brought it back to the office after the hearing. If I'm lucky, the tornado watch may have sent them all home early.

Aggie arrived at work long before anyone else. Fearful that Sybil would edit the information on the case before filing it, Aggie went directly to Sybil's office. Breathing a sigh of relief she saw that Sybil had left the case file lying on her desk. Aggie quickly faxed a copy of everything in it to Barry and said another prayer that he would find some evidence making it possible to stop the abortion—that is, if the health of the mother was not in jeopardy.

Later that morning at 9:00 Aggie heard a tap on her office door.

"Yes...come in."

Sybil Martin stood in the doorway looking nervous. "Hello, Aggie...uh...when did you get back?"

Aggie stared at her a moment then resumed working on something at her desk, ignoring the question.

Sybil walked in. "Sally said you wanted to see me?" she asked tentatively.

Making her stand before the desk and wait while she appeared to finish something, Aggie observed covertly Sybil's left hand, the thumb nail clicking the nail of the fourth. A nervous habit she'd seen often.

Slowly, Aggie lifted her head and gazed at her steadily, "Yes."

Sybil's eyes flickered. "What do you want to see me about, Aggie?"

Aggie looked down and returned to her work, "I'm giving you severance pay as stated in the contract. As of today, you're through. Clean out your office as soon as you can."

"What?!"

Still appearing preoccupied with the work on the desk, Aggie asked, "Do you need a hearing aid..." then looking up she continued, "as well as a *memory* check, Sybil?"

Sybil's mouth opened, her jaw working... "B..but..."

"Excuse me, Sybil, but I'm very busy. I'll leave a check with Sally for you. Pick it up after you've cleaned out your office."

Sybil knew she was no match for Aggie McBride. Turning abruptly, she clipped out of the office, her face hot with anger.

Aggie heaved a sigh through tight lips, relieved it was over—the first round, that is. She knew there would be another.

A tiredness swept over her. Putting her elbows on the desk, hands clasped under her chin, she stared into space, remembering the bounce of Sybil's gorgeous blonde hair as she retreated from the room. Odd—it reminded her of Gayle Harrington's hair on that first day of junior high in McKinney, Texas.

*August 25, 1980: Aggie found herself sitting in the desk behind Gayle looking at her long, shiny and carefully curled, blonde hair. She fingered her own thick, unruly hair that was pulled back tightly into a pony tail with an old rubber band.*

YANKING herself back to the here and now, Aggie wondered again why her mind was slipping back to the past these last two days. For whatever reason, it felt like some kind of a catharsis to her soul, and though she didn't understand, it seemed to have something to do with the hearing yesterday. She thought about this a moment. Something inside told her it was *vital* to go over her life and the events that brought her to this point—the point where her firm might be responsible for the needless death of an unborn child! She shivered in horror. What would Mama and Beth think if they were alive?

Aggie remembered when her sister, Beth, came home from school one day and related what her friend, Leslie, had told her in secrecy. Leslie had told Beth that she'd had an abortion. Aggie, twelve and in the seventh grade, knew the facts of life, but still did not understand. It was then that Mama sat her and Beth down and carefully explained about the development of a baby in the womb and of the miracle of birth.

*September, 1980: The fervent and intense expression in their mother's eyes got Aggie and Beth's attention immediately. "I want you girls to know that a small fetus is a baby in the eyes of God—that it is a sacred trust to care for as you would if it were fully matured and born."*

*They watched their mother get out the Bible, as she often did. She read to them from Genesis about God commanding Adam and Eve to multiply and replenish the earth.*

*"But Mama," Beth protested, "Leslie isn't married."*

*All of a sudden it was Mama's words that multiplied. Martha McBride, quiet and taciturn, was a woman of few words. A student of the Bible, Martha had read it to her daughters and taught them its principles, but only in a concise sentence or two. The words that rushed out of Mama that day were so astounding, Aggie knew she'd never forget them.*

*Aggie and Beth sat there, their mouths open, their eyes wide. Not only had they never heard a long speech from Mama, but never had she expressed so much emotion. She related horrific facts from the Old Testament—relating them to the present day!*

*"Aggie and Beth, listen to me and listen carefully. Moses led the Israelites through the wilderness. When they came to the land of their inheritance, they found that cities already occupied that land. What do you think God did about this?"*

*Aggie and Beth, their eyes still wide, looked at each other and then at their mother, shrugging their shoulders, wondering why in the world she was talking about Moses and the Israelite's land of inheritance.*

*Their mother answered the unspoken question. "He told Moses and the Israelites to destroy the people in the cities—to destroy every breathing thing."*

*"Why?" asked Aggie, shocked that God would command such a thing.*

*"Because those cities had become so wicked they worshiped idols—Satan, in other words. And they sacrificed people to these idols." The expression on Mama's face became so grim, Aggie held her breath. "They even sacrificed their own children!"*

*"They killed their own children?" gasped Beth.*

*"Yes. This had become their way of life; they sacrificed their children. Today, women and young girls are sacrificing their unborn children to their idols. Idols of materialism, idols of convenience, idols of selfishness. Abortion today—is sacrifice of children to idols. Someday, God in his wrath will take care of it in His own way."*

*Beth and Aggie sat there stunned, unable to say a word until, finally, Beth explained to her mother in hushed tones, "Leslie told me she was embarrassed about her pregnancy. She said that it would change her life if she had a baby."*

*"Boy, Leslie will sure receive hell and damnation, just like Preacher Jones says!" stated Aggie, adamantly. "Huh, Mama?"*

*Aggie wasn't prepared for Mama's indignant reprimand. "Aggie! We cannot judge Leslie. Don't ever judge others. God will do that."*

*"But Mama...."*

*"We can judge the sin, but not the person. Do you both hear me?"*

*They both nodded, struck mute at Mama's whole astonishing outburst.*

THE grown up Aggie found herself breathing faster as she contemplated the lesson Mama had taught so many years ago. She got up, walked to the window and stared out at the moving traffic, thinking. She felt the need to go over her life right now, even though it was difficult to do so here. Stepping out of her office and over to Sally's desk, she lowered her voice.

"Please hold all my calls, Sally, with the exception of any from Barry."

"All right. I've already held half a dozen calls from reporters."

"Good. Would you also tell Brenda and Jan that I want to see them when they're through with their appointments?"

"I will, Aggie."

"Thanks, Sally."

Aggie walked back into the office and closed the door. Now, she could think without interruption. Later, she would need to go over carefully what changes to make in her practice, and she certainly could use some solid, objective advice from someone she trusted.

"Miss Marks, where are you?" she whispered. Aggie couldn't count the times she'd asked this question through the years. Her first year at Slaughter Junior High, in Mckinney, Texas, Miss Marks was her English teacher—a teacher who had made an indelible impression upon her life.

They had known each other only nine months and then lost contact. Slowly, something became as clear as the crystal paperweight on her desk—not only did she need to go over the past, but she realized she could not make any far reaching decisions about her practice until she did! And now with Miss Marks coming to mind, she was certain the *past* she needed to review, in particular, were those nine months of her first year of junior high. Those wonderful and tragic nine months that were to change her life. It was true, the past *is* prologue to the future. The events which transpired during that time, influenced her to become what she was today.

What had she become? Tears surfaced; she blinked them back, letting her mind dwell on the beginning of that school year, the day she first met Miss Marks.

*August 25, 1980: Aggie wore hand-me-down jeans from Beth, and she'd always worn them to school. Her Dad had called her a "rough and tumble" girl because she loved to explore the outdoors, climb trees, play with the boys and hang upside down on the monkey bars. Besides, she only had two dresses and one was for Sunday School.*

*The metamorphosis began the first day of junior high when she walked into the first class of the day, English, taught by a new teacher, Miss Marks. Aggie stood just inside the door, in her old rolled up jeans.*

*Noticing her friends, Gary, Chris, Woody and a couple of others, all clustered together on one side of the room, she grinned and waved, then looked around for a seat.*

*It was then that she noticed something—something she'd only casually observed before. She noticed what the other girls were wearing. She stood there frozen, painfully aware that most of the girls were dressed like they were going to have their pictures taken or something! Some girls had on nice well-fitting jeans with new T shirts, others were wearing dresses. Then she saw Irma Hargrove and Gayle Harrington, the two girls who always made fun of her. They each were wearing a dress, expensive dresses, Aggie could tell.*

*By the time she could act, almost all the seats were filled up. Quickly moving down the aisle, she found one seat left, directly behind Gayle Harrington.*

*Gayle glanced across the aisle at Irma and they snickered. Aggie felt her face turn hot. It was then she noticed the teacher looking at her. Miss Marks smiled. Aggie knew, right then and there, she had an ally.*

~~~~~~~~~

*That night, Aggie approached her sister, who was in the ninth grade at Slaughter Junior High. "Beth, could I borrow one of your pretty clips for my hair tomorrow?"*

*"It's about time you wanted to do something different with your hair, Aggie. Can I brush it and put in the clip for you?"*

*"Would you, Beth?"*

*"Are you going to wear a dress, Aggie?"*

*"I thought I might."*

*"Good."*

*The two sisters, always close, were two years apart in age and two grades apart in school.*

*Beth came into Aggie's bedroom carrying the hair clip and brush. Moving to place them on Aggie's dresser, she recoiled at the sight of the row of chupsalis—the hard shell left attached to trees when the large, locust-like cicada emerges. Aggie and the boys she played with had a hobby of collecting them.*

"Aggie, when are you going to get rid of those things!?" Beth shivered. "I hate the horrible looking things! They look like they're alive—ready to pounce!"

"But Beth, Woody and I are having a contest to see who can collect the most. The loser has to buy the winner an ice cream cone."

"All right, Aggie, but they still give me the willies." Beth carefully avoided looking at them as she began to work with her sister's hair. After she had pulled out the old rubber band, loosened the pony tail, brushed and fixed her hair, Beth encouraged Aggie to put on a dress—the non-Sunday one.

Beth studied her. "Oh, Aggie, you're so beautiful."

"Beautiful?" Aggie asked, surprised and pleased.

"Yes, beautiful," Beth said, smiling.

"But, Beth, you're the beautiful one!" Aggie idolized her sister. Kind, gentle Beth who took after her mother. Aggie always thought of herself as 'rascally' like her dad, and she always wished she could be more like Beth.

"Aggie look in the mirror. Look at your long, dark lashes and your long dark hair. Your eyes are dark blue, mine are light blue. Your skin is creamy as a ripe acorn. Mine is pale."

"But, Beth," Aggie protested, "you have ivory skin like a princess. Mine is too dark because I play outside in the sun too much."

"We're quite the admiration society aren't we?" giggled Beth.

"We are for sure," Aggie said, then proceeded to compliment Beth some more, Beth returning it, each compliment becoming more full blown, more exaggerated until they both were laughing so hard, they fell over onto the bed.

~~~~~~~~~~

Aggie walked into class the next morning feeling quite self conscious. Soon, however, she realized no one really noticed how she was dressed, no one, that is, except, Gary, Chris and Woody, who all looked shocked.

Walking over to Woody, Aggie grinned. "What's the matter, Woodward?"

*"What're you all dressed up like a girl for?"*

*Aggie giggled. "'Cause I am a girl, Woody."*

*He let out a grunt of impatience. "I know that. But I thought we had a ball game going after school."*

*Before she could answer, Woody's attention riveted on the doorway, an expression of awe coming across his face. Aggie, turning to see what in the world could cause Woody to react like this, saw Gayle Harrington standing in the doorway looking around. It seemed to Aggie she stood there an overly long time—as if to draw attention to herself. As soon as Gayle was sure all eyes were upon her, she sauntered in and sat down at her desk.*

*Aggie grimaced in disgust. Of all things, Woody had a crush on Gayle! She turned on her heel and walked toward her seat, and as she passed the object of Woody's rapt attention, she said, "Hello, Gayle."*

*Gayle blinked a couple of times as if she couldn't believe her eyes, then muttered. "Oh...uh hi, Aggie."*

*After class, Miss Marks stopped Aggie on the way out. "Aggie, may I speak to you a moment?"*

*"Yes, Miss Marks."*

*"I just want to tell you how beautiful you look today."*

*"I do?" Aggie was thrilled. From then on Aggie became an avid student of English. And soon, to Aggie's delight, Miss Marks introduced the class to the art of writing stories. Aggie's mind, imagination and interest in words began to blossom under her tutelage.*

AGGIE found herself smiling. The times spent with Miss Marks were among the happiest in her life.

The short respite of nostalgia revived her flagging spirits, giving her the energy to delve into the work that had piled up while she was in Oklahoma. She worked fast and efficiently. At noon, she heard a knock at her door, then it opened. Jan and Brenda appeared.

"Glad to have you back, Aggie," Jan said.

"You wanted to see us?" Brenda asked.

"Yes. I want to hold a staff meeting tomorrow morning at 9:00 here in my office. Are you both free then?" They both nodded. "Also I wanted to tell you not to accept any cases that come as a result of the publicity generated by Sybil's case."

"What do you mean Aggie?" asked Brenda, sounding a little defensive. "You mean abortion cases?"

"That's exactly what I mean."

~~~~~~~~~~~~

Luke Barnes turned into the driveway of his house in southwest Austin—the house he'd built for Lila—the house they lived in for only a month. He still hadn't unpacked some boxes. Once more he could almost taste the bitterness of loss that welled up in his throat. It all started up again, he realized, when he heard that damnable newscast over the radio!

He sat in the truck, thinking. His mother would not be happy with the man he was now, the man he'd become. He recalled a discussion with her when he was fifteen.

*"What's the matter, Luke?" his mother asked as he came in from outside, slamming the kitchen door.*

*"It's Dad! I hate working with him. He doesn't trust me to make any decisions."*

*"Tell me about it."*

*"It's the same old thing, Mother. He has to hold all the reins and he holds them as tight as heck! He won't cut me any slack. I can't use my own initiative with the cattle, even when I'm out on my own. If I do, I'm always wrong and as usual, he chews me out."*

*His mother sighed. "I know, I know. It's hard isn't it?"*

*"It sure as hell is."*

*"Luke, please..."*

*"I'm sorry for cussing, Mother, but I can't work with Dad any more."*

*"Do you think your Dad is smart, Luke?"*

*Luke grunted. "Of course! How else could he have become so darn rich?"*

*"You've talked about becoming rich and powerful yourself someday."*

*"Yeah, so?"*

*"You can learn how from your dad. But can you learn when you're angry and bitter?"*

LUKE shook his head. I'm sure as heck angry and bitter now, Mother. But what can I learn from the hellish experience I've had with Lila?

# Chapter Four

Aggie drove into the protected, underground parking of the condominium complex at 5:30 P.M. Taking the elevator, she got off at the fourth floor, unlocked her condo, stepped in and locked it.

Entering the living room from the small entry hall, she dropped her briefcase and the Dallas Morning News she'd brought from the office, then literally collapsed on the couch, feeling drained. She stared at the unopened newspaper. At the moment she didn't have the courage to read it; she knew what would be there.

She felt edgy and anxious. Here it was Tuesday evening and Barry hadn't called. But why would he? He'd only had one day to investigate she reminded herself; still she reached for the phone on the lamp table. Before she could pick it up it rang.

"Hello."

"Yo there, Aggie," came Barry's gravelly voice. "I'm down stairs in the foyer with a pizza, open up the door."

"Barry! I just put my hand on the phone to call you." She pushed the button that released the lobby door. So relieved she could have cried, Aggie paced the floor until the doorbell rang.

Opening the door, she saw a grinning Barry juggling a large pizza, a liter of root beer and his briefcase.

Grabbing the briefcase out from under his arm, Aggie smiled and said, "Barry, you're the best sight I've seen today! Come in."

He stepped in and headed straight for the kitchen. "I called your office and learned you had just left. I took a chance that you might be hungry," he said, placing the jug and box of pizza on the table.

"Barry, you must have some news or you wouldn't be here."

"Don't get your hopes up too high, Aggie. But I do have news of a sort. You hungry?"

"I am now." She got mugs and plates from the cupboard, some napkins from a drawer, and placed them on the small table. "Thanks, Barry, I don't think I would have been able to eat tonight if you hadn't come."

After they were seated, and Barry had taken a couple of bites of pizza and a big swig of root beer, he smiled at her.

"You been prayin' again, Aggie?"

She smiled back. "Maybe."

"Well if this turns out to be something, it's your prayers, because it was just a fluke that I discovered it."

Aggie leaned toward him. "What did you find, Barry?" She had to wait until he had devoured a few more Barry-sized bites of Pizza and downed half a mug of root beer.

"Well," he said, wiping his mouth on a napkin, "after I read the account in the newspaper and read the papers you faxed me, I still had no clue where to start. When I had read it all for the third time, including Sybil's notes in the margins, I felt I was missing something. On the fourth go-round, I caught a name printed in very small letters in the margin, almost covered up by other notes. Marion Evans. It seemed to be there for no apparent reason, only that it was on a copy of the hospital records.

"That name sounded familiar to me, but I couldn't remember why. It came to me late this afternoon. She testified in a case three years ago in Houston. Sometimes I cut out newspaper articles and file them just in case I might need them. My file is full of newspaper articles, mostly useless, but now and then I need one."

"What case, Barry?"

"That's what I asked myself. I went into my file room and stood there trying to decide which file to look in." He grinned at her. "Well, I said to myself, 'Barry, you know that in your cases with Aggie, things just seem to fall into place so you'd better follow suit.' So I sent a quick prayer upstairs. You know, I found it in the second file I checked. The article even had her picture in it, she was so important to the case. It also was an abortion case, and when I reread it, I knew why I filed it. Things just didn't add up to me—more of a gut feeling than anything I could put my finger on."

"Barry, maybe..."

"Hold on, Aggie," he said reading her mind. "We don't have time to look into the Houston case yet, but I called the small hospital where the woman in the case here in Dallas supposedly had her tests made. I found out that Marion Evans had, coincidentally, worked there at the same time, but that she had just quit. They wouldn't give me any more information. Her name wasn't in the phone book so I visited the hospital. I wandered around until I found a sympathetic looking face. The young woman behind the desk was very helpful. I said: 'I would like to see my niece. I believe you have a Marion Evans working here.' It wasn't long before she gave me her phone number and address. I then asked what Marion's duties had been. It turns out that she is an outstanding medical technician, which made it easier for her to go from hospital to hospital. She was probably in a position to switch or alter medical records when and if needed."

Aggie laughed. "I don't know how you do it, Barry. Everyone trusts you."

"Sure, because I don't lie. You see, I didn't say Marion was my niece did I? The question is—where do we go from here? Marion may be perfectly innocent, but there are two things that might cause us to question: the news article about the case didn't quite add up, and the fact Marion quit right after Judge Wicken announced her decision."

"Somehow, we've got to find out more about her as soon as possible," Aggie said. "Wait a minute, Sybil lived in *Houston* before she came here."

"Did she have references?"

"Yes," she said returning to her seat. "A friend of mine gave her a referral letter, and I had no reason to question it."

They ate in silence for a while, then Barry said, "Call me tomorrow and tell me what firm in Houston she worked for and the name of your friend." He finished the last bite of pizza and drained his third mug of root beer. Scooting back his chair, he stood up. "Well, Aggie, I better go home and get to bed early. I've got a big day tomorrow."

"You eat too fast, Barry."

"I know. My wife used to tell me that," he said, walking out of the kitchen. He turned and grinned at Aggie, who had followed him to the door. "But I outlived *her*."

Aggie smiled at him. "Thanks, Barry, you've gone beyond the call of duty tonight. You're a real friend. I couldn't have done it these last four years without you."

"Thanks, Aggie," he grinned. "The feeling's mutual. Goodnight."

Aggie walked out of the small foyer into the living room, leaving her unfinished pizza in the kitchen, and sat down on the couch. Feeling so relieved that Barry found something at least to start with, she picked up the newspaper and opened it.

Right there on the front page of the second section was the heading of the article:

"THE IRON BUTTERFLY STRIKES AGAIN."
"Though not Agnes McBride herself, rather an attorney from her firm, Sybil Martin, has won a victory in the firm's most controversial case. The decision by Judge Wicken..."

Aggie's mind wandered back to when she was first called "The Iron Butterfly." It was the beginning of the second year of her practice. After a successful court case, the newspaper carried a small article about it on the back page of the second section. Before discussing the case, it had focused on how she was dressed, suggesting that she *"looked as out of place as an innocent and colorful butterfly fluttering around in a cold, gray, winter garden. On second thought, perhaps not so innocent. This tough and very capable woman might better resemble an iron butterfly."*

Aggie disliked the tailored suits and dresses many career woman wore, so she dressed like she wanted to—in beautiful clothes. At first, it startled the other attorneys, the judges and the juries. But it always seemed to buoy up the spirits of her female clients, giving them hope that they could be strong, as well as feminine. Her desire for pretty clothes began in August 1980, that first year of junior high, but her mother could ill afford to buy them. The *reason* for this state of poverty intruded painfully.

*July, 1978: Aggie was ten and Beth twelve when their father left them. One day he walked out to go to work and never came back. After a couple of days Aggie and Beth were scared. They were sure that something terrible had happened to him, that is, until Mama sat them down and told them he liked another woman, a younger, prettier woman.*

*"He went to live with her," she had told them, "so don't worry, he's safe. But he still loves you both, remember that."*

*They were so stunned, neither could speak for a few moments, then Aggie countered bluntly, "I don't believe you, Mama. Daddy wouldn't leave you! He wouldn't leave us!"*

*"I don't either," Beth said, finally.*

*Mama got tears in her eyes and pulled them both into her arms. "I know how you feel, but it's true and we must be strong. God will help us."*

*And that was that. Daddy never came back, never called, never came to see them—and Aggie knew he didn't love them after all.*

WIPING away a tear, Aggie recalled that her mother decided to remain in the small three bedroom frame house they were renting. However, in order to pay the rent and buy groceries, her mother had to go to work as a waitress on weekend nights. In addition, she took up cleaning houses during the day, but made certain she was there when they got home from school.

As time went on, the pain of their father's desertion began to ease. She and Beth settled into a comfortable routine, each taking on the household chores to lighten their mother's burden.

Two years after their father left, Aggie remembered how excited she and Beth were to attend school together again. Beth was entering the 9th grade at Slaughter Junior High and she was entering the seventh grade, her first year of junior high. They could now walk to school, see each other in the halls and walk home together on Tuesdays and Thursdays—the days Beth didn't have band.

Only three weeks into junior high, she was loving school, especially English under Miss Marks. Beth, who had always wanted to play the flute was learning it in band. Life had begun to feel golden when *he* entered their lives. Their dad had talked about his only brother, Chester, but they had never met him. She remembered she was in her bedroom sitting cross-legged on the bed studying as she always did, and Beth was in hers when they heard their mother call.

*September 15, 1980: "Beth, Aggie, come in here and meet your uncle Chester."*

*They came running into the front room and both stopped short. They hadn't expected him to look so much like their father, the daddy who left them without warning and without even saying goodbye!*

*When Aggie saw Uncle Chester, the old pain came back. She wanted her daddy back—and here he was—almost. It was too painful. She turned and ran back into her room and slammed the door.*

*"Aggie, come back here!" demanded her mother in her 'rare yelling voice.'*

*Aggie ignored her. She sat on the edge of the bed, arms folded tightly across her chest, listening to the muffled voices in the front room.*

*Then her bedroom door slowly opened. He didn't even knock! He was breaking a tight and fast rule of the family, Aggie thought in stunned silence. He just walked in without knocking! There he stood, with his arm around Beth, who was looking very uncomfortable. He smiled confidently at Aggie. She stared back at him, feeling angry and resentful.*

*Aggie noticed that his smile wasn't warm like her daddy's. But he was big, with wavy dark hair like him and his eyes were even deep blue like his. For some reason, Aggie couldn't take her eyes off his. Though they were the color of her daddy's, they were different, somehow. Then, she realized they didn't twinkle like Daddy's. Suddenly, she wondered if Uncle Chester might know where he was.*

*She stood up and faced him, arms still folded across her chest. "Where is my Daddy? Have you seen him?"*

*A slow smile spread across his face. "Why, as a matter of fact, I have seen him. Just a month ago, and he sends his love."*

*"Where is he?" Aggie demanded.*

*"Right now, I don't know."*

*"When is he coming to see us?"*

*"When he lands a good job, then he'll be back."*

*"Why didn't he tell us that? He didn't tell us anything when he left. He just left!" she shrieked.*

*"Aggie, Aggie," she heard her mother's soothing voice, and felt her arm around her shoulders.*

*Tears blinded Aggie's eyes. She pulled away from her mother's arm, backed away from all three and shrieked again, "I hate Daddy! I hate him, I hate him!"*

*"There, there," Uncle Chester's deep voice tried to soothe her. Then a big hand touched her shoulder.*

*Aggie angrily pulled away and screamed at him, "Don't touch me!"*

AGGIE jumped up from the couch and went to the window, looking out across Turtle Creek Blvd. to the green grass, the beautiful trees and flowers—watered by the creek flowing on the other side. Stepping out through the sliding door, she sat down in a patio chair on the small balcony and took in a deep breath. The view gave her no comfort. Uncle Chester walking into their lives was something she didn't want to remember, nevertheless—she knew she had to go over it all again. He had begun a campaign to ingratiate himself with the family, taking them all out for a hamburger and an ice-cream cone at Dairy Queen. It became a ritual every time he visited. She recalled what a wonderful treat for her and Beth, something Mama rarely indulged in after their father deserted them.

*September 1980: At least, Aggie thought, Uncle Chester made life a little cheerier for Mama and Beth because he joked with them. She refused to have anything to do with him, that is, until she saw him give Mama a little money, and only then did she begin to tolerate him.*

*On that first visit, he learned that Martha worked late on weekend evenings. After that he visited the next Friday, offering to sleep on the couch Friday and Saturday nights each weekend so the girls wouldn't be alone on those evenings. Martha didn't get home until 2:00 A.M. and was always a little nervous about leaving the girls alone. Still hesitating at the offer, she said they would try it one weekend and see how it worked. After that first weekend when Mama saw that all was well, she seemed relieved to have someone there when she was gone.*

*Tuesday, October 14: Four weeks into Uncle Chester's visits, Aggie and Beth were walking home together and Aggie was chattering about school. As usual, Beth quietly listened—not reacting or commenting, but since Beth was like that sometimes, Aggie didn't think anything about it.*

*When they walked into the house, they found Mama actually beaming.*

*"Come into Beth's bedroom, both of you, I have a surprise for you."*

*When they stepped into the bedroom, they both gasped. There on the bed was a treasure trove of clothes! Dresses, jeans, T shirts, regular shirts, tennis shoes, and skirts.*

*"Where did these all come from, Mama?" Beth asked.*

*"One of the wealthy women I clean house for has two girls about your sizes and she asked me if my daughters could use them. Some clothes they grew out of, but mostly they were clothes they just got tired of."*

*"Oh Mama!" Aggie exclaimed as she picked up a pair of jeans and studied them. Throwing them down, she picked up another, looking through the clothes, piece by piece.*

*Beth joined in, then said, "They're all expensive, name brand clothes. You'll look beautiful in these, Aggie."*

*"You will too, Beth."*

*Beth nodded and turned away, pretending to look at the brand names.*

*Aggie frowned and asked, "Beth, aren't you excited about the clothes?"*

*"Oh yes, Aggie, I am. Thank you, Mama."*

*It was plain to Aggie that Beth was not excited over the clothes. She looked at her mother and noticed that Mama was aware of it also—because her smile was gone.*

*"What is it, Beth, aren't you feeling well?" her mother asked.*

*"I'm fine, Mama, I guess I'm just tired that's all. I don't sleep very well on the weekends when you're gone waitressing. I guess I..." Her voice trailed off and she picked up a pair of jeans, "Look, Aggie, try these on."*

*After that, Aggie began watching Beth more closely. She seemed to get paler and more withdrawn everyday.*

*"What is the matter, Beth? Are you sick?" Aggie asked one day.*

*"No, Aggie...please don't worry. I'm fine."*

*But Aggie had a nagging fear in the pit of her stomach. Then one night it happened.*

THE memory now became too painful. Aggie got up and went into the house. Closing the sliding door, she slumped down in the over-stuffed chair and sobbed.

# Chapter Five

By 6:30 Wednesday morning, Aggie was sitting at her desk feeling the familiar tiredness as she fingered through the mail, and all the calls and messages that Sally had placed on her desk.

She noted something unusual—a window of time, a break. Not even one case pending in the future, though she was sure that the unreturned calls and unopened letters were from women wanting her to take their cases. Always the cases dovetailed or piled up. She had closed several cases just before leaving for Oklahoma and in her rush, she hadn't noticed the welcome break.

Maybe she should take Doris up on her suggestion to go cook for old Lucas Barnes. It sounded good to get away from the emotionality of her practice. The thought of being able to do the two things she never had enough time to do—write and cook—sounded wonderful. Then cold reality set in. Next Monday an abortion will be performed unless...

Aggie jumped up and went into Sybil's office to see if she had started packing. She found the room empty. Sybil had already moved out! This was just too abrupt, even for Sybil. An unusual amount of clutter covered the floor and desk top. Drawers were left open, the waste basket was tipped over on its side out in the middle of the room, the contents spread out upon the floor as if it had been kicked.

Aggie frowned and muttered aloud, "Why wasn't this room cleaned last night?" It was then she saw the note taped to the front of the open door. It said: "Do not clean this room." Was this the second round—Sybil's petty retaliation?

All of a sudden Aggie wilted. She turned and walked slowly out of the office and into her own, dropping into her chair. Sybil needed help. She knew it a year ago when she came here for a job. Aggie hired her because she was smart, capable and had been recommended by a friend. It soon became apparent Sybil didn't want help or couldn't accept it. Aggie felt helpless—but then in her chosen field, this feeling often came with the territory. There were women you could not help, anymore than she had been able to help Mama and Beth.

Aggie covered her face and grappled with emotion. Finally under control, she focused her mind on the serious agenda of the staff meeting this morning, making notes.

~~~~~~~~~~~~

Since there was no conference room, Aggie always used her office for the staff meetings. At 9:02 Jan and Brenda walked in.

"Good morning," Aggie greeted, smiling at each as they seated themselves. Though they both returned her greeting, she sensed a definite coolness, especially from Brenda.

"I called this meeting to cover some issues that apparently have not been spelled out clearly enough. Number one: No one is to accept a case concerning abortion."

"Wait a minute, Aggie," Brenda broke in. "We've received a lot of calls since Sybil's case and if you don't allow us to take them you're cutting down our income."

"You wait a minute," Aggie said, her voice low with censor, "I have your contracts of employment right here. May I remind you the contracts state that while you work in this law office, you only take cases that I approve of, or you will be terminated. May I also remind you that you both came to *me* for a job and you accepted the terms, including the fact you could not become a partner, that you would only remain an associate. I am the boss around here. This is *my* firm, remember?"

"We remember," Jan said, "but..."

"There aren't any 'buts,' Jan."

"Aggie," Brenda began testily, "We don't think you've been fair to Sybil."

"Do you think that too, Jan?"

Jan nodded, looking uneasy.

"Why, Brenda?" Aggie asked.

"Because she was just fighting for women's rights and by firing her, you're retreating from everything you believed in. You're also letting down Crystal Carson, you're mentor in college."

Aggie hid her shock. How did she know about Crystal Carson? She felt a stab of hope. Maybe Brenda might know something else. "I assume you know that Sybil had a letter of recommendation from a friend of mine, Leslie Bryant."

"Yes."

Aggie's heart quickened with excitement. "Then you possibly know that Crystal Carson was Leslie Bryant's mentor also."

Brenda took the bait. "Of course. Leslie Bryant has joined Crystal's law firm in Houston."

This proved even more of a shock to Aggie. Asking Brenda that question had been more of a lucky guess than anything. In college, she and Leslie had decided to pull out of Crystal's group because of the direction it was taking. And now Leslie was a part of Crystal's firm! She knew she had to call Barry immediately, and she had to end this meeting without questions.

"I need a little time to think over what you've said about my being unfair to Sybil."

"And," Brenda added, "think about letting us take the cases that have come as a result of Sybil's case."

"I will," Aggie said. "And we'll meet again soon. Oh, by the way, Brenda, is there anything about Sybil's case that might make me change my mind?"

"Only that Sybil was getting counsel from Crystal Carson's firm...in fact, I got the idea it was from your friend Crystal herself. Sybil was quite secretive about the case, so I don't know any more about it than what I've told you."

As her office door closed behind the two, Aggie reached for the phone and called Barry.

"Barry, I need to talk to you right now."

"Okay. Come on over and we can talk about it over a cup of coffee."

"I'll see you in two minutes. Thanks, Barry."

~~~~~~~~~~

Seated at the small table, Barry sipped his coffee, thinking, trying to digest the information Aggie had given him. Aggie took a swallow of her orange juice and waited for his questions.

"You aren't drinking coffee anymore, Aggie?" he asked as if that was what he'd been mulling over.

"No," she said looking a little grim. "I've become one of those health food junkies. I've been a little low on energy lately."

Barry's bushy eyebrows hovered over his eyes as he studied her. "Why don't you quit this damn business and get married and have children, Aggie."

Aggie's eyes widened in surprise. Barry was protective and at times fatherly in his manner toward her, but he never got on personal territory. She smiled. "Why, Barry, you know all the good men are taken— or old enough to be my father," she said, pointing a finger at him.

"I'm serious, Aggie."

"Marriage isn't in my plans."

"Why?" he asked with the abruptness of a reprimand.

"What's with you today, Barry?"

"Well, I'm wondering why you got mixed up with the likes of Crystal Carson."

"You already know about her?"

"Of course! Anybody who opens the paper, here in Texas, sees her mug now and then promoting everything and anything that's destructive to society, especially to the family. Anything that gives her a little more power."

"Oh."

"Well, answer my question Aggie."

Aggie took a deep breath. If it were anyone but Barry, she'd tell him it was none of his business—but out of respect for him, she had to answer.

Her shoulders slumped. "It's a long story, Barry, but I'll make it short. I met Crystal at SMU here in Dallas. I was planning on becoming a school teacher, then one day I heard Crystal on her soap box on the grounds of the campus. I stopped and listened. She was saying how women were victims of men—abusive, dominating and controlling men.

"When I heard this, Barry, it struck a note. She was saying out loud what I was feeling, for reasons I can't go into now. I began going to her meetings. She gathered in many young women who could also relate to what she was saying. I met Leslie Bryant at one of those meetings and we became friends. We both began attending Crystal's meetings regularly. Crystal was planning to become a lawyer and so was Leslie. As I thought about it, I realized that if I were to become a lawyer, I could maybe help women who were seeking aid but felt powerless to help themselves.

"After a year of attending these meetings, I became concerned over how Crystal was leaning. It became clear that she was becoming more radical and had adopted an unhealthy lifestyle and a frightening agenda. I talked it over with Leslie and found she was feeling much the same way. We both dropped out of the group. I'm shocked that Leslie has become a part of it again."

"How do you feel about men, Aggie?"

"Barry, I'm hiring you as a detective, not as a personal counselor," she said abruptly, then smiled to take the sting from her words. "Tell me, what we can do with this latest information?"

Barry shrugged and returned the smile, but the question in his eyes remained. "Maybe plenty and maybe not. I have a friend in Houston who has asked me to keep my eyes and ears open for anything in the papers about abortion cases here in Dallas. Apparently the authorities suspect Crystal Carson's firm in connection with some altered medical records. With this new information, I might be able to find out more about those medical records and Marion Evans."

"How soon can you find out?"

"I'll get right on it the minute you leave my office," he said. "But answer my question first, Aggie."

Aggie stood up, she sighed in exasperation. "I feel great about two men I know, Barry. You and Bob Biederman, the husband of my friend Doris."

"How do you feel about the rest of the male population?"

"Barry! What's up anyway?"

"Do you want me to get started on finding the info or not?"

"I don't know the rest of the male population."

"All right, Aggie," Barry said, leaning back in his chair. "I'll wait until you quit acting like an attorney."

Aggie simmered a moment then answered his question. "I don't trust men in general, Barry."

"Do you go out with men or are you too damn caught up with your feminist cause?"

"Darn it Barry, I *have* gone out on dates. But every man I've dated has made me not only less trustful, but quite cynical. There you have it. Now will you get to the job I'm paying you good money to do?"

~~~~~~~~~

Taking a coffee break, Luke Barnes settled back in his large comfortable office chair to read the morning newspaper. After reading the first page of the front section, he turned to the second page. He saw a picture of a woman that jarred his senses. Curious as to why this blonde-haired woman with features which would ordinarily be called attractive—wasn't. He read the caption under the picture; "Crystal Carson, leading Houston lawyer and president of the feminist group: the FPL, Feminist Power Leaders, is supporting..."

Luke slammed the paper down, got up, walked to the window and stared out. Ever since Monday when he heard that radio newscast about the abortion case in Dallas, he'd been as edgy and jumpy as his old stallion in a thunderstorm.

Part of it, he told himself as he paced the floor, was because he'd been working too hard, too many late nights. He needed some diversion.

Stepping back to the desk, he picked up the phone and dialed Joy Marshall.

~~~~~~~~~

Aggie stepped out of Barry's office feeling unnerved. All those questions Barry fired at her were so unexpected. She decided to take a short walk before returning to the office. Apparently the name Crystal Carson triggered Barry's outrage.

Crystal Carson was the person who had influenced Aggie's career choice, changing from education to law. She had always wanted to be a teacher like Miss Marks, except she wanted to teach first or second grade instead of junior high. She felt she could have more influence on younger children than the older ones.

An overwhelming feeling of regret came over her. If she had stayed with her first choice and become a teacher, she wouldn't be in the terrible situation she was in right now—her firm responsible for an upcoming abortion.

But would she have made any other decision under the same circumstances? She met Crystal when she was still grieving over Mama and Beth and feeling emotionally vulnerable. As Crystal said, becoming a lawyer would give her the legal know how and power to avenge women who had been abused by men. She remembered that she had mentally uttered a resounding yes! She couldn't help Mama and Beth now, but she could avenge them maybe—by helping other women.

Her new career choice made, Aggie went ahead with an impetus she hadn't had before. She had a cause! She graduated early even though she had to work her way through law school. After first working her way through college at the same restaurant as her mother; during law school, she switched places of employment becoming the first female waiter in one of Dallas' most exclusive restaurants.

It was there, one evening, that the master chef, unexpectedly short of help, exploded in a verbal rampage—threatening to lop off the fingers of one hapless apprentice. In one breath he excoriated the learning ability and incompetency of his associates, and vowed his own ability was so great he could teach any willing subject the supreme secrets of world class cuisine.

Though terrified, Aggie, who had always wanted to learn gourmet cooking, put on a brave front and challenged the great man to prove his boast. Perhaps he was too startled to reject her, or perhaps he recognized in her something that others missed; at any rate, she was given the opportunity.

Returning to the office building after her walk, she climbed the steps remembering when she first started practicing right out of law school. Cold, cruel reality set in. Things were far different than she thought during those college days of fiery idealism.

When she entered her office, she immediately felt uncomfortable. There was a strange feeling in the air.

"What's going on, Sally?"

Sally shrugged her shoulders and rolled her eyes at Aggie, warning her that something was afoot.

"Any messages or calls?"

"The usual—women calling, wanting you to take their cases, reporters and so forth."

Aggie went into her office and had just seated herself when Brenda and Jan appeared at her open door.

"Aggie," Brenda said, "may we talk to you?"

"Of course. Come in and take a seat."

"I'd like to get right to the point, Aggie," Brenda said.

"Please do," Aggie replied.

"Sybil called while you were out. She's rented an office and she wants us to join her."

Aggie had expected something might change, but not so quickly.

"Oh?" She waited for the rest, noticing how uncomfortable Jan looked.

"We've both decided to accept her offer," Brenda finished.

"Oh?" Aggie replied, surprised at the relief she felt.

Aggie's silences were always so unsettling, Brenda thought.

"Is this all right with you, Aggie?" Jan asked, uneasiness in her demeanor.

"Yes."

This was too easy Brenda thought. Suspicious, she asked, "Why are you taking this so well, Aggie?"

Aggie remained silent, a hint of a smile on her face.

This threw Brenda off balance. Impulsively, belligerently she blurted out, "We're taking our cases with us, even though..."

"That's fine." Aggie interrupted.

"Well uh...since we had the cases here at your firm...uh I mean since we won't be part of your firm anymore, we'd like to keep the whole fee."

"All right."

Brenda and Jan both looked shocked. It was Jan who responded, "Th..thank you, we appreciate that, Aggie...and will it be all right if we start moving out today?"

"Yes."

"Uh...thank you, Aggie," Jan said moving toward the door.

"Yes, thank you," Brenda said as they both left the office.

Aggie got up, closed her door and sat down feeling a little puzzled and suspicious. Sybil certainly got an office in record time, she thought, wondering if Crystal and her group were also giving Sybil financial support.

She was still amazed at how she was feeling. With the responsibility of Brenda and Jan no longer an issue, she was free to make any decision she wanted to! It felt as though a heavy load had been lifted from her shoulders.

Slowly, it became clear what she had to do, what she must to do. When she and Barry solved the present problem, and the necessary legal action taken, if warranted, she was going to close her law office temporarily. She was grateful she'd invested her money wisely; and that she had a little income with the monthly payments from quite a few of her dependable clients. She could at least pay her house payments, and a few other expenses. It was a perfect time to take that sabbatical Doris talked about, and she could certainly use an extra two thousand dollars a month.

Aggie smiled as she dialed Doris.

"Hello," Doris answered.

"Hi, Dor, is that offer to cook for old Lucas...what's his name...still open?"

Doris, surprised that Aggie had made a decision so quickly, didn't answer right away. "His name is Lucas Barnes, Aggie. Uh...to answer your question, I think so, but I'll call him and find out. What's up? What made you decide this?"

"I'm here at the office so I don't have time to tell you now. I'm going to call Bob and see if I can see him this afternoon, if not, later. I'm going to explain this to him and ask his advice."

"How soon shall I tell Lucas you'll be down?"

"I don't know for sure. I can let him know in about ten days to two weeks, depending on the case Barry and I are working on."

"This is amazing, Aggie. I hadn't expected your answer so soon. I'm sure Lucas will appreciate the news."

"A hitch could easily develop in our plans though, Doris, so be sure to tell him it isn't certain yet. If he doesn't want to take a chance and wait a couple of weeks to know one way or another, tell him to go ahead and look for another cook."

"I'll explain that to him and I'll get back to you, Aggie."

~~~~~~~~

Doris hung up the phone and sat there smiling. Won't Bob be surprised, she thought. He was sure Aggie wouldn't even consider her suggestion. The jingling of the phone interrupted her thoughts.

"Hello?"

"Doris, this is Amy."

"Amy! How wonderful to hear from you."

"How are Bob and the boys?"

"They're fine. How are you, Paul and the children?"

"We're all well. I'm calling to see if you've talked to my brother lately. I just got off the phone with him and I'm worried about him."

"Yes, I've talked to him several times of late."

"How did you find him?"

"Snarly...that is, until he hears my voice and then he's nicer."

"Has Luke talked to you about why he divorced Lila yet?"

"No. I wish he would. Every time I even hint about it he changes the subject or promises to tell me when he sees me. You know how stubborn Luke is, Amy, I just have to wait until he's ready to tell me. But, I do have some good news of sorts."

"Oh? I'll take any good news no matter how small."

Doris wanted to tell Amy everything but had decided beforehand not to. She didn't want to get Amy's hopes up. "As you know, Amy, Luke is trying to find a cook. I think I may have found him one. I wish I could hire her myself. I think Luke's spirits will get better when he can socialize more and you know his favorite way to socialize is having people over to his home, especially for dinner."

Amy sighed. "That's not very hopeful news, Doris. I'm afraid he'll just have Joy Marshall and her friends over."

"Joy Marshall? Luke has never mentioned her to me. Have you met her, Amy?"

"Yes. When I flew out to be with Luke a few months after the divorce, she was hovering around him like a bee over honeysuckle. Luke is very vulnerable right now and she's after him. She isn't the kind of girl Mother would approve of if she were alive. Joy is beautiful, charming, but ambitious and worldly—the opposite kind of woman Luke was always looking for and thought he'd found in Lila."

"Oh dear, I..." Doris stopped herself from telling Amy that she felt she had found the right girl for Luke.

"Another reason I called, Doris, is to tell you that Paul's work is taking him to Europe in ten days. He wants me and the children to go with him since he'll be gone a month, maybe two. I hate to leave the country with Luke feeling the way he is."

"Amy, you and the children must go. It's a wonderful opportunity for all of you. I promise, I'll look after him. I have something up my sleeve, but I don't want to tell you about it in case it doesn't work out."

"You do?" she asked hopefully. "You can't even give me a hint?"

"I want to, Amy, but not now. I promise, I'll let you know any good news; just call me and give me the address of where you'll be."

"I will, Doris, and thank you. You must know I'm dying of curiosity."

The minute Doris hung up, she decided to try reaching Luke at his office. She wondered how she was going to get him to wait for several weeks with the possibility that even then he might not get a cook.

She made a decision—a decision based on pure hope. She dialed Luke at his office.

An impatient "Hello" came over the line.

"Luke, this is Doris."

"Oh, hi, Doris." His voice warmed perceptibly. "This is my lucky day, Amy also called me this afternoon."

"She called me, too. She's worried about you, Luke."

"Uh-oh, you two planning to gang up on me?"

"Somebody should, Luke. What happened with you and Lila that you can't get hold of yourself enough to quit worrying your sister?"

"Plenty!" he barked, "And I didn't ask Amy to worry over me."

"I think you better tell me what happened, Luke, or quit acting so ornery."

The silence was so thick with tension, Doris expected Luke to hang up any minute. Finally he said, "I'm sorry, Doris. I don't mean to take it out on you, but something brought it all back to me the other day and

I..uh never mind. I'll get up to Dallas and visit with you face to face and tell you one of these days."

"Bob and I can come down there."

"No," he said quickly. "I'm not ready to talk about it right now."

"All right—for now anyway. I called to give you some good news. I just got off the phone with Agnes McBride. She would like to accept your offer. She thinks it will take about two weeks to get her affairs in order—is that all right?

"I guess it will have to be. We're trying it for six months, right?"

"Right."

"Tell me a little bit about her. Is she retiring?"

"No. She's burned out, she needs a change."

"What is her work?"

"Uh...she's been doing legal work in a law firm," Doris hedged.

"Oh...well that can be a grind. How old is she? I hope her health is good."

"She's tired right now is all. She loves to cook, Luke," Doris went on quickly. "You'll find her energetic enough."

"Good. Tell ol' Agnes I'm looking forward to meeting her and especially looking forward to her cooking."

"I will, Luke, and I'll let you know the date she'll be coming."

Doris hung up the phone and laughed—but quickly sobered. Three things she'd hedged on: Aggie's age, her vocation, and giving Luke the impression that she was coming for sure—any one of which could get her into hot water with Luke. For that matter, she could also find herself in hot water with Aggie and Bob. Oh well, she decided, I'll just keep it my own little secret for now, and hope for the best.

# Chapter Six

When Aggie called Bob Biederman and asked if she could meet with him, that she needed his advice, his curiosity was piqued. This much he knew, it must be important—Aggie asking for advice was a first. He had arranged things so he could see her as soon as she arrived.

Aggie, knowing what a busy attorney Bob was, felt grateful that he'd made time for her this afternoon. Bob had made a name for himself in the Metroplex and was sought after by many large corporations and had connections in high places. Aggie was hoping that somehow he could do something to help her with Sybil's questionable case. Even if he couldn't, she felt his advice was worth seeking.

Bob's office was in one of the new high rise office buildings only three blocks from hers. She walked briskly until she reached it. As she rode the elevator up to the tenth floor, she marveled at how circumstances seemed to be propelling her pell-mell into serious decisions.

It was 2:00 P.M. when she stepped into Bob's office. Julie looked up from her desk and smiled.

"It's nice to see you again Ms. McBride. It's been quite a while since you've been here. Please be seated, I think you timed it about right."

"Thank you, Julie." Aggie sat down and absently paged through a magazine. What an anomaly, she thought, to be sitting here, feeling safe in this office—the office of a male attorney while feeling she'd left the enemy camp back in *her* office of female attorneys. Even as short a time as a year ago, she would have laughed if someone had told her that this would come about.

Five minutes later, Bob Biederman's tall figure appeared at the door, looking clean-cut and honest as always. "Ms. McBride, come on into my office," he said, grinning.

She looked askance at him as she walked in. It sounded unflattering the way he always said 'Ms.' Secretly she hated the expression, but she'd never vocalized it to anyone. It hadn't seemed important.

"Have a seat, Aggie, and tell me—what's on your mind?"

Aggie related everything about the abortion case, about Barry's investigation of it and about his suspicions.

Bob's face reflected deep concern. "I know the Houston District Attorney, Aggie and I think you, Barry and I need to meet with him as soon as Barry feels he has something solid enough to investigate."

The feeling of gratitude and relief was so strong, Aggie felt close to tears. Finally, she murmured, "Thank you, Bob. Also," she continued, "I'm closing down my law firm temporarily and I need some advice about that."

~~~~~~~~~~~

Back in her office Aggie felt some semblance of peace as she started making a list of things she needed to do in order to close the office.

She had instructed Sally to help her keep an eye on Brenda and Jan. Aggie wanted to check on the files they took with them. She also had called a locksmith to change the locks tonight in case Sybil decided to come and go through the filing shelves and take files she shouldn't.

After this abortion case was resolved, one of the important things on her agenda was to write a letter to all her previous clients, telling them of her sabbatical and referring them to another attorney in her absence if they needed any further legal help. Bob had recommended a couple she could interview. The irony was—they were both male attorneys. Shaking her head in amazement, she realized she had to think, sort out and clear up some confusion that lay deep down in her own psyche. She felt on the verge of tears again. If only I could talk to Miss Marks, she thought, she's the only one who knows what happened. Where was she? Someday soon, she had to find her!

Startled by the buzzer, she quickly pressed the button. "Yes, Sally?"

"Mr. Slocum is on line one."

"Thank you, Sally. Hello, Barry, what do you have?"

"Plenty."

Aggie told him of her meeting with Bob. "Do you think you have enough information for us to meet with Bob and the Houston District Attorney?"

"I do," he stated firmly.

Aggie's heart pounded with excitement. "I'll call Bob and see if we can set the meeting up tomorrow sometime if possible."

The minute she hung up, she called Bob with the news.

A short time later, Bob called her back informing her that he'd talked to the Houston DA, who in turn called the Houston Chief Of Police. After a few minutes the DA called back.

"The DA said that the police chief nearly burst his eardrums he was so exuberant over what he'd told him. The DA is flying here tomorrow afternoon to attend the meeting, and has requested that we have the Dallas DA here also. I'll take care of it. The meeting is scheduled for 3:30 here in my office in order to avoid any undo publicity. I guess you know, Aggie, you're high-profile right now."

"I know. How can I ever thank you for helping me with this, Bob?"

~~~~~~~~~~

Before Brenda and Jan left, Aggie went over the files with them, allowing them the cases they were working on. After everyone left, she waited for the locksmith and then closed the office and went home.

She walked into the bedroom of her condo at 7:00 P.M. feeling emotionally and physically exhausted. Quickly undressing, she showered, washed her hair and slipped into her pajamas.

Feeling a little better, she fixed herself a light supper, after which she went into the living room, curled up on the couch and contemplated how things had come together today. There was still uncertainty. Tomorrow was Thursday—four more days! They had only four more days to legally stop the abortion. She let out the breath she had unconsciously been holding in, and took several deep breaths trying to release the tension in her neck and shoulders.

Barry had asked if she were saying her prayers. Until Monday in the courtroom, she had allowed her prayers to become as irregular as a baseball player at bat—hit and miss. She reflected on how Mama had taught her and Beth to pray. And that November up in her favorite tree she had prayed with all the fervency of her soul.

Aggie's shoulders suddenly straightened, as if stung by an electric shock; it wasn't Crystal Carson who had influenced her to choose law over teaching! It was that *resolve* she made at twelve years of age—up in that tree—long ago in McKinney Texas!

Painfully, this forced Aggie to reach back into her memory several weeks before that resolve—to the time her life changed forever.

*October 24, 1980: Early Friday morning, Beth tiptoed into Aggie's room and closed the door quietly.*

*"Wake up, Aggie," Beth whispered.*

*Aggie opened her eyes and blinked sleepily. "What are you doing up so early, Beth?"*

*"Ssh...Mama is still asleep and I need to talk to you before she wakes up," Beth said in hushed tones, her face flushed and fearful.*

*Aggie sat straight up in bed, alarmed. "What is it, Beth?" she asked in a whisper.*

*Beth sat down on the bed. "Aggie, I...uh...you are looking so pretty and grown up lately in all the pretty clothes Mama brought home that..." Beth stopped, unable to go on.*

*Aggie sensed that the compliment wasn't something to be pleased about. "That what, Beth?"*

*"That...that you should be careful when Uncle Chester comes today."*

*"Why?" Aggie asked, puzzled.*

*"Because...he's looking at you now like he looked at me when he first got here. I...I don't want you to get hurt...like...like he's hurt me."*

*"He's hurt you?!"*

*"Sssh! Mama will hear you."*

*"But if he hurt you, we need to tell mama!" Aggie whispered vehemently.*

*"No! No, Aggie, we can't tell Mama. Uncle Chester said Mama wouldn't understand. He also said if I told anyone, he might even have to hurt Mama."*

*Aggie was horrified, angry. "No! He'd better not! I'll call the police on him."*

*Beth's eyes were full of fear. "Please, Aggie no! You don't understand. He's been coming into my bedroom every night while Mama is at the restaurant and after you've gone to sleep."*

*"I know he's rude, Beth, he just walks in without knocking. Just tell him to leave!"*

*"Aggie, it's not that simple. He did things to me that..." finally Beth poured it all out, telling her sister everything.*

*Aggie felt sick to her stomach. "I don't believe you! He's our uncle. He looks like Daddy."*

*"It's true, Aggie. And I don't want him to do that to you...so you watch him like a hawk. Promise me, Aggie, that you'll scream if he tries anything."*

*"You're lying!"*

*Beth began to cry. Stricken with remorse, Aggie cried out, "I'm sorry, Beth. You don't lie...you never lie. I...I just don't want to believe it."*

*"I know. It's all right, Aggie," she said. "Just be careful." She got up and walked out of the room.*

*All that day, Aggie struggled to keep her mind on school. Upset over what Beth had told her, she dreaded school to end because then she'd have to go home. She was sure Uncle Chester would be there. He was always there on Fridays now.*

*Almost home from school, Aggie stopped. Even though Beth had band after school, she wondered why she hadn't waited for Beth so they could walk home and face him together?*

*Taking a deep breath, she reluctantly walked on. Sure enough, there was Uncle Chester's shiny red car in the driveway next to her mother's old gray car.*

*Slowly she climbed the steps of the front porch. Her heart pounding with dread, she opened the front door quietly and sidled in. There he was lolling on the couch reading the paper just as if he belonged there, she thought, resentment broiling up inside her.*

*He looked up from his paper. "Hello there, Sugar," he said, smiling.*

*Aggie remembered what Beth said about him looking at her now as he had her. She felt her skin prickle. She walked quickly into the kitchen to greet her mother.*

*When her mother left for work, Aggie and Beth worked on their* homework at the kitchen table until late, both dreading the time when they had to go to bed.

"Hey girls," Uncle Chester yelled from the front room, "I'm making my bed on the couch now so I need the kitchen light off."

Aggie looked over at Beth and squeezed her hand just before they separated to go to their bedrooms. Aggie pretended to go to sleep. She lay there tense and stiff as a rod, scared for herself, but more scared for Beth.

After some time, she opened her door a crack. She saw that Uncle Chester was no longer on the couch. She froze with fear. Finally, she managed to gather courage enough to tiptoe toward Beth's closed bedroom door, and listen. Soon she heard something that she couldn't make out...then suddenly she heard Beth cry out, "Please don't, Uncle Chester!"

Aggie turned and ran into her room feeling sick and frightened. It was true! She needed to stop him somehow. She lay there shaking, thinking, afraid to go to sleep. At last she drifted off to blessed oblivion.

~~~~~~~~~~~~

Aggie awakened with a start. The sun was streaming through the limp lace curtains, making a pattern upon the threadbare carpet. She sat bolt upright as she remembered last night. The sick, scared feeling came back, but it soon escalated into anger.

She lay back down and muttered into her pillow. "How dare he come into our house looking like Daddy and hurt Beth?! Oh, Daddy, why did you leave us so Uncle Chester could come and hurt us?" Great heaving sobs shook her small frame as she lay huddled up in bed.

When the sobs subsided, she lay there trying to figure out what to do. First, she decided she had to protect herself from Uncle Chester as Beth told her to.

An idea came to her—a terrible idea. She didn't have to wear her pretty new clothes. She didn't need to fix her hair nice. If she looked as ugly as her name, Uncle Chester would leave her alone, and then she could figure out a way to help Beth.

Since it was Saturday, Aggie decided to go to her tree and think. She dressed in the old oversized jeans, thinking how badly she wanted to wear the new name-brand jeans her mother brought home. And now she couldn't wear them or any of the other new clothes!

The tears wouldn't even wait until she got to the tree. They started as she grabbed her coin purse and stuffed it into her pocket. Opening the window, she climbed out. Her bike was leaning against the house as always. She got on and sped down Chestnut street until she came to Louisiana street where she turned right, peddling as fast as she could toward the edge of town, the tears blowing back into her flying hair. Furiously, she wiped at them with one hand.

"I hate men! I hate them! I hate daddy! I hate Uncle Chester!" she yelled into the wind.

The tears were coming so fast by the time she reached the old dirt road, she could hardly see. Turning onto it, she soon reached an area of trees. All she could do was jump off the bike and hunker down against the trunk of the tree and cry.

The tears finally dried up, leaving only shuddering spasms of breath. She climbed up into the tree, her safe place, her place to think. She had to figure out a way to protect herself from her uncle other than just wearing her old jeans. At last an idea came; an idea so abhorrent, she wondered if she could muster up enough courage to do it.

How she wished their lives were like they used to be before he came. They were getting used to being without their father. Her mother had brought all those pretty clothes home which would have made Beth so happy—but because of him, they didn't! Now, instead, she was sad, quiet and scared all the time.

"How dare he come into our house and ruin everything?!" she shouted angrily. Hate welled up inside her so strongly, physical pain gripped her chest. "I'll find a way to make him leave and never come back!"

The hate suddenly gave her the courage to do what had to be done. She climbed down, jumped on her bike and peddled toward the town square. When she reached the square, she turned west on Tennessee Street, stopped at the barber shop, pulled her bike up onto the sidewalk and leaned it against the building.

*She clutched her chest trying to stop the pain as she opened the door and stepped in.*

*The barber was just taking money from a customer. Aggie sat down and waited for the man to leave, then stepped up to the barber.*

*"I want a hair cut. How much are they?"*

*The man was startled. "Uh..." He looked at her beautiful, long, dark hair. "There is a beauty salon a few doors down from here. They're better equipped to cut such nice long hair."*

*"I don't want to go there. I want a man's hair cut. I want to look as ugly as my name...Agnes."*

*The barber looked shocked, then concerned. "I...uh does your mother know you're here?"*

*"No, but I'm twelve and I'll soon be thirteen. This is my decision. I have five dollars in my coin purse. Can you cut it for that?"*

*"Yes, but, Miss..."*

*Aggie climbed up into the chair and folded her arms tightly across her chest. "I'm not moving until you cut it like I want."*

*Concerned, the barber studied her, then he said, "I'll make you a deal. I'll cut your hair for two dollars if you'll consent to let me cut it short—but like I want. You can go home and get used to it. If you want it shorter—just like a man, I'll do it for no further charge."*

*Aggie thought about it a moment. "It's a deal."*

*Relieved, the barber put the plastic apron over her, pumped up the chair, got his scissors and began cutting just about two inches below the ear and straight across.*

*Aggie sucked in her breath when she saw the first long lock fall to the floor. She clamped her teeth tightly and closed her eyes for the rest of the haircut.*

*"You can open your eyes now," the barber said, smiling. "I'm through."*

*She looked into the mirror and almost didn't know herself. Her thick hair, with the blunt cut, stuck out like a bush!*

*Mutely paying the barber, she left. She got on her bike and headed for home. Tears of sadness collected into one big lump in her throat. Reaching the house, she drove around back, leaned her bike in its customary position and crawled back through the bedroom window.*

*She heard muffled voices and the clink of spoons on dishes, and knew everyone was eating a late Saturday breakfast. She swallowed hard, squared her shoulders, walked out of her room and into the kitchen to face her family.*

*Her mother, Beth and her uncle were seated around the table eating cold cereal. When they saw her, they stared at her as if they didn't recognize her.*

*Finally, her mother gasped, "Aggie!"*

*"What in the hell did you do to yourself?" Uncle Chester demanded.*

*Facing him with all the fierceness of her soul, she said, "What does it look like?"*

*"You look disgusting!"*

*"That's the plan, Uncle Chester!" she yelled, her eyes full of hate.*

*Abruptly turning away from them, she ran out of the kitchen, out the front door, and around the back to her bike. She got on and peddled around the neighborhood as fast as she could until she calmed down.*

~~~~~~~~~~

*At dinner Saturday night, Aggie asked, "Beth will you sleep with me tonight and tomorrow night? I've been scared lately."*

*"Scared, Aggie?" her mother asked, surprised. "Your uncle Chester will be here tonight."*

*"I guess I've had some bad dreams or something. Will you, Beth?"*

*Beth's eyes were wide and fearful as they darted toward her uncle and back again to Aggie.*

*Before Beth could answer, their uncle pressed them, "Hey girls, your uncle Chester's here to protect you. You don't need to sleep together."*

*Aggie felt sick again and wished she could throw up all over him. "Sorry, Uncle Chester, but Beth and I have some girl talk to do anyway—you know boys n' stuff."*

*He glowered at his plate and stuffed food into his mouth in his usual gluttonous manner. When he was through eating, he stood up and faced their mother.*

"*Martha, I just dropped by to see you all, but I can't stay tonight, I have some things to do. I'll be back next week.*"

"*Do what you have to do, Chester,*" she said.

Aggie breathed a big sigh of relief and looked over at Beth who gave her a small, pathetic smile of thanks.

After their uncle left, their mother got ready for work. As she always did before she left, she cautioned them to lock the doors and call her at the restaurant if they needed her.

The evening didn't go as Aggie had planned. Beth agreed that Uncle Chester was definitely repulsed by her appearance then began to cry. "*I'm so sorry, Aggie, that you had to do this.*"

Aggie, who could never stand to see Beth cry, said, "*It's all right, Beth, because now we have time to plan how we can keep Uncle Chester from coming to see us anymore.*"

Beth insisted she had to study all evening, fearfully refusing to discuss any plans for getting rid of Uncle Chester permanently.

Sunday morning turned out even worse. Her mother, who hadn't had time to discuss Aggie's drastic actions before going to work the night before, now found time at the breakfast table.

"*Can you tell me,*" she asked as patiently as she could, "*why you went and had all your beautiful hair cut off, Aggie?*"

Beth threw her a fearful look and shook her head ever so slightly.

Aggie frowned at her then looked down at her bowl and spooned at her cooked cereal. "*I...I wanted a different hair style for a change.*"

"*Why did you yell at your uncle Chester?*"

"*I don't like him, that's why.*"

"*That is no excuse to be discourteous to him—and after he's done so much for us.*"

Aggie's lips pressed tightly together, smoldering as she stared at her bowl. She looked up and muttered, "*Yeah, he's done so much...*"

"*Aggie,*" Beth interrupted, her face anxious, "*what dress are you wearing to Sunday School?*"

"*I'm not going to church,*" she said flatly.

"*Why?*" her mother asked, shocked.

"*Because my new hair style only looks good with my old jeans and I can't wear jeans to church.*"

Her mother's displeasure was evident. "And after I brought home all those pretty clothes you aren't going to wear them anymore?"

Aggie shook her head and looked down, close to tears.

# Chapter Seven

Monday morning, Aggie didn't walk to school with Beth, explaining that she wanted to go the long way around in order to avoid running into any of her friends. This made her late for Miss Mark's English class.

If it weren't for the driving force of the anger and hate toward her uncle, she wouldn't have had the courage to even walk into class—especially walk in late!

Her lips pressed tightly together, Aggie took a deep breath, slowly opened the closed door and stepped in. All heads turned in her direction. There was silence for a fraction of an second, then several girls gasped. Her only girl friend, Betsy, covered her open mouth with her hand and stared in wide-eyed shock. Even Woody and the group were shocked.

The distance to her seat seemed endless. When she reached it, she was aware that Irma Hargrove and Gayle Harrington were whispering about her and snickering.

After she sat down, Aggie hesitantly raised her eyes and looked at Miss marks. If her teacher was shocked at her appearance she didn't show it because she just smiled at her.

All that day, Aggie felt like a zombie, walking to classes, listening to the teachers, and doing homework without thinking or feeling.

After school, when she stepped out of her last class, she found Miss Marks waiting for her.

"Aggie, may I give you a ride home?"

Aggie was so surprised, she just stared at her a moment then stammered a yes. She wouldn't be walking with Beth because she had band after school.

"Wait for me out in front. I'll be there as soon as I gather up some papers."

While waiting on the front lawn, she heard Irma Hargrove's voice. "There she is. Good ol' saggy, baggy pants Aggie!" Then there was laughter.

*Gayle joined in the next time. "Yeah! saggy pants Aggie!"*

*Aggie didn't look at them. Turning away, she vainly struggled to blink back the flowing tears.*

*It wasn't long before she felt Miss Marks' gentle hand take hold of her arm, and together they walked to the parking lot. Miss Marks opened the door for Aggie and she slid into the seat. Her teacher's sympathy and kindness only brought on more tears, which Aggie unsuccessfully tried to stop.*

*By the time Miss Marks had opened the door and settled herself behind the wheel, Aggie's sobs were totally out of control. Soon, she felt Miss Mark's arm around her shoulder, and heard her say, "Just cry it all out, Aggie, it's all right."*

*When Aggie was able to stop, she said, "I don't want my mother to see my red eyes. I can't go home right now."*

*"All right, let's just sit here for a while. Irma and Gayle are very unkind, Aggie, please try not to let it hurt so much. I know how you feel. I had girls who hurt me when I was young." Miss Marks told her about it. "And sometimes, even when you're grown up there will be times when you'll run into unkind people. The important thing is that you are not the one doing the hurting."*

*"Thank you, Miss Marks, for telling me that. I think I'm ready to go home now."*

*Miss Marks started the engine and drove out of the parking lot onto the street. "Isn't it beautiful weather?" she asked. Aggie nodded. "Miss Marks continued, "As many years as I've lived in Texas, I still can't get over how grand it is. Where I lived as a little girl it gets very cold in October. Now give me directions to your house."*

*Aggie directed her until they drove into the graveled driveway of her house. Before she could thank her, Miss Marks asked if she might meet her mother.*

*Aggie nodded. They got out of the car and walked across the yard. For the first time, Aggie became uncomfortably aware of her home, of the weed filled front yard, the sagging front steps and the peeling paint.*

*"What a wonderful big porch, Aggie. All you need now is a porch swing to make it perfect."*

*Immediately Aggie felt better. She led her teacher into the house.*

*Martha McBride, who had been standing by the window watching anxiously, turned toward them.*

*"Hello, Mrs. McBride. I'm Alice Marks, Aggie's English teacher. I gave her a ride home so I could meet you."*

*Martha's face relaxed. She smiled. "I'm glad to meet you, Miss Marks. Aggie has spoken highly of you."*

*"Why thank you, Aggie," Miss Marks said, smiling at her and then at her mother. "Mrs. McBride, is it all right if I invite Aggie to dinner at my apartment tonight?"*

*Martha's face registered surprise, then she said, "Why...I think that would be nice for Aggie."*

*Miss Marks turned her attention to Aggie, whose eyes were wide with wonder. "Would you have dinner with me, Aggie?"*

*Aggie nodded, speechless.*

*Aggie noticed that Miss Marks' apartment was cheery and neat as a pin.*

*"Let's go into the kitchen and have a snack, Aggie. It's only four o'clock so we won't eat for awhile."*

*Aggie followed her into the kitchen, feeling shy, not knowing what to say.*

*"Please have a seat at the table and I'll get us the cookies I made last night. Do you like milk with your cookies?"*

*Aggie nodded. The cookies tasted good and the milk soothed her stomach which had been in knots all day.*

*Alice Marks talked about where she grew up in Maine, and how beautiful it was. She explained how she thought Texas was just as beautiful in its own way, asking Aggie questions about how long she'd lived in Texas, and how she liked living in McKinney.*

*At last, Miss Marks said, "I see you had your hair cut. I think if it were shaped a little, short hair would enhance your big blue eyes, high cheek bones and your pretty delicate chin."*

*The cookies quit tasting good. "I don't want it shaped. I want it just like it is," she said, shoving the plate of cookies away.*

*"Why, Aggie?"*

*"I want to look as ugly as my name, Agnes."*

*"Would you please tell me why?"*

*"I can't tell you."*

Miss Marks was silent for a long time, and Aggie stared at the table, fingering some cookie crumbs.

*"Who lives in your house, Aggie?"*

*"Mama and my sister, Beth."*

*"Is your Dad living?"*

*"Not as far as I'm concerned he isn't. He just picked up and left one day—didn't even say goodbye."*

*"I'm so sorry to hear that, Aggie. Do you have any relatives who come and visit?"*

*"Just my uncle Chester."*

*"When was the last time he visited?"*

*"Last Friday and Saturday."*

*"Do you enjoy his visits?"*

All the fear, anger and sick feelings came flooding back, cancelling all her inhibitions. *"I hate him!"* Aggie sucked in her breath and covered her mouth, shocked that she'd blurted it out. She noticed that Miss Marks' kind blue eyes and expression didn't change.

She just calmly asked, *"Have you always felt this way?"*

*"I didn't like him from the very first time I met him six weeks ago. He looks too much like my daddy, but he's been good to Mama. He gives her a little money now and then, and jokes a lot and sometimes takes us out to Dairy Queen to eat. So I've tried to like him—until last Friday night and now I hate him."*

Aggie saw great concern come over Miss Marks' face who then asked, *"Did he hurt you, Aggie?"*

The desire to tell her became an overwhelming need. *"No. He hurt Beth!"* The tears suddenly came out in torrents.

Alice Marks pulled her chair around next to Aggie's and held her until the sobs subsided.

*"D-don't tell anyone, Miss Marks,"* Aggie said suddenly fearful. *"Beth said Uncle Chester told her he might have to hurt Mama if she told anyone. The only reason she told me is she saw him looking at me*

like he did her when he first came to our house. She told me to be care-ful."

For the first time, Aggie saw anger on Miss Marks' face. "Is that why you had your hair cut?"

"Yes. I told the barber I wanted a man's hair cut because I knew Uncle Chester would hate it. The barber didn't want to cut it like that and said he'd do it later if I still wanted him to."

"How do you feel about your hair cut?"

"I hate it, just like I hate wearing Beth's hand-me-down jeans." She blinked furiously at the insistent tears.

"Listen to me carefully, Aggie," Miss Marks said slowly. "There is another way to protect yourself and your mother and Beth. Are you interested in hearing it?"

"What do you mean, Miss Marks?"

"I mean you don't have to try to look ugly. You can dress in your pretty clothes and be beautiful, and still take care of the problem of your uncle Chester."

"I...I can?"

"Yes. How about we get dinner now and eat, then I'll tell you about it. First, though, let me tell you this. I have a hobby. I can cut and style hair. I put myself through college that way and I have a great idea for a hair style that I think you'll love, Aggie."

"You have?"

"Then you're interested?"

"Oh, I am, Miss Marks...if"

"All right, then, come and help me get dinner and I'll show you how to make the best spaghetti sauce you ever tasted. I got the recipe from an Italian friend of mine."

Aggie expelled a big, tremulous breath. "I would like that, Miss Marks," she said, feeling like the whole world had been lifted off her shoulders.

The spaghetti sauce was delicious. Aggie asked if she could have the recipe so she could make it for her mother and sister. After the dishes were done and the recipe copied, Miss Marks and Aggie remained at the kitchen table.

"Now, Aggie," Miss Marks began, "what your uncle Chester has done to Beth is a crime and if Beth will tell a policeman what he did, and if you tell him what you know, saw or heard, the policeman can arrest him."

"How do you know that, Miss Marks?"

"I've known others who've been through this. You know, Aggie, sexual abuse is getting to be more and more common in today's world, though there is still a great reluctance to bring it out in the open."

"It is?"

"I'm sorry to say so, but yes. Now, Aggie, do you think you can get Beth to tell a policeman about your uncle?"

"If she knew that the policeman would arrest him so he couldn't hurt Mama, I'm sure she would. She has to!" Aggie's blue eyes flashed with the fire of determination. "We can't let him come to our house ever again!"

Miss Marks smiled. "Fierce little Aggie McBride. I'm glad I'm on your side. Now for the plan. Ask your mother tonight if you can spend a little time with me after school tomorrow night. If she says yes, you and I will go to the police station and talk with a policeman who will be on duty for the next couple of weekends. Is that all right with you, Aggie?"

Aggie, almost speechless with relief, nodded her head vigorously.

"When your uncle Chester comes again, call me. We'll use a code. Say: 'Miss Marks may I hand my assignment in late?' This will tell me that your uncle Chester is there and that I'm to call the policeman. He and I will come right over."

Aggie's heart pounded with anxiety. "I'm afraid this will frighten Beth and Mama."

"Would you feel better if I came before the policeman and told your mother what you've told me?"

"Yes, then Mama can get prepared before the policeman comes. If only I hadn't promised Beth I wouldn't tell Mama, I could tell her myself before you come. It will have to be you, Miss Marks, who tells Mama so I won't be breaking my promise to Beth."

"Aggie, you have had a health class in school. Did you understand everything?"

"Yes, I think so, and Beth explained a lot more when she told me about Uncle Chester."

*"All right, we'll do it that way. However, Aggie, don't expect Beth to be as brave as you. Her boundaries have been violated. Your boundaries haven't, so you are stronger."*

*"Boundaries?"*

*"Sexual boundaries. Did you know, Aggie, that sexual boundaries are spiritual boundaries?"*

*"They are?"* Aggie's eyes were wide and questioning. *"What uncle Chester has done to Beth has made me think that...that sex is something to be ashamed of, something—dirty."*

*"Don't allow him to influence your thinking and feeling, Aggie. The privilege of procreation, that is, the privilege of having babies is a God given gift, so sexual relations are special and sacred and are to be saved for marriage to show our husband how much we love him and to bear his children. Therefore, sexual boundaries are spiritual boundaries. When someone like your uncle invades the boundaries of a young innocent girl, it is an abomination before the Lord. Do you understand, Aggie?"*

AGGIE stood up and stretched. She went into the kitchen and poured herself a glass of apple juice, sat down at the table and sipped it...thinking about what Miss Marks had told her. She remembered feeling totally amazed that sexual boundaries were really spiritual boundaries. She'd accepted that profound statement with all her heart and it had stayed with her all these years. It went along with what her mother had taught her about abortion and what Reverend Jones had preached on Sundays.

Through the years of dealing with wounded women, Aggie had used Miss Marks' wisdom and understanding, and it gave many women courage to strengthen themselves.

Aggie recalled how Miss Marks had turned her awful bush-like hair cut into an attractive hair style. As much as she loved having long hair, Aggie remembered, when she stared into the mirror that evening, how much better she looked in short hair. That's why she continued to wear the same style to the present day.

Miss Marks had washed her hair, parted it high up on the left side, layered it, trimmed it, and cropped it close at the back of her neck to show off the natural peak at the neck line. She exclaimed what beautiful, thick shiny hair she had and what a nice natural wave it had to it. In front of the ear she left short tendrils that curved up slightly in the hollow of her cheek. Miss Marks explained how her hair just naturally went the way she was styling it, the cow-lick holding her hair to the right without a clip but allowing a few sprigs of bangs to hang down on her forehead on the left. Next, she blow-dried her hair turning it all under slightly.

Aggie smiled, remembering when she walked into class for the first time with the new hair style.

*The next morning, dressed in well fitting name-brand jeans and a pull-over knit shirt the color of her colbalt-blue eyes, Aggie walked into Miss Marks' English class promptly at 9:00 A.M. Her head held high with a confidence she'd not had before, she stood at the door a moment as Gayle had done. The class members, who saw her, stopped what they were doing and stared. When Gayle and Irma noticed her, their jaws dropped, their eyes wide with astonishment. She turned and smiled at Miss Marks, who was beaming, then she slowly sauntered to her seat.*

*"Hello, Gayle...Irma."*

*"Uh...hello, Aggie," Gayle muttered. Irma couldn't say anything.*

*After class, Woody was there—standing by her desk. "Uh...Aggie, could I walk you to class?"*

*This time it was Aggie's turn to be astonished. Her first impulse was to blurt out...why? That is, until she saw Gayle's head whirl around and stare, her face frozen in a mask of incredulity.*

*Aggie smiled sweetly at Woody. Her baseball buddy, who had suddenly assumed a new role, was looking a little gaga at her. "Thank you, Woody, I would like that."*

*This is the way it went all week and Aggie enjoyed it immensely because it put Gayle into one big, long ill-humored pout. However, she wondered why Woody wasn't feeling as awkward and self conscious as she was. After all, they were really only buddies, not boyfriend and girlfriend—at least in her mind. Apparently Woody had forgotten all about this—but she hadn't. She had always liked boys better than girls. They were a lot more fun, but that was all, and she was eventually going to* have to break it to Woody that she wasn't into liking boys in any other way yet.

As the week wound to a close, Aggie's euphoria—pretending life was normal and happy—came to an abrupt halt. The gnawing fear that Uncle Chester would be there when she got home from school that afternoon felt like a lump inside her stomach.

As she turned the corner and saw that Uncle Chester's car was not in the driveway, her relief was overwhelming. Maybe he'd caught on that she knew about him and he didn't dare come back. She told Beth this when she got home from school, hoping it would cheer her up.

The next week, Woody was still acting love-sick and Miss Marks smiled and winked at her. Wednesday after class, she pulled Aggie aside. Woody stood back a short distance, waiting.

"Aggie, I'd like to invite your mother, Beth and you to dinner tomorrow night. Would you ask them and call me tonight?"

"Oh, I know they'd like to, Miss Marks. I will, Thank you!"

She turned to Woody and said, "I'll race you to class."

"You know we're not supposed to run in the halls, Aggie."

"I know it, Woody, but I'm so happy I'd like to try it—I'll race you after school then."

"Ah, Aggie, you always beat me."

"I'll let you win this time, Woody," she said, batting her eye lashes like she'd seen Gayle do.

~~~~~~~~~~

When Aggie told her mother and sister about the invitation for dinner at Miss Marks' place, her mother's face brightened. Unfortunately Beth's reaction was the opposite.

"What's the matter, Beth?" her mother asked.

"I don't want to go, Mama."

"Why for goodness sakes, Beth, it will do you good to get out of the house. You don't act like yourself lately."

"I know, Mama. Maybe another time I can go to dinner at Miss Marks."

"Well, then I'll stay home with you. Aggie, go call your teacher and accept the invitation for yourself. Express our regrets and thank her."

*Tears almost betrayed Aggie's deep disappointment. She turned around quickly and went to the phone. She'd been pretending that things were getting better at home and now she knew they weren't.*

~~~~~~~~~

*Wednesday night turned out to be special anyway. Miss Marks had assigned the class to write a story and she had brought Aggie's home with her. After dinner as they were seated at the table, she handed it to Aggie. There was a big red 'A' at the top.*

*"Aggie, you have a talent for writing. Were you aware of that?"*

*"No," Aggie responded in awe.*

*"Well, my dear, you do and you need to develop it."*

*Aggie was thrilled. She loved writing stories. This way she found she could create her own happy world.*

*Again, on Friday after school when Aggie turned the corner, relief flooded her whole being. Uncle Chester's car wasn't there! She could hardly wait to tell Beth, when she came home from band practice, that this probably meant their uncle wouldn't be coming anymore.*

*Aggie found her mother lying down in her room resting when she came home. "I made your favorite cookies, Aggie. You may have one now, but hadn't you better change first?"*

*"I'm so hungry, I'll change later, Mama."*

*Aggie poured herself a glass of milk and sat down to enjoy her chocolate chip cookie and a book. After a while, she heard the front door open, and she looked up expecting Beth. "Uncle Chester!" She felt as though someone had kicked her in the stomach.*

EXHAUSTION suddenly hit Aggie; she couldn't think about that time in her life anymore tonight. Another day, she'd go over it, she decided, inhaling deeply and letting it out in a heavy sigh. She got up from the kitchen table. Her feet felt heavy as she walked into the bedroom to get ready for bed.

# Chapter Eight

Aggie returned to her office at 5:30 Thursday evening, elated over the success of the meeting at Bob's office. Both of the District Attorneys were impressed with the evidence Barry had accumulated, and shocked at the scope of Crystal Carson's illegal activities.

She found Sally preparing to leave. "Do you have a moment, Sally?"

"Of course, Aggie, what is it?"

"Come into my office and sit down. I have something to tell you."

Aggie broke the news to Sally of her pending leave of absence and asked her if she would continue to stay in the office for a month or so to answer the phone and forward the mail. Explaining to Sally that she would receive a full salary each month and in the event she decided to close her office permanently, would receive an additional six weeks severance pay as well as a letter of recommendation. "I already have several possible job opportunities for you starting two or three months from now."

Sally was stunned. "B...but you are starting to have such a lucrative practice here, Aggie."

"I know, Sally, but this is what I need to do right now. Can I count on you to stay for a month or two?"

"You certainly can, Aggie, and thanks. I'll bring some cross stitching to work with me to fill in the time—also some reading."

After Sally left, Aggie wrote a check for Barry and stepped out of the office to take it to him. His grinning face greeted her as she stepped into his office. "I'm still in a state shock at what came out at that meeting, Barry."

"So am I, Aggie. So am I."

Aggie reached into her purse, pulled out the check and handed it to him. "If it hadn't been for you, Barry, we would have never had evidence to appeal this decision. Thank you."

Barry looked at the check and whistled. "You're overpaying me, Aggie."

"No, Barry. I don't think I could pay you enough to tell you how grateful I am."

"Save your thanks for the Man upstairs, Aggie. He was the one who helped us both."

"I know. I intend to take care of that tonight."

"Bob Biederman called just before you walked in. He told me the Dallas District Attorney called him and informed him that they will probably arrest Sybil Martin and Marion Evans tomorrow morning first thing. At the same time, in Houston, they're arresting Crystal Carson."

"Sybil may not have known about the collusion, Barry."

"They'll find out if that's the case."

"What I want to know is...when are they meeting with Judge Wicken, to request that she vacate her previous order allowing the abortion?"

"The DA has arranged a meeting with Judge Wicken tomorrow afternoon at 2:00."

Aggie let out a sigh of relief. "Good. That's cutting it close. I guess Bob will find out the final verdict. I'll let you know, Barry, if he calls me first. I'm afraid I won't rest easy until that meeting is over with and the verdict is what I want it to be."

"I'm afraid I won't either, Aggie. Judge Wicken is known for her sympathies with the feminist movement, but I don't think she'll put up with breaking the law. I'm just glad that the District Attorneys both thanked you and stated unequivocally you weren't involved in the case anymore, that it's in their hands now."

"For which I'm grateful, Barry!" Aggie then told Barry her plans to close her office for an indefinite period of time.

~~~~~~~~~~

After showering and getting ready for bed, Aggie curled up on the couch musing over how pressed she felt to continue reviewing those nine months of long ago—wondering if she realized all the reasons why.

If only she could dwell on the happy times with Miss Marks, she wouldn't dread going over it as she was dreading it right now.

*October 31, 1980: Uncle Chester's large hulk seemed to hover over her like a big, black grizzly bear. "Hello, Sugar, you look good enough to eat in your pretty dress."*

*Aggie flushed with uneasiness and resentment. She had become so engrossed in the book, she had forgotten to change like Mama had asked her to.*

*"You here alone, babe?"*

*"No, Mama is resting and Beth will soon be home from band practice."*

*"Come here, Sugar, and give Uncle Chester a big hug."*

*"No!"*

*"You mad at me 'cause I jumped you about cutting your hair?"*

*"No."*

*"Good. Because I like it better now. You look prettier and more grown up than you did when it was long."*

*His smile made Aggie shiver. She got up and quickly eased passed him to the kitchen door. She turned and found him following her. Backing away from him, she yelled, "Leave me alone!"*

*"What the hell...." He stopped in his tracks, and glared at her.*

*She turned around to find her mother standing in the doorway. She was so relieved she hugged her. "Uncle Chester is here!"*

*Her mother looked puzzled for a moment then loosened Aggie's arms and walked on into the living room.*

*"Hello, Chester. It has been a couple of weeks. Nice to see you."*

*"Thanks, Martha." He chuckled nervously. "I think I startled Aggie."*

*"Oh?"*

*Just then, the front door opened slowly and Beth peered in nervously, her eyes large and fearful.*

*"Beth!" exclaimed Uncle Chester. "Come and give your uncle a hug."*

*Beth obediently started toward him.*

*"Don't Beth!" yelled Aggie.*

*"Aggie, what in the world is the matter with you?" her mother asked, casting a nervous, half-apologetic glance at her brother-in-law.*

*All three were staring at her. She swallowed hard and shrugged her shoulders.*

"Hey!" Chester's voice broke the uneasy silence. "Everybody get ready, I'm going to take you all out to dinner at a nice restaurant."

"I have to be ready to go to work at the restaurant by 7:00, Chester," Martha explained.

"What say I take you all there?"

"But that's too expensive, Chester," Martha protested.

"I've done real well these last two weeks, Martha. Let's celebrate."

"Well, all right," Martha said. "Thank you. It will be nice for the girls."

Aggie ran into the kitchen to phone Miss Marks. As soon as she heard her comforting voice, she said, "This is Aggie, Miss Marks. Can I hand my assignment in late? Uncle Chester wants to take us out to dinner tonight."

Miss Marks understood. "I'll be right there and the policeman will be there about twenty minutes later. Bye, Aggie."

Her mother and Beth were in their rooms getting ready and Aggie in hers when the knock came. Aggie ran into the front room and opened the door, relieved and happy to see Miss Marks' kind, but serious and concerned face.

"Come in, Miss Marks."

Alice Marks stepped inside and glanced at Aggie's uncle. Aggie ran into her mother's room. "Miss Marks is here, Mama." She opened Beth's door. "Beth, Miss Marks is here, she wants to see you."

She ran back over to stand by her teacher. Her mother and Beth entered the front room.

"Why hello, Miss Marks," her mother said, smiling. "Are you here to see me or Aggie?"

Alice Marks, her arm around Aggie's shoulder, stood in front of the door facing Chester, Martha McBride and her daughter, Beth.

"Go on, Aggie," she whispered.

Aggie's heart felt like it was going to leap right out of her chest. "Beth...t-tell Mama."

Beth's face turned white. Her eyes darted over to her uncle. His eyes bore into Beth unmercifully.

"I can't breathe!" Beth gasped grabbing her chest, and dropping onto the sofa. "I can't breathe..."

"Mrs. McBride, get a small paper sack. Beth seems to be hyperventilating," Alice said with calm authority.

Martha ran into the kitchen and came back with a sack. Alice knelt beside Beth and asked her to breathe into the sack. Soon, Beth's breathing became normal and Alice stood up.

"Mrs. McBride, your brother-in-law, Chester here, has sexually molested your daughter, Beth."

All the color drained from Martha's face and Beth, still sitting on the couch, started shaking. She stared at Aggie in horror.

"What the hell?!" Chester blurted out.

Martha turned toward him slowly. "Is...this true, Chester?"

"Hell! What is this?!"

"Don't swear, Chester. Just answer me. Is this true?"

"Do you think I would do that?"

"Answer me." Martha's voice was almost inaudible.

"Ask Beth." He turned abruptly and glared down at her huddled figure. "She'll tell you that this meddling school teacher's a liar."

Martha looked at her oldest. "Beth, is it true?"

Aggie held her breath waiting...watching Beth's terrified face. When nothing was forthcoming, Aggie screamed at her sister, "Tell Mama!"

"It's true," she whispered, then covered her face and sobbed.

Martha was stunned; unable to speak.

"It's a lie! See how scared she is, Martha. These two have coerced her. She's afraid to go against them."

A loud knock on the door startled them. Aggie quickly opened it.

"Hello, Miss, I'm Sergeant Wills."

"Please come in," she whispered breathlessly, her heart pounding in her ears.

Martha, her daughter, Beth and Chester were shocked. Silence hung heavy for a moment. Finally Martha asked. "What is the problem, officer?"

"I called him, Mrs. McBride," Alice said. " Sergeant, this man has been molesting this fourteen-year-old girl here, Beth McBride."

"That's a lie, officer!" Chester bellowed.

Officer Wills ignored him and studied Beth instead. "Is this true, young lady?" he asked gently.

*"Are you going to tell a lie, Beth, so your uncle Chester has to go to jail?" her uncle asked in a hurt voice.*

*The officer spoke, his voice low with anger. "I would advise you to keep quiet, mister, or I'll arrest you for interfering with an officer. Now, Beth, tell me," he asked, his voice gentle again. "Is it true?"*

*Beth looked like she might hyperventilate again, but instead she looked down and picked at her nail, apparently unable to answer.*

*Aggie went over to the couch where Beth was sitting and knelt in front of her. "Beth, it's all right. It will be all right, just tell the policeman the truth."*

*Beth refused to look at her sister, and tears dropped onto her shaking hands.*

*Aggie grabbed Beth's hands and shook them. "Tell him, Beth! The policeman will arrest him and put him in jail and he won't hurt you anymore. He won't hurt Mama."*

*Beth began to sob.*

*"Tell him!" yelled Aggie.*

*"Aggie, stop it," her mother reprimanded.*

*"Mrs. McBride," Sergeant Wills began, "Is it true? What do you know about this?"*

*"I just learned about it tonight. I...I think I'm going to have to have some time with my girls and my brother-in-law to ferret out the truth."*

*"Do either of your daughters lie, Mrs. McBride?" he persisted.*

*"No. They are truthful girls."*

*"Do you think they are lying now?"*

*"No...I mean...as I said, I...I need some time, this is a terrible shock to me."*

*"But Mama!" Aggie exclaimed, feeling close to tears.*

*"I want you to hush right now, Agnes!" her mother demanded.*

*Aggie noticed that Sergeant Wills and Miss Marks looked as frustrated as she felt. She also noticed the smirk on her uncle's face. She wanted to kick him on the shins as hard as she could, then go shake Beth.*

*"Well, I'm going to have to leave now," Sergeant Wills said, "but if you change your mind, Beth, please call me. Good night."*

*After the officer left, Miss Marks hugged Aggie and said loud* enough for everyone to hear. *"Don't feel badly, Aggie. You tried your best. At least,"* she glared at Chester, *"I think we scared him."*

*"Like hell you did!"*

*"Chester! This is the last time I'll ask you to stop swearing,"* Martha demanded, her voice filled with anger.

*"I'll be leaving now, Mrs. McBride,"* Alice said, *"I'm sorry for you and your daughters that this couldn't be resolved tonight. I hope for your sakes that you will decide to go to the police. Good night."* She turned and left.

Before Martha could say anything more, Chester said, *"I'm going to leave too, Martha. Here I came to take you all out to a nice place to eat and this is the way I'm treated!"*

He stepped over to Beth, towering over her, reminding Aggie of a dark, menacing bull about to trample his victim. *"I was going to buy your mother a new car and you ruined it, Beth, by not denying that meddling woman's lies."*

Aggie stepped over to Chester, facing him defiantly. *"I don't believe you! You're the liar!"* she yelled, pounding him with her fists.

His face purple with rage, Chester lifted his hand to strike Aggie. Martha screamed, *"Stop it, Chester!"*

He glanced at Aggie with hate filled eyes, and slowly lowered his uplifted arm, while fending off her blows with the other.

Martha pulled Aggie away.

*"Go to your room right now, Agnes,"* her mother ordered, her voice shaking with anger and anxiety. *"And, you are to stay there the rest of the evening!"*

*"But Mama!"*

*"Go on!"*

Aggie ran into the bedroom and slammed the door as hard as she could, angry tears streaming down her face. Soon, she heard Beth's bedroom door shut. She stood in the middle of the floor, arms folded tightly across her chest, listening to the muffled voices of Mama and Uncle Chester.

She couldn't stand hearing their voices any longer. Changing quickly into jeans, a T-shirt and sweater, she slipped out of the window. Walking over to a scraggly bush she sat down behind it and let the tears come.

*She made a decision. If Uncle Chester stayed there this weekend she was going to run away.*

*Shortly, she heard Uncle Chester's car leave, then a little later she heard her mother leave for work. Shivering from the chill of the night air, she crawled through the window, moved to the bedroom door and peered carefully out. The house was dark.*

*She tiptoed to Beth's door. Opening it, she looked in and saw her sister huddled up—apparently asleep. Relieved, she tiptoed back to her own room.*

AGGIE stood up and moved to the window looking out at the evening twilight—feeling tense and shaken. Things were never the same after that night. Mama smiled even less, Beth became more pale and withdrawn. Neither would talk about that night or—the forbidden subject.

Miss Marks and a few friends at school made her life bearable. Miss Marks taught her the love of good literature, the art of writing stories and in general helped her feel a zest for life—still the pain in her chest seemed always to be there.

One day when she was over to Miss Marks for dinner, the pain became unbearable.

*November 5, 1980: "You still have that pain in your chest, Aggie?"*

*She nodded. "It's worse. Do you think I need to go to a doctor, Miss Marks?"*

*"We need to try something first, Aggie. But before I tell you about it, I need to tell you something about myself. For years, someone hurt me over and over. I tried to work it out with her each time and each time I forgave her. Finally, not too long ago, it was too much and suddenly I hated her. The hate became so intense I felt actual pain in my chest. It was then I realized that this hate would destroy me if I didn't get rid of it. I knew there was only one person who could help me get rid of it. God.*

*"For three days I prayed incessantly for the hate to leave. I read from the Bible every day. At the end of three days, God literally plucked it right out of my heart, and I was eventually able to forgive her." Alice*

looked deeply into Aggie's wide and wondering eyes. "Do you think the pain is caused by the hate you feel for your uncle?"

All Aggie could do was nod vigorously.

"Do you want to try what I did?"

"Yes."

"If the pain doesn't leave, then you must tell your mother about it so she can take you to a doctor."

~~~~~~~~~~

Aggie tried getting rid of the pain, doing as Miss Marks had directed. After three days, it miraculously disappeared. That night, she knelt beside her bed and prayed and cried as she thanked her Father in Heaven. When she told her teacher, Alice Marks' eyes filled with tears, and she hugged Aggie tightly, her heart aching with both joy and sadness.

November 18, 1980: Alice continued to try to include Beth in her and Aggie's study sessions and spaghetti dinners, but she refused. One day she drove Aggie home and invited both Aggie's mother and sister for dinner the next night. Martha thanked her, but turned the invitation down. After Miss Marks left Aggie turned to the two of them.

"But Mama...Beth it would be so much fun. Why did you turn Miss Marks down again?"

"Beth is embarrassed to be around Miss Marks, don't you see? Don't ask again, Aggie."

"Why is she embarrassed? Miss Marks said it is no one's fault, but Uncle Chester's."

"I don't want to discuss it, Aggie."

"Beth, say something!" Aggie pleaded.

"Mama is right, Aggie," Beth said in a thin voice.

"Mama...Beth, Miss Marks said that you were victims of Uncle Chester—but that you don't have to continue to be victims, you can get some help."

"Go to your room right now, Aggie."

"You told Uncle Chester not to come back, didn't you?"

"Yes, Aggie, but I don't want to discuss it any further. Go to your room."

*"All right I will!" she yelled. "You and Beth can just go ahead and be victims, but I won't be one!" She turned and ran into her room.*

*She sat down on the bed feeling so frustrated and miserable she thought she would die. It wasn't long before these feelings propelled her off the bed. Quickly changing into jeans, she opened the window and climbed out. Straddling her faithful old bicycle, she sped off toward her tree.*

*Reaching it, she ascended and settled herself crossed legged on her favorite limb. Though the leaves of the old red oak had turned red and orange, they hadn't yet fallen. They hid her while the tears flowed down her cheeks—tears of sadness because she couldn't share Miss Marks with Mama and Beth. When the tears finally stopped, she prayed for them, prayed for herself and prayed for Miss Marks.*

*Two resolutions burned deep in her bosom that November afternoon. First she decided that her life was going to be different than Mama's. She would go to college as Miss Marks had encouraged her to do. She would become a school teacher like her.*

*The second resolution was spoken out loud, "I'll take care of you, Mama and Beth, even if you won't take care of yourselves!"*

AGGIE found herself blinking back tears—weeping for the idealistic young girl that she had been. Then a shuddering sigh escaped as she realized, after all this memory searching, why she had become depressed, or so physically tired all of the time. She was sure now—it was emotional exhaustion.

The moment she'd changed her major in college from teaching to the study of law, the battle began. Avenging the wrongs committed by Uncle Chester and her father became her driving force; getting through law school, achieving honors and scholarships.

Out in the real world, she began her law career battling. Each man she punished was Uncle Chester or her father—while each woman she protected or nurtured was Mama or Beth!

Unfortunately, out of all the legal cases which had come to her, only a few women really pulled themselves up and out of the mire of victimization. The rest returned to the abuser or remarried the same kind of wife beaters, adulterers and child molesters.

They continued to give in to their own destructive behavior, allowing circumstances to control their lives. It was like watching Mama and Beth over and over, resulting in the same feelings of frustration and helplessness.

Suddenly, a profound awareness exploded inside her mind and heart, jarring her very soul—*she* was a *victim*! From that November afternoon up in the tree, at twelve years of age when she resolved to protect Mama and Beth—until recently when she decided to dissolve the law firm, *she* had allowed herself to become a *victim* of the victims! In her own way, she had been no different than Mama and Beth.

# Chapter Nine

Friday at the office Aggie tried to keep her mind occupied. In spite of the things she had to do, paying bills, catching up on loose ends, and calling to reserve a secure storage unit for her files, desk, chairs and tables, the day dragged unbearably. Sometime after 2:00 this afternoon a decision would be made that would have a great impact on her life, on other's lives—for good or ill. Every little while, she uttered a prayer.

Eventually, she made lists of what she needed to take with her to Austin. She also set a tentative date to leave.

After Sally left at 5:30, even though she wasn't hungry, she ordered a small pizza to be delivered to her office. She didn't dare leave. She wanted to be there when Bob called.

Luke Barnes slid his long frame into the Lexus, turned on the motor, drove out of the underground parking of his office building and turned toward the country club. Joy Marshall had called him at the office, asking if he could meet her there for dinner. He'd taken her to dinner a few days ago hoping it might ease his restlessness and irritability. Though he had enjoyed himself at first, the evening droned on, leaving him feeling empty. Knowing he hadn't been good company for Joy, he wondered why she wanted to try it again.

He enjoyed people more when entertaining in his own home. He liked people around—he needed them, in fact. The busier he kept himself, the sooner he could come to grips with his situation.

Maybe if he sold the house he would feel better. But where did he want to live? Perhaps it was best he couldn't decide right away. He'd promised the cook Doris was sending him that they would give it a try for six months. If he liked her and her cooking, and if she was happy working for him, maybe she would cook for him wherever he moved.

It was 7:30 and Aggie had just decided to go on home when the phone rang. She reached for it, answering before it could ring a second time. "Hello?"

"Aggie, Bob. I called your home and of course I discovered you weren't there, so I called here."

"Tell me everything, Bob," she said, straining to keep the anxiety out of her voice.

"Well, the arrests were made this morning as I said they might. The doctors involved were innocent of any wrong doing and were very concerned about the altered medical records. They said that the patient whose record was used could be in a serious health condition because of the switch. Also, the DA, in consultation with Judge Wicken, figured they had enough evidence to vacate her previous order and incarcerate the woman until she has delivered the baby. After the birth, the father will get full custody. They think the mother was involved in the conspiracy."

Tears of relief spilled over as Aggie mentally uttered a quick prayer of thanks. "Thank you, Bob. I'm so grateful to you and Barry for bringing this about."

"You're the one responsible for it, Aggie, and I relayed this to the DA. He's going to call and thank you."

"When are they going to tell the father?"

"Tonight."

"Oh good!"

"As a sidelight, Aggie, the authorities have discovered that Crystal Carson only arranged medically approved abortions for those with big money. Apparently there are those who don't want the taint that abortion invariably brings when and if found out by their social peers. Though subtle in this era, the stigma is there—even for those who believe in it. So, Ms Carson and her bunch of malefactors have made big bucks."

"Interesting, but I'm not surprised. Tell Doris the news and tell her I'll be calling her with the date when I'll be leaving for Austin. It will be sooner than I thought."

"Good! You need a break, Aggie."

# *Chapter Ten*

One week later, Friday night, Bob and Doris brought over dinner and helped Aggie pack her van in preparation for her move to Austin. Bob carried her computer, table and printer down on the elevator and then came back for the second load—things she used to cook with—pots, pans, condiments, spices and utensils. After a few more boxes of sundry things, suit cases and clothes bags, the van was finally loaded.

Aggie followed her friends to the front door. "How can I say goodbye to you both?"

"Don't say it, Aggie," Doris said, smiling. "Let's just say we'll be seeing each other soon."

"Let's do. I hate goodbyes."

"By the way, Aggie, I have a message from Lucas for you—or a request."

"Oh? What?"

"He had Mary, the Hispanic woman who works for him, call and ask if you could cook dinner for a party tomorrow night at 6:30. Mrs. Butler, the one who cooks for the parties once in a while, sprained her ankle. Mary said the menu is planned and that all the food has been purchased for the meal."

Aggie bit her lip. "Well, that's jumping into it fast. I suppose I can manage it—if I leave a little earlier in the morning."

"Also," Doris continued, "Lucas is out of town and he'll arrive just in time for the dinner. He said to tell you that he'll meet you after dinner. Oh, and one more thing, Aggie. Don't tell Lucas you are an attorney."

"Why?"

"Well," Doris hedged, "it might make him concerned about you being his cook if he knows."

Aggie frowned in concern. "Why would my personal life concern him if I just cook for him? It doesn't make sense..."

"Aggie, I told him you did legal work in a law firm." She rushed on, "That's all he needs to know. Promise me you won't say anything about your profession until we talk about it again."

Aggie looked over at Bob, who just shook his head and shrugged his shoulders.

"Well, all right," Aggie agreed reluctantly, "but I'm only going along with this for a short time."

Doris hugged her friend. "Thanks, Aggie. Goodbye and good luck. We'll talk on the phone."

~~~~~~~~~

Aggie woke up at 5:00 A.M. feeling more rested than she had expected. Mixed emotions bubbled inside her as she lay there contemplating the drastic change she was making in her life. She felt both excitement and nervousness over this new adventure, wondering what lay ahead.

A feeling of loneliness washed over her. "If only Mama and Beth were here to wish me well." A few tears trickled down her cheeks, dropping onto the pillow.

She stepped out of bed and into the shower. An hour later, she was in the van. Heading south on I 35 E past Cedar Hills, she felt a flutter of excitement. How odd, she thought, this feels like a vacation! Savoring the sensation, she remembered the other time she'd experienced this excitement. It was when her family went on their one and only vacation a year before her father left. Many times she'd tried to simulate this feeling, this excitement as she took short trips to see different parts of Texas, but with no success.

Turning her attention to the countryside, Aggie knew that the state of Texas produced more wild flowers than any other state, but it was May 22nd and most of the wild flowers had come and gone. She wished it were April or early May so she could enjoy the sprawling fields of Texas Blue Bonnets and Indian Paint Brushes. She'd read that Bluebonnets signal to the bees when their pollen is ready for gathering or has already been gathered. The white mark on the flower's banner petal turns to magenta when pollen has been foraged by bees.

Her eyes searched for Indian Blankets or Fire Wheels which bloomed from April to June in some parts of Texas, but she couldn't see any. However, she did see some cut leaf Daisies along the roadside here and there.

Aggie, born and raised in Texas, loved its many areas of beauty. She passed farms of maize and field corn. Cattle grazed on the grassy hills and meadows. Approaching Hillsboro, where I 35 W from Fort Worth joined I 35 E, there were larger farms of maize. All this was comforting to her spirit after the stress she'd just been through. To have her mind free from the cares of her profession, with no pending cases hovering over her, seemed unreal.

Coming to Temple, Texas, she noticed homes in the middle of expanses of grazing land. She delighted in the fields of sunflowers and the forests of trees. Georgetown came next and almost before she knew it she was at the outskirts of the growing city of Austin, Capitol of Texas.

Edginess soon replaced her peaceful vacation feeling. She pulled over to the side of the road and stopped to look at the directions Doris had given her. Back on the highway she continued south on I 35 through Austin, crossing over Town Lake and getting off at Riverside, Exit 233 West. By diligent attention to the directions, she found her way to Bees Cave road and a few miles further she came to a sign saying Barton Creek Road. With a sigh of relief she turned into what was obviously an exclusive subdivision of custom homes in a wide variety of styles.

It was a beautiful area of rolling hills covered with lush green trees and foliage. Each home sat well back on a very large lot—at least four or five acres by Aggie's estimate—the only clue to the occupant, a mail box standing guard at the curb.

At last she found the name of Lucas Barnes. She drove into the private paved road which divided as it approached the house. One fork led around the right of the building, the other led to a wide U shaped driveway which she took, stopping at the apex of it directly in front of the house. The only landscaping was wild and wooded except immediately around the house, where raised light brick planters curved aesthetically. But they were empty—no plants—no flowers. Aggie felt a bleak emptiness that was more than just barren planters. She frowned, wondering why. Studying the house itself, she noted that it was a two-story, constructed mainly of native Texas limestone. Aggie found it architecturally interesting. From where she was sitting, she could see at least six gables to the roof, including the pitched roof overhang of the wide front porch with its square stone pillars on either side.

It was time to get out of the car and go to the door, she told herself. She felt relieved that Lucas Barnes was out of town. This would give her time to get her bearings and settle in a little before meeting her employer. She had worked so long for herself, having an employer sounded foreign to her. How would she feel, she wondered, receiving orders rather than giving them?"

Slowly, hesitantly, she got out of the van and walked to the front door...stood a moment then pushed the bell.

Shortly the door opened. The woman who appeared asked, "Yes? May I help you?"

Aggie couldn't speak for a moment. She wasn't sure what she had expected, but certainly not this lovely, well dressed, genteel person standing in front of her. The gray at the temples of her well coiffured black hair lent an air of sophistication. The thought flashed through her mind—hardly the usual housekeeper type.

Finding her voice, Aggie said, "Uh...this is the Lucas Barnes' residence isn't it?"

"Yes, it is."

"I'm the new cook," she blurted out, feeling stupid that she was so nervous.

Mary Gomez reacted with suspicion. She studied this petite young woman, dressed in light blue denim knee-length shorts and a white T shirt, who couldn't be more than eighteen. "I'm sorry, miss, you're mistaken, Mr. Lucas has already hired a cook."

"He's already hired one?" Aggie asked, confused. "But...just last night someone contacted Doris...and..."

"Doris Biederman?" interrupted the woman.

"Yes. My name is Agnes McBride and Doris..."

"*You* are Agnes McBride?" the woman interrupted again.

"Yes, I am."

"Why...you can't be. Agnes McBride is an older woman."

"I don't know what you mean by older, but I'm thirty-one."

"Thirty-one?" Mary was shocked. She eyed the girl's short dark hair, her large questioning blue eyes, certain that she was looking at a teenager.

"You look...uh no more than eighteen."

Aggie laughed nervously. This had happened to her before, but today it unnerved her. "Someone called Doris last night and asked her to tell me that Mr. Barnes would be out of town, and asked if I could possibly take over for the cook he usually uses because she had sprained her ankle."

That was proof enough for Mary. "Please forgive me for keeping you standing on the porch. Do come in, Miss McBride, or is it Mrs.?"

Aggie stepped into the lovely foyer. "It's miss, but call me Aggie."

"Glad to meet you, Aggie, I'm Mary." Her smile was beautiful and radiant.

"I'm happy to meet *you*, Mary, and...I'm glad to finally be here."

"Have you had lunch, Aggie?"

"No, I haven't."

"Come into the kitchen and see where you'll be working. I'll fix lunch while we get acquainted."

Aggie smiled. "Thank you," she said, looking around.

"I'm sorry for rushing you, Miss McBride, please, go ahead, take your time and look around. This will be your home for a while I understand."

"Thank you, Mary. I guess I expected to see stone and marble everywhere because of the outside appearance of the house."

"That's what Mrs. Barnes wanted, but she became so busy in her work, she didn't have time to help Mr. Barnes choose, so she gave him carte blanche, as one would say. He chose solid oak floors."

"I like his choice," Aggie said. She also liked the rugs placed in the center of the foyer, and the rugs down the hall. They were cream color, sprinkled with a pattern of light browns and several shades of green.

To her right was a large formal dining room, with a long, light colored oak table and eight oak chairs padded in forest green.

Turning to the left, she saw a small formal living room, which—like the planters outside—was empty, totally devoid of furniture. Only a cream hued carpet lay on the floor As she stared into the room, the same bleak feeling came over her, mingled with a sense of sadness, of loss. Again she wondered why. These emotions seemed to come from the house itself as though some great sadness lingered here. She pulled her eyes away.

Across the foyer on the right a lovely staircase wound upward. The wooden steps were covered with a taupe runner rug with a light cream border, matching the background of the other rugs.

Aggie smiled. "It's all very nice, Mary. I think I'm through examining this part of my employer's house."

Mary led her down the hall to the kitchen, smiling to herself. Luke was going to get the shock of his life and she was *not* going to prepare him!

Aggie gasped in delight as she stepped into the kitchen/family room combination. "I love U-shaped kitchens. They are so efficient."

The kitchen floor was the same golden brown oak and the cabinets were white, with shiny, speckled-granite counters. The kitchen table was a round oak, with a single carved pedestal base, placed in a large bay window. Aggie was delighted. The whole area was cheery and light.

The family room area, with its large stone fireplace, was partially furnished; there were no pictures or other decor, but the furniture was comfortable and practical. The couch was golden beige; the two large chairs were upholstered in forest green tactile fabric. A rug with a unique pattern of neutral tones, rust and rose, gave warmth to the room. The floral pattern of the throw pillows on the couch had the same warm colors as the rug. In front of the couch was a large old chest of dark distressed wood on which some magazines were neatly piled.

Aggie sighed. "How nice."

"Come and let me show you the deck, Aggie."

Aggie followed Mary out one of the doors to the deck. "How wonderful!" she exclaimed, admiring the expansive two-level, redwood deck with a redwood retaining wall incorporating planters and benches.

Just beyond the deck were the woods. The trees and foliage, clustered close together, were wild and pristine looking, Aggie felt, just as they must have a hundred years ago.

Her eyes were drawn back to the planters. They too were barren. If this house were mine, she thought, the first thing I would do is plant flowers! And the second thing I would do is get some deck furniture. Mentally she shook away these thoughts, reminding herself that she was here only to cook, not to garden.

"I know," Mary said, as if reading Aggie's thoughts. "The deck could use some furniture, but at least there are the benches." She gave no apology or explanation. Leading Aggie into the house she asked, "Do you like tamales, Aggie?"

"Yes, I do!"

"I have some freshly made ones, also beans and homemade flour tortillas."

Aggie's eyes lit up. "That sounds so good, Mary. I've always wanted to learn how to make authentic Mexican food," she said, watching Mary warm the food and then fill the plates.

"Mr. Barnes is quite tired of my Mexican fare, but I don't cook any other way. He's been looking forward to *your* cooking. Please have a seat at the table, Aggie," she instructed, placing a plate before Aggie then one for herself.

"When does Mr. Barnes expect me to begin the regular cooking?"

"Monday night. You'll have time to unpack and maybe shop for anything you might need for your menus and for yourself. Mr. Barnes told me to tell you that if you want to eat breakfast and lunch in your own place, you may, but that you're welcome to eat here. You will want to eat here at least until you go shopping for yourself. Also he would like to meet with you tomorrow, Sunday, so you can get acquainted and so he can tell you what kinds of meals he likes and expects—and how often he entertains and so on."

"All right. This food is delicious, Mary. Will you show me how to make it?"

"I would be glad to, Aggie," Mary said, pleased.

After lunch, Mary got into the van with Aggie and directed her to drive around the house to the little cottage where she would be living. Surrounded on three sides by dense growth, the small house bordered the driveway which continued on in a small loop to the garage at the back of the main house.

The cottage actually turned out to be a small brick home with an attached carport into which Aggie now drove the van. They got out and Mary unlocked the front door. Aggie was delighted. The front room was charming and cozy with one flowered couch of blue, white and rose and one upholstered chair in plain blue. My colors she thought. There was a small cheery kitchen, one bedroom and one bath.

"This is very nice, Mary. I'm going to be quite comfortable here."

"Good. Now, may I help you carry things in from your van?"

"No, thank you, Mary. There really isn't anything that I can't handle myself."

"All right, Aggie, but let me know if you do need help in any way."

"I will, Mary. Thanks again."

Mary walked the short distance back to the main house, and Aggie began unloading. When she had finished carrying everything in, she made several trips to the Barnes' kitchen, finding places for her cooking utensils, spices, and condiments.

"What is the menu for tonight, Mary?"

"Mrs. Butler planned to have fried chicken, mashed potatoes and gravy, peas and Jell-O salad. She's already made two apple pies."

"Sounds good, but do you think Mr. Barnes would mind if I changed it a little?"

"Oh my, no. He's the most adventuresome eater I know."

"Good. That's the way I like to cook."

Aggie foraged around, found what was available in the wonderful walk-in pantry and in the refrigerator. She decided that instead of fried chicken she would marinate the chicken breasts in herb and lemon, cut them in strips and coat them with a combination of bread crumbs and Parmesan cheese and saute them in olive oil. The garnish would be artichoke hearts and tomato fondue.

Aggie realized she was actually humming as she began the preparations. Instead of mashed potatoes, she decided to peel and slice the potatoes, mix them with rings of fresh onions and a little Italian dressing and bake them. The raspberry jello salad was already done. Finding some frozen raspberries, she decided to garnish the molded salad with a dollop of whipped cream with three raspberries on top. A sprig of parsley propped up in the middle added a note of *joie de vivre*—joy of life.

Several hours later, when the food was mostly prepared, Aggie walked up to her little house and showered. She changed into white cut offs and an indigo blue T shirt. When she returned to put the finishing touches on the meal, she found that Mary had set the dining room table for four.

"Who does Mr. Barnes prefer to have serve the meal, Mary?"

"I will serve it tonight, but he has certain peculiarities when he entertains. He'll explain everything tomorrow."

"My aprons are still packed, do you have an extra one, Mary?"

"I don't, but Mrs. Butler left hers here yesterday." Mary opened the small broom closet and pulled off the hook a flowered apron and handed it to her.

Puttin it on, she and Mary laughed; it almost reached the floor! "Oh well, I'll make it do."

At 6:30 the doorbell rang and Mary left to answer it. She came back smiling. "Mr. Barnes got here just as his three guests arrived. He said they'd be ready to eat in about ten minutes."

"Does Mr. Barnes serve cocktails beforehand?"

"He offers one to his guests, but most decline because they know he doesn't drink. He was raised by a mother who taught him otherwise."

"Good. I like people completely sober when they eat my cooking."

Mary placed the salad by each place and returned. Ten minutes later, Aggie prepared the plates, placing the food decoratively on each as Mary watched. She'd never seen this way of serving. Aggie looked up and smiled. "I learned this from a master chef."

"I see. It looks so colorful and appetizing, Aggie," she said, picking up a couple of plates and carrying them in.

Returning after taking the next two in, Mary said, smiling, "You're getting rave notices about how it looks, anyway."

"I suppose Mr. Barnes knows I'm here, then?"

"I really don't know, he didn't ask, he's too busy visiting with his company."

"May I fix you a plate, now, Mary?"

She shook her head. "Later, Aggie."

After Mrs. Butler's apple pie was served, Aggie relaxed. "Why don't you sit down now, Mary, and eat dinner."

"I will if you'll join me."

"I couldn't eat a bite, Mary, I'm still too keyed up. Go ahead and eat," she said, fixing Mary a plate. "I'll start the dishes, and eat a little later."

"Mr. Barnes usually has me hire someone to clean up the kitchen, but he's been out of town." She sat at the table and began to eat. "My, this is good, Aggie. I think I'm going to enjoy your stay here."

"Thank you," she said, scrubbing on a pan. "It's quite a change for me—a change I needed."

Shortly thereafter, Luke Barnes, with one of his guests, Joy Marshall, walked into the kitchen to meet and compliment the new cook. They looked around, clearly puzzled. Luke frowned, staring at the young girl at the sink, wrapped in Mrs. Butler's oversized apron, busily washing pans. He looked over at Mary quizzically.

Aggie glanced over her shoulder and saw a handsome couple, but turned back to the sink quickly. She wasn't in the mood to meet any of Lucas Barnes' friends.

"Who is this, Mary?" he asked, gesturing to the dishwasher.

Mary smiled and shrugged her shoulders.

Irritated, Luke asked, "Where's old Agnes? Did she limp off to bed with lumbago or something? I expected to meet her. Now."

Aggie turned around slowly staring at the man and asked with just a touch of ice, "*Old* Agnes?"

Mary was unable to contain her laughter. All three looked in her direction. "Mr. Barnes," she said, finally. "Meet Agnes McBride. Agnes meet your employer, Lucas Barnes."

Aggie's eyes widened in shock, then she spoke in a tone to match his. "You are *old* Lucas?"

Mary was still having a good laugh over their reactions when Luke abruptly turned to her.

"Mary! This is no laughing matter, she's just a kid!"

The woman thus addressed couldn't answer—she was convulsed with laughter.

"Joy, will you please excuse us? I need to settle something here."

With obvious reluctance, Joy left.

Luke turned back to Mary, but before he could say anything, Aggie addressed him.

"Mr. Barnes, if that is who you are, I'm not just a kid, I'm thirty-one."

Luke scrutinized her face only, since the apron covered the rest of her from neck to toe. She had the largest and bluest eyes he'd ever seen. Why, they were actually cobalt blue, he thought. He opened his mouth to say something, then closed it and shook his head. "You're really thirty-one?"

"Yes."

"At least that's better than seventeen—but for some reason I thought you'd be older."

"And for some reason I thought *you* would be older."

Luke turned thoughtful. "Hmm, I think we've been hoodwinked by my cousin."

"Your cousin?" Aggie asked, shocked again.

"Yes, didn't Doris tell you?"

"She said you were a *friend.*"

He smiled. "Well, that's true, too. We were close friends in high school, as well as cousins."

Aggie's brows drew together as she tried to take it all in, then they rose in amazement, a small smile on her face. "You're right, she *has* hoodwinked us."

"Why do you think she didn't tell you we were cousins?"

"She knows I wouldn't have come if I'd known."

"Why?"

"Doris is a dear friend and if my working for you didn't work out, I...I just wouldn't have wanted to jeopardize our friendship."

"I'll have to admit, I wouldn't have had you come, had I known everything."

"Don't feel obligated, Mr. Barnes, I haven't even unpacked."

"I didn't mean that I didn't want you to stay, I mean....I uh...need to talk to my cousin."

"I think I need to talk to her, myself," Aggie said, narrowing her eyes, an uncompromising smile on her face.

"Luke, your guests are wondering what's keeping you," a sultry voice spoke from the doorway.

For the first time, Aggie looked at the woman. She was strikingly beautiful. Tall and slim with light brown shoulder length hair, layered in the latest style, light green eyes and an ivory complexion.

"Excuse me, Mrs. or is it Ms.?" Luke asked.

"It's Miss," she emphasized.

"Yes...well, Miss McBride, please excuse me. We'll pursue this tomorrow after lunch here in the kitchen. Is that all right with you?"

"Yes, Mr. Barnes," Aggie said. She watched him walk out of the kitchen, with the woman holding on to his arm possessively.

Aggie turned to Mary. "You knew what was coming I see."

"Yes. I didn't want to warn you, I wanted Luke to have a surprise."

"He certainly got one, and so did I! In fact, I'm still in a state of shock." She smiled. "My friend, Doris, certainly did pull one on us." Suddenly Aggie wilted and sat down at the table.

"You're tired, Aggie. Let me get you something to eat now."

"Thanks, Mary, it's been quite a day and a long one."

Mary placed a plate of food before Aggie and sat down to finish hers.

"You call Mr. Barnes 'Luke,' Mary?"

"Yes." She smiled. "I just called him Mr. Barnes to you because you were new. I helped raise that boy, along with my own two sons when I worked for his parents. My husband worked for Luke's father at the ranch and I helped in the kitchen. We had a house behind the ranch."

"Is your husband living?"

"No, he died four years ago."

"I'm sorry. Where are your boys?"

"They are both married and have children. One is a doctor in El Paso and one has a successful farm in East Texas."

"And you work for Mr. Barnes now?"

"Yes. He won't let me do heavy cleaning anymore. I just oversee the cleaning and ironing. I do the wash, take care of his social engagements, sometimes serve when he's entertaining as I did tonight. I do some of the cooking, but he likes variety so he hired you. When Luke built this house, he added on special quarters for me. I have a small sitting room, bedroom, bath and kitchenette down the hall from the kitchen."

"It sounds like he cares about you."

"He does. He treats me and my children and grandchildren like family, and we think of him as family."

Aggie became silent and thoughtful as she ate. When she was through, she pushed back the chair. "I feel much better, Mary, I'm going to finish the dishes. You go on to bed."

Mary stood up and carried her plate to the sink. "It won't take long if we work together. You've already washed the pans. I'll put away the food and you can load the dishwasher."

~~~~~~~~~~

Aggie opened her suitcase, pulled out her nightgown and put it on. After she'd brushed her teeth and washed her face, she turned off the overhead light, turned on the lamp beside the bed and got in. She could tell by the pleasant scent of the sheets that they were freshly washed. Propping herself up with both pillows, she sat thinking about this strange new situation.

She smiled as she deliberated on how Doris had managed to fool both her and Lucas. "Clever girl you are, Dor," she said aloud. She had noticed that there was a phone in the kitchen. "If it weren't so late, I'd call you right now!" However, Aggie felt more like thanking Doris than chastising her. For some strange reason, she felt at home here—and more than that—she felt relieved that a new case wasn't hanging over her head, along with others that invariably interlocked or overlapped each other. It felt good to put her practice on hold. Doris was right. She needed the rest—much more than she'd realized.

"Well, Mr. Lucas Barnes," she suddenly decided, "I'm staying whether you like it or not. We made an agreement to try it for six months and that's what we're going to do—even if you did expect an older woman—and even if I expected an older man." With that, she turned off the light, removed the extra pillow and snuggled down in bed, feeling more of a healthy exhaustion than the usual emotional exhaustion. Promptly remembering something important, she slipped out of bed onto her knees, and again thanked God for helping her, Barry and the authorities put a stop to the abortion—and for her friend, Doris, who cared enough about her to arrange this new job—this respite.

# Chapter Eleven

Sunday morning, Aggie woke up feeling disoriented. Where was she? She remembered and smiled. She also felt displaced. She had no idea where to go to church; she didn't have any food in the kitchen; she didn't even know where to buy groceries! And she was hungry. She didn't feel like running into Lucas Barnes up at the house so she decided to unpack and wait for lunch.

Aggie, used to moving fast, was completely unpacked by 10:30. After showering, she threw on a pair of jeans, tennis shoes and a T shirt. What could she do now? she asked herself. She looked out her bedroom window and studied the woods around the small house. "How beautiful," she murmured. Walking quickly to the back door, she stopped, realizing she'd awakened without that terrible feeling of exhaustion! "Well, chalk one up to Doc Davis. He was right." How good it felt to have energy! She opened the door and went down the steps to explore the woods.

~~~~~~~~~~

Mary returned from Catholic Mass at 11:15 and dialed Aggie to come and have brunch. No answer. Sure that Aggie must be in the shower, she waited until 11:30 and tried again, then at noon. Still no answer. Mary guessed that Aggie may have gone for a drive. Deciding to leave a note on the door for her, she walked up to the cottage. Seeing Aggie's van still in the carport, she rang the bell. No answer. Mary began to worry. Where could she be?

Back home, Mary called again at 12:30. Thoroughly alarmed, she waited for Luke to get home from church. The minute he arrived she told him of her concern.

"I'm sure she's fine, Mary. But I'll change and go look around for her. He ran upstairs and took off his suit, and put on a pair of jeans, feeling more concern than he'd let Mary see.

Luke ran out the kitchen door across the patio and down the steps to the driveway. He walked briskly up to the cottage and rang the door-bell. No answer. Glancing at his watch he saw that it was nearly 1:00. He frowned and went around the back and called Aggie's name. No answer. Noticing some small foot prints leading into the trees, he relaxed. The woods were approximately five and a half acres. The neighbors on both sides of him also had five acres and none of it was fenced. He figured she probably got a little turned around.

He walked in the direction of the footprints, lost them and picked them up again. Finally, he lost them entirely. He called her name now and then and listened, hoping he didn't have to walk his whole five acres as well as the neighbor's to find her!

As he got deeper into the woods, he came to a spot where there were a bunch of foot prints, going and coming. He stood there a moment trying to decide which way to go.

"*Old* Lucas Barnes, what are *you* doing here?" came a voice from somewhere.

Startled, Luke looked around. "What...where are you?!"

"Up here!"

Luke looked up; there up in a tree, Agnes McBride was sitting cross-legged on a large limb.

"What in the blazes are you doing up there?"

"I do my best thinking up in a tree," she said, grinning. "You taking your morning constitutional, Mr. Barnes?"

"No!" he exclaimed with impatience, "I've been looking for *you*."

Aggie looked surprised. "You were?" She looked at her watch and was immediately contrite. "Oh-oh, I didn't realize it was so late. I'm sorry. I thought I heard someone call my name, but I thought it must be my imagination. I was sure it was a neighbor calling to someone."

Her apology cooled his agitation. "Are you sure you're thirty-one? You look about thirteen sitting up there," he said, a teasing twinkle in his eyes.

"I think so, but I feel younger today."

"Are you hungry?"

"I'm starved. I was hungry when I woke up, but my cupboard was bare."

"Why didn't you come up to the house and get something?"

"I didn't want to face you this morning," Aggie said, with candidness.

He grinned. "Do I scare you?"

Aggie grinned back, thinking. After Uncle Chester, she had never let any man intimidate her, but—Lucas Barnes was a man to take seriously. "Maybe."

Luke threw back his head and laughed. "I can be ornery sometimes, but I'm really harmless."

Watching him as he approached the tree unaware of her presence, Aggie had studied him. He was a magnificent looking man, she thought. He was over six feet tall. Even though he was slim, his wide shoulders accentuated his narrow hips, and his T shirt revealed tan, muscular arms. His eyes, and the smile she'd seen last night were certainly something that could cause a girl to catch her breath, she mused. High prominent cheek bones, and a substantial jaw left his cheeks hollow, giving his face a look of ruggedness and character. Yes, Doris my friend, your cousin is wonderful looking. And Aggie was sure the reason she allowed herself to examine him was because he *was* Doris' cousin.

"Well, Miss McBride, are you going let me get a crick in my neck from looking up? That's a pretty high limb you're on," he said. His eyes full of mischief, he held out his arms. "Shall I catch you?"

Aggie eyed his inviting arms and surprised herself—for an instant she wanted to jump into them. She swallowed hard and responded a bit stiffly, "I can get down, thank you."

Luke watched her quick agile movements as she moved down to one limb then to the next. He also noticed her nice curves, her small waist. Shaking his head slightly, he tried to dislodge the compelling image from his mind.

She jumped the rest of the way. "There," she said breathlessly, "I made it."

He looked down at her. "You did. You look like a professional tree climber."

Aggie laughed. "I used to be. It feels good to climb a tree again, and to walk around in nature. This is beautiful country."

"I'm glad you like it," he said, pleased. "I like it, too. Follow me and I'll lead you out. Mary has lunch ready for us."

"Sounds good!" Aggie, following behind, found she had to trot to keep up with Luke's long steps, and also found herself admiring the back view of Doris' cousin. His brown hair lay nicely against his handsome neck. Aggie always wondered why a man would allow his hair to grow long enough to cover his neck. The back of a man's neck was such a masculine part of him.

When they walked into the kitchen, Mary's expression of relief was unmistakable. "Aggie, I'm glad you're safe. You scared us."

"I did? I'm sorry. I was having such a good time exploring the woods behind the cottage, I forgot the time."

"If you'd like to freshen up, Aggie, there's a half bath down the hall, first right."

"Thank you."

"I think I'll run upstairs and do the same, Mary," Luke said as he stepped toward the hall.

When they were all seated around the table, Aggie exclaimed, "Oh, good! More tamales, beans and tortillas."

"I'm glad someone around here appreciates them," Mary said casting a glance at Luke.

~~~~~~~~~~

After the kitchen was cleaned up, Luke suggested that he and Aggie sit down at the table. He invited Mary to join them, which she did.

"First thing, Miss McBride, since we have a mutual 'friend,' and since we're close to the same age, we might use first names. How do you feel about that?"

"I feel fine about it. Shall I call you Lucas or Luke?"

"Luke. And may I call you Agnes?"

"You may, if you prefer, but I think Agnes is an ugly name."

"It is?"

"Surely, you don't think other wise?" her smile daring him to tell the truth.

"Well...by itself, it isn't the most melodious name, but on you, it's rather nice."

She raised her brows, doubting his statement. "No one has ever said that to me before. I don't know you very well, obviously, so I can't tell if you're trying to make me feel better about my name or if..."

"When you get to know me better, you'll learn I don't say things I don't mean. What would you like me to call you?"

"I prefer to be called Aggie."

"All right, Aggie, shall we phone our mutual friend, and put her on the spot?"

"Oh, let's do!"

"I'll put her on the speaker phone." He dialed and waited. Doris answered. "Hello, Doris." he said, "where's *old Agnes*?"

"She didn't get there?" she asked, alarmed.

"No, she didn't."

"Oh, Luke, something's happened to her!"

"Something happened to her all right, because the only person who arrived was a girl who looked seventeen—claiming to be old Agnes." Aggie was enjoying this immensely.

"Luke! How dare you scare me like that?"

"How dare you deceive us like you did?"

"I didn't deceive you. If you'll remember, you called her 'old Agnes.' I didn't."

Aggie spoke into the speaker. "Why did you call Luke an older gentleman?"

"Aggie! Hi! Well...Luke *is* older than you, he's thirty-two. And he's a gentleman—sometimes." She laughed. "Besides, I didn't say he was a gentleman."

"Clever, Dor. I'll have to hand it to you, you managed to pull it off quite well."

"Thank you...I guess. Are you both mad at me?"

In the silence that followed, Luke winked at Aggie.

"Come on, you two, quit giving me the silent treatment. Are you going to stay, Aggie?" she queried, obviously quite unrepentant over the deception.

"Luke hasn't asked me to—he's still in shock."

"Luke?" Doris questioned.

"I don't know yet, she's a little odd. She disappeared from the cottage this morning. We couldn't find her anywhere. It scared Mary. I had to go looking for her." He let another silence follow.

"Well...where did you find her, Luke? Quit this!"

"I saw some small footprints leading into the thick stand of trees behind the cottage. I followed them but soon lost them. I called and called. I had to walk over a whole ten acres searching. Finally a voice startled me. I looked up and there she was, high up in a tree sitting cross-legged on a limb. This time she looked thirteen." Aggie and Mary were trying to stifle their laughter as they listened to Luke's exaggerated version of the events.

This time the silence was on the other end of the line. At last Doris asked, "Is this true, Aggie?"

"I'm afraid so."

More silence. "Why?"

"I do my best thinking up in a tree."

"Aggie, is this you I'm talking to or an imposter?" She heard Aggie laugh. "I guess I don't know you as well as I thought I did."

"To ease your mind, Dor. I'm staying—even if your cousin here hasn't confirmed it. I've unpacked. We made an agreement to try this for six months and I'm not going to let him renege." Luke raised his brows in surprise.

"Oh, good," Doris said, sounding relieved. "Then you like it there?"

"I do. Mary has been so nice to me. The cottage is very comfortable." She looked over at Luke. "I *feel* comfortable here."

"Thank you for telling me that."

"Thank you, Dor, for caring enough about me to arrange this break for me. And tell Bob thanks for everything."

"I will, Aggie."

"And my thanks, cuz," Luke added. "She's a great cook."

The moment Luke hung up the phone, Mary excused herself to go take a nap. Luke suggested that he and Aggie seat themselves in the more comfortable chairs in the connecting family room.

Aggie slipped off her tennis shoes and curled up in a chair while Luke sat across from her on the couch. During the meal she'd had an opportunity to study Luke Barnes a little closer. His eyes were chestnut brown, the color of his hair. They were gentle eyes and they spoke of vulnerability. They were deep, and unfathomable, but wonderfully attentive when listening to some one. His smile was big and heart warming, crinkling the corners of his eyes, softening his rugged features.

"I'm curious, Aggie, you are so young, why did you need a break? Doris said you worked in a legal firm and I know that can be tedious and stressful at times, but why not just a vacation?"

Aggie thought a moment, trying to decide how much to tell him since Doris had quite strongly suggested that she not tell Luke she was an attorney. "I would rather not go into it if you don't mind, except that some of the cases were stressful to me."

"Oh, you worked for trial lawyers. That explains a lot," he said with a slight grimace. "Now, to explain a few things to you. I don't entertain a lot, just now and then. When I do, I'll have Mary hire a couple of Hispanic girls she knows to clean up the kitchen. There will be times I'll want you and Mary to join us when I have guests. I'll have the girls serve in this case."

"Why? I don't know your friends," she asked, knowing that she wouldn't want to join them when he entertained the woman who had come into the kitchen with him.

He smiled. "You can get to know them."

"But...I don't want to get to know them."

Luke frowned, irritated. "You don't have a choice if you work for me. This is the way I do things."

Aggie stiffened perceptively. Her old reaction to men, in general, flared up. She felt the quick heat of anger. Biting back a sharp retort, she looked down trying to gain control. If he weren't Doris' cousin, she told herself, I wouldn't take this! She looked up at Luke and saw him staring at her with an expression that startled her. If she read it correctly, it was hostility or a close cousin to it. She returned his stare, silent for a few moments; finally and with great difficulty she said, "All right."

# *Chapter Twelve*

The meeting with Luke Barnes had so disconcerted her, Aggie paced through the small house, thinking. What was the matter with the man? Why would her reaction to his request turn him into a such a different person? He'd been kind and gracious until then.

She stepped out onto the back porch. It was almost June and the heat of the afternoon sun was heavy and laden with humidity. In spite of it, she went down the steps and walked through the trees thinking. Soon, she stopped and sat down under the shade of an old oak tree, leaning her back against it, listening to the birds.

A crushing loneliness descended upon her. Her mother and Beth were gone. The only two people she had in the world were Doris—and Miss Marks—wherever she was. Every time Aggie had planned to have Barry look for Alice Marks, a pressing case would come up—or was it something else? She seemed to feel blocked every time she thought of it. Her mind slipped back to when she lost contact with her teacher.

*May, 1981: Aggie hugged Miss Marks fiercely, fighting back tears. It was the last day of school and Miss Marks was going home.*

*"I'll miss you, Miss Marks."*

*"I'll miss you, Aggie, more than you know."*

*Aggie looked up into her teacher's face and saw tears in her eyes.*

*A week after Miss Marks left, her mother planted a bombshell. She informed them that she had accepted an offer to hostess at a very elite restaurant in Dallas, explaining that it would mean much more money for her. "We'll be moving to Dallas," she added.*

*"No!" exclaimed Aggie. "We can't leave. I want to be here when Miss Marks comes back next year."*

*"Did she say she was going to be back, Aggie?"*

*"No. But I know she will!"*

*"Aggie, the moving truck will be here in a week. We are moving to*

Dallas out of necessity. I have to save money to help you and Beth
through college.

"I'll earn my own money, Mama, please don't make us move," she
pleaded, fighting back tears.

"I'm sorry, Aggie, I know how much you've learned under Miss
Marks and how close you've become, but we have to move."

"Beth," Aggie pleaded, "you don't want to move do you?"

Beth looked down and nodded.

Aggie was inconsolable. "I can't leave! I'll...I'll find another family to live with for the winter, then I'll come home in the summer."

Tears welled up her mother's eyes. "I can't do without you, Aggie,
even if you could find a place."

Mama's tears were few and far between, but when they came, they
tore Aggie's heart out. Her determination crumbled. "All right, Mama,
I'll go," she said, her heart aching.

"It will be fun and exciting, Aggie, you wait and see," ventured
Beth.

But it wasn't fun and exciting. Aggie hated the big city of Dallas.
She couldn't ride her bike anywhere except close to home. Mama had
found a small house in a poor neighborhood close to downtown Dallas
and close to the restaurant.

The hot summer dragged on that year with Beth hardly stepping
outside because of her tender skin. Her mother worked every night and
rested most of the morning. Aggie took over the cooking completely.
She and Beth did all the cleaning. In the evening when it was cooler,
she and Beth walked to the small grocery store on the corner and
shopped. The worry over leaving her daughters alone every night
began to take a toll on their mother. The neighborhood was not as safe
as it was in McKinney.

August, 1981: Beth and Aggie found themselves in large, impersonal schools with overcrowded classes. It was a time of social
upheaval, with schools seemingly more committed to social engineer-
ing than to quality education.

However, Aggie was glad that school had started. Now she could
contact her teacher. She wrote a letter to Miss Marks in care of
Slaughter Junior High in McKinney. A week later the office personnel

*returned her letter in a larger envelope and added a short note saying that Miss Marks didn't renew her contract and that they didn't know her home address. Aggie felt desolate and heartbroken. However, worse than these feelings, was the fear Aggie felt over Beth. Beth was getting paler and more listless. One day Beth didn't get up for school. "What is it, Beth?" her mother asked, "don't you feel well?"*

*"I just feel so tired, Mama."*

*Beth stayed home that day and for the next three days, then her mother took her to the doctor. After a thorough examination, the doctor said he could find nothing physically wrong.*

*The next morning, Beth said, "I don't want to go to school anymore, Mama, some of the students there scare me."*

*After much persuasion, Martha realized that Beth would never return to school. The principal agreed that it would be best, at least for now, that Beth study and take her tests at home.*

*When Martha went home that afternoon and explained to her oldest daughter about home study, Beth was excited about it. "But, I wish Aggie could take home study with me."*

*Aggie jumped at the chance. "Can I, Mama?"*

*"We'll see what the principal has to say. I would certainly feel better if Beth had someone with her."*

*Aggie's principal agreed, so for the next three years, Aggie and Beth studied together, and in this small protected cocoon, Beth seemed to lose some of her fears—even able to laugh occasionally.*

*Progressing rapidly, Aggie almost caught up with her sister.*

*May, 1984: Beth graduated quietly and unceremoniously in the small rent house with only Aggie and her mother there to celebrate. It was then that Martha asked her oldest about college. "I have a small college fund put aside for you Beth. If you work just a few hours a week, you'll be able to make it."*

*"Mama, may I help Aggie until she graduates and then we can go to college together?"*

*Martha felt relieved at the suggestion. It eased her mind. "Yes, I think that would be a good idea."*

*May, 1985: As Aggie completed her senior year a year early, Beth became even more lethargic and weak. Aggie began to lose hope that Beth would ever be able to venture into the real world again.*

AGGIE painfully remembered that it was when the summer peaked its hottest in July, that Beth just faded away and died. For two days Beth had remained in bed. Her mother, frightened at the way she looked, called the doctor for an appointment. She got one for the next day.

The next morning, the day of Beth's death, Aggie and her mother were sitting on her bed. Their hopes rose, for Beth smiled and seemed happier than she had for years. She held her arms out and hugged her mother, then her sister, telling each how much she loved them.

That afternoon, before the doctor's appointment, Beth lapsed into a coma. Her mother called an ambulance, but just before it arrived, Beth peacefully slipped away. At first, her mother blamed herself, blamed the doctors, but soon realized that Beth had been slipping away from them, and life ever since Chester McBride entered their lives.

Neither she nor her mother could imagine life without their sweet, kind Beth. Her mother's faith in a hereafter, sustained her, but Mama was never the same after that. Aggie suspected that she suffered doubly over Beth's death because of the terrible thing her brother-in-law had done.

It was strange, Aggie thought, though the grief and loneliness she felt over the loss of Beth seemed unbearable, she remembered feeling relieved that her loving, fragile sister had gone home to Jesus where she would be safe from men like her father who deserted her—and men like Uncle Chester.

In her imagination, she saw Beth smiling and happy with roses in her cheeks, running through a beautiful garden of flowers. She kept this in her mind constantly as she enrolled in Southern Methodist University a year early, riding the bus there and back.

After the first year in college, at eighteen, she began working as a waitress at the same restaurant as her mother. She smiled as she remembered working with her mother. How proud she was that Martha McBride was her mother and how pretty she looked dressed up— always smiling at the customers.

One evening at the restaurant, her mother collapsed. An ambulance was called and Aggie rode with her to the hospital. It was shortly after the doctors examined her, that her mother died. There had been one brief moment when her mother's eyes opened, focusing briefly on Aggie's face, smiling weakly, trying to hide her great sadness. Two lonely tears rolled down her cheeks. She never spoke. The doctor explained to Aggie that her heart just gave out.

An overwhelming feeling of grief and loneliness came over Aggie. "Oh Mama...Beth how I miss you both." Leaning against the tree, hugging her knees, Aggie lay her head down and gave in to her grief.

Some time later, she heard the snap of a twig. Her head flew up and she found herself looking into the face of Luke Barnes; so deep in to her grief, she couldn't react.

"Aggie," Luke said, "are you all right?"

His sympathetic voice made her want to cry—she wasn't through crying—she needed to cry. "Please leave, I need to be alone."

"Did I hurt your feelings by the way I talked to you?"

Aggie shook her head, fighting tears. "I'm grieving for my mother and sister who died—please leave."

Luke sat down beside her, slipped his arm around her and pulled her head over onto his shoulder. "Cry, Aggie. Go ahead and cry it out."

His arms felt strangely comforting and so safe, Aggie sobbed as she never had before. Not even when Beth died, not even when her mother died had she been able to let go like this. It was as if she'd been holding these tears back for years, needing only a sympathetic voice and a comforting arm to break the dam.

After some time, Aggie, pulled away, reached into her jeans for a tissue and wiped her nose. "Thank you. I've never cried like that."

Luke removed his arms, pulled out a tissue from his own pocket and blew *his* nose.

Aggie looked over at him in surprise. He'd been feeling her grief! She studied him a moment. "Luke, have you lost someone?"

"Yes. I guess that's why I could empathize. I, too, go through bouts of grief. When did your mother and sister die?"

Aggie briefly told him of their time in Dallas. "It was almost fourteen years ago—but I have no other family and..."

"You have no family?" Aggie shook her head. Luke's brow twisted in concern. "And I made it worse by acting so unbending and dictatorial."

"Dictatorial yes, but I also felt some hostility."

Luke was silent a moment. "I'm sorry, Aggie."

"Thank you, Luke. Who did you lose?"

"Five years ago my mother and father were killed in their small private plane."

"Oh, no! I'm sorry, Luke. Were you close?"

"I loved and respected my father, but we were too much alike. My mother was the most selfless, giving, loving person I have ever known. We were very close."

"I'm sorry." Impulsively, Aggie did something totally foreign to her. She put her arm around Luke's back, leaned her head against his hard shoulder and cried again—for reasons she didn't quite understand. All she knew was she felt bereft for Luke—a man who was practically a stranger to her.

Luke was so taken back at *her* empathy, he didn't quite know how to react, except to blink and try to hold back his own emotion.

Aggie removed her arm and wiped her nose once more. "Do you have any other family besides Doris, Luke?"

"I have a sister, Amy, who is married and has four children. I also have a grandmother. Doris' parents are living so I have an aunt and uncle. Also, Doris has two brothers so I have cousins."

"I'm glad you have family."

They both fell silent, each feeling how strange it was that they could cry together—grieve together and yet not know each other.

Luke's thoughts strayed, unsettling him as he thought of how good Aggie had felt in his arms, and how tender he felt toward her. He told himself it was probably because they had a special link—Doris. The disconcerting thing was—he realized he wanted to take Aggie into his arms again and hold her for a long time.

He jumped to his feet. What was he thinking?! Amy told him that right now he was vulnerable and to be careful. No way was he going to get involved with a woman again—at least not for a long time—if ever.

Aggie watched him stiffen, becoming hard all over. In her line of work, through the years, she'd become a student of body language—and Luke had just put up a wall as firm and as impenetrable as the stone walls of his house. She stood up and looked up at him. "Luke?"

He looked down at her, noticing, again, how small she was."Yes?"

"You must have been hurt deeply by your wife."

He was startled. "Who told you?" he asked gruffly.

"No one."

His expression softened. "Would you like to go for a ride and see the country around this part of Austin?"

"Oh, I would love to. Thank you!"

Luke was pleased at her reaction. "Come on then, let's go."

# Chapter Thirteen

A week later, Sunday afternoon, Aggie curled up in a chair and looked out the front window thinking back over the week. She had become acquainted with the stores and gourmet shops of the city, shopping for the one meal she cooked at night, and for her own kitchen for the other two meals. She thought it better to eat breakfast and lunch in the cottage on the weekends so Mary and Luke could have their privacy. But during the week a couple of times she had gone up to the house and had lunch with Mary.

So far, Aggie had cooked a variety of meals: that southern favorite, black-eyed peas, French cuisine, Chinese and plain American. Luke waxed eloquent over her cooking and she found herself feeling great satisfaction in pleasing him.

Often during the week, she thought of the episode in the woods behind her house. She was still amazed over it and over the fact that she'd allowed herself to show that kind of emotion with anyone, let alone a man, and a man she scarcely knew! Because of it, however, she felt closer to Luke than she thought possible in such a short time.

Mary was a great help to her in many ways—the most important was helping her to understand her complicated employer.

Aggie thought of her attendance at the church service this morning. She had tried to remember the name of the church to which Mama had taken her and Beth. She knew it was a small break-off from a Southern Baptist church—realizing now that it was probably one of a kind. She had attended the church closest to Luke's house. The minister wasn't like the one in that little church in McKinney and it made her feel lonely. Nevertheless, she was comforted by the words spoken, by the hymns sung.

A pensive feeling came over Aggie. Ever since reviewing those wonderful and terrible nine months of her life, she was satisfied that she had finally understood and made peace with herself. "So why am I feeling this way?" she asked aloud.

For some reason, all through the church services, she thought of her mother and how she never seemed to be bitter or angry—as she had every right to be. She often marveled over this and now today, she marveled once more. How did she do it? Once during her first year in college, she remembered asking her mother this question. Her mother answered, "The Bible tells us we must repent and forgive." That's all she said. Bewildered, she remembered asking herself what in the world Mama had to repent for? It was her father who needed to repent! But she knew her mother must have forgiven her husband and his brother, Chester. How else could she be so free of bitterness and anger? The minister's talk this morning mentioned repentance and forgiveness. Had *she* forgiven and repented for the anger and hate she felt toward her father and Uncle Chester? Or was it the other way around? Could she really forgive without *repenting first* for her bitterness and anger?

Getting up, she walked into the bedroom and picked up her mother's old Bible that she'd brought with her. It had been some time since she had read in it. She felt the need of reading it now, hoping it would bring her mother closer.

Slipping her shoes off, she put a pillow behind her back and sat cross-legged on the bed leafing through the pages, reading passages her mother had underlined lightly in pencil. Finally, after reading an underlined passage in Ephesians 4:31, Aggie noticed water marks on the page. Were those her mother's tears? She felt her own tears flowing down her cheeks. If her mother had to repent, surely she had even more need to do so! But could she?

Closing the book, she slid off the bed to her knees and prayed for help to repent so she could forgive. Suddenly, she felt terrible remorse for all the hate and anger that had driven her through the years—each prosecution of an abuser an unconscious form of revenge. She begged her Father in Heaven to forgive her. Soon, great sobs seized her, shaking her body and soul until she felt weak and spent. Finally the sobs subsiding, she begged Him to help her forgive.

Slowly, a peace came over her. With a feeling of awe, she ended her prayers with a prayer of thanks, and then one of gratitude that she could be here in this new situation where the atmosphere was conducive to thinking and pondering, giving her time to make her life right.

She got up off her knees and lay down, resting. Realizing once more that men, in general, were not to blame for the ills of women as she had been led to believe and as she herself wanted to believe, anymore than women, in general, were to blame for the ills of men. Both were the offender at times and both were victims at times.

After years of struggle, pain, loss, depression, watching one person's cruelty to another, and the cavalier attitude toward the sanctity of life—she had, at last, *a redress of the heart.* Because of this, she knew she could go back to her law practice and help women in a way she couldn't before. But did she want to? She was enjoying her time here; down the road she would carefully reexamine her future.

# Chapter Fourteen

It was June 11th, three weeks since Aggie had moved into her new little home. She was amazed at how easy it was to settle into her new life and how she looked forward to eating dinner every night with Mary and Luke. They had stimulating and pleasant conversations and often found things to laugh at.

With her energy returning, she went back to work on her children's books, feeling happy and content—and grateful to Doris.

It was Friday evening after dinner, and everything was planned for the meal tomorrow night. Luke had informed her he was having a few guests over. He'd requested that she and Mary dine with them and let the two girls, Sarah and Evie, serve. Aggie no longer felt resistive to this; she was even looking forward to it.

She turned on the printer preparing to print out the pages she had written during the week. She was almost through the tenth book of her series.

~~~~~~~~~

It was 7:30 P.M. and Luke felt restless. He wondered what Aggie did with herself most of the day everyday when she wasn't up at the house preparing for the night meal. He had become more than curious about this young woman. She only talked about herself whenever he asked questions, answering briefly then changing the subject by asking questions of him or Mary. Impulsively deciding to pay her a visit tonight, he headed out the door to the cottage.

Looking out the window while waiting for all the copies to be printed, Aggie was admiring the beauty of nature around her and across the driveway. She had placed the computer table and printer in front of the window in the small front room so she could see out and watch Luke, Mary and their friends come and go. At that moment, she saw Luke coming down the driveway, his long legs striding purposely. He was turning up her walk! She was surprised. He hadn't attempted to come over since their emotional encounter at the tree three weeks ago.

He knocked and she opened the door. "Hi," she said, smiling. "What brings you here to my humble little abode?"

Luke grinned and leaned his arm high against the door frame. "Just checking to see how you like it here in your little hideaway."

"Come in, Luke, and have a seat. It's nice to have a visitor."

He frowned. "Are you lonely here?"

"No, I keep busy."

Luke seated himself on the small couch and Aggie sat in the chair.

"What are you doing, Aggie?" he asked as he noticed the printer churning out the last page of something. "Or is it private?"

"I have a hobby writing children books."

"Interesting," he said sounding impressed. "Have you had any published?"

"I've had nine published. I'm working on the tenth now. It's been a while since I've had time to write and I'm enjoying it immensely."

"Imagine—I'm in the presence of an author," he stated, smiling.

"Don't be impressed. I had some connections through my work. In other words, I had some *pull*. Actually, what really sells them are the Victorian illustrations by my friend." What Aggie didn't tell him was that the illustrations were done by a client who had been a battered wife. Because this young woman was one who sincerely tried to change her life, Aggie pulled some strings and got her a position back east with a publisher as an illustrator—far away from her ex-husband.

"May I see a finished book?"

Aggie got up and took one from the small book case and handed it to him.

He looked through it. "These are beautiful illustrations. And I'm sure the writing is good, too."

"Thank you, Luke," she said, taking it from him and returning it to the bookcase. "I had a teacher in junior high who awakened in me a love for writing."

Luke was silent, contemplating this new knowledge about this unusual young woman. After a few moments, he asked, "Aggie, would you like to go for a walk with me? Or do you have to work on your book?"

"I'd love to go for a walk with you. Just let me turn off the printer and save the document. He watched her, thinking, as he had more than a few times, what a feast for the eyes she was.

Luke opened the door for her, and together they walked down the driveway and veered off to a walking path that followed the road, but was hidden from it by trees and bushes.

"How nice, Luke. I think I'll use this for exercising. I used to run for 40 minutes everyday in Dallas. I need to get back to it."

They walked side by side, silent. Strange, Luke thought, the restlessness he'd been feeling, before he visited Aggie, was gone. He also noticed that his long steps were almost making Aggie run. He slowed down.

"Thanks," she said laughing. "You have the longest legs." She drew in a deep breath, "Doesn't the air smell fragrant? And I believe you have as many birds here as in Dallas. As a young girl I spent a lot of time outdoors, enjoying nature, but I haven't taken time to enjoy it for several years."

"Where did you live when you were a young girl?"

"In a small town. Where did you grow up?"

He noted her nonspecific answer and how she turned the subject back to him. "On a ranch." He, too, could be nonspecific!

She smiled. "What do you do for a living, Luke?"

"I inherited the ranch. I oversee it now and then, but I have an investment company in downtown Austin."

"Do you enjoy that more than ranching?"

"I do. But, like you, I enjoy the outdoors. If I stay inside an office for too many days, I get stir crazy. That's when I go out to the ranch and check on things. When did you and Doris become friends?"

"A little over two years ago."

"How did you meet, Aggie?"

Aggie was silent a moment thinking how to answer this question since Doris had suggested she not tell Luke she was an attorney. She felt annoyed that she had to sidestep again. "I worked in a law firm and I met Bob because he asked me to do some work for him. I refused to accept pay for it since he was doing a friend a favor. Apparently he told Doris about this, and she invited me to dinner to thank me. We liked each other immediately."

"I'm curious about why you haven't married before now, Aggie. Or have you?"

"No."

"Well?"

"Well, what? I only heard one question."

"Why haven't you married?"

There was no way Aggie could answer that and no way would she even if she could.

Aggie's silence was deafening—and also irritating. "You could at least give me some kind of answer, Aggie."

"I'll answer you with a question. Why did you divorce your wife?"

"That's private," he snapped.

"I know. Why I haven't married—is also private."

Luke's jaw rippled in anger. "I think we better turn around," he said, abruptly doing so and walking quickly toward home. Soon, he realized Aggie hadn't followed him. He stopped and turned around. She was still walking in the other direction. "Aggie!"

She stopped and turned around.

"Come on back."

"I want to continue on the walk."

"It will be dark around nine, and it's dangerous to be out walking alone."

"I have a watch, Luke. I'll turn around before it gets dark."

"Come back, Aggie!" he demanded. "I feel responsible for you."

She smiled. "Come and walk with me then."

"No. I want to go back," he responded in a tone that ordered her to do the same.

"All right, see you." She turned and proceeded on the walk.

"Stubborn woman!" Luke muttered under his breath. He wrestled with himself a moment, then turned and walked toward home feeling angry. By the time he reached the house, he was feeling edgy as well as angry. Today a woman isn't safe anywhere. "Why in the heck did I show her the path in the first place?" he chastised himself loudly. Soon, he realized she would have found it on her own—the way she explored!

He went into the garage and got a folding chair and placed it where he could watch for her return. The longer he waited, the more impatient he felt. He got up and paced back and forth. His impatience turned into worry as the sun went down and the sky slowly darkened. He jumped up from the chair and headed toward the walking path to find her. He had just turned the bend when he saw her walking toward him.

"You said you would turn around before it got dark, Aggie," he stated angrily.

"I did, but it got dark before I got here."

"Yeah, I can see that."

Aggie walked past him to the door of her house. She turned to the smoldering man. "Goodnight, Luke," she said cheerfully. "See you tomorrow night." He didn't answer, so she opened the door, went in and closed it. Stepping quickly to the window, she watched him. He stared at her door for a moment then viciously kicked a stone that lay in front of him on the driveway.

Aggie frowned, wondering—concerned. Why was there so much anger inside Luke? Her concern slowly turned to amazement. Why was she able take his reprehensible actions in stride, especially when she knew she would never put up with that behavior from any other man?

# Chapter Fifteen

Seeing Luke leave in his truck Saturday morning shortly after breakfast, Aggie went up to the house to start preparations for dinner. She found Mary finishing up the breakfast dishes. "Hi, Mary."

"Oh, hello, Aggie. You're here early."

"This meal takes a little more preparation time so I thought I'd better start early. How's Luke this morning?" she asked, trying to sound casual.

"He's a little glum. I noticed you two going off for a walk last night. Did anything happen?"

"Not really, Mary. But I get the distinct impression Luke Barnes is used to getting his own way."

Mary smiled. "He's a strong personality like his father, but he also has some of his mother's traits—fortunately."

Aggie got out the eggs, flour, salt and other ingredients and started on the dessert. "Luke asked me a personal question and he became quite irritated when I wouldn't answer. I turned the tables on him and asked him why he divorced his wife. This brought the conversation to a screeching halt—which was my purpose. I knew he wouldn't like it, but I didn't expect him to become so angry."

Mary remained silent, so Aggie continued. "It was more than anger at me—he seems to be a man full of anger."

"He's quite bitter, Aggie, but he has reason to be."

Hoping Mary would explain, Aggie worked in silence.

When Mary was through cleaning up, she sat down at the table and watched the preparations. After a while, Mary said, "You seem professional, Aggie. Have you ever owned a restaurant?"

"No, it's just a hobby I enjoy. I put myself through law school working as an apprentice to an excellent master chef at an elite restaurant in Dallas. I've also entertained friends during my career so I could have an outlet for it."

"You...you are an attorney?"

It had just slipped out. She noted surprise on Mary's face and then concern. Annoyed that she had to hide it in the first place, Aggie sat down at the table and faced Mary directly. "Mary, Doris asked me to keep this information from Luke. Why?"

"I think we both better continue to keep it from him."

"Why, Mary? I may slip again since much of the community of Dallas knows. It's hard for me to be secretive about something so innocuous and impersonal."

"It's knowledge that, right now, won't seem innocuous to Luke."

Since Mary remained silent, offering no more information, Aggie got up and returned to her preparations, wondering how long this job was going to last.

"Aggie, please sit down a minute. I don't feel I should divulge anything personal about Luke, but I think you should know something."

Aggie wiped her hands on a towel and returned to her chair.

"Aggie, the short time you've been here, Luke's spirits have been better than I've seen them in a long time. I love that boy—I helped raise him and I want him to be happy. His wife hurt him terribly. She deceived him in the cruelest way. What she did was unforgivable!"

"Not telling him I'm an attorney is also deceiving him, Mary. This makes me even more uneasy about not being up front with Luke."

"But, Aggie, Luke didn't get married for years because he couldn't find a woman who didn't want a career. When he met Lila, his wife, I think she already knew this from a friend of his. As it turned out, Lila had a career, and a consuming ambition to get to the top. As you may guess, women go wild over Luke. She was no different. She went after him, convincing him that she only intended to work until she got married."

"What has this to do with *my* career, Mary? I'm just an employee!"

"But you are an employee who has lifted his spirits."

"Is that part of my job, Mary?" Aggie asked a little shocked.

"No, of course not, but please, Aggie, just keep your career to yourself a little while longer and then I'll ask Doris to tell him."

"All right. But surely that wasn't why Luke divorced her?"

"No. There was something else—something much more serious, something that isn't my place to divulge."

Abruptly getting up, Aggie began working rapidly, her lips

compressed. She didn't need this! Just as quickly, she wondered why she was reacting on such an emotional level.

~~~~~~~~~~~

It took most of the day to prepare the meal and when she could do nothing more until the last minute she slipped out of the kitchen to go shower and change, leaving Mary to set the table. She was back in the kitchen in forty-five minutes, explaining to Sarah and Evie what they would be serving first. Even though she had to dine with Luke and his guests, she had to prepare each course before Evie and Sarah served it—regardless of Luke's wishes—this of course, would mean a talk, perhaps a confrontation, with Luke.

At 7:05 the door bell rang. Mary went in to answer it and Aggie put the finishing touches on everything. Placing the hearts of romaine on the salad plates, stems facing outward, with cherry tomatoes in the center, she poured a touch of her special vinaigrette dressing, then sprinkled a few garlic croutons over each. She heard voices and laughter. She told Evie when to put the rolls in the oven. Another ring of the doorbell, brought more guests.

Shortly, Luke walked into the kitchen and stopped short, momentarily taken back at Aggie's appearance. She had chosen to wear a soft royal blue dress with lapis, sterling silver and pearl earrings. Regaining his composure, he asked in a formal tone of voice, "The guests are here, Aggie, will you please come in?"

"And, hello to you, too, Luke," she replied.

He gazed at her a moment, then turned and walked out. She followed him, wondering why she was allowing this man so much rope.

Luke took hold of Aggie's arm. "I would like you all to meet a friend of my cousin Doris—and, my new cook, Aggie McBride. Aggie, I would like you to meet my friend, Joy Marshall and her three friends: Victor Wolfe, Ted Lafferty and Shawna Carter."

Both men's eyes lit up in open admiration. Joy Marshall, wide-eyed at the change in Aggie from teenager to glamorous woman, was able only to nod. After everyone acknowledged the introductions, and visited a few minutes, Luke informed them that dinner was about to be served, suggesting the seating arrangement. Luke stood at the head of the rectangular table, set with dark green place mats, hand blown clear glasses, and sterling silver. He waited for everyone to be seated: Joy to his right, Mary, who had been introduced earlier, sat at his left, and Shawna next to her. Aggie was asked to sit at the other end, Victor to Aggie's left and Ted to her right.

When they all were seated, Luke told the group that he would offer a prayer over the food. Joy smiled in acquiescence, and bowed her head as did the others. Afterward, Luke nodded at Sarah, who had been told to stand by the door.

Presently, she and Evie placed a salad in front of everyone. There was silence for a few moments while everyone began eating, then Victor broke it.

"This is an attractive salad, Aggie, and I like the dressing. Why can't I find a cook like you?"

"I second that," Ted said. "Do you ever put her out for loan, Luke?"

Before Luke could answer the inane question, Joy broke in. "Yes, Miss McBride, this is delicious. I would like the recipe for the dressing. If the rest of the meal is as good as this, I'm so-o-o glad Luke hired you."

"I thank all of you. I hope you're pleased with the rest of the meal."

Mary gave Aggie a comforting smile and Luke showered his attention on Joy, including the others when possible.

Aggie couldn't figure out if one of the men was Shawna's date. If so, someone was being very rude, because both men talked to her and ignored Shawna.

"Has cooking always been your profession, Aggie?" asked Victor, leaning over and flashing a smile, his expression and dark good looks reminding her of his last name—Wolfe.

"I've been cooking since I was thirteen years old."

"Where did you come from, Aggie? I thought I knew all the beautiful women in Texas."

"I've been hiding in that small brick house the third little pig built."

Victor Wolfe looked puzzled. Ted Lafferty laughed. "That's a good one, Aggie. She gotcha there, Vic."

Victor catching on, laughed. "Clever, Miss McBride, clever."

Before Victor could say anything else, Aggie turned to Ted and conversed with him.

When everyone was through with the salad, Sarah and Evie cleared off the plates. Aggie excused herself and went into the kitchen to take care of the main course. She quickly and professionally arranged each dinner plate with slivered, sauteed potatoes on top of which she arranged lobster pieces which had been marinated in a light orange sauce. She placed a colorful lobster claw on top then arranged three skinned and peeled orange sections vertically. The last touch was a sprig of green tarragon. Placing freshly baked rolls in a linen-lined basket, she returned to the dining room.

Aggie glanced at Luke as she seated herself. Returning his glower with a smile, she turned to Shawna and asked her questions as Sarah and Evie placed the main course before everyone, offering a roll to each, leaving the basket on the table.

Joy's brows rose as she eyed the attractive and tantalizing plate before her. Shawna gasped in delight. "Oh, how wonderful! I feel like I'm in the snootiest restaurant in Austin."

Victor buttered and bit into a roll. "Mmm, these are the lightest and best tasting rolls I've ever tasted, Aggie."

"Thank you, Victor," she said.

"I'll have to agree with Victor for a change," Ted added, "these are the best rolls I've ever put in my mouth." In between bites, he kept up a running commentary.

Victor, annoyed, blurted out, "Hey, Luke, we need to make a toast to the cook. This is great! Where's the wine?"

Joy intervened with more practiced smoothness. "Luke doesn't drink, Vic. Besides, you had enough before you came."

At this, Luke decided to be more of a host, asking questions of everyone, except Aggie, bringing up sports, the market and so on. Relieved, Aggie ate her dinner in peace.

When everyone was finished, Aggie again excused herself and went into the kitchen to tell the girls to clear off while she prepared the dessert. Placing a piece of the chocolate hazelnut flat cake on each plate, she dropped a dab of whipped cream on each and then one raspberry in the middle. Taking a small glass pitcher of raspberry sauce from the refrigerator she poured it in decorative swirls on the plate, around the cake. The last touch was a couple of green peppermint leaves on each plate. After Aggie returned to the table, Evie and Sarah carried the dessert into the guests, who reacted effusively.

The conversation shifted to Joy and her small chain of lingerie shops. Victor, bored with the conversation, leaned over to Aggie, "Hey beautiful, how about going to dinner with me next Monday?"

"Sorry, Victor, I have to cook for Mr. Barnes."

"How about going for a drink after dinner."

"I don't drink."

"How about us going to a movie then?"

Ted, tired of this, butted in, "Vic, can't you see she would rather go out with me?"

"You? You aren't even divorced yet. I am."

Luke was getting more and more irritated with the two men. "Aggie, this dessert is unsurpassed." Everyone agreed, each complimenting her.

She smiled. "Thank you."

Luke continued taking charge of the conversation, annoying Victor because it kept him from focusing his attention on the beautiful woman to his right.

When everyone was through with dessert, and the after dinner coffee had been served, Aggie made her escape to the kitchen. She quickly put the food away, said goodnight to Sarah and Evie and left.

Locking both her doors, she turned out the lights and went into the bedroom to get ready for bed. Deciding that if these were the kind of people Luke entertained, she didn't want any part of it.

Picking up a book, she turned on the lamp and climbed into bed. Soon, finding she was unable to concentrate on the book, she closed it. Victor Wolfe gave her the creeps and somehow, sometime she knew he'd ask her out.

She wasn't sleepy in the least, so she got up and put a robe over her night gown, turned out the lights and went into the front room. Curling up on the couch she sat in the moonlit room, thinking.

Victor, Ted and Shawna were Joy's friends—not Luke's, she reminded herself. There was so much more to Luke than all of them put together. Why does he associate with them?

An hour passed, and she was about to get up and go to bed when she saw Luke's tall figure walking down the driveway. He was turning into her place! His knock was loud and impatient.

She opened the door. "Hello, Luke."

Luke, surprised the door opened so quickly just stood there, silent. Finally, he asked, "What...were you sitting in the dark watching for me?"

She laughed. "I was sitting in the dark, but hardly watching for you. I was sure you and your friends were still up at the house having a jolly good time."

"Why did you leave so abruptly, Aggie?" he asked curtly. "When I asked you to dine with my guests, I intended that you stay."

"Come in, Luke."

He stepped in and helped himself to a seat on the couch. "Aren't we going to have any lights?" he asked as he saw Aggie pulling her legs up under her in the chair.

"I'd rather have only the moonlight so I don't have to look at the displeasure on your face. You did glower at me at the table, you know."

"I asked you to let Sarah and Evie serve."

"I should have made it clearer, Luke, but with my kind of cooking, there is an art to placing the food on the plates and I need to do that myself."

Luke, understanding, relaxed. "Oh. Yes, I can see that. Well, the food certainly was attractively arranged—and very good, I might add."

"Thank you. But, Luke, do I have to dine with you and your guests?"

"You don't have to...no, but I would like you to."

"That's nice to hear. You practically ordered me to before."

"I know. I don't know what gets into me sometimes."

"Why do you want me to dine with you and your friends?"

"I like all my family and friends around me when I entertain."

"Why?"

"I don't know. I've always been that way."

"But Luke, I'm neither family nor friend."

There was a long silence, both feeling comfortable in spite of it. Luke, at last responded to her remark. "Since you and Doris are friends, why can't *we* be friends?"

Another silence followed, after which a slow smile spread over Aggie's face. "I guess we can, Luke. When I was a little girl, I always liked boys as friends more than girls anyway. But," she shook her head, "somehow it's different when we become adults. It isn't as easy for a man and a woman to be—just friends."

Luke gazed at Aggie. Her deep blue eyes had turned into large unfathomable black opals in the moonlight, her hair raven black, her face pale. She appeared as mysterious as Luke had already found her to be. He remembered how beautiful, how glamorous she looked tonight at dinner. Though small in stature and build, she seemed to fill the room with her quiet strength and aura of mystery. Victor and Ted eyed her like a tantalizing confection in a candy store. He ground his teeth in irritation just thinking about it.

"I'm concerned, Aggie. I watched Victor Wolfe come on to you. Don't have anything to do with him."

Aggie was surprised—but even more surprised that she felt so grateful for his concern. "Why, Luke?"

"Surely, Aggie, you can see that he's a low-life can't you?"

"What about Ted? He kind of asked me out, too."

"He's still married."

"Why don't you invite *your* friends to dinner instead of Joy's?"

"Why?" he asked, surprised at the question.

"Because Joy's friends aren't your caliber."

He smiled. "I think that may be a compliment."

Aggie smiled back. "Just a fact, Luke."

Luke heaved a sigh, leaned over, placed his elbows on his knees, lacing his fingers together. "My friends are all married and have children, Aggie—I'm way behind. We don't have as much in common anymore."

"Do you think you might have more in common with them than with Victor and Ted?"

Luke smiled at her and shook his head. "Good thinking, Aggie. What do you think of Joy?"

"I don't think of her."

He laughed. "Would you try?"

"I'd rather not."

"Why?"

"Because I might say something I'll regret. After all, your love life is none of my business."

"There is no 'love life' there."

Relief swept over Aggie. "I'm glad to hear that."

"Why?"

"All right, you asked for it. She doesn't seem to be your caliber, either."

Luke smiled and leaned back, putting his arm over the back of the couch. "What caliber am I, Aggie?"

"The kind your mother thought you were."

Luke threw back his head and laughed. Aggie smiled. She liked his laugh. It was deep down gut-level enjoyment, pleasing and infectious.

"You should have been a lawyer, Aggie, you ask and answer questions with a mixture of frankness and obliqueness."

Unease prickled her skin. "Do you like female lawyers, Luke?"

The pleasant look of relaxation and enjoyment left his face. He looked down a moment, then abruptly stood up. "I believe it's time I let you go to bed. Mary said you've been in the kitchen all day preparing dinner."

Aggie stood and gazed up into his face. Trying to end on a light note, she said, "That's nothing. Some meals take two days."

"They do? Well, I won't be entertaining for a couple of weeks at least. I'll let you know. Thanks for the visit, Aggie." He opened the door and stepped out.

"I enjoyed it, Luke. Come and visit my little palace any time."

He turned and studied her face a moment, feeling reluctant to leave. "I will. Goodnight, Aggie."

# Chapter Sixteen

Mary and Luke had just finished cleaning up the lunch dishes Sunday when the phone rang. Mary left the room to go to her quarters and Luke picked up the phone. "Hello?" he said, sitting down at the table.

"Hi, Luke."

"Hey, Doris! It's great hearing from you."

"How are you, Luke?"

"I'm feeling more up-beat lately. How are you? How are Bob and the boys?"

"We're all well. How is Aggie?"

"She seems to be fine."

"Does she have a phone in her little house?"

"Yes." He gave Doris the number.

"You sound better, Luke."

"It must be Aggie's cooking. You were right, she was worth waiting for."

"I'm glad, Luke. Have you heard from Amy?"

"Just a couple of cards, have you?"

"Same here. Apparently she and the children are enjoying Europe. Well, since you're fine, Luke, I think I'll give Aggie a call."

"Wait, Doris. Could I ask you a couple of questions?"

"Of course."

"Why hasn't Aggie married? She's a beautiful and intriguing woman."

"Oh? That's interesting."

"Don't get any ideas, Doris. Any man would notice her beauty. He'd have to be blind not to."

"Aggie has very high standards, Luke. She's dated some, but I guess she hasn't met a man who interests her."

"I can't find out much about her. She won't talk about herself very much. But she's certainly patient with me, Doris."

"She is?" Doris asked, sounding surprised.

"Didn't you think she would be?"

Doris hesitated a moment, then said, "I've seen Aggie in action, and she can chew a man up and spit him out."

It was Luke's turn to be surprised. "She can? Give me an instance."

"We took Aggie out to dinner one night and this friend of Bob's stopped at the table ostensibly to visit with Bob, but he couldn't take his eyes off Aggie. Bob liked this man and thought Aggie might like him, so he invited him to join us. Bob, having never associated with him except in legal circles, was shocked to see what a conceited jerk he was socially. He came on thick to Aggie—bragging and making outrageous statements and so on. Aggie, cooly, verbally, turned his own words right back on him in a way he didn't fully realize at first. Finally, he caught on—not only was he not making progress, but he was in a verbal sword fight and losing badly. He soon excused himself."

"Hmm, I would have liked to hear it. At dinner last night, I heard her put a guy in his place." He smiled, remembering.

"Oh? And she hasn't put you in *your* place yet?"

"No. In fact, she's taken my 'snarliness,' as you call it, Doris, with uh...I don't know quite how to explain it. It's as if she can see right through me and understands—but of course that can't be the case. I mean, that's the only way I can explain it."

Doris was so happy to hear this, she almost clapped her hands, however, she certainly wasn't going to let Luke know how she felt.

Luke quickly went on. "Maybe it's because I'm a cousin of yours, Doris."

"You think so?"

"I don't know, Doris, you tell me."

"I don't know either, Luke. I guess you'll just have to get to know her better and find out for yourself."

"You're a big help, Doris! Go call Aggie."

~~~~~~~~~~

Aggie was about to pick up the phone to call Doris when it rang.

"Doris! I was just going to call you. How are you all doing?"

"We're all fine, Aggie. How are *you*?"

"Dor, your doctor was right. It was emotional stress...or depression, as he called it. My energy returned almost as soon as I began working here. Amazing, huh?"

"Then you like it there?"

"I do, very much. I'm writing again and enjoying it. Mary is wonderful to me, and Luke is uh...is a good man. He's been very nice to me."

"Nice? I...I'm glad to hear it," Doris stated, trying to conceal her surprise.

"You didn't expect him to be?"

Doris was silent.

"You don't have to answer, Dor. But could you tell me why he has so much anger inside him?"

"Oh...you see it," she said, slowly. "I wish I knew. His sister, Amy, knows, but she won't tell me because Luke wants to tell me. I've asked him several times and he keeps promising to come up to Dallas and tell us why he divorced Lila. I'm sure that's the cause of it...or at least most of it."

"Mary is careful not to say anything to me. I suspect, though, Doris, that Luke is by nature a little volatile and difficult at times."

Doris was silent, again. Finally, she responded. "You are so astute, Aggie, it's a little scary. He gets this from his father, but—what saves his bacon is that he's also very kind and has a big compassionate and understanding heart—like Aunt Ann, his mother."

"I can see that."

Luke's insight was right, Doris thought, Aggie *can* see right through him. But then, why was she surprised? She, herself, felt understood when first getting to know Aggie, finding that she was amazingly intuitive.

"Dor, you still there?"

"Yes, Aggie—just thinking how amazing you are."

"I don't know why you say that, but I want to thank you for duping me into coming here. You are a real friend. I realize now how badly I needed it."

Doris smiled and let out a sigh of relief. "I took a big chance arranging it, Aggie, as you know, so can you imagine how relieved and happy I am that it's turning out well for both of you."

Aggie hung up the phone smiling, thinking how good it was to talk to her friend again. She missed her. She went into the small front room and stared out the window at the main house, feeling lonely—wishing Luke would come down. As she was mentally examining this thought, she saw Luke's car drive by and off toward the highway. Uneasiness came over her again. Why hadn't she asked Doris to go ahead and tell Luke that she was an attorney? The answer was simple. She didn't want to push Doris.

What should she do? Her natural inclination was to go up to the house and tell Luke as soon as he returned. What could it hurt? So Luke would get upset—that would be his problem, not hers. He'd have to take care of what was eating at him! No. She wasn't going to tell Luke until she talked with Mary again, she decided. Returning to the kitchen, she picked up the phone and dialed Mary's private number.

Mary's low, cultured voice answered. "Hello?"

"Mary, this is Aggie. Could you come down here? I need to talk to you."

"I would be glad to, Aggie. I'll be right there."

Aggie went into the front room to watch for her, opening the door before Mary could ring the bell.

"Thank you, Mary, I appreciate this."

"Sundays drag when I don't get to see my children or grandchildren so this is a nice change for me."

"I'm glad. Please have a seat, Mary."

When they were both seated, Aggie began, "I'm getting more uncomfortable about not being up front with Luke. I know you asked me not to tell him about my profession, Mary, but I think I have to. He even jokingly said I ought to be an attorney."

Mary rubbed her forehead, thinking. "I understand, Aggie, but I wish you would hold out for a while longer."

"I'm sorry, Mary, but I can't."

"Well...it may not matter *too* much if you tell Luke, unless—let me ask you this, Aggie. What kind of an attorney are you? What do you specialize in?"

"I'm an attorney for women. I specialize in women's issues."

"Oh my! Oh dear...I was only asking that to be sure...I didn't dream..." Mary covered her face with one hand.

"What is it, Mary?" Aggie asked, shocked at her reaction.

Mary looked up. "Aggie, Doris doesn't know or she wouldn't have sent you here. Luke should have told her long before now."

A cold dread came over Aggie. "Please, Mary, tell me why this upsets you so."

Mary got up and looked out the window for a few moments, then slowly walked back to her seat and sat down heavily.

Suddenly, Aggie felt impatient with it all. "Mary, why do you dance around, Luke? Is he so temperamental that you have to tiptoe around, not daring to do or say anything for fear of upsetting him?"

"I just don't want him hurt anymore than he has been."

"But, Mary, he's a big boy. Surely what I specialize in can't hurt him more than he's already been hurt."

"It will."

"Why?" she asked, feeling totally out of patience now.

"Luke will just have to forgive me for divulging his private life. I'm going to have to tell you. After you hear it, you may do what you wish about telling him."

"Would it be better if I just pack up and leave, Mary?" Aggie asked, thoroughly frustrated over Mary's *and* Doris' coddling of Luke.

"Oh no...no, Aggie, that would be worse! Let me tell you, and you judge for yourself."

"All right, go ahead, Mary."

"Luke made it plain to Lila, his wife to be, that he hadn't married because he couldn't find a woman who didn't want a career. He made it clear to her that he had nothing against a woman having a career, but *he,* personally, wanted a woman who had the desire to be a full time wife and mother, in spite of the pressures of the outside world to do otherwise. Well, as I told you before, Lila deceived him. I think that Luke was looking at the time-clock. He was getting so anxious to get married and get on with his life that he didn't see through her—which wasn't like Luke at all. Besides, she was very clever.

"They had dated two months when he asked her to marry him. Luke wanted to get married right away, but Lila asked if she could wind up her work as an anchor woman for a major Austin television station and get married in three months. Luke reluctantly agreed. One month later, Lila changed her mind suddenly, and wanted to get married in two weeks. Luke was thrilled. I was concerned about it. I think Lila sensed that Luke's ardor might be cooling, so she decided to move faster.

"Needless to say, we had to scramble to get ready for it. Amy flew out to help Lila and me with preparations, Doris also came up early and then their families joined them for the wedding. Lila wanted an expensive and ostentatious wedding in the church she attended—a church favored by the upper-crust of Austin. Afterward, they had a magnificent reception at the top country club in the city.

"After their honeymoon, Lila broke the news that a regional group of stations wanted her to be a journalist for them covering Austin, Houston, San Antonio and Dallas. Her base would be Austin, but she would have to travel. Apparently she told Luke that she was only going to take it for six months. After a heated discussion in front of me, Luke gave in again—but only if she would leave after six months.

"When six months came, Lila didn't leave—always promising that it would be soon. They built this house, even though it was more Luke's plan and idea than hers. She wanted to remain closer to town, but she gave in, and they moved here.

"A month later, Luke just happened to talk to someone who knew the head man who hired Lila and it came out that Lila had signed a five year contract. Luke wouldn't believe it at first. He was sure the man was mistaken. Then an even greater bombshell hit.

"Luke wanted children, but Lila was having some kind of female problems and had been seeing a doctor. She told Luke that she had endometriosis and treatments would be necessary to clear it up before she could get pregnant. It was taking so long, Luke became concerned for Lila and made an appointment with her doctor so he could to talk to him personally.

"After asking about Lila's condition, the doctor informed Luke that the abortion had caused complications and that she probably wouldn't be able to have any more children. Luke told me that he was so stunned he couldn't even speak for a moment, then blurted out, 'What abortion?'

"The doctor was shocked that Luke hadn't known. He said Lila had told him that she and her husband decided to abort the pregnancy because of her career. That they intended to have children later."

Aggie was horrified. Her hands flew to her mouth, her eyes closed.

Mary nodded. "It's too terrible to believe, isn't it? I guess the doctor was upset that Luke didn't know anything about it. He assured Luke that he had nothing to do with the abortion, that she'd only been coming to him for the last two months.

"Luke confronted Lila with the abortion and the five-year contract. Of course, they talked in the privacy of their bedroom so I don't know how she tried to explain it. The next morning, Lila packed her things and moved out.

"Since Luke instigated the divorce proceedings, I don't know how he managed to keep from paying alimony, but I gathered from Amy that he had threatened to go public with the whole story. That, apparently took care of it—though none of us knew why. Anyway, Lila makes enough money, she doesn't need it."

Mary waited for Aggie to say something. Aggie's brows knit together in troubled thought, her eyes downcast. Slowly, she looked up at Mary. "You know, Mary, I've handled cases of spousal abuse, child abuse and many others. At first, my world was narrow—believing such things came entirely from men. As years went on, I began to see things a little differently. However, I consciously didn't allow myself to accept it because all I had known in my own family was male cruelty. The turning point began when I became acquainted with Doris and Bob. I began to do a lot of self examination and I've had a change of heart.

"Now that I hear what Luke has been through, I feel angry. I'm angry that so many women today are denying their gentle, nurturing natures and are becoming selfish, and hard." Aggie knew that she herself had become hard—isn't that why they called her the 'Iron Butterfly'? "In Lila's case," she continued, "I'll add—cruel."

"Do you see why I don't want you to tell Luke about your profession?"

Aggie fell silent, thinking. Of course she didn't want to tell him. Wasn't she almost involved with an abortion case? For some reason, she didn't want him to know about it...yet. Soon, however, she *had* to tell him. She still felt that Mary and Doris were too protective of Luke.

"I won't say anything, Mary. For now, anyway."

# Chapter Seventeen

After Mary left, Aggie wandered around the house thinking about everything she had been told. She felt smothered and closed in. Finding herself in the bedroom, she changed from the cool cotton dress to jeans and a white T shirt, then went out the kitchen door to take a walk among the soothing sights and sounds of nature. It was late afternoon and hot. In spite of the heat, it felt good to get out.

She walked for some time. Stepping over dead limbs and twigs, she wound around the clumps of junipers, and went through a growth of stately oaks. The song of a Golden-cheeked Warbler reached her ears and she followed the sound. Soon she heard water trickling and suddenly there before her was a beautiful cypress-shaded creek. She knew the trees were cypress because of the curious cone shapes growing upward from the roots. Sitting down on one of the large limestone rocks that lined the creek she watched the flowing water, gradually relaxing, peace flooding through her. She sighed, wishing she had someone here to enjoy it with her. Who? she asked herself. Luke! She wished Luke were here; he seemed to love nature as much as she. A troubled frown appeared as thoughts of what he'd gone through penetrated her consciousness—disturbing her moment of peace.

Getting up from the rock, she started back through the trees, glad that she had a good sense of direction. As she walked, her thoughts became more and more troubled. Impulsively, she stopped and climbed the first tree that was possible to climb, the small dead limbs scratching her arms until she found one on which she could sit. Something was nagging at her, but it wouldn't come to her. All she could think about was how terrible Luke must feel to lose his baby in such a cruel and barbaric way. "That was it!" she exclaimed aloud, then whispered, "It wasn't Luke's baby!" That was what had been gnawing at her! She wasn't sure, but she could almost bet on it.

That would explain why Lila all of a sudden wanted to get married in two weeks. She discovered she was pregnant! Aggie, used to thinking the worst of the other side in her cases, did so now. Had Lila given the executive of the television station, who hired her, a few of her favors to get the position and then several weeks later found herself pregnant?

The big question was: since Lila moved up the date of the marriage to hide it from Luke, why didn't she go ahead and have the baby? She'd have to talk to Mary about that. And, she knew herself well enough to realize she had to find out the truth. She would definitely call Barry tomorrow and talk with him about it and see if he thinks there is any way to find out whose baby Lila was carrying. If she could find out, and *if* it turned out that it wasn't Luke's, then, at least, Luke's grief would diminish greatly.

A voice, a distance away, startled her. "Aggie! Are you out there?" It was Luke!

"I'm here, Luke!" she yelled.

"Where?!"

"I don't know!"

"Keep talking and I'll find you!"

"All right! Why are you trying to find me?! Did you think I was lost again?!" she yelled.

"No," came a voice a few feet away.

"I'm up here, Luke."

He stopped, looked up and grinned. "There you are, my little wood nymph. Is this going to be a regular thing, Aggie?" he asked chuckling.

"I think so."

"I went to your house and you were gone, so I came looking for you to ask if you wanted to come up to the house and have a bowl of ice cream with Mary and me?"

"That sounds good, Luke. I would love it. Thank you."

"Well, come on down then."

Aggie started down. "Ow," she muttered as a small leafless branch scratched her arm again, leaving a thin red line.

"Why did you climb a tree with so many dead branches sticking out everywhere?"

"I didn't notice them at first," she said as she stepped on the second to the last limb.

"Why don't you jump and I'll catch you?" he enticed.

Aggie looked down at him and smiled—sorely tempted. The desire, she realized, was greater than last time. Her smile vanished as she studied his face, wishing she could help his pain and grief go away.

Luke, noticing the change in her, asked, "What is it, Aggie?"

She stepped onto the last large limb. "Are you ready to catch me?"

Luke grinned with surprise. "You bet! Come on."

She jumped and Luke caught her easily. She smiled at him. "You certainly are *strong*," she said softly, her heart pounding with a feeling of excitement she'd never felt before.

Luke looked into her large blue eyes, his heart thumping with the unexpected thrill of holding her. "You are so small, Aggie, so beautiful."

They gazed into each other's eyes for several seconds. Aggie, wishing she could ease his grief in someway, impulsively tightened her arms around his neck, pressed her cheek upon his for a moment, then kissed it. "Please put me down now, Luke." she added quickly.

Taken by surprise by Aggie's expression of tenderness, his eyes studied her face, her full, uniquely shaped lips. The desire to kiss her almost overwhelmed his resolve.

"Luke, please put me down."

"Not until you tell me why you did that, Aggie."

"I'll have to think about it."

Luke smiled. "I'll hold you while you think."

"No, Luke, let me down," she demanded, squirming so hard, he gave in.

"Well, for what ever reason, thank you for the kiss, Aggie. It was the sweetest kiss I've ever had."

Now feeling slightly embarrassed, she looked down and spoke softly, "You're welcome."

He reached for her hand and they began walking toward the house.

~~~~~~~~~~

Joy Marshall looked out the window of her luxurious condominium, seething with frustration and anger. Luke had not called her since Saturday night. She had asked him to call her today, suggesting

maybe they might go for a drive out to Fredericksburg. He only nodded absent-mindedly. She wondered if he'd even heard her. He was
probably thinking of that black-haired vixen he called his cook. She'd
noticed he could hardly carry on a decent conversation with her at dinner he was so busy looking at Aggie McBride and trying to listen to her
conversation with Vic and Ted.

She had worked long and hard to find some one who could intro-
duce her to Luke Barnes; and after the introduction, she had finagled
ways to run into him, here and there. Finally he'd asked her out. They
had been dating a little for about six weeks and no way was she going
to let that—that runty little cook of his get in the way!

Aggie McBride. Something about the name was familiar What was
it? she wondered. Aggie—was her name Agnes? Agnes McBride—that
sounded even more familiar. Where had she heard it or where had she
seen it? She'd think about it. It would come to her eventually, she was
certain.

~~~~~~~~~~

Luke opened the door for Aggie and she stepped into the kitchen.
"Have a seat at the table," he said to her, "and I'll get the bowls down
and then go get Mary." Placing the bowls on the table, Luke stopped
and stared. "Aggie!" he exclaimed.

Startled, Aggie looked up into Luke's scowling face. "What?"

"Look at those scratches on your arms!"

She looked. "Oh. I did scratch myself." She smiled up at him. "You
know the old adage: 'no sense, no feeling.'"

"Yeah, no sense." He turned, went to a cupboard, pulled out a box
of small plastic bandages and a bottle of antiseptic and sat down beside
her. "What were you thinking to climb a tree like that?"

"Apparently, I wasn't thinking—about the tree anyway."

"Look next time. Hand me an arm."

"I can do it, Luke."

He ignored her, wrapping his long, firm fingers around her arm and
squirting antiseptic. Taking the other arm, he did the same.

The touch of his strong but gentle hands was soothing, but at the
same time, sent a disturbing sensation clear through her.

"What was on your mind, Aggie, that you didn't notice the kind of tree you were climbing?"

She gazed into his inquisitive brown eyes, noticing their depth. Her face became pensive.

"Not happy thoughts I take it," he said, undoing a bandage and placing it over a scratch.

Mary walked into the kitchen. "Oh my! What happened to your arms, Aggie?"

Aggie rolled her eyes. "You both are making too much of it, after all they're just scratches."

The phone rang and Mary excused herself to answer it. "Yes, he's right here." She handed the phone to Luke, a look of displeasure on her face.

"Hello?....Oh, hello, Joy....We were? Since when?....You did? I didn't hear you....I can't, Joy. I'm helping a friend....I'll call you....I don't know my schedule next week....All right....Talk to you later," Luke said, putting the phone back.

Aggie raised questioning eyes at Luke. "Don't let me interfere with your social life, Luke."

"Not a chance, Aggie, I'm having a great time playing doctor," he replied, grinning and placing a bandage on the last scratch. "Now, let's have a bowl of ice cream."

# Chapter Eighteen

The first thing Monday morning, after observing Luke drive off to work, Aggie went up to the house to quiz Mary more about Luke's ex-wife. She found out where Lila worked, who hired her, and also found out that Lila had taken back her maiden name, Lee. Afterward, back at the cottage, she made some phone calls. At last, armed with more information, Aggie rang Barry's number in Dallas.

"Aggie!" Barry exclaimed. "I've been wondering about you. How are you?"

"I'm doing much better, Barry. How are you?"

"I'm fine, but the detective business isn't as challenging with you out of town. You like it there, then?"

"Yes, I do. It so happens, that 'old Lucas Barnes' is only a year older than I am. It was quite a surprise for both of us since he thought I was 'old Agnes.'"

Barry chuckled. "Sounds like your friend, Doris, pulled a fast one."

"She did, but Luke and I played a part in it. We both jumped to conclusions. You'll have to admit that the names, Agnes and Lucas, both sound like they could belong to senior citizens—and Doris took advantage of that."

"Was she match-making, Aggie?"

"Maybe...I don't know. Luke Barnes is her cousin."

"Is that right? Do you like him?"

"He's a nice man, an attractive man, but sometimes he has all the charm of a pit bull."

"Some description, Aggie, and a nice noncommittal answer. What's up?"

Aggie sucked in a big breath and told him everything Mary had told her, as well as everything she'd found out on her own.

Barry whistled. "You taking on men's issues now, Aggie?"

"Only that of Doris' cousin, Barry," she replied testily.

"Okay...okay. Not much to go on, Aggie. Let's dissect it. I can see two red flags: the too quick marriage and her backing down when Luke mentioned going public with the story. Luke was probably too gullible when he believed that just the threat would scare Lila. Today that's no big deal. So there has to be more to it. It's obvious Lila wanted the whole thing to die down for reasons other than Luke's threat."

"That's exactly what I thought."

"Off the top of my head, Aggie, the only avenue I can see is bluffing some one, either Lila Lee or the VIP who gave her the job. What's his name?"

"Brian Gold. From what I could find out, I believe he lives in Dallas. He's the president of Gold Communications which owns three stations in Texas including KNTK here in Austin. I called the station and found out that Lila Lee has moved to Houston."

"Okay...any thoughts, Aggie?"

"I was wondering why Lila Lee moved the marriage date up so suddenly if she had intended all along to abort the pregnancy."

"Good question. Maybe she wasn't intending to abort. Maybe Mr. Gold reneged on the offer of the job after Lila married."

"Could be if he has a wife and family."

They were both silent, thinking. Aggie finally spoke. "The only way she could possibly blackmail him is with DNA."

"You know, Aggie, this is awful 'slim pickins', but I'll see what I can do and get back to you."

Late that afternoon as Aggie prepared dinner, her spirits were up—not that she was confident anything could be solved, but because she was doing something toward trying to solve it.

When she had asked Mary earlier how she would feel if they could prove that the baby Lila carried and aborted was not Luke's, she exclaimed, "Oh, Aggie, that would ease Luke's heart in a way nothing else could!"

Aggie hummed as she prepared the lighter summer menu of roasted potato wedges with salsa de cilantro a la presilla, black bean salad with chipolte vinaigrette, topped with crumbled goat cheese and her special cole slaw.

Luke leaned back in his chair and stretched, then looked at his watch. It was 4:30, almost time to go home. His pulse quickened at the thought of going home and seeing Aggie, of finding her in his kitchen cooking for him. It was like having a wife to go home to—almost.

It was the beginning of the fourth week since Aggie arrived. Ever since she had come, he found it comforting to go home and walk into a kitchen redolent with the smell of dinner being prepared. It reminded him of the times when he was a boy coming into the kitchen starved and always finding his mother there preparing dinner. This had nurtured his spirit as well as his body.

The whole family sat down for the evening meal at the same time every night—at the same time every morning they ate a big breakfast together. No matter what, his mother was up and preparing breakfast for the family. Luke was convinced that this comforting routine, this consistency and constancy, also nurtured everyone's spirit even more than their bodies.

Along with this, his mother was always there when he came home from school, whenever he came in from play, and when he came in from work. She was there when he needed her even before he himself realized it; she could tell by the way he held his head, by a look in his eyes, by the way he sat. As a boy he often wondered if his mother was a mind reader; it was uncanny the way she always knew when he was troubled—no matter how he tried to hide it from her. His mind went back to a time when, at age eleven, he had questioned her about this.

*"Mom, are you psychic or something? You always know things. My friend's mothers never know when they're up to something. They can get away with things—I never can!"*

*His mother smiled. "If I remember, Luke, the mothers of your friends work outside the home."*

*"What difference does that make?"*

*It was then that his mother told him something so profound he never forgot it—something that had never before entered his head.*

*"Luke, there are many women who have to work—single mothers, widows, those whose husbands have health problems and so on. Children understand this. They can instinctively tell the difference*

between a mother who has to work and a mother who wants to work in order to afford a bigger house, a newer car or nicer clothes.

"Nevertheless, those mothers who have to work outside the home and those who want to, both face an impossible task to perform. They have to juggle two full time jobs in one day."

"So?"

"What do you think is the most important thing they can't do even if they are trying their very best? Something that no one else can do."

"Clean house?"

"Can children clean?"

"I guess so. Go grocery shopping?"

"Depending on the children's ages, do you suppose they could do some of it...or the father?"

"Maybe. I can't guess, Mom."

"Try," she encouraged.

In frustration, he blurted out, "Cook? Oh, never mind others can help with that. Uh...I can't think of anything."

"Thoughts! Luke."

"Huh?"

"A mother who is trying to run two different worlds in one day can't give her children her—thoughts."

"Sure she can!"

"Luke, listen and listen well because I want you to learn this. When a working mother gets up in the morning, she has to dress for work, see that everyone is dressed for school or for day care. Her thoughts are on getting to work on time. She may have to throw on cold cereal. Maybe she has to iron a dress for work, maybe one of the children can't find a shoe, maybe a child forgot to tell his or her mother that he or she needed a notebook for school and she has to run to the store before school. What is she thinking about, Luke?"

He frowned, "Ah, Mom, why all these questions? You know—she's thinking about all the things she has to do."

"Exactly, Luke, she's thinking about surviving the crisis' of the moment and making it to work on time. The same thing happens at night. Driving home, maybe she's thinking about what to have for dinner, wondering if she has to run to the grocery store and so on. At *home, it's a scramble to get dinner on, even if her husband helps, even if the children help. Maybe she has to go to a school program, or go buy her daughter a dress for a party, maybe she has to iron something for work tomorrow, maybe she has to get after her children to do their homework, and help them with their homework, maybe her son needs some new shoes and so on."*

*"I don't want to hear all this, Mom," he complained.*

*"It's tiring isn't it?"*

*"It sure is!"*

*"Can you see why maybe your friends get away with things?"*

*He thought a moment, the light dawning. "Yeah, their mothers don't have time to think about what they may be up to."*

*"That's right, Luke. She can only manage the bare necessities of their physical needs. Do you think she can give any thought to their emotional and spiritual needs?*

*"Housework is boring, Luke, but it gives me time to think about you, Amy and your father. I can stop any time and kneel down and pray about anything I'm concerned about. Thoughts are powerful, Luke, and children can feel them. It takes a lot of thought, pondering and prayer to raise children."*

LUKE got up from his desk and stared out the window. Was it unreasonable to want for his own children a mother like he had? Lila had been so convincing; he thought she wanted this too.

And why was he letting himself get maudlin over having Aggie there cooking for him anyway? She wasn't doing it because she cared about him—he was paying her! He didn't even know her—and she won't even talk about herself. Just because she likes to cook doesn't mean she would give up her career anymore than Lila. Distrust and bitterness overrode the anticipation of going home and seeing her. He steeled himself against any further feeling.

~~~~~~~~~~

Aggie, her cheeks rosy from the heat of the stove, looked over at Luke when he walked in. She could see it immediately. He had put a wall up around himself again.

"Good evening, Luke," she said lightly.

"Good evening, Aggie," he returned stiffly, only a suggestion of a smile on his face. He strode quickly to the hall where he took the stairs, three at a time.

Mary came in, set the table and poured the water while Aggie put the finishing touches on the food.

"Will you call Luke down for dinner, Mary?"

"Of course." Even though there was an intercom, Mary refused to use it. To her, it was invading Luke's privacy. She walked to the bottom of the stairs and called him. Five minutes later he came down in khaki pants and a green knit shirt.

During the meal, instead of the relaxing conversation they usually had, Luke read the evening paper. Mary looked at Aggie and shrugged her shoulders.

Aggie thought she understood why Luke was distancing himself from her. She felt that the intimacy they experienced the day before, when he caught her in his arms, must have had an emotional impact on him as well as her. He was simply afraid of trusting again.

Although she understood this very well, it was easier to put up with him getting ornery than shutting her out. Her father had shut her out of his life; she didn't need this! Her heart was full of amazing tenderness toward Luke Barnes; and he was the first man she'd ever felt attracted to—yet she had to pull back. Somehow, some way she was going to have to shield her own heart as Luke was shielding his. The lump in her throat made it hard to swallow.

"Mary," she asked quickly, "when your children and grandchildren visit, I would like to meet them. When are they coming?"

"They had each visited just before you came, so it won't be for a while. Do you have pictures of your family, Aggie?"

"I do; not many, however."

Aggie's and Mary's conversation was spotty—uneasy. Luke was such a powerful presence, his silence was palpable, making it difficult to ignore.

When they finished with the main course, Aggie served the dessert to Mary and Luke, reserving hers for later. She excused herself, washed up the pans, and put the food away as quickly as she could. Excusing herself quietly to Mary, she left the kitchen for home.

The minute she stepped inside her house, tears stung her eyes. "What is the matter with me?" she asked aloud. Why was she feeling so emotional? She squelched the desire to go for a walk in the woods. If Luke, again, began to worry whether he had hurt her, he'd come looking for her as he had before. She felt too vulnerable; she couldn't face him.

Grabbing her keys and purse, she stepped out of the kitchen door to the carport where the van was parked. She got in, backed out and drove down to the highway, turning left toward the area that was less populated. She drove aimlessly, trying to focus outside her own pain.

~~~~~~~~~~~

Luke turned into his driveway at 10:00 P.M. after a short, early evening round of golf and visit with Joy Marshall. He noticed that Aggie's van was still gone. His brows creased in annoyance. "Where could she be at this hour?" he mumbled to himself.

When he entered the kitchen, he went to Mary's door and knocked. She opened it and smiled. "Hello, Luke, have a good game?"

"No. Do you know where Aggie went?"

Mary's brows rose in surprise. "I didn't know she was gone."

"Her van has been gone all evening."

"Don't worry about her, Luke, she's been on her own for years."

"Nevertheless, I'm going to watch for her."

Luke paced the kitchen floor, repeatedly stepping out onto the patio to check on Aggie's carport. At last he saw her van pull in.

~~~~~~~~~~~

It was long after dark when Aggie arrived home. She felt calmer and more self contained. While driving, she had attained a semblance of objectivity and made some important decisions—decisions she couldn't have made before. She decided that after the six months commitment cooking for Luke, she would give up her law practice, go back to school and get a teaching certificate. She needed the association of children. For the first time, since becoming an adult, she longed to have her own. Until then, she would enjoy other's children.

She stepped out of the van and went into the house. Feeling more tired than usual, she went into the bedroom to prepare for bed.

Luke waited until Aggie had gone inside, then his long stride ate up the distance to her front door. He knocked. Soon the door opened.

Not seeming surprised at all, Aggie said, "Hello, Luke. Why the visit at this hour?"

"May I come in?"

"Of course," she said stepping aside.

Luke remained standing. "Where have you been, Aggie? I was worried about you."

"There's no need to worry, Luke, I'm a big girl."

"Not very," he said, smiling.

"Well, you can see that I'm all right, so you may say good night."

"Where did you go, Aggie?"

"Luke, that is not your concern."

"But...I feel responsible for your safety, Aggie."

"Why?"

"I don't know. Maybe it's because you are in my employ."

"Please don't. I've been on my own for a long time. You have your life—I have mine. Let's leave it that way."

Luke frowned in consternation. Aggie was different tonight; there was a perceptible aloofness about her. A far cry from yesterday! "What's the matter, Aggie?"

"What makes you think something is the matter?"

"You're acting—different tonight—different than yesterday."

"Did you act different at dinner tonight?"

Luke turned silent, contemplating the situation. "You are acting aloof because I read the paper?"

"Do you think that's why?"

"Don't answer my questions with another question, Aggie," he warned. "One would think you were a lawyer!"

Aggie bit her tongue once more. "I've been around enough of them."

"Answer my question, Aggie."

"Do you think we're getting anywhere, Luke?"

"No! Not when you answer my questions with a question. Goodnight, Aggie."

"Goodnight, Luke," she said softly to his retreating back.

# Chapter Nineteen

It was late Tuesday morning when Barry called. "Barry! what do you have?"

"Not much. I've been investigating every source I know to find out about Brian Gold. I'll tell you what little I've got, but first, if possible, you need to find out if Luke and Lila were intimate before marriage. In this day and age, that's usually the case, so if they were, it would be impossible to find out the things you want to know. Unless, of course, you could find DNA evidence."

"Stay there, Barry and I'll call you right back. I'm going up to the house and talk to Mary. It's likely she won't know anything so private as that, but she's worked for the family for years and loves Luke like her own."

"Okay, I'll stay put."

Aggie ran out of the house and entered the kitchen in a rush. Mary was sitting at the table drinking a glass of ice tea and reading. She looked up in surprise.

"What's all the hurry, Aggie?" she asked.

"My investigator called. He's been doing some checking for me, but he can't continue until I get some more information. It's probably something you'll know nothing about. It's very personal, I hate to even ask."

"Go ahead, anything to help Luke."

"If Luke and Lila were intimate before marriage, it would be impossible to find out anything unless we had DNA evidence."

"They weren't."

Aggie let out a breath of relief. "Are you certain, Mary?"

"Of course I'm not, but almost. Ann, his mother, had very strong beliefs and she instilled them in her children. Luke was determined to live her standards and go into marriage that way."

"What about Lila Lee?"

"Amy and I both felt she wasn't up to Luke in any way, especially in that area."

"Could she have broken Luke down even once?"

"As I said, I can't be certain, but I'm almost positive he wouldn't respect her if she tried. I cautioned Luke along this line. I felt I owed it to Ann and he promised me."

"Good! I'll let you know the minute I find out anything."

"Thank you, Aggie. I can't tell you how much this means to me."

Back at the cottage, Aggie dialed Barry.

"Barry Slocum here."

"Barry, I've talked to Mary. Without extraneous details, the answer is no, they weren't intimate. She's not a hundred percent positive, but almost."

"Amazing. All right. I've found out that Brian Gold is quite the womanizer. Apparently, women are attracted to his looks as well as his money and power." He blew out a gust of breath into the phone. "This is not my kind of case, Aggie, but for you I'll do it. The only possible way I can handle it, since we lack any real evidence, is to try to bluff Brian Gold. Can you see any other way, Aggie?"

"No, I can't, Barry."

"Say one of those prayers of yours, then."

"I will, Barry. Thank you!"

~~~~~~~~~~

Brian Gold was furious when he read the note from Barry Slocum: "MR. GOLD, IT IS IN YOUR BEST INTEREST TO SEE ME" All week he'd been rebuffing Slocum's requests to see him. The note sent acid into his stomach. Slocum was known throughout Dallas as an astute and cagey private investigator—but his reputation as an honest man bothered Brian the most.

"Who in the hell hired him?" he growled to himself. He'd find out one way or another!

The buzzer on his desk was like an ice pick in his nerves. "Yes?"

"Mr. Slocum is here."

"Send him in."

Entering the luxurious office of Brian Gold, Barry looked around and whistled. "Some domain you have here, Mr. Gold."

Brian's eyes were slits. "Cut the small talk, Slocum. What was the meaning of that note?"

Barry studied the man standing behind the desk. He looked to be in his early fifties, blonde, tan, well built and handsome by any female standard, Barry was sure.

"May we sit down, Mr. Gold?"

"Only if you make it quick, Slocum."

"Do you know Lila Lee?" Barry asked, seating himself.

Gold flinched only slightly. "Of course. She works in my Houston station."

"Do you know anything about...DNA, Mr. Gold?"

The blood left Gold's face, but he remained composed. "What are you getting at?"

"Do you know for certain the DNA was destroyed?"

"This is double talk. Get out of my office!"

"All right," Barry said rising from the chair.

"Hold it. Do you have a tape on you?"

"Search me," Barry offered.

Brian Gold did exactly that. When Gold sat back down at his desk, Barry asked, "Satisfied?"

"I won't be satisfied until you're out of my sight!"

"I'm going to be frank with you, Gold, I'm not here to shake you down or blackmail you."

"Who hired you?"

"I can't divulge that."

Brian Gold swore. "Why are you here?"

"To get a truthful answer from you, if that's possible. I'll sign a note that the person who hired me will not use it against you."

"Why in the hell would you want an answer to anything if you weren't going to use it against me?"

"Not very trusting are you, Gold?"

"Spill it, Slocum or get out!"

"I give you my word that the answer you give me will not hurt you, but it will relieve some pain for some one else."

"You talk in riddles. Who is that some one else?"

"Lila Lee's ex-husband."

Brian Gold's eyes were slits again, seething with anger. He spewed out some unsavory adjectives describing Lila Lee.

"There's no need for that, Gold. Just tell me that it was your baby Lila Lee aborted."

"How dare you! I have a wife and family."

"Okay, I'm outa here," Barry said rising.

"Sit down!" thundered Gold.

Barry sat down and waited.

Brian Gold weighed the situation. If it were anyone but Barry Slocum, he wouldn't trust him. "If I had let you leave, Slocum, what would you and your client have done?"

"I can't divulge that."

"Write the damn note, then," he barked, handing him a paper and pen.

Barry wrote it, signed it, and handed it back to Gold who studied it carefully.

"Are you going tell Lila Lee's ex that it was mine?"

"No. I'm just going to tell him I know it wasn't his. I give you my word."

"Who hired you?"

"A friend of Lila's ex."

"It wasn't Lila?"

"No."

"How did you find out then?"

"I can't divulge that."

"All right, you have the information, get the hell out of here!"

~~~~~~~~~

It had been exactly a week since Aggie had last talked to Barry. She and Luke were playing emotional stand-off—polite and casual in conversation.

She was looking out her kitchen window when the phone rang. She grabbed it, "Hello?"

"Hey, Aggie," came Barry's welcome voice.

"Barry! I've been standing on one foot then the other."

"Mr. Gold was playing hard to see so I sent him a note."

"Tell me everything."

"You were right, again, Aggie." He related everything. "So what do I do with this information?"

"Come here to Austin and tell Luke. However, I don't want Luke to know that I had anything to do with it. I'll pay you well above expenses—and a bonus because I know this was something you disliked doing and I know you only did it for me."

Barry was silent.

"Barry?"

"You care for this man, don't you, Aggie?"

"Of course. He's Doris' cousin."

"Sure... When do you want me to come?"

"As soon as you possibly can."

"All right, Aggie. I'll call him tonight. I'll call you back and let you know."

The minute she hung up, Aggie ran up to the house to tell Mary, exacting a promise not to tell Luke her part in it. Mary cried in relief and then thanked her profusely.

# *Chapter Twenty*

The next day, Barry called Aggie, informing her that he had an appointment to see Luke at his home in the early evening, Thursday night. Aggie relayed this to an excited and happy Mary.

Thursday, the weather had turned so humid Aggie had to shower twice. Putting on a sky blue cotton dress, she hoped to feel cooler in the kitchen while preparing dinner. Luke had informed them that he had an appointment at 5:30 and wanted to eat dinner after that.

When Luke arrived home at 5:15, he looked strikingly handsome in his sandy-brown suit. He seemed preoccupied, giving them a perfunctory greeting, while loosening his tie, then added, "I'll be in the study, Mary. A gentleman is coming to see me at 5:30."

"All right, Luke."

Aggie and Mary smiled at each other as he left the room.

~~~~~~~~~~

Luke took off his suit coat, hung it over the back of his chair and sat down at his desk, feeling anxious. When he threatened Lila, she had given in too easily. He wondered when the other shoe would drop. This may be it, he thought. Soon, he heard the doorbell ring and presently Mary and the expected visitor appeared at the door.

"Thank you, Mary. Close the door as you leave."

Luke stood up and reached out his hand, "I'm Luke Barnes."

The man shook his hand firmly. "Barry Slocum here. Glad to meet you, Mr. Barnes."

"Please have a seat, Mr. Slocum."

"Call me Barry."

"All right. What is it you want to see me about, Barry?"

"Well, Mr. Barnes," Barry said, smiling amiably, "I'm a private investigator and this is the most unusual assignment I've ever had."

Luke lifted his brows in surprise, not quite sure how to assess the man in front of him. "As you might guess, I'm anxious to get this over with."

"I'm the bearer of good news, Mr. Barnes, no need to feel anxious."

"Who hired you?"

"I can't divulge that."

"Was it Lila Lee?"

"No. A friend of yours hired me."

A look of tentative relief came across his face. "A friend? Male or female?"

"I can't divulge that."

"All right, give me the good news," he stated skeptically.

"I might as well say it outright. The baby your wife, Lila, aborted was not yours."

Luke was so dumbfounded, he couldn't say anything. This was the last thing he expected to hear! And it was too good to be true. Besides, who knew about the abortion besides Mary and Amy?

"I certainly want to believe you, Barry, but I'm afraid I can't. None of my friends knew anything about it."

"It's true, I assure you."

"How could you possibly find out a thing like that?"

"I'm a private investigator, I do this for a living."

"That isn't an answer."

"My client and I put our heads together and made an educated guess who the man was who fathered the baby. It was a difficult assignment, but I went to see this man and bluffed him into admitting it. I signed a paper saying that the person who hired me would not use the information against him. I told him, the only person I would tell was you, and I gave him my word that I wouldn't divulge to you who he is."

Luke was silent for some moments, trying to internalize what Barry had told him. "This is a farfetched story, Barry. It's hard to believe. Why would he admit such a thing?"

"I mentioned something about Lila Lee and DNA."

"You threatened him?"

"No, but he assumed I was threatening him. That's how his mind works."

Luke frowned and shook his head. "This is a little hard to swallow, Barry. You went to this man not really knowing?"

"That's right. I insinuated a couple of things and he looked like a guy who'd just received the death sentence. It was pretty obvious."

"You're some investigator. I...I'm still having difficulty believing the 'good news.' Can you tell me how you and your client put it together?"

"No, I can't, and I have to ask you to help me keep my word. If, by chance, you happen to put it together yourself, you can't confront this man or your ex-wife Lila."

"Why would I help you keep your word?"

"Well," a slow smile spread across Barry's face, "because my client apparently thinks you are an honorable man."

Luke studied the man before him. He liked his face; it was an honest face. "You must be an honorable man yourself to want to keep your word."

"I try to be."

"It would be easier to believe if there was proof."

"I figured it was almost impossible to find proof, but if we could, it would take a long time. I think one would have to gain the friendship of your ex-wife and then it would be a long shot."

Luke thought about this then slowly nodded his head. "You are probably right. It would take a long time to become friends with Lila, even if she allowed the attempt in the first place."

"Well, I believe I've completed my mission, Mr. Barnes," Barry said, standing up.

Luke stood up and came around the desk and held out his hand to Barry. "Even though I still feel a little doubtful, I can't tell you what this news means to me, Barry. Thank you!" He shook Barry's hand vigorously. "And...thank your client for me."

"I will, and good luck to you. I hope your future will be brighter now."

Luke walked with Barry to the front door, and watched him leave, then went into the kitchen.

Mary studied his face anxiously, trying to read what was there. "What is it, Luke?"

"I've just been given some astounding news. News, I'm afraid, I can't quite internalize yet."

"Good or bad news, Luke?"

Aggie, who had quickly eaten dinner while Luke was with Barry, excused herself. "I'll be back to help you clean up, Mary. I've got something I must do at home."

"Go ahead, Aggie. Don't worry about coming back." She turned back to Luke who was staring after Aggie. "Can you tell me, Luke?"

He sat down at the table, looking mystified. "I want to believe it, Mary."

"Believe what, Luke?"

"That it wasn't my baby Lila aborted."

"Is that what he told you?" she asked, trying to pretend surprise.

"Yes."

"How would he know that?" she asked placing his dinner in front of him.

"That's what I wanted to know."

"Eat your dinner, Luke, then tell me everything he said."

~~~~~~~~~~

Aggie hadn't told Barry to call when he got to the motel, but she was certain he would, and she wanted to be home when he did. She also wanted to give Luke and Mary their privacy so they could talk about what Barry told him. Luke's expression told her that it would be a while before he could let himself believe it completely. She knew, when he thought it through carefully, he would put it together as she and Barry had, and in the end, with the information Barry had given him, wouldn't doubt it."

Her heart felt easier now. To pass the time until Barry called, she turned to her writing. The phone finally rang. She ran to the kitchen. "Hello?"

"Hello, is this the resident of the Good Samaritan, Aggie?"

"Barry, thank you for calling. Tell me everything."

"First, I want to tell you I like Luke Barnes—and I trust him."

"I'm glad. You know your opinion counts with me."

Barry related everything. At the end, he said, "Luke asked me to thank my client so—thank you, Aggie, from Luke."

"Barry, you're an amazing man. You are more than my investigator, you are my dear friend."

"Thank you, Aggie. The feeling's mutual."

"Send me your expenses and I'll mail you a check."

"Okay, and keep me posted on how things go for Luke, will you, Aggie?"

"I will, Barry."

Aggie hung up smiling—feeling grateful and relieved. She knew in order to pay Barry his expenses, salary and bonus she would have to sell some stock. It had been a month since she arrived here and she needed to call Sally and ask her if she would stay a little longer—long enough to put an ad in the paper and sublease her office space. Without the expense of rent and Sally's salary, she could go back to school.

# Chapter Twenty-One

Luke stared out the window of his study, thinking of Aggie. He knew she left so he and Mary could talk. Strange, he thought, he wished he could tell Aggie his good news. It was comforting to have Mary to talk to, she'd been like a mother to him, even when she was raising her own children. But it wasn't the same.

When he was dating Lila, she seemed to listen intently to anything he had to say. He thought she was listening when he told her of his desire to get started on a family as quickly as possible. He thought she was listening when he said he wanted his wife at home. She led him to believe she felt as he did.

Clenching his fists in sudden anger, he thought of what Barry Slocum had told him: of Lila being unfaithful to him while they were engaged, of her allowing him to believe the baby she had carried for a short time—was his. "What a fool I've been!"

Through the years he had tried to find a wife; he'd been so careful in his search—only to end up marrying a deceitful, selfish woman! He no longer had confidence in his ability to judge. He left the study abruptly.

Upstairs in his bedroom, he angrily grabbed a small bag, threw in a change of underwear and his shaving kit, then changed to jeans.

He stopped in mid-movement. "Why am I so angry? If Barry Slocum is right, the baby wasn't mine!" A sudden rush of gratitude came over him as he realized that the terrible feeling of loss, over what he thought was his, was gone. He uttered a silent prayer of thanks and went down stairs.

He found Mary sitting at the table reading the evening paper.

"Mary, I'm going to spend the night and most of the day tomorrow at the ranch. Tell Aggie that she needn't cook dinner for me tomorrow night. Joy Marshall has invited me to a dinner dance at the country club."

Aggie, sitting at the computer, saw Luke drive by in his truck, and wondered where he was going. She was anxious to study his face and see how he was feeling. After all, he had been dealt another blow learning that his fiancé was untrue to him. But, she hoped the news Barry brought far outweighed the hurt.

She stared out the window, unseeing, wishing she could have met Luke before he fell for Lila Lee; before he was hurt; before he built a wall of distrust around himself. But, was *she* ready to meet Luke Barnes two years ago? No. She must go on with the plans she made the other night. She would go back to school and become a school teacher.

Mary came walking up the driveway to her door. "Come in, Mary," Aggie yelled.

Mary stepped in. "I came to tell you I'm on my way to the airport. I forgot to tell you, but I'm flying to El Paso tonight to visit my son and his family for three or four days."

"How nice, Mary. May I drive you to the airport?"

"Thank you, Aggie, but I've called a taxi. Luke always pays for it."

"All right, but I'll miss you. How is Luke?"

"I think he's swung from hardly daring to believe it to a kind of peace I haven't seen in him for a long time."

Aggie sighed in relief. "Maybe he's believing it faster that I expected. If so, it's probably because Barry Slocum is so credible and likeable. Where did Luke go, Mary?"

"He went to the ranch. He's staying there tonight and most of tomorrow. He said to tell you that you don't need to cook for him tomorrow night. Joy Marshall has invited him to a dinner dance at the Country Club."

Aggie's brows crinkled in irritation. "Joy Marshall is an aggressive woman."

"I know. I don't dare say this to Luke, but I don't approve of her at all." She shook her head and changed the subject. "You are going to be alone here tonight, Aggie. Will you be all right?"

"I've been alone for many years, Mary. Don't worry, I'm used to it."

"All right then. Lock your doors, Aggie. I'm leaving now."

"Have a nice time with your family, Mary."

"Thank you, I will."

Aggie sat back down at her computer and watched Mary walk back up to the house, thinking about how she really felt. The truth was, she didn't want to be alone. She was disappointed that Luke left and that she wouldn't get to see him tomorrow at all. She wanted to see for herself how he was after Barry's visit.

The loneliness that suddenly engulfed her felt unbearable. Maybe she could go to a movie or to the musical she'd been wanting to see. She looked at her watch. It was too late for either one.

She tried to turn her attention to the book, but couldn't concentrate. Deciding to go get a snack, she got up and went into the kitchen.

Five minutes later the door bell rang. Maybe it's Luke, she thought. Excitement coursing through her, she walked quickly to the door. To her shock and disappointment she found Victor Wolfe standing on the door step.

"Hello, Aggie," he said, grinning.

"Hello, Victor. This is a surprise."

"What are you doing tonight?"

Aggie thought quickly. "When the door bell rang, I thought it was Luke."

"You have a date with him?"

"No, but I was expecting him."

"Okay. I won't ask to come in then. I came over to see if you would go to the country club dinner dance with me tomorrow night."

"Victor, I don't know you well enough."

"We can get to know each other at the dance. Besides, you should feel comfortable, Luke will be there. He's Joy's date."

Several thoughts raced through Aggie's mind: she would be able to observe Luke; and maybe if he saw her with Victor, he would let down his reserve with her. Dare she chance it? Victor Wolfe still made her skin crawl. In the grip of her loneliness, she made a rash decision.

"All right. I'll go if you will drive within the speed limit—and if you'll let me drive on the way home."

His eyes widened in surprise. "Who's been squealing on me?"

Aggie couldn't help but laugh. "Just a guess, Victor."

He grinned. "Not only are you beautiful, you're smart."

"Thank you. What time will you pick me up?"

"6:30. By the way it's formal."

"All right. See you at 6:30. Good night, Victor."

# Chapter Twenty-Two

Aggie woke up to the peculiar sound of her favorite bird, the Grackle. She lay there listening to it, remembering how it used to fascinate her with it's scraping, raspy sound that turned into a throaty and melodic 'coguba-leek.' This morning, it eased her feeling of isolation.

In all the years of living alone, she had never felt like this. This morning, the feeling was different than when her mother died, leaving her totally alone in the world. The desolation and grief she felt then, eased with time as she buried herself in studies and made friends at school.

The desolating loneliness this morning felt as though it would never cease. Only one person could relieve it—Luke! She needed Luke. She *needed* him! She closed her eyes, completely wonder-struck. She had steeled herself not to need anyone—much less a man!

It was only five weeks ago that she first met Doris' magnificent cousin. It was the very next day that a bond began to grow between them, beginning when he went searching for her, worrying that he'd hurt her feelings. The bond cemented when he found her crying and sat down beside her, tenderly putting his arm around her shoulders—holding her tightly, encouraging her to cry.

Even in the midst of her grief that day, the bewildering question hung at the edge of her consciousness; how could a near stranger break down the dam of sorrow she'd held in for years? Mystified, she asked herself; did Luke feel the bond? It didn't seem so. Fear clutched at her heart. She pushed it back as quickly as it came.

Putting her hands behind her head, she lay there thinking. Waiting for Luke to come home each night her feelings gradually escalated; first to anticipation, then to excitement. The minute he walked into the kitchen, a peace would settle over her. All this had happened so subtly, she had hardly been aware.

By necessity, she had developed a spirited independence. Though she had rebuffed Luke's protectiveness, she was surprised at how comforting it felt. She had rarely seen protectiveness in a man through the years in her work. The men she prosecuted were not 'real' men; they were the cowardly and cruel who took out their anger, or their aberrations on those physically weaker—women and children.

Aggie found Luke's manly protectiveness more than attractive. While in the feminist movement at college, all the young women not only sneered at the idea of a man safeguarding them, but bitterly denied their need of it.

Contemplating the possible results of this upon men, Aggie picked up a thread that had, over the years, subtly woven itself into her subconscious. Today, it *pressed* upon her mind. Did aggressive, independent women who felt they no longer needed the protection of men, putting themselves on the same footing, demanding equality in *every area* of life, make men feel emasculated? Was this the cause of so much coarseness and insensitivity toward women in the work place and other areas of life? Whatever the reason, the result seemed to spawn its own energy, producing momentum, spinning it into a *vicious cycle.*

Then there were gentle women like Mama and Beth who were so deserving of a protective, caring husband and father, and who would have blossomed under such guardianship. Tears sprang to her eyes, sliding down her temples onto the pillow.

~~~~~~~~~~

Luke, up at the break of day, had saddled his old black stallion, Savage, and headed out to the range to look things over, to check on the cattle—and to think.

Three hours later, he headed back, pulling Savage to a stop under a big old tree. Swinging off the horse, he sat down, leaned his back against the wide trunk, and rested his arms upon his knees. The shade as well as the gentle breeze cooled the beads of perspiration covering his forehead and neck.

He had made one decision—not to dwell on Lila or try to figure out *whose* baby she was carrying. What point was there now that he knew it wasn't his? After going back over everything concerning Lila, he had come to the conclusion that Barry and his client were correct, especially since the man—father of the baby—was willing to accept

Barry's signed note. Even though he didn't know Barry Slocum, he sensed he could trust him; he believed him. In his gut, he knew he could figure out who Lila had been unfaithful with—but as he had decided, there was no point. The child he thought he lost was not lost. Tears came, and here in this unguarded moment, his chest heaved with sobs of relief and thankfulness.

Twenty minutes later, feeling the catharsis of hours of thinking, of releasing emotion, he turned his mind to some one he'd neglected, his grandmother Barnes. He had a strong feeling that he needed to go see her this morning. He didn't want to. Since a teenager, he had rebelled against her dominating ways. She dominated his grandfather, his father and tried to dominate him. But most of his resentment came from the grief she had caused his mother. Nevertheless, he had an obligation to look after her.

He got up, mounted Savage and headed back to the house.

~~~~~~~~~~~

Driving back to Austin, Luke thought about the visit with his grandmother. It turned out to be more pleasant than he'd expected, probably because his attitude was better. She was so happy to see him he felt guilty over his neglect and vowed to do better by her. Amy was much more forgiving than he. When visiting, Amy was very attentive to her grandmother.

The trip to the ranch had been fruitful in other ways also. He had spent time with Bob Burke, his foreman, advising him on some help problems, and together they had made some important decisions on the business. They had decided to take several hundred acres and put in a commercial tree farm, fast growing yellow pine, to help satisfy the voracious appetite of the building industry.

Glancing at his watch, he realized he was running late. He needed to be at the country club at 7:00. He dreaded the evening and chastised himself for accepting Joy's invitation.

It was 6:45 when he turned into his driveway. Aggie's van was there. She was alone last night and she'd be alone all evening. He felt a pang of uneasiness. He wanted to check on her, but realized he didn't have time.

His heart and mind freer, he allowed his curiosity to run rampant as he showered and got ready. Who was Barry's client? Who could have known? Who could have cared enough to spend that kind of money investigating something so important to him? He knew he would never rest until he found out.

~~~~~~~~~~~

It was 7:45 when Luke entered the Hyacinth room of the country club. The background dinner music was almost drowned out by the talking and laughter of the guests who were seated in groups of eight around white linen covered tables. Luke noted that they were already being served the main course.

His eyes searched for Joy. She saw him first. Excusing herself from the table, she came over to him, her eyes full of anger.

"Where have you been, Luke? You are my guest of honor!"

"I'm sorry, Joy. I had to go out to the ranch and there was more to take care of than I realized."

"Couldn't it have been taken care of next week?"

"No, it couldn't."

"All right, then," she replied testily, "come and sit down. You'll just have to do without the hors d'oeuvres and salad."

"Fine with me," he stated grimly.

Aggie, who had been watching for Luke, sighed with relief when he walked in. He looked so attractive in his tuxedo, it almost took her breath away. She felt at ease now, but nervous over how he would react upon seeing her with Victor since he'd made a point to warn her against him. Joy was certainly shocked when she arrived with Vic because she immediately pulled him over and spoke to him. Overhearing a word here and there, she gathered that Joy definitely did not want her here. Nevertheless, Vic showered her with attention in between cocktails.

Aggie wore a rose, scooped-necked, form fitting dress with a swirled A line skirt—jacquard-woven with tone-on-tone roses. Her earrings were a delicate square and a plump heart of rose quartz backed by sterling silver with a fresh water pearl interspersed between the stones. Vic had complimented her effusively, telling her how the color of the dress matched her rosy cheeks and accentuated her dark, lustrous hair.

After everyone had finished with dessert and coffee, couples gravitated to the dance floor. Victor asked her to dance. As they walked toward the dance floor, Luke, who was also heading in the same direction with Joy, saw Aggie for the first time. He blinked a couple of times, then his jaw dropped. He pulled Joy to a stop as Aggie did Vic.

"Aggie?"

"Hello, Luke," she said, smiling.

He glowered at her. "What are you doing here?"

"That's what I wondered, too," Joy said, with distaste. "Don't bother with your hired help, Luke, let's dance."

"Just a minute, Joy," he stated with irritation.

"I'm here with Victor, Luke," Aggie answered.

He glared at her a moment longer then, his voice low in angry dismissal, said, "Well, I hope you have a good time. Come on, Joy."

Glad the interchange was over, Victor took Aggie's arm and propelled her to the dance floor. He put his arm around her waist, pulling her close, and pressing his cheek against her temple.

"Mmm, you feel and smell good, Aggie," he whispered.

"Thank you, Vic," she replied distractedly, her eyes searching for Luke and Joy. At last she caught a glimpse on one of their turns. Joy had both her arms entwined about Luke's neck, forcing him to look only at her. Aggie's stomach knotted up in frustration and annoyance.

When the music stopped, Aggie pried Victor's arm off her waist. She was about to suggest they sit the next one out when Luke appeared at her side, still glowering.

"May I have the next dance, Aggie?"

"She's with me," barked Victor.

"I know, Vic. I just want to borrow her for one dance."

"All right," he said reluctantly. "But only *one!*"

Dancing with Luke was difficult. He was so much taller, he had to bend to put his arm comfortably around her upper waist. She looked up and smiled. "Hi."

"Hi yourself!" His voice was low and menacing. "Whatever possessed you to accept a date with Victor Wolfe? I warned you!"

Tenderness for Luke welled up in Aggie. Grateful for his concern, she smiled and spoke softly. "Thank you for being concerned about me,

Luke, but—for some reason I felt terribly lonely this weekend. Mary gave me your message and when Victor came to my door and invited me to go to the same dance, I felt safe in accepting because I knew *you* would be here."

Luke's face softened, totally disarmed by her voice, her expression and by what she said. His hand gripped hers harder.

"Let's go out to the patio, this is awkward."

"All right."

Luke maneuvered her quickly through the dancers and out onto the patio, leading her to a secluded spot behind a large potted plant.

"Let's sit here on this bench, Aggie."

"I'm glad you finally got here, Luke," she said, seating herself. "I was worried."

"I'm glad I got here, too," adding quickly "I can't let you go home with Victor, Aggie, he's a drinker."

"I know. I accepted the date only if he would drive the speed limit on the way and let me drive home."

Luke looked surprised. "Smart girl."

"That's what Victor said."

"But, I'm worried about more than that. Vic has the reputation of forcing himself upon women, Aggie. I still can't let you go home with him. Let's go home—now."

Aggie frowned in disapproval. "No, Luke, that wouldn't be kind to Joy...or to Victor."

"To hell with what's kind."

"Luke," she said, her voice a soft reprimand.

Luke's chest heaved then fell. "All right, Aggie. I'll think of something else. Don't let Vic take you home until I tell you what I've come up with."

"I won't," she said, a hint of a smile on her lips, her blue eyes warm and affectionate. "Thank you."

Luke's heart thumped against his chest as he studied her stunning face, remembering when he first saw her this evening. He was sure that he'd never seen such a beautiful sight. "You look wonderful, Aggie."

"Thank you, Luke."

Suddenly, his hands reached out and gripped her shoulders, turning her towards him. His eyes gazing into hers, he bent down and kissed her lips hungrily. She returned his kiss. Several moments later, he reluctantly pulled away. Dropping his hands, he groaned inwardly.

"So this is where you're hiding!" came Victor's angry voice. "When I couldn't see you dancing, I came looking for you. You said you wanted a dance, Luke, so what are you doing out here?"

"Settle down, Vic," Luke's calm, deep voice was a contrast to Victor's strident one. "We came out here because it was awkward dancing together. I'm too tall for Aggie."

Victor's anger deflated. "Oh. Come on, Aggie, it's almost our dance now."

The three of them entered the room together, running into a fuming Joy.

"Where have you been, Luke?"

"Out on the patio, Joy. Let's dance." He quickly led her toward the dance floor.

The evening crawled by for Luke. Trying to be courteous to Joy while watching Victor drink and loll all over Aggie in the name of dancing, was almost more than he could take.

Looking at his watch, he saw that it was 11:05. "Joy, I'm afraid I'm done in. I was up at dawn this morning."

"But Luke, I'm the hostess of this party and it doesn't end until 1:30. You are my escort—I need you here."

"I see." Just then, he saw Aggie struggling with Victor on the dance floor. He had both his arms around her waist and she was trying to free herself. "Excuse me, Joy. I'll be right back."

Joy, furious, watched Luke stride over to Victor and talk to him until he let go of Aggie. All Luke could do this evening, Joy thought with deep resentment, was stare at Aggie, giving her, his date, only cursory attention. Well, Ms Aggie McBride, you *may* be getting the surprise of your life next week!

Luke came back over to her. "Joy, I'm going to drive Vic and Aggie to Aggie's place and then I'll drive Vic back here to his car. He'll need someone to drive him home. I'll remain here at the party with you until it's over."

Joy's resentment deepened. He hadn't even asked her if this was all right with her! "All right, Luke, but hurry back."

"Thank you, Joy," he said, "I'll hurry."

Joy again watched Luke trying to reason with Victor. Finally succeeding, he took hold of one of his arms while Aggie took hold of his other one. Together, they helped Victor along toward the door.

~~~~~~~~~~

When Luke drove into his driveway at 2:30 A.M., the emotional exhaustion far outweighed the physical. He noted that Aggie's place was dark. Never had he been so glad to have an evening over with! After the party, he had to spend another half hour trying to appease Joy. At the same time, he vowed never to take her out again or accept an invitation from her!

As he drove into his garage, he groaned out loud, suddenly remembering that a week ago Joy had asked to be invited to another one of Aggie's dinners. Though reluctant, he had invited her and Shawna to dinner next Friday night. He got out, slammed the car door, angry at himself. He had allowed Joy to run the show long enough! Friday night would be the last.

# Chapter Twenty-Three

The first thought that came to Luke's mind as he awakened Saturday morning was Aggie. Trying to quell his growing excitement, he jumped out of bed. He had been painfully deceived once; the last thing he needed was to jump into a relationship as fast as this one with Aggie was going!

"How in the devil can I slow it up at this point?" he asked himself out loud. That kiss last night had almost been his undoing. Aggie's soft lips felt so darn delectable against his—and her warm response was a balm to his bruised and lonely heart.

He paced the floor trying to calm his runaway emotions. For one thing, he decided with firm resolve, he couldn't chance kissing her again until he knew her better—until he spent more time with her. He decided, if she were willing, he'd take her out tonight and as often as possible next week. With just the two of them, in a relaxing atmosphere, it would be easier to get acquainted. His spirits soared as he slipped into his jeans.

Downstairs in the kitchen, he grabbed a box of cold cereal and poured himself a bowl. Tired of waiting for the builder to take care of things in and out of the house that needed fixing, he planned to take care of some of them himself this morning.

~~~~~~~~~~~

Slivers of light through the mini-blinds awakened Aggie. She squinted at her watch and saw that it was 8:00. She stretched and basked in the sunlight as well as the memory of last night. Never had she felt so taken care of, so watched over, so protected. A part of her still resisted this because for twelve years she had taken care of herself. Nevertheless, it felt wonderful to let go and allow Luke to take care of her for a while, which he did—gallantly. How safe she felt, even in the clutches of Victor Wolfe. Many times during the evening she'd caught Luke watching her and Victor, watching like a hawk.

And—there was the kiss out on the patio. She closed her eyes reliving it. Her heart beat wildly. How many times had she asked herself during the years—am I capable of falling in love?

During her college years she had dated and had allowed a kiss here and there, never really enjoying it. During her career, she had accepted a few dates and had allowed only two different men to kiss her once, not enjoying it either time. Many times she'd wondered—even if I *could* trust, will a man ever come along that I can love?

Now, she thought, the amazing question is—*am* I in love? She didn't know; she had no way of measuring it.

~~~~~~~~~~

While sitting at her computer, Aggie watched Luke working on the loose boards of the redwood deck. Her heart beat faster as she watched Luke's male physique move quickly, his strong hands move skillfully, both so attractive with every move he made. She drew in a deep breath. In all her adult life, she'd never felt this way. Was it because she had been distrustful of men? Or was it because she had never met any single man as outstanding as Luke Barnes? Certain it was the latter, she breathed out a, "Thank you," to Doris.

Forcing herself back to her writing, she tried to concentrate, but one anxious thought overrode any creativity: Don't count on anything as far as Luke is concerned; he might, at any time, put up another wall. "I must return to school for a teaching certificate," she reminded herself aloud.

The phone rang. Getting up, she moved quickly to the kitchen. Could it be Doris? she wondered.

"Hello?"

"Hi, Aggie," came Luke's deep resonate voice.

"Luke!" Her heart did a double beat. "I just saw you outside fixing the deck."

"You been watching me, Aggie?"

Aggie felt herself flush. "As a matter of fact I was," she confessed. "I was trying to write, but the scenery outside was much more compelling."

Luke laughed. "Now that gives me more courage to ask you."

"Ask me what?"

"I called to see if you're doing anything tonight."

"Yes. I'm cooking dinner for you."

"Is that all?"

"Yes."

"Good. I thought maybe that Wolfe character had asked you out for tonight."

"No chance, Luke. That is, unless you'll agree to be our chaperone again."

Luke chuckled. "Oh no! No chance of that, either. That was one of the most miserable nights I've ever spent in my life, Aggie, except," his voice turned husky, "for that moment out on the patio." He cleared his throat. "I would like to take you out to dinner tonight, Aggie, if it's all right with you."

Her heart thrilled. This was more than she dared hope for. "It's more than all right, Luke," she said.

"Thank you, Aggie," he said. "I would like to take you out to one of my favorite restaurants. I'll be wearing a suit. Is 6:00 convenient for you?"

"It is, Luke."

"Good. I'll see you tonight."

Luke went back to work, *his* excitement giving him a surge of energy. Aggie's excitement sent *her* to her closet to look over her wardrobe.

~~~~~~~~~~

At 5:45, Aggie studied herself in the mirror. The violet dress with its flowing skirt of crinkled rayon, made her hair look almost black. The square, silver earrings matched her favorite sterling silver locket hanging on her neck by a silver snake chain.

Feeling her heart pulsating in her throat, she folded over her arm a silky rayon jacket that matched the dress, picked up a black clutch bag and went into the front room to wait for Luke.

Promptly at 6:00, Luke stopped his car in front of the cottage, got out and walked to the door. Aggie opened it before he could ring the bell.

"Good evening, Luke."

Luke grinned. "Now, that's what I like—a woman who's right on time."

Aggie stepped out and locked the door. When she turned back to him, his eyes traveled over her. "You look lovely, Aggie."

"Thank you, Luke."

Luke's hand held her upper arm gently as they walked to the car, sending a flutter of excitement through her.

Driving toward the downtown restaurant, Aggie studied Luke's strong profile, noticing how nice his thick brown hair looked with his charcoal brown suit. She also noticed something else. "You have a nice tan, Luke. Did you get it yesterday at the ranch?"

"I guess I did. I saddled ol' Savage and spent at least four hours out on the range, counting the time it took to get back to the ranch."

"Tell me about Savage."

"He's my old stallion, but he still has a lot of spirit in him."

"I've always wanted to learn how to ride a horse, but never got around to it."

He looked over at Aggie. "I'll teach you."

"You will? And I'd love to see the ranch sometime. Did your parents live there?"

"They did. Their house is still there. My foreman and his wife and family keep it up for me. They live in a newer home nearby."

"Where is the ranch located, Luke?"

"It's between Austin and Bastrop."

"Where does your grandmother live?"

Luke, surprised that Aggie remembered, said, "About two miles down the road from the ranch. I went to visit her Saturday and tried, as I have before, to talk her into selling her place and moving closer to me so I can look after her, but she still refuses. It's too large a house for her to take care of at this age, and she's all alone."

"How nice of you to look out for her."

"Not really, Aggie. I've neglected her. I've had resentments toward her for years. She's a dominating woman who's caused our family a lot of pain, especially my mother."

"I'm sorry to hear that. I would have loved to have even one grand-parent."

"You know that man that came to see me Thursday night?" Aggie nodded, holding her breath. "Well, he told me some very good news and I needed to go out to the ranch to think it all over—like you have to climb trees to think." He looked over at her and smiled. "To get right to the point, it ended up that I felt so grateful for the good news, I even felt I should go see Grandmother Barnes, and I made a vow to myself to go see her more often. Mother long ago forgave Grandmother as did my sister, Amy. I'm the unforgiving one in the family."

Aggie closed her eyes a moment, feeling happiness, knowing how the news from Barry had affected Luke.

Luke turned into the parking lot of the restaurant. "This is a steak house, Aggie, but they have delicious appetizers and vegetables with special sauces—a little like you cook—except your meals are better."

"Why thank you, Luke. You didn't have to take me out to eat, you know, I could have cooked for you as usual."

Luke shut off the key and turned to her, gently touching her hair. "Aggie, I'm taking you out because I feel we need to get to know each other better. Things are...uh happening rather fast." He thought of the kiss last night which sent fire through his bones. "That kiss last night warmed my heart," he said aloud.

Aggie's heart filled with joy that Luke could let down the wall enough to be so frank. She whispered, "It affected me the same way, Luke."

"It did?" he asked, almost in disbelief. She nodded. His eyes reflected happiness as he traced her face with his two fingers, lingering a moment on her lips. He exhaled. "I think we need to go in."

After they were seated and had ordered, Luke asked, "Is that a locket?"

"It is."

"Any pictures in it?"

"Yes. One of my sister Beth and one of my mother."

"May I see them?"

"You may." She pulled the locket and chain over her head and handed it to him.

He opened it and studied the two pictures. "Beth is lovely. She looks like your mother." He raised his eyes to Aggie. "You don't look like either one. Do you look like your father?"

"I have his hair, eyes and skin, but there the resemblance ends. My features resemble my mother's mother who I never knew."

"Is your father living?"

"I don't know."

"Why don't you know?" he asked surprised.

"He deserted us when I was ten and Beth was twelve."

Luke, shocked and dismayed, asked, "Permanently?" She nodded. "You mean, he hasn't made contact with you at all?" She shook her head. "Did...did you have any idea he was going to leave?"

"No. One day he was there joking and laughing with us and the next day he was gone. Beth and I became very frightened when he didn't come home. It was then that Mama explained that he went off with another woman."

Luke looked down at the table, his hand rubbing his mouth, his brows creased. Slowly, he looked up at Aggie, handing her back the locket. "That's terrible. How could he do that? I don't understand it."

"I remember my father losing job after job. I've wondered if he just couldn't cope with the responsibility of a family."

"What did your mother do to support you?"

"She didn't want to be gone when we came home from school so she cleaned houses for some of the wealthy women in town. On the weekends, she waitressed at night in a well known restaurant and later became a hostess there."

The waiter placed a plate of small, deep-fried cheese puffs on the table. "These are what I come here for, Aggie. Have one."

Aggie took one and tasted it. "Mmm these are good!" After several bites, she said, "I think I may be able to figure out how these are made."

"If you can, I'll raise your wages," he said, grinning.

"I'll remember that, Mr. Barnes."

The rest of the meal was just as good as Luke had promised, but he hardly gave her time to eat; asking about herself and her life. As it turned out, he asked questions she could freely answer, questions about how she put herself through college, and about her relationship with her mother and sister. Next, he asked about her tree climbing habits. This led to the subject of her other tomboy activities, such as baseball and bicycle racing with the boys. This insight into Aggie, made Luke chuckle.

During dessert, she asked him about his friendship with Doris and all about his sister Amy.

While the waiter cleared off the dessert dishes, Luke studied Aggie's face. He felt that he knew her a little better, yet there was still so much about her he didn't know. How did she feel about having a career? About marriage and family? But could he throw these questions at her now? After all, he couldn't make this a crash course in getting acquainted, though, for some reason—he felt a sense of urgency to know as much about Aggie as soon as possible.

Aggie smiled at his serious face. "What are you thinking, Luke?"

"Many things, Aggie. I want you to know how much I've enjoyed this evening with you. May I have another?"

"Definitely." She grinned. "I like getting paid for cooking dinner when you take me out instead. Doris didn't tell me about these special little perks."

"Hmm, it is a good job you have isn't it? I don't know if you would consider these perks or not, but the boss is smitten with you. In fact, he looks forward to coming home everyday to his beautiful cook."

"He does?" Her heart catapulted with joy. "Those are nice perks. Your cook looks forward to her boss coming home every night, also."

Luke's eyes burned into hers as he reached for her hand and held it. "I can't tell you how happy that makes me, Aggie. But Amy warned me. She said I was vulnerable and not to rush into another relationship too fast, and here I am wanting to take you in my arms and ride off into the sunset."

Aggie laughed. "Can ol' Savage carry both of us?"

"You bet," Luke said, chuckling. "How about it?"

"I'll have to learn to ride first."

"Week after next, I'd like to take you to the ranch and give you a riding lesson."

"I would like that very much, Luke."

Luke stopped the car in front of the cottage, turned off the key, but made no move to get out. Aggie watched him stare through the windshield, and wondered what he was thinking. Because it was only 9:30, her first impulse was to invite him in for a while, but for some reason she thought better of it.

Luke felt her eyes on him. Turning to her, he smiled. "What are you thinking, Aggie?"

"I was wondering the same thing about you."

He grimaced. "Maybe I should keep my thoughts to myself, but here goes: I was thinking it is way too early to drop you off, but—in order to keep my hands off you, I'd better call it an evening."

Aggie was silent. The moonlight upon her face revealed an expression that made his heart race. With no response forthcoming, Luke quickly opened the car door and stepped out.

They walked together up to the porch and stood there gazing at each other. At last, Aggie spoke, "Thank you for dinner and for the evening, Luke. I enjoyed it very much."

"Me too, Aggie. May I reserve all your evenings next week?"

"You don't have to reserve them, Luke," she said with a small laugh.

"Oh yes I do. I saw quite a few other men giving you the eye at the dance the other night."

Aggie laughed. "You didn't!"

Luke raised his brow, giving her an authoritative sideways glance. "I did, so I'm not taking any chances. Can I have every night next week?"

"You've hired me every night anyway."

"But only for dinner; I want all evening."

An uneasiness came over Aggie. She got by tonight without discussing her vocation, but in casual conversation she was bound to slip—eventually. A call had to be put in to Doris right away. She was going to ask Doris to call Luke and tell him that she'd asked her not to tell him she was an attorney. This couldn't be put off another day!

"Aggie?"

"Uh...what?"

"You were deep in thought." He leaned his right arm above her, against the house, placing the back of his left hand against his hip. With a small smile on his face, he asked, "Is your calendar that booked up or don't you want to spend all week with me?"

"I would love to spend all week with you, Luke, but there is something I have to check on. What did you have in mind to do next week?"

"There are at least two things I have in mind. One is the musical *Les Miserables.* It's on now if you'd like to see it. The other is going to a restaurant I like that has a band which plays country western."

"They both sound wonderful," Aggie said, relieved that at least with these two activities there wouldn't be too much opportunity for personal conversation.

"All right. I'll make reservations for *'Les Mis'* probably on Thursday and the restaurant on Friday. Darn! I forgot, Aggie. About ten days ago, Joy Marshall asked to be invited to one of your dinners again. I invited her and Shawna for next Friday night. I think I'll call and weasel out of it."

"No, Luke, I'd be glad to do that."

"All right," he said, hesitantly, his face turning grim, "but this is the last!"

"Let me check on something, Luke, and we'll talk later about the other evenings. Is that all right with you?"

"Okay. And I'll be thinking of some other things we can do."

He picked up one of her hands and held it a moment, studying her face, aching to hold her, to kiss her. Instead, he lingeringly kissed her hand, then said, "Good night, Miss Agnes McBride." He turned and quickly strode to his car.

Aggie unlocked her door and stepped inside. Leaning against the door, she placed her hand over her pounding heart, and sighed, thinking what 'heart trouble' she was having lately. She smiled. Never had her heart acted so erratically!

Soon the reality of her precarious situation asserted itself. Walking quickly into the kitchen, she turned on the light, picked up the phone and dialed Doris. Sitting down at the table, she let it ring and ring. They must be out, she thought. But where were the children? Are they out this late with the children? Deciding to try again after she was ready for bed, she went into the bedroom.

Thirty minutes later, Aggie went to the phone again and dialed Doris. No answer. "I'll try first thing in the morning," she said aloud. "But what if they're out of town?" Uneasiness settled over her again.

# Chapter Twenty-Four

The first thing Sunday morning, Aggie picked up the phone, sat down at the kitchen table and dialed Doris. No answer. "They *are* out of town. What am I going to do?" she muttered, panic welling up inside her. She should have taken care of this when Doris called! But—she had no way of knowing that Luke would all of a sudden want to see her every night next week. Still...

Luke hadn't asked her to spend Sunday with him, maybe—no, she couldn't chance it. She had to leave for the day. But, where could she go? As far as she knew, she didn't have any friends located in Austin.

The phone rang, jarring the early morning silence. She picked it up before the second ring.

"Hello?"

"Aggie, how are you this morning?" Luke asked.

There was an intimate warmth in his voice she hadn't heard before and it set her heart to racing. She felt out of control; she hadn't had time to formulate her plan yet!

"Aggie?"

"Good morning, Luke. I...uh was just thinking how nice your voice sounded to me this morning."

"Hey, that's what I like to hear, but it makes it harder for me to tell you why I called."

"What is it, Luke?"

"I've had a call from my foreman at the ranch. Apparently, my grandmother was there ranting about his management of the ranch and causing quite a scene. His wife touched Grandmother trying to calm her down and found that she was burning up with fever. I've got to go down and take care of her—take her to the doctor, put her in the hospital, whatever is needed.

"Of course you do, Luke," Aggie said, feeling great relief. An answer to prayer, she thought a bit guiltily.

"I wish Amy lived closer. I don't like being the one solely responsible for Grandmother," he said quietly, as if to himself. "This may mean I'll have to stay down there a couple of days, Aggie. If so, there goes two evenings we were going to spend together."

"I know, but you have no choice, Luke."

"Okay, I'll see you whenever. I'll miss you, Aggie."

"I'll miss you, too."

"You'll be here alone, Aggie. I don't like that. Take care and promise you won't accept a date with anyone."

Aggie smiled. "I promise, Luke."

Luke hung up the phone feeling disgruntled. He wanted to ask Aggie to accompany him, but felt it wouldn't be wise at this time in their relationship. At the same time, he wished she had offered—but then wasn't that one of the things he liked about Aggie? She wasn't aggressive in their relationship, allowing him the prerogative. Unlike Lila...or Joy...or most other women he'd associated with.

Aggie hung up the phone feeling grateful for the added time given her to reach Doris. She went to the front room to watch for Luke's departure. Twenty minutes later, Luke's pickup drove by leaving her feeling lonely, however, not as devastatingly lonely as the last time he left. This time, she had the assurance that he cared for her a little, and that there was hope for the future, nebulous though it was. She felt vulnerable when it came to Luke so she tried not to let herself think of the future in specific terms concerning him. She had learned this mental skill during her life as a protective mechanism; she hoped it would work now.

With most of the uneasiness gone, she felt more able to work on her book. The deadline for the tenth of the series was coming up.

Aggie fixed herself some breakfast and went into the bedroom to get ready for church.

~~~~~~~~~~

Monday morning, Aggie called Doris' number. Still no answer. Disturbed, she dialed Bob's office. His receptionist answered.

"Julie, this is Aggie McBride."

"How are you, Ms. McBride? Do you like it down there in Austin?"

"I'm very well, and I'm enjoying it very much here. Is Bob there?"

"No, he isn't. He and his family have gone on a two week vacation. This is the second week so he'll be home next Saturday."

Aggie sucked in a breath. "Is there a phone number where I could reach him or Doris?"

"No. He purposely didn't give me one. He didn't want anyone calling."

"Do you have either of their parent's phone numbers?"

"No, I don't. I'm sorry."

"All right, thank you, Julie."

Aggie got off the phone feeling more grateful than ever that Luke was out of town, hoping that he'd be gone at least a couple of days.

~~~~~~~~~

Tuesday evening Luke still had not returned home, but he called. "Aggie, everything all right?"

"Yes, Luke. How is your grandmother?"

"She's fine. When I arrived, she was still at the ranch. She had collapsed. I called the ambulance and they admitted her to the hospital. The doctor found that she had bacterial pneumonia. They treated her with antibiotics and she responded so quickly, I was able to bring her home this afternoon."

"Good! I'm so glad she's all right."

"I hired a woman to stay with her for a few days, in spite of Grandmother's protests. I'll stay overnight here, then tomorrow morning I'll go straight to work from here. Is our dinner date still on?"

"Of course, Luke."

"Good! Let's make it Wednesday night since Friday is out."

"All right, Luke."

The restaurant we'll be going to is a very casual one. As I said the other night, the band there plays country western, so I suggest we both wear jeans."

"That sounds fun."

"Great. I'll be working later so would 7:00 be all right with you?"

"Yes. And I'll be looking forward to it, Luke. See you soon."

~~~~~~~~~

Joy Marshall sat at the desk in her study looking through the material she had received in the mail today. She had lucked out! Her sister in Dallas had sent her copies of some newspaper articles concerning the law firm of Agnes McBride. Did Luke know that his precious cook was a lawyer? And one who owns her own firm? And did he know that she was involved in an abortion case in Dallas? On a couple of occasions at parties she and Luke had attended, a discussion concerning abortion had come up. Luke became unusually quiet, excusing himself both times with an unmistakable expression of anger on his face. She was almost certain that he knew very little about Aggie. She was also certain how he was going to react when he heard these interesting details about her!

Joy had begun to suspect and later came to believe that maybe his divorce had something to do with abortion because of his reaction when she asked him why he got divorced. He had refused to discuss it, his anger boiling over at her for asking about it. She was quite sure Luke was ignorant of Aggie's background.

Joy smiled. "Now, Ms Agnes McBride, I'll be seeing you and Luke this Friday with a big surprise for both of you! Soon, you'll be history—if I know Luke."

# Chapter Twenty-Five

Wednesday, because of Aggie's excitement over her upcoming date with Luke, she accomplished a lot. She had finished the final revision of her tenth book. It was almost ready to send off to the publishers. This was the last of that series. The next series would begin with the small heroine leaving her childhood and turning twelve. The first series was inspired by herself as a child living in a poor run down house while some of her friends lived in lovely old Victorian homes. Gayle Harrington lived in a grand old remodeled Victorian home on Virginia street and Irma Hargrove lived in one on West Louisiana. In McKinney, there were many old Victorian style homes. Today, people with money buy them and fix them up, turning those blocks into lovely upper-class neighborhoods.

Aggie remembered how often she used to ride her bike past those beautiful homes, admiring them. One day when riding past Gayle's house, she stopped and picked a magnolia from the huge old magnolia tree on her front lawn, and smelled it all the way home.

The first book began as therapy for Aggie, transporting her mind into a lovely, simple world she could live in for a while, away from the reality of abused women and children. Soon, however, it turned into the pure love of writing delightful stories for children, stories with morals to them—morals she'd learned from her mother and Miss Marks.

All day as she was writing, the excitement of seeing Luke that evening billowed inside her, and now the time was almost here. After showering, she picked out her best jeans and chose a wine colored cotton chambray, three-quarter sleeved shirt with pleated cuffs. Because of the silver buttons down the front, she wore her silver concho belt and silver earrings. Adding the final touches, she combed through her hair, dabbed perfume on her neck and went into the front room to watch for Luke.

Soon, Luke's Lexus stopped in front. She watched him get out and walk up to the door, the jeans hugging his narrow hips, his shoulders looking very broad in the butter cream shirt. The sleeves rolled up just short of his elbows revealed his strong tan arms. Quickly taking a couple of big breaths to calm her heart, she opened the door.

"Hi, Luke," she said softly, her eyes sparkling with happiness.

The expression on Aggie's face thrilled Luke. He looked her over and smiled appreciatively, "Hi to you, my beautiful Aggie." Holding out his hand he said, "Shall we go?"

The drive to the restaurant was punctuated only by Aggie's questions about Luke's grandmother, the rest of the way they savored each others presence in silence.

Seated at a table at the back away from dance floor and band, Aggie looked around at the rustic, comfortable decor. A country western singer was belting out the forlorn song of an unfaithful lover. She smiled at Luke. "This is fun."

"I hope you'll enjoy it."

After they had each ordered a meal of fried chicken, mashed potatoes, okra, black eyed peas and corn bread, Luke asked, "What have you been doing while I've been gone, Aggie?"

"Writing. I finished revising the tenth and final book in my series. It's ready to send to the publisher."

"What are you going to write now?"

"I am starting a new set with the same little heroine who will be twelve now. Before, the main character was a grade school child."

"What made you start writing children's books, Aggie?"

A safe subject Aggie decided. "As I mentioned, my first year in junior high, I had an English teacher who told me I had a talent for writing and encouraged me. I owe it all to her. Actually, the stories in some of the books are a little autobiographical. As I've told you we were very poor and there were two girls who lived in large elegant Victorian style homes who always made fun of me because I had to wear Beth's hand-me-down jeans. Since Beth was taller, they were always saggy and too long." Aggie smiled, "They taunted me with 'Baggy, baggy saggy pants Aggie.'"

Luke frowned, "How unkind!"

"Thank you for your sympathy, Luke. But I've found that trials give richness to our lives if we use what we learn to help ourselves. I don't think I would have written that series, if I hadn't had that experience.

Now tell me, " she asked quickly, "have you had someone who has particularly influenced your life?"

"I've had a few—no teachers, but I've had Doris' mother and father, Aunt Edie and Uncle Jim—but mostly my mother. She blessed everyone's life who knew her."

The waitress brought the food and they concentrated on it for a while, then Aggie asked, "Tell me how your father influenced you."

"He taught me how to manage money, how to make money and how to work hard, and how not to treat a son."

"Oh? What do you mean."

"He was critical and I never could please him until I was older and after...never mind, I'd rather not go into that. His mother was critical and dominating with him and he carried it on with me. Later, I learned that he loved us even if it was hard for him to show it."

"Was he a little volatile?"

"Why...yes. How did you know?"

"Because you are and I don't think it came from your mother."

Luke scrutinized her. "You...you're right. Why do you go out with me, knowing this?"

She smiled. "I've asked myself that. If it had been any other man, Luke, I wouldn't because I've..." she almost slipped, telling him that she'd seen a lot of that and worse in her cases. She breathed in a tremulous breath and continued. "I mean, you have a lot of other wonderful qualities, Luke, that far surpass that tendency you have, and I know that's not the real you."

"Thank you, Aggie. I'm grateful you feel that way."

They finished their dinner in silence. When Luke saw couples starting to line dance, he asked, "Shall we dance now and eat dessert later?"

Aggie grinned, "Let's do. Do you know how, Luke?"

"No," he said grinning, "do you?"

"No."

They laughed. "Let's go learn together, Aggie."

They caught on quickly, laughing at each other's mistakes and having a wonderful time. Each time the music stopped the crowd clapped for the band, encouraging them to play more. As the evening wore on they learned several country western dances.

Finally, Aggie begged to sit out and order dessert.

~~~~~~~~~

It was twelve when Luke walked Aggie to her door. "I have never had so much fun, Luke. Thank you."

"Same here, Aggie. We'll have to go there again. Is tomorrow night still on for the musical?"

"It is, Luke, and I'm looking forward to it. I could see *'Les Mis'* over and over."

"What about dinner?"

"I think we ought to eat some left-overs before they go to waste, rather than go out before the musical."

"That's a good idea because I am a little behind at work. The musical starts at 8:00. I think we had better leave at 7:15."

"All right, I'll have dinner ready whenever you get home."

"Aggie..." he touched her face, studying it in the porch light, then putting his fingers under her chin, he tilted her face upward, burning with the desire to take her into his arms—to kiss her, to hold her. He dropped his hand. "Goodnight, Aggie." He turned abruptly and walked over to his car, got in and drove the few yards to his garage.

Aggie watched the car disappear into the garage. Stepping inside, she turned off the porch light and sat down in the darkness. She had seen Luke's struggle, could see his desire to kiss her, matching her own desire. How she admired his principles, his will power, his moral strength! She had never seen this. Watching from the sidelines in her many cases, she gradually became aware of the powerful sex drive inherent in a man. From these experiences and her experience with Luke, a true principle dawned on her—apparently a lost principle with men and women today, she thought sadly, but certainly not lost on her tonight. A man who harnesses his powerful sex drive to protect his virtue as well as the virtue of women he associates with—until he finds that special woman—and only on the wedding night unleashes that sexual drive, is a man of *power* and *strength*—a *man* in the real sense of the word. A man so *profoundly attractive* and *desirable* to a woman, it's amazing that today's men and women are ignorant of it and the principle behind it! Aggie uttered a prayer of thanks for the privilege of knowing Luke Barnes.

# Chapter Twenty-Six

The day moved on in a magical way for Aggie. She started the first book in the new series. Creativity began stirring inside as she wrote; yet the memory of last night and the anticipation of tonight hovered at the periphery of her mind, constantly lifting her spirits. She wondered how Luke was feeling.

At 5:00 P.M. she went up to the house, and went through the refrigerator, putting together some leftovers for a quick dinner when Luke came home. She went back to the cottage, showered and began getting ready for the evening. Pulling over her head a natural color linen/rayon tank top, she wrapped around her hips a natural color, long, mock sarong skirt with red poppies covering it. Next, she slid on a poppy red boxy little jacket with duel pockets. Red heels and red earrings went on next.

She went to the mirror, finished the makeup and brushed her dark hair that always went back in the same simple style that Miss Marks designed for her many years ago.

By the time she returned to the kitchen, Luke was there sitting at the table reading the paper. He looked up as she walked in. His jaw dropped at the sight of her. He stood up and went over to her, took her hands in his and smiled.

"You are the most beautiful sight I've ever seen! I love you in red."

Aggie smiled, "Thank you, Luke, you've started the evening out nicely for me. Sit down and I'll get you a plate of leftovers." After Aggie put on an apron, filled a plate for Luke, and filled one for herself, she sat down.

Luke offered a prayer over the food and they began to eat. "Even your leftovers are better than restaurant food, Aggie."

"But, Luke, I prefer getting paid for cooking for you while eating out with you—so don't become too effusive over my leftovers."

Luke laughed. "Cushy job you have here, Miss Agnes McBride."

~~~~~~~~~~

The usher led Luke and Aggie to their reserved seats on the thirtieth row, the best seats in the building Luke felt.

"How was your day, Luke?" Aggie asked after they had settled into their seats.

"It turned out to be very productive? How was yours?"

"The same. I think knowing you has inspired me, Luke, because I can write better since I've come here."

Luke thought about this a moment. "I've never had such a nice compliment, thank you, Aggie."

She smiled at him and let out a big sigh. "I've looked forward to this all day."

"I have too, Aggie," he said, reaching for her hand.

The theater filled up, the lights dimmed and the music began. Aggie couldn't remember feeling so happy, so content.

It wasn't long before Aggie reached into her purse for a tissue. Luke, noticing her tears, used this as an excuse to put his arm around her and pull her as close as possible.

Aggie let out another big sigh, her contentment even greater.

As the production moved on, Aggie's heart swelled with the love and romance of the story—transferring it to the special man beside her, and for a brief moment lay her head upon his shoulder. Luke gave her a squeeze and they smiled at each other.

At the end, their hearts and minds filled with the uplifting thoughts and feelings the music had inspired, they silently eased out of the theater through the crowd, holding hands until they reached the parking lot where Luke opened the car door for Aggie.

They were silent nearly all the way home until Aggie blurted out, "Luke I really don't want to put effort into making a gourmet meal for Joy Marshall."

Surprised by the outburst, Luke couldn't answer for a moment, then he threw back his head and laughed. "Why?" he asked finally.

"I just don't."

He laughed again. "Do I detect a little jealousy?"

"No! Well...just a little."

"Oh, Aggie, Aggie, that does my poor heart good to hear. I'm all for putting on just an ordinary, easy meal. Hopefully that will cure her of inviting herself to dinner."

"Thank you, Luke."

Luke drove into his driveway and stopped in front of the cottage, making no move to get out. With their seat belts undone, it was possible for Luke to put his arm around Aggie and pull her closer to him. They sat there for some time, savoring the tender feelings the musical had left them with. The unspoken feeling of closeness that had slowly developed between them day by day, culminated in this moment of heartburning desires and dreams—left unspoken by each.

Luke wanted to throw all caution to the wind and allow himself to examine his feelings toward Aggie. With all the strength he could muster, he decided to give it a little more time; after all, he had only known Aggie for about six weeks. He leaned over, kissed her forehead tenderly then quickly opened the door and walked around, opening the door for her.

Slowly they walked hand in hand up the walkway to the small porch. He looked down at Aggie and smiled. "There is so much I want to say to you, Aggie—but I can't. We need to get to know one another better—after a failed marriage, I...."

"You don't have to explain, Luke, I understand." What she didn't tell him was that she desperately needed to talk to his cousin Doris before he said what was on his mind!

"Thank you again, Luke, for a wonderful evening. The musical was superb and the company was even better."

Luke, grasping her shoulders, fought a feverish desire to kiss her, to hold her and never let her go. Instead, his eyes devoured her hair, her face, her lips, then he bent down and once more kissed her forehead.

"Goodnight, my beautiful Aggie."

"Goodnight, Luke," she said. "Thank you for that tender kiss." She turned quickly, and unlocked the door and went in.

Luke stood looking at the closed door a moment, wishing she hadn't left so quickly. If it had been Lila standing there, she would have initiated a kiss and begged him to come in. "Thank you, Aggie." he whispered as he turned and walked back to his car.

# Chapter Twenty-Seven

Friday morning, after Aggie was sure Luke had left for work, she went up to the house to decide what to fix for dinner that night. When she entered, she saw Mary.

"Mary! How nice to have you back."

"Hello, Aggie. Thank you. It's wonderful to visit but it's always nice to be back home. How did you and Luke manage without me?"

"Quite well, Mary. He's taken me out on a couple of dates."

Her eyes lit up. "Really? Now I put my stamp of approval on that."

"You do? Your opinion is very important to me, Mary. Thank you!"

"I understand Joy and her friend Shawna are coming to dinner tonight."

"Yes, I told Luke I didn't want to spend time making a gourmet meal for her."

Mary laughed. "Good girl. So what are you having?"

"Something easy—spaghetti, salad and a bowl of plain vanilla ice cream for dessert. Oh, and I do have some french bread in the freezer."

"Sounds good to me and too good for Joy."

Aggie looked around in the pantry and pulled out canned tomatoes, tomato sauce, and mushrooms. "It looks like we have all the ingredients so I don't have to run to the store. You see, I haven't had to cook much since you've been gone. I'll be back this afternoon, Mary, and start the spaghetti sauce."

~~~~~~~~~~

Aggie spent the morning writing. In the early afternoon she took a shower, threw on an exotic Italian print dress, went up to the house made the spaghetti sauce and allowed it to simmer slowly. She cut up the salad and put it back in the refrigerator, wondering where Mary was when she heard the vacuum. Leaving the kitchen, she found Mary vacuuming the hallway. Motioning for Mary to turn it off, she said, "Mary, why are *you* vacuuming? Where is the housekeeper?"

"She can't come, she's sick."

"Luke doesn't want you to do this anymore, Mary, let me do it."

"No, Aggie, I'm perfectly fine."

"I have dinner under control, please let me."

"All right then, I'll finish the dusting."

After Aggie finished the bare front room, she cleaned Luke's office, looking around as she did, imagining that she could smell his wonderful cologne. When she was through there, she pushed the vacuum to the foot of the stairs just as Mary finished the dusting.

"Has the upstairs been vacuumed, Mary?"

"No."

"All right, I'll do the stairs then go on up."

"Thank you, Aggie. I need to get another housekeeper as a back up. My back can't take too much vacuuming," she finally admitted. "I'll follow you up and do the dusting upstairs."

Aggie vacuumed the hall and two of the four bedrooms, then she entered Luke's bedroom and Mary followed with the dust cloth. Aggie looked around. "This furniture is quite masculine, surely Lila didn't choose it."

"No. He didn't want any of the furniture she had picked out up here, he gave it to her and bought his own."

Aggie resumed vacuuming for a few minutes until some pictures on top of a chest of drawers caught her attention. She turned off the vacuum. Family pictures! That, even more than decorative pictures, is what this house is lacking, Aggie realized. "Why aren't there any pictures of Luke's family downstairs?" she asked.

"He hasn't unpacked them yet, they're still in the garage."

"Is the large one in the middle a picture of Luke's parents?" Aggie asked as she walked over and gazed at it. She didn't hear Mary's answer, her shock was too great. She gasped, her breath came fast and short. So weak she felt she might faint; she reached out to the dresser for support. "Who...who is the blonde woman?" she gasped.

Mary, surprised by Aggie's reaction, walked over to her. "The older or younger one?"

"The older one."

"That is Ann Barnes, Luke's mother."

Aggie's hands flew to her mouth, her disbelieving eyes were soon filled with tears. "She's dead! No! No." She slumped to the floor and sobbed.

Mary was so astonished, she didn't know what to do. Kneeling down beside her, she asked, "What is it, Aggie? What is it? You knew Luke's mother was dead."

"I know. I know. I should have tried to find her sooner!" More sobs shook Aggie's shoulders. Several minutes later, just as suddenly as the sobs began, they stopped. "It's impossible, Mary." She stood up and studied the picture again. "It can't be Miss Marks, she didn't have any children!" She turned to Mary. "This woman is Miss Alice Marks my English teacher, she can't be Luke's mother!"

Mary stood up and stared at Aggie, now shocked herself. Gently, she guided Aggie to the small couch and made her sit down, then sat down beside her. "Aggie, the woman in the picture is Alice Ann Marks Barnes, Luke's mother."

"It is Miss Marks—it is!" Grief shook her once more. Mary, holding her tightly, patiently waited until the sobs finally waned. Aggie looked over at Mary. "*Miss* Alice Marks taught me English my first year in junior high. How...how could she be Luke's mother, Mary?"

"It's a long story, but Ann, she went by Ann, not Alice—Ann left her husband and children for those nine months she taught you. No one knew where she went. She left a note for her children, Luke and Amy and one for her husband. She told her husband, King, not to search for her. She explained that she would return when he decided to think for himself, to be a husband to her and a father to his children without the interference of his mother. You see, Mae Barnes became unbearable when the children got older. She was determined King should do this and King should do that with his children, not even considering Ann, their mother. King had always been dominated by her and was allowing it more and more, causing problems with the children and with Ann. Nothing Ann could say or do could get King to see what was happening. She decided that the only way to wake him up was to leave him for a while. It nearly broke her heart to leave the children at such vulnerable ages. Luke was thirteen and Amy was twelve. She began planning this some time before she did it because she had to take classes from the University to renew her teaching certificate. Apparently, she renewed it under her maiden name—Marks.

"Before she returned nine months later, King became desperate enough to listen to her and after he did, he realized what he had put her through. It was hard for him to change, but he was so grateful to have her home, he quit allowing his mother to interfere in their lives anymore."

Aggie's attention had been riveted on Mary and the incredible story she related. Again, her eyes filled with tears. "Miss Marks never let on what she was suffering. She was always so cheerful and loving to me. Yet, how she must have missed her children all the while! She saved my life in a way. I don't know what would have happened to me if she hadn't been there. At the end of the school year she left and we moved to Dallas. I wrote to her in care of the school the next year but they returned my letter saying Miss Marks didn't renew her contract. I was beside myself with disappointment that I had lost contact with her. I have wanted to find her all these years, Mary—and now I have, but it's too late!" Aggie put her hands over her face, her body shaking with emotion. Mary put her arms around her once more, comforting her the best she could, totally amazed at the story.

Aggie pulled a tissue from her pocket and blew her nose. "Mary, Miss Marks had an impact on my life in so many ways. No wonder I love Luke."

"You *love* Luke?" Mary asked, her eyes wide.

Aggie, startled at what had slipped out of her mouth, turned silent, thinking. Then she spoke slowly, "I've never loved a man, Mary, or even thought I did, so I didn't know how I felt about Luke—until now. Yes! I *do* love Luke!"

It was Mary's eyes that glistened with tears, now. "I'm so happy to hear this, Aggie. You will be so good for him."

Aggie hugged Mary. "Oh, thank you, Mary." She jumped up and gazed at the picture again. "Amy looks like her mother." Excitement finally found its way through all the myriad emotions. She turned and clasped her hands together, holding them over her heart. "Mary, I can't believe it! How strange it all happened as it did; how wonderful that, besides my mother, the woman whom I have loved the most in my life is the mother—of the man I love!

"How strange that I should meet Doris. No wonder we loved each other immediately. Doris—dear Doris, if it hadn't been for her, I wouldn't be here. Just wait until she and Bob hear this story!"

Aggie walked around the room so full of excitement she could hardly contain herself. She stopped in front of Mary, took her hands in hers. "You must promise me, Mary, that you won't tell Luke any of this. I want to tell him myself. And I must contact Doris tomorrow and ask her to call Luke and set things straight. I've tried to call her, but she and Bob have been away on vacation. I've been so worried all week for fear Luke would ask me questions I couldn't answer. Oh, why must we have company tonight? I guess I better finish the vacuuming and get down to my dinner."

Mary laughed. "I've never seen you so excited and talkative, Aggie. We both better finish up and get out of Luke's room before he catches us." Just then the phone rang. Mary answered it there in the room.

"Hello?"

"Mary, tell Aggie, that I won't be home before the company. Joy called and told me that Shawna can't come tonight. Joy was going to ride with her because her car is in the garage being repaired, so she has asked if I could go pick her up."

"All right, Luke. See you later." Mary relayed the message to Aggie.

"Oh no! That means he'll have to drive her home, too. I can't wait to tell Luke, but it will just have to wait until he comes back from taking Joy home." Aggie frowned. "Maybe I had better wait until I can contact Doris before I tell him. I guess that means it will have to wait until tomorrow sometime. But I don't want to tell Doris any of this wonderful news until I can tell her in person. I want to see her face!"

~~~~~~~~~~

Mary set the table and Aggie put the finishing touches to the salad. Both were filled with the excitement of the discovery. As Aggie tasted the sauce again, another amazing thing occurred to her. This spaghetti sauce is the very sauce Miss Marks taught me how to make! How could it all come about like this? Just then, she heard the front door open and Joy's vivacious chatter.

Shortly, Luke stepped into the kitchen, his face filled with happiness at seeing her. "How's my favorite cook?"

"I'm wonderful, Luke." Her eyes were filled with wonder and excitement as she gazed up at Miss Marks' *son*!

He studied her a moment. "Yes, you *are* wonderful. More ways than one, my little wood nymph. What's up? Something's different with you."

"You better join your company, Luke. Dinner is ready and Mary and I are serving."

"Fine with me, just as long as you and Mary dine with us."

Aggie had to smile at Joy's face when she placed the plate of spaghetti and a bowl of salad before her. "Don't you care for spaghetti, Joy?" she asked.

"Oh yes, but this is...uh not your usual meal, Aggie."

"I know, but it is a very special sauce."

Luke took a bite. "You know, Aggie, this tastes like my mother's favorite spaghetti sauce."

Aggie wanted to scream at him: IT *IS* YOUR MOTHER'S! SHE GAVE IT TO ME. Instead, she just smiled and thanked him for the compliment. Joy's conversation, directed mainly to Luke, made it possible for Aggie to watch Luke, to look at him now out of different eyes. He was Miss Marks' son! It was too unbelievable to sink in. All she wanted to do was stare at him and try to internalize his relationship to her beloved English teacher. Her impulse was to go over to him, hug him and tell him that she knew and loved his mother!

Luke felt Aggie watching him. Glancing at her as often as possible, he sensed an excitement he'd never seen in her. His eyes were curious and questioning as they locked with hers. Mary watched them both, intrigued with the drama that was happening and that which was about to unfold.

When they were through with the main course, Aggie and Mary excused themselves, went into the kitchen and came back, each carrying two small bowls of vanilla ice cream. Aggie set the ice cream in front of Joy, enjoying the expression on her face.

"This isn't up to your usual fare, Aggie."

Aggie, aware of the sudden hostility and venom in Joy's voice, smiled sweetly. "No, it isn't, is it?"

When Aggie sat down and had taken a bite of ice cream, Joy asked, "Are you getting bored with cooking now, Aggie?"

Surprised that Joy had condescended to include her in the conversation, replied. "I never get bored with cooking, Joy."

"I thought it might be getting dull after your exciting life in Dallas as a well known attorney for women's causes," Joy stated, a triumphant expression on her face.

Aggie felt the blood drain from her face. She looked at Luke who only stared at Joy, confusion on his face.

"What are you talking about, Joy?" Luke asked.

"Why don't you ask Aggie?" she smirked.

Luke turned his gaze to Aggie. Noting her ashen face, his heart froze. "What does Joy mean, Aggie?"

Aggie's heart pulsed so heavily in her throat, she wondered if she could speak. Swallowing hard, and taking several cautious breaths, she spoke hesitantly—almost in a whisper, "What...Joy said, Luke, is...true."

"That can't be! You told me you were a paralegal."

"No, I didn't, Luke," she contradicted gently.

"You did!"

"She didn't, Luke." Mary stated firmly, totally distraught at the turn of events.

"Stay out of it, Mary."

"Luke, Doris told you I worked in a legal firm."

Joy, delighted at Luke's reaction, added further information. "The firm of Agnes McBride and Associates was the firm that handled that controversial abortion case not too long ago where the father was suing for custody of the baby at birth and..."

"Aggie!" Luke exclaimed, interrupting Joy. His face, gray with fear, he spoke tentatively. "I was in my truck some weeks ago when I heard a newscast about a woman, Sybil something I believe, who won an abortion for a woman. I turned it off—I couldn't listen. Was...was that..."

"Was that my firm?" Aggie quietly finished for him. "Yes, Luke, but..."

"I can't believe it." There was desolation in his voice, pain on his face. "I can't believe you deceived me, Aggie—not *you*! But worse—that you would have anything to do with winning an abortion case!"

"Luke,..." Mary began, pleading...

"Be quiet, Mary. This is between Aggie and me."

"Listen to me, Luke..." Aggie begged.

"No, Aggie. I...I don't...want to...hear anymore from you." It was apparent to everyone that the words were something he didn't want to say. His face, a mixture of pain and disappointment, slowly turned hard with anger. "I think it would be best if you left the cottage as soon as possible. Leave your forwarding address and I'll send you a check with severance. Come, Joy, I'll drive you home," he said, ignoring their uneaten ice cream.

Aggie watched Joy gaze up at Luke with a sickening expression of sympathy. "I'm sorry, Luke, I didn't know the news would upset you like this."

"Cut it, Joy," he spit out.

She blanched at how he spoke to her, but soon, her head held high, she stated with confidence, "I just thought you might want to see these articles from a Dallas paper that my sister sent me about the cases." She held them up for Luke to see. He took them and looked at them, one by one, his face becoming more grim, more bitter. His jaw rippled as he stuffed them into his shirt pocket.

"Come on, Joy, I'll drive you home now." Walking quickly to the front door, Luke opened it, and waited for Joy to step out. He closed it, not even glancing once in Aggie's and Mary's direction.

They both sat there, still in shock. Finally, Mary got up and went to Aggie and put her arms around her. "I'm so sorry, Aggie."

"Thank you, Mary. But, I guess you are shocked also."

"Only surprised about the abortion case, but you see, I know more about you than Luke. I know what you did for him. Sometime you can tell me your side, not that I need it, though. And I know Luke; he'll come to his senses and will want to hear your side."

"Thank you, Mary. I...I need to go up to the cottage. Do you mind cleaning up alone?"

"Not at all, Aggie."

"Remember what you promised, Mary. You are not to tell Luke about my part in having Barry visit him, and you aren't to tell him my discovery today."

"It will be hard, Aggie, but I promise."

"Thank you." Aggie stood up and kissed Mary on the cheek. "See you later," she said, then walked quickly into the kitchen and out the door, running to the cottage. Stepping inside, she locked it and sat down on the couch. She couldn't believe that just after her wonderful discovery this terrible thing had happened.

"What have I done to your son, Miss Marks?" The tears came softly at first, then shuddering sobs shook her body. "Dear God," she uttered in between sobs, "help me. Bless Luke." As she calmed down, she asked, still in the mode of prayer. "Why didn't I follow my dreams of becoming a teacher like Miss Marks? If I had, I wouldn't have caused this hurt to her son!"

Getting up, she ran into the bedroom closet, pulled out a suitcase and cosmetic case and began to pack quickly. She had to leave. If she knew Luke, he'd be back tonight or tomorrow morning to talk to her. His refusal to hear her side hurt too much; she couldn't face him now. She had to leave for a few days, and then when she had gained some semblance of calmness and objectivity, she'd be back for the rest of her things and go back to Dallas.

As she packed she wondered where to go. The reality, that there was no place for her to go, that she had no one, left her feeling so devastatingly alone, she knelt beside the bed and cried for help. Slowly, a strange idea began to form in her mind, an idea so improbable, so unexpected it startled her; yet for some unfathomable reason—it felt right. She would stay there for a few days before coming back to pack up. Shocked at herself for feeling so positive that she *could* stay there, she, nevertheless, went about planning it. First, she'd have to find a motel for tonight and leave town tomorrow.

Through packing, she changed to jeans and carried the suit cases out to the van. She came back in for only one reason—to write a note to Luke. Sitting at the kitchen table, she wrote: "Luke, as you will understand, I had to get away from here quickly. I will be gone for a few days, then I'll be back to pack up everything and move back to Dallas. Aggie."

Taking the note, she propped it up on the couch so Luke would see it just as he came in. She unlocked the front door, left through the kitchen door and got into her van. Backing up, she drove down the driveway, and turned right toward the motel.

# Chapter Twenty-Eight

Luke drove Joy to her condominium in grim silence. Her efforts to comfort him came over for what they were—insincere—serving only to make Luke angrier. When she started to say something, he cut her off. "I don't want to talk, Joy. You've delivered your message, there is nothing more I want to hear from you."

When Luke drove into her driveway, he sat there waiting for her to let herself out. Joy, panicky, not wanting to leave on this note, said, "Luke, I..."

"Please get out, Joy. We're through. Don't call me and I certainly won't call you."

"But Luke, I was only thinking of your welfare."

He glared at her. "Get out, Joy!"

Furious, Joy opened the door and got out. "All right, Luke, just go back to your deceitful, runty little cook!" She slammed the door shut.

Luke backed out, and burned rubber as he sped off.

~~~~~~~~~~

As Luke turned into his own driveway, he noticed that Aggie's van was gone. He frowned. "She couldn't have packed up and moved already," he mumbled. Parking his car in the garage, he entered the kitchen, his heart heavier than he could remember. Mary was sitting at the table waiting for him.

Distraught over all the secrets and wishing everything could be brought out into the open, Mary had tried to think what she could say to Luke when he came back. She realized there was really nothing she could say without breaking her promise to Aggie. Though upset at Luke over the way he had talked to Aggie, the way he'd refused to listen to her side of the story, as she looked into his stricken face, her heart ached for him.

Luke sat down at the table, pulled the newspaper articles from his pocket, his eyes, haunted, sought hers beseechingly. "Did you know anything about these?" he demanded, slamming the articles down on the table, "that she is a feminist attorney? Did you know she'd been involved in an abortion case?"

"I was shocked, Luke, but I wish you had agreed to listen to her side of the story." She quickly added so as not to get into a discussion, "I'm tired Luke, I'm going to bed. Goodnight." She got up and started down the hall.

"Mary!" His voice cracked. "Where did Aggie go? Where could she be? Her van isn't in the carport."

She turned around and walked back. "I didn't know she had gone anywhere."

"She couldn't have packed and left so soon, Mary."

"Luke, I'm sure she'll be back soon. It's getting late—where could she go at this time of night?"

"That's what I want to know. I'm going up there and check. Taking an extra key to the cottage from a hook on the wall, he headed for the door."

"I'm going with you, Luke."

Out of caution, Luke knocked on the door. Waiting a moment, he turned the knob and found the door wasn't locked. They entered, turned on the light and immediately saw the note on the couch. Luke stepped over and picked it up. He read it out loud. He looked at Mary and frowned, both anger and desperation etched into his face. "Where could she have gone, Mary?"

"Luke, Aggie is used to taking care of herself, so don't be concerned. She said she'd be back and pack up in a few days."

"Don't concern myself?" His voice rose. "As long as her things are here, I still feel responsible for her safety, Mary!"

Mary had known this is what he would say. "Of course you do, Luke, but what are you going to do—go looking for her?"

"No, of course not! I wouldn't know where to start. But—in a few days, if she doesn't return, I might call the police." He turned and stalked out and Mary followed, locking the door behind her.

~~~~~~~~~~~

Saturday morning as Mary entered the kitchen, she found Luke in his robe sitting at the table, his head in his hands.

"Good morning, Luke."

He looked up, "Oh, good morning, Mary."

Mary was concerned. His eyes looked heavy and tired. "How did you sleep, Luke?"

"I didn't."

Mary busied herself making breakfast. How many times had she and Ann gone through this kind of thing with Luke? His quick temper and impetuous reactions always ended up causing him deep remorse—remorse only he could take care of. He always tried to straighten it out afterward. Luke's big, compassionate heart was his saving grace, but, she shook her head, this was much more serious. Luke's emotions ran deep concerning Aggie. She had known this for some time.

As the day wore on, Mary's worry increased. Luke had closeted himself in his study and had not even come out for lunch. She had to talk to some one. Going back to her apartment, she closed the door, sat down on the couch and picked up the phone to call Doris, but changed her mind. "Maybe Amy is back." She dialed Amy instead.

After three rings she was about to hang up when Amy answered, "Hello."

"Amy! I'm so glad you're home! When did you get back?"

"Mary, it's good to hear from you. We got back last night late. We are all so worn out, we've hardly had the energy to unpack, but we're beginning to now. What's up? How are you? How is Luke?"

"I'm fine, but Luke isn't."

"What's the matter, Mary?" she asked, concern in her voice.

Mary thought a moment. Amy knew about Lila so she could tell her everything—everything but Aggie's discovery that Ann was her beloved Miss Marks. That was Aggie's story to tell. "I don't know where to start, Amy, so much has happened."

Fear in her voice, Amy asked, "Has something happened to Luke?"

"He's fine, physically, Amy. Emotionally he's a wreck. You know that Doris sent a young woman here to be a cook for Luke didn't you?"

"I knew she was going to but didn't know it had taken place—and I didn't know she was a *young* woman. Go on, Mary."

Mary related everything as thoroughly as she could. She even told her about Aggie hiring Barry and sending him to see Luke.

Amy was silent for a few moments. "How wonderful to hear that it wasn't Luke's baby that Lila..." She couldn't go on. When she was able, she asked, "It sounds like Aggie is quite a person. How does she feel about Luke?"

"She didn't realize until recently, but she loves Luke."

"I'm concerned about her firm having something to do with an abortion, Mary."

"Knowing Aggie, I can't believe it happened as Joy said. We owe it to Aggie to hear her side. Maybe Doris knows her side."

"I'm going to call her right now—and after I talk to her, I'm making reservations to fly out. I don't know why exactly, but I have a strong feeling I need to be there, Mary. Paul was going to take a week off before returning to work, so he can stay with the children. I may fly into Dallas if Doris can drive me to Austin. I'll let you know—but don't tell Luke I'm coming, he'll just call and tell me not to come."

"All right," sighed Mary. Though very relieved that Amy was coming, she was upset at having to keep yet another secret.

~~~~~~~~~~

The next morning, Aggie was on highway 71 between Austin and Bastrop. Unable to go to sleep until after 3:00 A.M., she had awakened late and stopped only long enough to get a glass of orange juice and a piece of toast.

She couldn't believe that she was just about to arrive at the King Barnes ranch where Ann Barnes, her Miss Marks, had lived and raised her children. A mixture of sadness and loneliness welled up inside her as she slowed down, pulled off the road and stopped at the mail box a few yards off the highway. It said, *Luke Barnes*. Directly behind it was an impressive entry to the ranch. Two stone pillars holding up a large arched wrought iron sign announced: KING BARNES RANCH.

Aggie followed the winding road over hills of grass land and clusters of trees. At last she arrived at a ranch house. She felt that this must be it, so she pulled up in front and studied the house. In her mind it looked just as she thought it should; a typical Texas ranch house with a wrap around covered porch. It had a nice lawn and landscaping with trees all around it. She ached to go inside and look around, feeling that it might bring Miss Marks closer. If only she were here, she would understand everything. Tears rolled down her cheeks. Miss Marks, she knew, would have given her the benefit of the doubt—why couldn't her son?

Backing up and turning the van around, she drove back to highway 71 and pulled onto the road, turning toward Austin. She drove on, slowly, watching. After a couple of miles she saw a large imposing two story white house, Victorian style, set back on the crest of a small hill. She had missed seeing it on the way to find Luke's place. Slowing down, she turned in and stopped to read the mail box. Sure enough, it said *Mae Barnes*. She drove toward the house, again wondering why this idea, this inspiration had come so forcefully to her mind and why it felt right. From what both Luke and Mary had told her about this woman, she should be nervous—but for some reason she wasn't. Strange, she thought as she arrived at the house. Parking in the drive-way, she looked at her watch. It was 11:00 A.M.

She had changed to a blue shirt and white pants and put on her favorite silver locket and earrings. Walking up the steps to the porch, she stood at the front door a moment. Her heart fluttering a little, she took a deep breath and pushed the bell. It seemed a long time before the door opened. A tall, broad-faced, austere looking woman stood in the doorway. Aggie's eyes studied her quickly, estimating that she was in her seventies, but still attractive with chestnut brown eyes, the same as Luke's. Her hair, that once may have been brown like Luke's, had now turned to a slightly wavy gray.

Her thin lips pressed tightly together, she cooly scrutinized Aggie, then her brows rose imperiously, "Yes?"

"I'm here to see Mrs. Mae Barnes."

"I'm Mae Barnes, what can I do for you?"

My name is Aggie McBride. I'm a friend of your grandson, Luke."

Her eyebrows rose again, but this time in surprise. "Oh?"

"I know this will seem strange to you since you don't know me, but I need your help. I don't know whether Luke told you or not, but he hired me as a cook."

"Oh, yes, he told me he had hired one, but he didn't tell me you were so young and attractive," she stated in a disapproving and slightly suspicious tone of voice.

"He didn't know. He thought I was older and I thought he was. When Doris told us about each other we both jumped to conclusions. You see my name, Agnes and his name, Lucas sounded...."

"Come in, Miss McBride," Mae Barnes said, interrupting any further explanation.

"Thank you."

"Come this way, Miss McBride."

Aggie followed her through the entry way, noticing how straight-backed and dignified she carried herself. Her wavy gray hair was pulled back into an attractive bun. Turning right, Mrs. Barnes led her into a large front room. To Aggie, it looked more like an old fashioned parlor with its magnificent antiques. Among them was a comfortable looking dark green velveteen sofa, one matching overstuffed chair and two green and rose floral wing-back chairs. Crocheted doilies protected lamp tables from the lamp bases, and lace napkins shielded the arms of the sofa and chair. Lace curtains covered the tall windows, muting the summer sun, and the room carried the scent of cedar and old lace.

"Please have a seat, Miss McBride," she said, pointing to the sofa. Mae Barnes sat on the chair, ramrod straight. "Now, how may I help you."

For some absurd reason, Aggie had the desire the cry. Why was she feeling this way? Mae Barnes was not a woman most people would say had a 'soft shoulder' to cry on. "Mrs. Barnes, it...it's such a long story, I don't know where to start. I..." she couldn't help it, the tears started flowing. She covered her face and sobbed. Soon, she felt a hand on her shoulder. She looked up to see Mae Barnes handing her a lace handkerchief. She took it and blubbered a thank you, sensing that this was her way of showing sympathy. Mae sat back down and waited.

Finally able to gain control, Aggie sniffed and wiped her eyes. "I can't believe I broke down in front of you. Actually, I don't know why, but when I tried to think of where I could go, I thought of coming here to you. For some reason, it felt right."

Mae Barnes' eyes reflected surprise. "Would you like to freshen up or would you like something to drink?"

"Thank you, no."

"All right. You may start this long story of yours."

"I'll try to be brief and if there are questions you need to ask, please feel free to do so." Aggie thought a moment, deciding to tell Mrs. Barnes a brief history which would lead to the information that would bring her, she was sure, great comfort and relief. She began with the fact that she was an attorney for women. She told her of the abortion case her firm was responsible for and how it had turned out, how her health had gone down hill, how Doris had become a friend, how she had suggested a six month sabbatical—cooking for Luke and so on. At last, she related the hiring of Barry, what he found out, explaining that Barry had gone to Luke's house and told him personally.

At this information, Mae Barnes showed a great deal of emotion. "Oh! Oh my!" She covered her face with her hands a moment, then clasping them together, her eyes glistening with tears, she said, "Thank you, Miss McBride, thank you!"

Aggie smiled and nodded, hardly believing she could so easily confide in this woman, even though this is what she had planned to do when the idea had come to her. Finally—she confessed how she had grown to love her grandson. Next, she told her what Joy Marshall had revealed to Luke—and his reaction. The only thing she left out was why she had become a lawyer and the unique story of Miss Marks.

There was silence when Aggie was through. Mae Barnes did not reveal by the expression on her face how amazed she was that this young woman would want to come to her—nor did she reveal how touched she was that she had. Instead, she said, "Come with me, Miss McBride, I think it's time for us to go eat some lunch."

"Please call me, Aggie."

"Thank you, Aggie."

Aggie stood up and looked around the room. "I love this room. And it smells like a grandmother's house should smell—though I never had grandparents."

Mae Barnes' eyes softened. Without a word, she turned and led Aggie into the dining room and on into the large, bright country kitchen, with a big round oak table surrounded by six chairs.

"I think I will take your invitation to freshen up now, Mrs. Barnes."

"There's a half-bath right next to the laundry room by the back door."

When Aggie returned, Luke's grandmother had set a glass bowl filled with cut up watermelon and cantaloupe on the big round table, and was preparing ham and cheese sandwiches.

"What can I help you with, Mrs. Barnes?"

"You can set the table and get a pitcher of ice water," she said, pointing to a drawer and cupboard where Aggie could find utensils, plates and pitcher.

As they sat down to eat, Aggie sighed. "Thank you, for letting me talk to you and literally cry on your shoulder. I feel better—and more at peace here in your home."

Mae looked down at her plate, and quickly blinked the tears away. It had been so long since she'd felt needed. She looked up at Aggie.

"What are your plans now, Aggie?"

"I'm not sure. In a few day I think I'll be able to go back to the cottage and pack up to go back to Dallas, but I can't face Luke right now."

"Would you like to stay here for a few days, Aggie?"

"Oh, I would, Mrs. Barnes! I was hoping I could when I first thought of coming here."

Mae tried not to show Aggie how happy this made her feel. "After we finish eating and cleaning up, you must go out and get your suit cases. You did bring them didn't you?"

"I did."

How strange, Mae thought, that Aggie McBride would think of coming here. Even though Luke had been to see her and had helped her when she was ill recently, she knew how he felt about her, so how could Aggie feel she could come here? Strange or not, it felt good having this young woman in her home. She liked her—and she did say she loved Luke.

~~~~~~~~~~

Aggie looked around the room Mae had brought her to; it was upstairs and had a private bath. Flowered wallpaper covered the walls. White batiste curtains were pulled charmingly back from the window.

The furniture consisted of an old mahogany dresser with a beveled glass mirror, an old oak rocker with a rose pad, and a night stand with a porcelain lamp next to an old mahogany, four poster bed. The rose bedspread was a soft quilted comforter. She opened her suit case and hung up several dresses, and blouses. She felt so much at home here! As a child, she had longed for a grandmother and grandfather. If things had turned out differently with her and Luke, maybe Mae Barnes could have been *her* grandmother, too. Tears stung her eyes, then a strong feeling came over her that she must tell Mae the rest of the story—the rest no one knew—not even Mary.

Mae was resting in her room down stairs and had suggested Aggie do the same.

Aggie pulled her earrings off, laid them on the dresser and went over to the bed. Pulling down the bedspread, she lay her head on the soft down pillow and curled up. Before she could even think one thing, she was asleep. Two hours later, Aggie awakened. She looked at her watch, amazed that she had even slept, let alone for two hours!

Quickly getting up, she pulled up the spread, freshened up and ran down stairs. She found Mae in the kitchen drinking a glass of lemonade. Mae smiled at her as she entered. "You must have been tired, Aggie."

"I was. I couldn't sleep last night. I felt so peaceful upstairs that when I lay down on that soft pillow, I went right to sleep."

Mae looked pleased. "I'm glad you felt comfortable enough to sleep. Would you like a drink of lemonade?"

"I would, thank you, but I'll get it."

Aggie sat down at the table with her lemonade and took several swallows. "Mm, this is refreshing, thank you. Mrs. Barnes, upstairs I...I had a strong feeling that I should tell you something that I have not told Doris. Even Mary doesn't know all of it, and Luke knows nothing."

"Oh?" Mae, surprised again, felt pleased. "Then you must tell me."

"Before I do, I must ask you not to tell anyone until I can tell Luke—that is, if he will give me a chance. If not, then when I've returned to Dallas, you may tell him."

"I will respect your wishes, Aggie. Go on with your story."

"Again I'll try to be brief for it's another long story."

Aggie began with the first day she walked into junior high school, the first day her teacher had smiled at her. Aggie purposefully did not tell Mrs. Barnes the name of the teacher, leaving it until the last. She told of her father deserting them several years before and as briefly as she could everything that happened that year—including the tragic story of Beth and Uncle Chester. She stressed how her English teacher had helped her, in what ways, what an impact she'd had on her life and how much she loved her. She explained how they had lost contact, and how badly she wanted all these years to find her.

Aggie noticed how intently Mae Barnes listened, though it was obvious that she was puzzled, wondering why Aggie would feel that it was important for her to hear this story. Aggie finished by telling her of helping Mary vacuum and seeing the pictures in Luke's bedroom. "As I walked over to take a closer look, I asked Mary if the center picture was of Luke's parents. Mrs. Barnes, I couldn't believe my eyes! Right there in front of me was a picture of my beloved English teacher Alice Marks." She waited until this information had sunk in.

Mae Barnes gasped. "Ann...Ann was your teacher?"

"She was! Tears filled Aggie's eyes. All I could do, was fall on the floor and sob because my beloved Miss Marks, who I have wanted to find all these years—was dead!"

Aggie's revelation was such a shock and so fraught with emotion, something inside Mae Barnes crumbled causing her to do something she had never done before in front of anyone. She covered her face with her hands and sobbed quietly.

Aggie got up, went around the table and put an arm around her shoulders, feeling that it was a rare thing when this woman let down her guard and allowed anyone to see her vulnerability. When Mae's tears were spent, she wiped her eyes and asked, "Did Mary tell you the reason Ann left that year?"

Aggie wiped her own eyes and sat on a chair next to Mae taking one of her hands in hers. "Yes."

"I don't think Luke has ever forgiven me for running his mother off."

"Mrs. Barnes, if she hadn't left and taught that year, I hate to think what would have happened to me. Because of her, I was able to make it through the year. Because of her, I learned to love writing. I've had nine children's books published. Most importantly, Mrs. Barnes," Aggie squeezed her hand. "I came to know and love the mother of the man I love—Luke. I never would have known her otherwise. Because of the wounds from my childhood caused by my father and uncle, I wondered if I could ever trust a man again, let alone love one. Luke is the kindest and most wonderful man I've ever met, Mrs. Barnes. His moral strength is almost unheard of today. I don't know if Luke can get over the shock and bitterness enough to hear what I have to say. No matter, I'll always love him."

"I know it was a terribly difficult time for you and your son's family when Ann left, but something good has come of it. I've learned the hard way that trials have a way of bringing us blessings when we remember to pray for help during them—as my mother and Miss Marks—Ann, taught me."

Mae Barnes, her eyes full of tears, gazed at Aggie. "I...I can't tell you what this means to me—you telling me all this. My son turned against me, Luke would have nothing to do with me—only Amy forgave me. Oh, yes, Ann—dear Ann also forgave me. But I never told her thanks before she died." For the second time in her adult life, Mae Barnes covered her face and sobbed. Aggie held her tightly until her grief had worn itself out.

# Chapter Twenty-Nine

Sunday morning Luke found himself in an emotional tug-of-war. Aggie hadn't returned. Not that it made any difference he repeatedly assured himself, but he did feel some responsibility for her safety.

Luke didn't go to church. When Mary went to Mass, he got the key to the cottage and went up to see if he could find any clue where she could have gone. He looked through her neat belongings but with no luck. He sat down on the couch wondering why he was even caring. He was hurt more than he could have imagined possible by what Aggie had held back, what her firm had been responsible for—something so terrible, so unforgivable! He hated Joy for telling it. He was angry at Doris for sending Aggie here. No—he was angry at himself for not telling Doris why he divorced Lila. If he had, she wouldn't have suggested Aggie for his cook—but then he couldn't stand the thoughts of not ever having met Aggie. Maybe he should have listened to her. He tried to push the thought away. It was too painful.

He glanced up at her children's books. He picked up the first volume and began reading. It hurt; he could see Aggie in the little heroine of the book. Finishing it, he continued until he had read them all. He felt emotional because he felt he knew Aggie better now, but did it help? Did it excuse what she did?

By Sunday night, Mary was weary. She had watched Luke prowl around the house like a mother bear who had lost one of her cubs. She was grateful he had to go to work tomorrow. Later that night on the private line in her room, she received a call from Amy telling her that she had arrived in Dallas and was staying with Doris. She told her that as soon as Doris could take the boys to Fort Worth to her mother, they would be down—either Monday night or Tuesday sometime. Amy reminded her that she still wasn't to tell Luke.

After hanging up the phone, Mary, tried to think where Aggie would have gone. It couldn't have been very far, because the note to Luke indicated she would be returning in a few days. In that case it didn't seem reasonable that she would have gone so far that returning would have been time consuming.

She decided that they would all just have to sit around here and wait until she came back. Then a thought struck her. Putting herself in Aggie's shoes, she would want to go see the home of the one she loved so much, her English teacher. To Mary that was the most likely thing for Aggie to do, but she could only look at the house. Maybe she could even get the Burkes to let her in, but that wouldn't take very long. If that were the case, she'd be back by now—still...

~~~~~~~~

Monday afternoon, Luke came home from work telling Mary he was going to call the police.

"Luke, the police won't consider her missing if you think it through carefully."

He frowned and thought a moment. "I guess they won't. What shall I do, Mary?"

"Go back to work and wait until she comes back."

"I can't."

Mary decided to tell Luke her hunch. "Did you ever tell Aggie where your ranch is?"

"Yes, why?"

"Oh, I don't know, maybe just to get away and think for a few days she may have driven down that way as a place to go."

"I can't figure out why she'd do that."

"Did she care for you, Luke?"

"She acted like she was beginning to."

"If she did, do you think she might drive to the ranch or down that way?"

Luke thought about it. "Well, it's the only place that even sounds plausible. I'm going down there. I'll call work, pack up a couple of things and leave right away."

~~~~~~~~

Doris and Amy were just entering Austin when something started to nag at the back of Amy's mind. On the way, Doris had told her all about the friendship between herself and Aggie, and also about Aggie's history in Dallas. Amy was impressed, thinking that Aggie sounded like a wonderful girl for Luke. Because her errant brother hadn't told Doris why he'd divorced Lila, she had to tell her and tell her now! Under the circumstances, it was important for Doris to know.

When Amy had finished telling Doris about the divorce, Doris was concerned, wondering what she had gotten her friend into.

They arrived at Luke's place just five minutes after he had left for the ranch. Mary was delighted to see them, hugging each a little tearfully, informing them where Luke had gone.

"All right, let's go, Amy, maybe we can arrive there about the same time he does."

"Okay, but first, I have to find something in one of those boxes out in the garage. Something is bothering me."

All three went out into the garage. "What are you looking for, Amy?" Mary asked.

"I left mother's diaries here for Luke to read, but apparently he hasn't gotten around to it because he told me they were still packed up in the garage."

They found them in the second box they opened. "I need only one journal," Amy said, looking at the dates. "Here it is! Let's go."

Mary declined to go with them, she had gone through enough emotional stress to last a year. She waved goodbye to them as they drove off.

On the way, Doris asked, "What is it that is bothering you, Amy?"

"I would rather not say until I'm sure. I need to read something in this before we get there, and as soon as I find what I'm looking for I'll tell you."

~~~~~~~~~~

Aggie was excited. Mrs. Barnes had offered to call the Burkes and tell them to let her into the ranch house so she could look around, explaining that she was a good friend of Ann Barnes. Since it was such a hot, humid day, she slipped on a sky blue cotton sheath dress, with short peaked sleeves. She ran down stairs and into the kitchen. Mrs. Barnes was just putting down the phone.

"The Burkes will watch for you," she said smiling at the radiant girl.

"Oh, thank you, Mrs. Barnes. I don't think I'll be very long. Bye."

Aggie went out the kitchen door to her van, that was now parked behind the house, and got in. It wasn't a very long drive and her heart was beating fast with excitement. She drove through the impressive entry gate of the ranch. Finally reaching the house, she drove around back as Mrs. Barnes had instructed her to do in order to meet the Burkes.

She pulled up behind the ranch house and got out. Bob and Cherie Burke greeted her, introducing themselves. "Just go right into the back door, Aggie, and look around all you want," Cherie said.

"Thank you, I appreciate this."

She stepped up onto the porch and into a mud room then on into a large attractive blue and white kitchen. She wandered around the kitchen, looking at everything, opening cupboards and drawers, trying to imagine Miss Marks here working, cooking, taking care of her family. With a pang, she thought of young Luke who had such a hard time with his father, but who was close to his mother. She looked at all four bedrooms then entered the large room in front with the big stone fireplace, the mammoth blue leather couch and chairs, and the ebony grand piano. Under the furniture a blue and rose rug covered the shiny stone floor.

Pictures on the mantle caught her eye. She quickly stepped over to look at them and there in the middle was Miss Marks, her tall good-looking husband and her two children, Amy and Luke. Suddenly the front door opened and there stood Luke.

Luke blinked a couple of times, shook his head not believing his eyes— "Aggie?"

Aggie was so startled, she couldn't speak. Her heart swelled with happiness at seeing him, but the last place she wanted him to find her was *here*!

"What are you doing here, Aggie? This is private property," he added curtly, immediately regretting it.

"I know, Luke. I'll leave." She turned to leave.

"Wait, Aggie! I didn't mean that. Finding you here was so unexpected, I..."

Aggie stopped and gazed at Luke. With all her heart she willed him to say the words that would make everything all right, but he was silent. She could see that he still struggled within.

Again she started for the door.

Luke reached her in one long stride, his fingers closing on her arm. "Aggie, don't go..."

The touch of his fingers worked their old magic. She felt almost helpless. Finally she asked, "Why, Luke?"

The front door burst open and Doris and Amy entered.

"Doris! Amy!" Luke exclaimed, obviously bewildered. He jerked his hand from Aggie's arm.

Amy ignored Luke and stared at Aggie's surprised face. "You've found her! You've found little Aggie McBride!" Tears pooled up in her blue eyes and she turned to Luke. "You've found little Aggie McBride!"

Luke looked dumbfounded. "What? I've *found Little* Aggie McBride?"

"Yes!" Amy walked over to Aggie, the tears now rolling down her cheeks. "We've found you!" She held out her arms and hugged Aggie, who looked almost as puzzled as Luke.

Amy held Aggie away from her and studied her. "You are as beautiful as Mother described. Oh, if only Mother could be here now!"

At last Aggie realized that Amy knew of the relationship with her mother. She enthusiastically returned Amy's hug. Blinking back tears, she saw Doris standing back, tears rolling down her cheeks also. She knows too! thought Aggie.

Luke stood there totally stupefied. "What the hell is going on here?!"

"Don't cuss, Luke," Amy said through her tears. "You know Mother didn't like it and—she may be here right now."

"Will some one tell me what is going on?!"

Aggie went over to Doris and hugged her. "Can you believe it all, Doris?"

"No, I can't." Doris replied. "When did *you* learn about it, Aggie? Amy and I wondered if *we* were going to be the ones to break the news to *you*. Did you discover it today as you looked at the pictures?"

"Hold on, everybody!" Luke roared. "Will everybody quit ignoring me, and tell me why you two are here and what you all are talking about?"

"Sit down everybody," Amy said "and I'll be right back, I have to get something out of the car."

An uncomfortable silence settled over the three of them until Amy came back with her mother's diary. "I don't know quite where to start. Aggie, do you have anything to say to Luke before I start?"

"Yes." She looked at Luke. "I could hardly wait to tell you what I had discovered Friday afternoon when I was helping Mary. I was vacuuming your room when I noticed the pictures on your chest of drawers. I...I couldn't believe it. I have ached to find her all these years and there she was...but," Aggie fought for control, "but it was too late, she's dead!" She stopped, unable to go on for a moment, then she stood up abruptly. "I think I had better leave. Amy, you can tell your brother." Her eyes, hurt and accusing, focused on Luke's. "He told me he didn't want to hear anymore from me." She turned and ran out of the room into the kitchen.

Amy started after her. Luke moved to follow.

"No Luke!" Amy stated firmly.

"But I don't know where she's going!"

"You stay here. I'll find out."

Reluctantly, Luke walked back and sat down, thoroughly confused and upset.

Through the kitchen window, Amy saw Aggie about to get in her van. She ran outside. "Aggie, wait! Where are you staying?" she asked as she stepped over to her.

"I'm staying with your grandmother Barnes."

Amy's mouth dropped open. "You are certainly going to have to tell me how this came about! But first, don't you want to stay long enough to watch Luke's reaction when he learns about you and mother?"

Aggie nodded, a small grateful smile on her face. "Thank you, I would like that, but I wish to leave right after—for reasons I'm sure you understand."

"I do, but come on..."

"Wait, Amy, when you three have had your talk, I'm sure your grandmother would like you to stay with her. You were planning to weren't you?"

"Yes, we were, Doris and I, anyway. Luke may stay here."

"Amy, I'm so grateful to you for flying out and bringing Doris with you."

"You're welcome, Aggie. I had a strong feeling it was important I come."

"I'm so glad! All of you come to dinner. I'll help your grandmother prepare it."

Amy gazed at Aggie in wonder and smiled. "You are a treasure, Aggie. Let's go in." They both went back in the house and into the front room.

Aggie remained in a chair near the door of the kitchen so she could observe everyone and be free to leave when she needed to.

Luke glanced at her, hiding his relief that she'd come back.

Amy sat down, looked at Luke and said, "Let's talk about Aggie and her English teacher."

"Her English teacher?" he asked, puzzled.

"Has she talked about her?" Amy asked.

"Her English teacher? I'm sure she's had more than one English teacher."

"Has she mentioned an English teacher?" Amy persisted.

"Why are you asking me this?" he asked, irritated over such a seemingly unimportant subject, especially at this time.

"Please answer me," Amy requested quietly.

A smile tugged at his lips. "You are pulling one of Mother's 'quiet' tactics." He blew out an impatient gust of air. "Let me think."

Aggie found herself enjoying this tremendously—watching from where she was sitting, almost as if no one knew she was there.

"Yes," Luke said. "She's talked quite a few times about a teacher influencing her in different ways. One she mentioned opened up the world of writing to her. As a result, she's written a series of children's books." He glanced back at Aggie, but saw no reaction.

"Oh?" smiled Amy. "How wonderful."

"Is that really important?" Luke asked, a little impatiently, looking at both Amy and Doris.

"I'll tell you the name of the English teacher and see if you think it is important, Luke. Her name was Miss Marks."

Luke looked puzzled.

"Miss Alice Marks."

"That's a coincidence. That's our mother's first name and maiden name."

"It *was* our mother, you dunce!" Amy almost shouted. She and Doris smiled at each other, waiting for his reaction.

"That's impossible...wait a minute, that year she went off and taught school, she didn't say anything about using her maiden name."

"She didn't want Dad to find her, remember?"

Luke's eyes widened in shock as he thought it through. Stunned, he asked, "*Our mother* taught Aggie?"

"Yes. If you had read mother's diaries like I asked you to, you would have found out, and also you would have found out a lot about Aggie."

Aggie was startled to hear this.

"I can't believe it!" He shot to his feet and moved quickly to the mantle. He stared at his mother's picture, which was taken just before she left that year, then turned and gazed at Aggie, his disbelieving eyes questioning her. She smiled and nodded. His jaw dropped, and he shook his head ever so slightly as if trying to make it all sink in. He turned and faced his sister and cousin. "What a strange coincidence! Everything—you, Doris, becoming good friends with Aggie and then you arranging for her to come and cook for me...."

"Yes, it is. I can't believe I had a hand in it," Doris stated, an expression of incredulity on her face, then she added, "Luke, Mary told Amy about Joy Marshall and her tactics; telling you in front of Aggie about her being an attorney and about the abortion case."

Luke's face turned hard. "Yes, she did." He turned to face Aggie, but found her gone. This upset him inordinately, but he immediately tried to convince himself that it was probably for the best.

"And Luke," began Amy, "I'm sure you will understand why I had to tell Doris the reason you divorced Lila."

He nodded slowly. "Now you know why it upset me that Aggie would deceive me by not telling me she was an attorney and..."

"Luke," Doris interrupted, "I was the one who told her not to tell you she was an attorney for a while. We've been gone on a vacation and Bob found out from his secretary that Aggie had been trying to reach us. I'm sure she wanted me to call and tell you. She didn't want to keep that from you in the first place."

"At least I'm glad to hear that," he said, relief flooding through him— "but—" his face became troubled, "how could she be part of an abortion case, an abortion case her associate won?!"

"Did she try to tell you something, Luke?" Doris asked.

"Well...yes, but what in the world could she tell me? How could she explain that away?!" he asked angrily.

"I'm sorry, Luke, that you didn't give her the courtesy of listening to her side of the story."

"There's no excuse for what her firm did, Doris!"

"Not her firm, Luke, one attorney in the firm. Sybil took this case against Aggie's wishes while Aggie was out of town on another case. That's why she fired Sybil Martin and hired an investigator to check on the evidence."

"She did?" Profound relief coursed through him, then his heart sank like a heavy stone in the ocean, irretrievable. What had he done?

"Here, Luke," Doris said, handing him a couple of newspaper articles. "I'm sure Joy didn't want you to see *these*."

He read silently the caption of the first one:

"INVESTIGATION PROVES
ABORTION NOT NECESSARY.
Agnes McBride hired investigator,
Barry Slocum to...."

Luke jumped up. "It was *Aggie!*" He paced back and forth. "It was Aggie who hired Barry Slocum to find out it wasn't my baby Lila was carrying." His sister and cousin watched the full weight of remorse come down upon him. "But how did she know about Lila's abortion? Who told her. That was private information!"

"Luke," Amy said softly, "Mary had to tell Aggie, in order to protect you. Aggie, told Mary that she was an attorney and that she was going to tell you. Mary happened to ask what kind of an attorney she was and when she found out that she was an attorney for women's issues, she begged her to wait. Nevertheless, Aggie was determined. So that you wouldn't be hurt anymore than you had been, Luke, Mary told her about Lila. That stopped Aggie. I don't know what Aggie was thinking, of course, but since her firm had almost allowed an unnecessary abortion to take place, maybe she was afraid of your reaction—and from what I've seen, rightly so."

Luke sat down heavily, his face stricken with grief and concern at what he'd done to Aggie. He finished reading both articles. One ended with the information that the District Attorneys of both Dallas and Houston had formally thanked Agnes McBride.

Doris added more to the weight of his remorse. "Luke, because of this case, Aggie closed down her office. It was then she told me she would accept your offer to come and cook for you. I don't know what she was planning to do at the end of the six months; go back to Dallas and practice, go somewhere else and start over—or what."

His elbows on his knees, Luke leaned his head into his hands, and stared at the floor. Silence filled the room while Amy and Doris waited. It was a long time before Luke looked up, and when he did, they saw anguish on his face. "Amy, you gave me the advice not to get involved too soon because you said I was vulnerable, but I couldn't help it. I was drawn to Aggie immediately—not because of her beauty, but because...because of so many special things about her. I *love* Aggie," he confessed miserably. "And I've ruined everything! I know, she's a career woman—she's an attorney. I can't believe I'm saying this, but in spite of it, I don't want to lose her."

"Do you want me to read our mother's diary about her and Aggie?" He nodded.

Amy looked at her watch. "You know, it's really time for dinner. Let's go over to grandmother's place and eat there." Amy smiled to herself. Luke was in for another surprise—Doris too.

Luke was so emotionally exhausted, he was glad to have a change. "All right. I'll follow you and Doris over in my truck."

# Chapter Thirty

Mae Barnes opened the door to her grandson, granddaughter and Doris. Smiling, she opened her arms, embracing each. "How good to see you, Amy and Doris—you, too, Luke." The three exchanged glances, surprised at this uncharacteristic display of affection.

"How are you feeling now, Grandmother?" Luke asked.

"I'm feeling much better, Luke. Thank you. All of you come into the dining room. You are just in time; dinner is almost ready."

"Something smells good, Aunt Mae," Doris said. "But since you weren't expecting us, are you sure you have enough?"

"I'm sure of it," she said, smiling.

When they entered the dining room, Doris and Luke were surprised to see that the table was set for five. Luke asked, "Are you expecting company?"

"No. I was expecting you three," she stated, a sly smile on her face.

"You were?" asked Luke surprised. "How could you know we were here? Did the Burkes tell you?"

"No, I did," said Aggie, carrying in a bowl of potato salad. "We're having a picnic right here in your grandmother Barnes' dining room."

Mae Barnes, her granddaughter, Amy, and Aggie took delight in watching Doris' mouth drop open and Luke gape at Aggie—momentarily speechless.

"What...what are you doing here, Aggie?" Luke managed to ask.

"That's the second time you've asked me that question today, Luke. I told you, I'm helping your grandmother prepare a picnic for you all."

Mae Barnes was enjoying this. "Do you have a problem with that, Luke?" she asked.

"No...but...I don't understand...I..."

"Don't try, Luke. Let's all sit down and enjoy the meal together," his grandmother instructed.

Aggie went back into the kitchen and brought out a plate of fried chicken and a basket of hot rolls. Mae, who had followed her in, brought out a large bowl of cut up honeydew melon, cantaloupe, water-melon and green grapes.

Luke stood there, still struggling to grasp what was happening. Amy smiled conspiratorially at her grandmother and Aggie as they sat down. Luke remained standing, looking dumbfounded.

"Are you going to join us, Luke?" his grandmother asked, enjoying his reaction.

"I guess," he mumbled, pulling out a chair.

"May we pray?" Mae asked.

Everyone bowed their heads while Mae gave thanks.

The food was passed around while Doris, Amy and Mae conversed with each other and Aggie listened with interest.

Luke ate in silence, studying Aggie every chance he could. Several times he caught her looking at him. The question was still eating at him—why was she here of all places? But more importantly, he wondered if he had a chance with her after the way he'd treated her? For some reason, the fact that she was here in his grandmother's home gave him a flicker of hope that there might be. She looked so beautiful in that blue dress. It enhanced the deep blue of her eyes, and her countenance was that of an angel. He yearned to take her in his arms, cover her with kisses and beg her for forgiveness.

"This food tastes great, Gram. I didn't realize I was so hungry," Luke heard Amy say.

"It is, Aunt Mae," Doris said, using the affectionate name she had always called her even though she and Mae were not related.

"Thank you," Mae said. "Aggie prepared the chicken and the potato salad. I had the rolls in the freezer."

"Did anyone call Mary to tell her we found Aggie?" asked Luke, suddenly remembering.

"I called her, Luke," Aggie said.

Luke gazed at her, his eyes soft with gratitude. "That was thoughtful of you, Aggie. Thank you."

When the meal was over, everyone helped clean up, and put the food away. With this done, Mae suggested they all go in the living room and visit.

When they were all settled in their seats, Amy said, "Gram, Mother kept a diary as you may know. She kept one covering the nine months she was away from us. It's important for Luke and Aggie to hear some of it. I know Doris would like to hear it. The question is, Gram, do you want to hear it?"

Before Mae could answer, Aggie spoke out, "*I* want her here when we hear it, that is, if you don't mind, Mrs. Barnes."

There was a moment of silence before Mae replied. Her voice broke when she answered, "Thank you, Aggie, for wanting me here." She turned to Amy and continued, "Though it was a painful time for all of us, I would like to hear it."

"All right," Amy said pulling the diary from her purse. "I will begin at the beginning, reading only parts. Any of you are welcome to read all of it later." Before starting, she looked over at Aggie, who was sitting by her grandmother on the couch, and smiled.

Aggie almost trembled at times when she looked at Amy, especially when she smiled. She looked so much like her mother. She was pretty, tall and slim, like her mother with stylishly short blonde hair. Her blue eyes held the same light in them, the same deepness, the same kindness. Her smile, like her mother's, lit up her face, making her beautiful. Now that she thought about it, Doris resembled Amy.

Amy looked at Luke, knowing how he was suffering—but Aggie was here! Here in Gram's house. There was hope. Next, she smiled at Doris—the person who was most responsible for discovering the long lost Aggie McBride.

Amy opened the diary and began reading:

*Sunday August 24, 1980:* (the first diary entry since coming to McKinney) *I feel so lost, so lonely here in this little apartment. How I miss Amy and Luke—and yes, King. Tomorrow is my first day of teaching English to junior high school children—children the same age as Amy and Luke.*

*Monday August 25, 1980:* *My first day of school was successful and uneventful except for one thing in my first class. It was five minutes before nine when at the door appeared a most enchanting child. Her hair was so dark it looked almost black. It was pulled back into a pony tail. Her deep violet eyes looked almost too large for her face with its high cheek bones and small pointed chin. She wore an old T shirt tucked into blue jeans much too large for her and tied at the waist with an old ribbon. The jeans were rolled up several times to make them short enough. I watched her look around the classroom. She grinned and waved at a group of boys all seated in the same area. As she scanned the room, looking for a seat, her face turned from eagerness to soberness. She looked down at her clothes and slowly raised her head, her face flushing with embarrassment. By the time she got her bearings, there was only one seat left behind a nicely dressed girl named Gayle. Across the aisle from Gayle was her friend, Irma, who was just as nicely dressed. It was obvious that these two girls were snickering and whispering about this girl. As she sat down behind Gayle, she nervously looked up me, her new teacher. I gave her a reassuring smile and she smiled back. Her name is Aggie McBride.*

AMY stopped and looked at Aggie, who was looking down at her lap, touched beyond words that Miss Marks would care enough to take the time to write about her. Amy noticed Aggie steal a glance at Luke whose face was a mixture of amazement and tenderness as he gazed at Aggie.

"Do you remember this, Aggie?" Amy asked.

"Very well. I'm touched that your mother took time to write about me in her diary. She saved my life that day when she smiled at me. I felt as though I had an ally."

Amy glanced at Doris who was smiling and shaking her head in amazement.

To anyone who noticed, Mae Barne's face had turned stoic, unreadable. Hearing Ann's journal was both cathartic and painful. She'd had five years to grieve over the death of her only child, her son and his wife—five years to relive her mistakes and wish she could turn the clock back. Now, she had to relive them again, but—with tangible support from a stranger, this young woman beside her who miraculously appeared on her doorstep seeking her help.

Amy began reading again.

*Tuesday, August 26, 1980: I wonder if I'm going to be able to make it for nine months away from my family...*

*Today little Aggie McBride came to her second day of junior high in a pretty dress. Her naturally wavy hair was brushed and loose, held back with a pretty clip. Immediately, she walked over to her friends, the group of boys she'd waved at yesterday. I overheard one named, Woody, ask, "Why are you dressed like a girl? What about our ball game after school?" I suspect Aggie has been a tomboy and perhaps has never thought of wearing anything to school but jeans—until yesterday. This idea surprised me since she is so petite and feminine. Later, I had an opportunity to tell her how nice she looked. She seemed very pleased.*

*It's only Tuesday and already I wonder what I'm going to do when the weekend gets here. My heart is aching with loneliness. What have I done?*

*I had to remind myself that it was only after much agonizing and after much prayer that I decided to make this sacrifice for the good of my family unity. I knew is would be painful for all of us, but I felt this was the only answer—the only way to get through to King—the only way he'll be able to see what he's doing to his family by allowing his mother to interfere in the raising of our children.*

AMY stopped reading and an uncomfortable silence settled over the group. With the exception of Luke, the three others were concerned for Mae. Luke felt this was good for his grandmother to hear, and it satisfied some of the feelings he'd held inside him toward her. Even now, he thought, he could not see any remorse on her tight-lipped face.

Aggie spoke into the silence, addressing Amy. "Did your mother contact you in any way during those nine months?"

"Yes. She called us every week, but at first only when she knew Dad was out working. We begged her to come back home. She always assured us she would, but only when it was the right time. Finally, she began calling Dad. At first he would only rail at her, accuse her. I learned later that all she would say to him was: 'I guess it isn't time for me to come home, King.'"

Studying her grandmother, Amy asked, "Are you all right, Gram? Shall I go on?"

Mae, steeling herself inside, replied stiffly. "Yes, to both questions."

Amy breathed a sigh of relief, feeling that it all needed to be brought out into the open once and for all—especially for Luke's sake and for her grandmother's as well. Turning to Aggie, she said, "Is it all right with you, Aggie?"

"Since it's all right with your grandmother, it's all right with me." She slipped her hand into one of Mae's and held it tightly for a few moments.

Mae swallowed back the lump in her throat. This tender physical support from Aggie was so unexpected—but so needed.

Luke noticed this action on Aggie's part and felt a mixture of betrayal and confusion. Why, he wondered, did Aggie come here in the first place? And why would she comfort the woman who drove off his mother?

Amy continued. "After about six months, Mother called Dad. I answered the phone. I went to get him and then unbeknown to both, I listened in on the other phone. The conversation went something like this: 'All right, Ann, I'm going to go tell my mother to stay out of our business. Now will you come home?'"

"Mother answered, 'That isn't what I want, King. I want you to recognize that *we*, you and I, need to make decisions together—to be one in what we want for our children. Yes, you need to talk to your mother, but very kindly—firm but kind. Until you can show me that you really understand, I can't come home.'"

Amy sighed. "Dad became so angry, he slammed the phone down. Then he was beside himself for doing so because he didn't know how to reach her. We didn't hear from Mother for a month. I could tell Dad was scared. I think he thought any moment she'd come for us kids and leave him for good. I told Luke about the conversation and told him not to worry—that Mother would call again.

"When I grew up, Amy continued, I learned that Dad felt totally lost without Mother, and that after that incident, he went to a psychologist for counseling. This was an amazing step for him. None of us, including Mother, knew exactly what he said to you, Grandmother and when. Would you mind telling us?"

Mae's posture turned rigid, her lips pressed together tightly. Both her pride, and the old habit of wanting to control battled inside her.

Everyone's eyes were on her, waiting, but it was Aggie's gaze that prompted her to look in her direction. Aggie smiled, encouraging her with an almost imperceptible nod. How can I do this? Mae agonized. Often, she wished she could apologize to Ann, but that was an easy wish—Ann was gone. And she found she couldn't apologize to Ann's children *now*. She was barely able to tell what Amy requested. She took a deep breath.

"Your father, my son, came to me a month before your mother returned. He told me that he and I had run his wife off, but said he felt it was more his fault for not being man enough to..." Mae struggled a moment, swallowing back emotion, "man enough to withstand me— my interfering in his family affairs. I...I don't know exactly what he said, it has been so long."

"Gram," Amy began gently, "did he speak kindly to you?"

With eyes downcast, her chin quivering ever so slightly, Mae said in almost a whisper, "Yes, he was kind, but firm, just as Ann had requested."

In the charged silence everyone digested this healing disclosure.

Aggie realized Ann Barnes' courage had helped her husband, King, become a loyal husband and father, while at the same time teaching an invaluable lesson to her children, hard as it was.

Thinking back, Luke remembered that after his mother returned, the atmosphere in their home was more peaceful and happy. As a young boy he had attributed it only to the fact that his mother had come home.

Amy wished that her grandmother, for once, could say: "I'm sorry." Since it wasn't forthcoming, she said, "Thank you, Gram. We appreciate how difficult that was, but I'm sure you realize how important that was for us to hear."

Mae nodded.

It was clear to Amy looking at her grandmother's drawn and haggard face that she was totally exhausted. "You look tired, Gram. Why don't we all go to bed and resume the reading of Mother's diary tomorrow morning?"

"I believe I am a little tired, Amy. Thank you. Of course you are all welcome to stay the night here."

"Thank you, Aunt Mae." Doris chimed in. "It will be kind of like old times. Remember when Amy and I slept over every chance we could get?"

Mae smiled. "I remember."

Luke stood up abruptly. "I think I'll sleep at the ranch tonight, Grandmother."

"All right, Luke,"

He turned his gaze on Aggie a moment, then spoke to his sister. "What time are you going to start tomorrow, Amy?"

"Right after breakfast about 8:00 if that's all right with everyone."

"Fine. I'll be here after breakfast." He walked to the arched entrance of the room and stopped. He spoke over his shoulder. "Aggie, may I see you outside for a moment?"

Aggie didn't answer.

Luke slowly turned to face her. "Aggie?"

"Yes?"

"I asked you a question."

"I expect to see your face when you address me, Luke."

Amy smiled inwardly. This girl won't run to Luke with the crook of a finger like all the others.

"Now you see it," he said with an edge to his voice, "may I speak to you a moment?"

"What is it you want to speak to me about?"

"May I speak to you alone? Please?" His voice held an undertone of pleading.

Aggie hesitated a moment, then nodded. She followed him through the dining room, the kitchen and out the back door.

They stood on the porch looking at each other.

"What is it, Luke?"

Several emotions gripped Luke: Gratitude to Aggie for paying Barry Slocum to discover the truth. Pain and remorse for how he'd refused to hear her side Friday night. The desire to take her in his arms and hold her—to keep her from running away from him again. A sense of betrayal that she'd come to his grandmother. He acted only upon the last.

"Why did you come to my grandmother, Aggie?"

"If I remember correctly, Luke, you told me very adamantly that you didn't want to hear any more from me."

"I know. I...I'm sorry, Aggie...I'm sorry I didn't let you tell me. It's unbelievable that you knew my mother—that she wrote about you in her diary. I can't quite take it all in."

Aggie's silence drove him on. "But—why did you come here of all places?"

"I don't know, Luke."

"What do you mean you don't know?" he asked more abruptly than he intended.

"I don't, that's all."

"Don't you realize, Aggie, it was that woman in there who drove my mother away from me for nine months?"

"No, Luke, it was your father who drove your mother away."

"Yes, he did. That became even more apparent tonight, but my grandmother was part of it. It bothers me that you came here."

"Your mother chose to take me into her life—so I have a right to come here and if it bothers you, that's your problem. Goodnight, Luke." She turned quickly and went inside, leaving a disgruntled and unhappy Luke.

# Chapter Thirty-One

Mae's steps had a bounce to them as she started breakfast early. Her big old home once again housed a family after so many years of emptiness. Strange, she thought, Ann *long ago* made Aggie a *member* of the family—that's the way it felt today.

A sharp stab of unease entered her heart as she remembered what was ahead in the reading of Ann's diary. Quickly putting it out of her mind, she returned to the enjoyment of cooking for her family as she had done so many times in years past.

The aroma of cooking sausage reached Aggie's nose as she opened her bedroom door to go downstairs. She felt the excitement one must feel when visiting a grandmother. First to enter the kitchen, Aggie saw the round table set for four. A small glass of orange juice was placed in the middle of each plate. A glass bowl in the center held what looked like homemade peach jam.

"Good morning, Mrs. Barnes. This looks wonderful and smells wonderful."

"Good morning, Aggie. Did you sleep well?"

"I did. There is something comforting about your home, Mrs. Barnes—about that bedroom upstairs. Why do you suppose I feel this way?" Aggie asked.

Apparently Aggie was as puzzled as she herself was, Mae thought. "I find you coming here to me very strange indeed, and having you feel my home comforting is also puzzling." Mae wanted to tell Aggie how grateful she was for her support last night, but she couldn't. She had never learned how to express gratitude or love. She had come to realize that the austerity of her own parents—their inability to express feelings was a form of cruelty that had stunted her—had robbed her of the ability to express her feelings.

Doris came in with Amy. Both exclaimed over breakfast. Pulling out a pan of biscuits from the oven, Mae suggested they seat themselves. After Mae had offered thanks, the girls complimented her over the sausage, biscuits and gravy and fried eggs, which pleased Mae immensely. Aggie was effusive about her peach jam.

"Peach jam is one of Gram's specialties," Amy explained. "She makes it with Texas peaches grown in Weatherford."

"You'll have to show me how to make it, Mrs. Barnes."

The girls were finishing up the dishes and Mae was resting at the table when Luke opened the back door and stepped into the kitchen.

"Smells like I missed a good breakfast, Grandmother," he remarked without a smile.

"You did, Luke," Amy gloated. "But then you look so glum, and since your powerful personality affects everyone around you, we wouldn't have had nearly as much fun visiting at breakfast if you had eaten with us."

Luke glared at his sister, but she returned it with a smile. "Go wait for us in the front room, Luke. We'll be there shortly."

He glanced at Aggie and found her smiling to herself. He walked out of the kitchen feeling thoroughly annoyed. Only his agonizing love for Aggie kept him from walking out the door and driving back to Austin.

~~~~~~~~~

Once more they were seated in the same arrangement as last night with Aggie sitting beside Mae.

Aggie was feeling apprehensive. It was possible Miss Marks had recorded the unhappy and painful episodes she had so recently emotionally and mentally reviewed. She didn't relish reliving them again—especially in front of Luke at this difficult time of their relationship. Pulling herself up short, she realized that anything she heard today couldn't be as hard as what Mae had gone through last night.

"Is everyone ready?" Amy asked, receiving different but affirmative reactions from each. "Remember, I'm only reading the entries which have to do with Aggie."

*Saturday September 25, 1980:* *Aggie has been coming to school in some very pretty clothes lately. I complimented her and she told me that a rich lady her mother cleans houses for gave them to her for her daughters.*

*Aggie makes me think of my Amy. I know they would be good friends if they knew each other. I'm about to give in and tell King where I am so he can bring the children to visit. Being separated from them gets harder each day!*

<u>*Monday October 27, 1980:*</u> *Today I had a terrible shock. Aggie came to class in her old over-sized jeans with all her beautiful hair cut off just below the ears. It was a straight across hair cut, no tapering or feathering whatsoever. Since her hair is so thick it stood out all around, dwarfing her petite face. The most shocking thing to me, however, was the expression on her face. Her large blue eyes looked fearful and haunted. I knew something terrible must have happened over the weekend. I waited for her after her last class to find out how I could help.*

AMY stopped reading, knowing the other two must be feeling as she was because they were looking at Aggie—concerned.

"Shall I go on, Aggie?"

Aggie, staring at her lap, overwhelmed at her teacher's concern, muttered, "Go on, Amy."

Amy went on, and as Aggie suspected, Alice Marks had recorded everything. First in retrospect, the happy times—their spaghetti dinners—then came the other, her father and the painful episodes concerning Uncle Chester. A couple of times during the reading, Aggie stole a glance at Luke and each time found his wonderfully attentive eyes gazing at her full of anguish. She had to look away quickly because her love for him brought a lump in her throat the size of a golf ball.

An amazing thing happened as Amy was reading—Mae Barnes did something Luke and Amy had never seen. She showed spontaneous affection; she put her arm over Aggie's shoulders. They had always hugged their grandmother, but she had never responded, had never returned their embrace until yesterday—and now she had actually initiated it.

As the diary neared the end of the nine months, Amy read one last entry.

*Friday May 29, 1981:* I'm in awe when I think back on the courage it took little Aggie McBride to go the barber and request that he cut off her beautiful hair, and to put on the old over-sized jeans in order to protect herself from her uncle...while trying to find a way to protect her sister, Beth. How she had the courage to walk into class that Monday morning is beyond me.

This kind of courage, along with the fighting spirit Aggie displayed the day her uncle returned and the policeman and I confronted him, was amazing! It was an inspiration to me. I have learned a great lesson from this child. If Aggie can do what she did, I can go home now and face whatever lies ahead. King seems to have changed—yet I know there will still be some rocky roads ahead.

I grieve that I've had to miss out on nine months of my children's lives—but I'm grieved about something else—leaving Aggie. I've become so attached to her...almost as if she were my own. I haven't dared tell her that I won't be back. I'll write her. Maybe down the road, Aggie's mother will let her come and visit us—but then there is Beth, dear sweet, fragile Beth who won't allow me to get close to her. Still, I can't lose contact with Aggie. I need to see her grow to womanhood.

AMY stopped and looked at Aggie, who, was by now, fighting back tears. "There is more throughout the diary recounting Mother's anguish at losing contact with you, Aggie." Amy turned her attention to her brother. "Now you know, Luke, why I exclaimed 'You've found little Aggie McBride' when I first walked in the door at the ranch."

He nodded, mute with emotion.

"And here's a returned letter Mother wrote to you, Aggie. Do you want me to read it?"

"She did write me then! Oh yes, please read it."

*Sunday September 15, 1981*
*Dear Aggie,*
*I guess you know by now that I won't be back teaching this year. I'm so sorry that I can't be there to watch you progress in your writing. I miss our times together.*
*I must confess something. For reasons I can't go into, I couldn't tell*

*you that I am married and have two children, Amy and Luke. Amy is your age and Luke is a year older. My married name is Alice Ann Marks Barnes. I go by Ann Barnes. My husband's name is King Barnes.*

*Someday, maybe I can help you to understand why I had to be apart from my family for those nine months. But if I hadn't, I never would have met you, Aggie. Though I grieve over missing out on that time in the lives of my children, blessings have come from it, one of the greatest is meeting you.*

*Soon, my husband and I with our children will be taking a trip to McKinney to see you.*

*How is Beth? How is your mother? I pray for them. I pray for you. We must never lose contact with each other, Aggie.*

*I love you,*
*Miss Marks (Mrs. Barnes)*

THE room was filled with emotionally charged silence. Only Aggie's quiet sobs filled the void. Mae handed her another lace handkerchief.

Luke, a totally stunned man, rested his elbow on the arm of the big chair, his hand rubbing his brow as if trying to help his mind absorb all he'd heard this morning. A few moments later, he glanced at Doris. She gave him a small smile while shaking her head, telling him she also was trying to internalize what had come about by suggesting Aggie work for him.

Amy watched everyone's reaction, feeling moved all over again.

Wiping her eyes with Mae's lovely hanky, Aggie broke the silence. "I, too, wrote a letter that was returned to *me* by someone in the office of Slaughter Junior High. I have it upstairs. Would you all like to hear it?"

"Yes, we would," Amy quickly replied for all.

Luke's eyes followed her out and watched for her return.

Moments later, Aggie returned with a letter in her hand and seated herself again beside Mae. All four gazed upon this young woman, seeing her through the eyes of her teacher of long ago. Taking the letter from the envelope, Aggie began:

*September 8, 1981*
*Dear Miss Marks,*
*We had to move to Dallas so Mama could work at a restaurant that pays her more. I begged her not to move so I could see you this fall and take another class from you. She said we had to move so she could help Beth and me go to college. I told her I would earn my own money, but she said she had already hired a moving truck!*

*I told her I had to see you—that I would find a family to live with for the school year. Mama got tears in her eyes and said she couldn't do without me. Mama hardly ever cries, so when she does, it makes me sad. I had to quit begging.*

*Beth said it would be exciting to move to Dallas, but I hate it because Mama is afraid of letting us go very far from home. I miss getting on my bike and riding anywhere I want and riding out to my special tree.*

*The school is so big and Beth gets frightened because some of the kids are scary. (But none of them are as scary to me as Uncle Chester was.)*

*Mama said as soon as you write back and tell us where you are living in McKinney, she'll take me up there to visit you.*

*I miss you.*

> *Love,*
> *Aggie*

AGGIE started to fold the letter to return it to the envelope, when Luke got up and stepped over to her. "May I see your letter?"

Surprised, Aggie nodded and handed it to him. Luke knelt on one knee beside her and looked at the thirteen-year-old Aggie's writing—reading it again. He swallowed with difficulty, then slowly raised his head. His eyes, poignant with tenderness, gazed into hers. Finally, he handed it back to her and returned to his seat.

"Thank you, Aggie, for sharing that," Doris said. "but why did you bring it with you to Austin?"

Smiling at her friend, she said, "I've always taken it with me when I traveled anywhere, Dor, always hoping I'd run into Miss Marks somewhere, sometime—and at last, I did," her voice broke, "in a matter of speaking."

"Yes, you did," Amy agreed. She turned to her brother. "Luke, you may read mother's diary as you have time. She mentioned trying to find Aggie in several places, but I will read one more entry she recorded a few months before she was killed."

*Sunday September 10, 1994: For some reason tonight I am think-ing about Aggie McBride and wondering where she is. I was terribly disappointed when my letter was returned marked: 'Unknown, No Forwarding Address.' My call to the school told me only that she had not returned for the 8th grade, and they had no knowledge of her whereabouts. I so want to see how she has turned out. Has she learned to trust men? Is she married? Does she have children? But more than anything, I want her to meet Luke and Amy and become part of their lives as she was and is a part of mine."*

AMY closed the diary, and for the first time Mae spoke, "How strange the way things have happened, for Ann now has *part* of her desire fulfilled. Aggie has met Amy and Luke. And more than that, has become good friends with her niece, Doris." Looking pointedly at Luke, she continued, "It remains to be seen whether Aggie will become part of your life, but as far as I'm concerned, she has become part of mine. I am inviting Aggie to stay here as long as she wishes—until she decides what she wants to do, where she wants to go."

Everyone was struck silent, including Aggie. Doris marveled as she realized the roll she had played in bringing all this about. She could hardly wait to inform her skeptical husband about everything!

Amy reflected on the first moment she saw Aggie. It had been a spiritual experience for her. Her mother taught her and Luke that there was a hereafter and there had been a couple of times since her mother died when she felt her presence. Could her mother somehow be aware of what was happening? It gave her comfort to think so.

Luke, pondering the things his mother wrote in her diary, wished he could tell her that not only have I met your Aggie, but I'm terrified she won't *let* me be a part of her life after the way I treated her! His elbows on his knees, he pressed his forehead into his clenched hands. I've really screwed up, Mother. If only you were here, I know you could smooth it over for me with Aggie.

Aggie, deep in thought, stared at the floor. In her wildest dreams, she could never have imagined sitting here in the parlor of Miss Marks' mother-in-law, with Miss Marks' niece, her daughter and son—listening to Miss Marks' loving diary entries about her!

Aggie was vaguely aware that Mae had gotten up and left. After some time, she looked up to find that Doris and Amy had also slipped out. Only Luke was there, his arms resting on his knees, leaning toward her. His eyes, deep pools of misery, were gazing at her intently.

Somewhat startled, she gasped, "Oh! We're alone."

"Yes, we are, Aggie, and now that we are, I don't know quite what to say—there are so many thoughts and emotions, so many things to absorb."

Aggie's face bore a far away expression. "I know what you mean. It's all rather incredible."

"Incredible only begins to describe it. The first thing that comes to mind is I need to thank Bob and Doris for bringing you into our lives."

"Oh?" she questioned in a tone of skepticism.

Luke's eyes pleaded for forgiveness before he expressed it again. "Please forgive me, Aggie, for the way I reacted when Joy told me those things. I can't believe the way I talked to you."

Aggie's expression was unreadable, her eyes downcast, so he got up and sat down beside her. "Aggie, look at me."

Aggie turned to him. He scrutinized her face still unable to fathom how she was feeling. "*Can* you forgive me?"

"I have already forgiven you, Luke."

Relief flooded his features. "You have? Ah...Aggie, thank you!" He put his arm around her and pulled her toward him, but she pulled away."

Luke slid off the couch. Kneeling on one knee in front of her. "What is it, Aggie?" he asked, fear knawing at his insides.

Aggie could only gaze at him in perplexed silence, wondering herself what was the matter. She loved Luke, she knew, but where was the thrill at his touch? The pounding of her heart? She could feel nothing.

"You haven't forgiven me."

"Yes, I have, Luke."

"Then why are you pulling away from me?"

"I don't know."

"You felt *something* for me, I know. Did I kill it, Aggie?"

"Luke, I have a problem right now—please give me some time."

"How long, Aggie?"

"Give me until later tonight, Luke—to think about it."

"All right." He took both her hands in his. "Aggie, I love you."

Her blue eyes widened, awe-filled, then softened. "You...do?"

He nodded wordlessly. "After you left, Aggie, I thought I'd go crazy with worry. I've never felt so miserable in my life." When Aggie didn't respond, he thought a moment, then grinned. "Though I wouldn't admit it to myself, I was smitten when I saw you for the first time—in Mrs. Butler's over-sized apron, looking like a wide-eyed teenager. I fought it because I was still suffering from the effects of my disastrous marriage—but when I saw you up in that tree, I knew I was hooked."

Aggie's brow twisted in concern. What is the matter with me? she asked herself. A short time ago, she would have been ecstatic over Luke's admission of love. It hurt her heart to see the smile fade from Luke's face, so she smiled and confessed, "I wanted to jump into your arms that very first time, Luke."

"You did?" His face brightened. "With that happy thought, I'll go on over to the ranch and let you think. What time shall I come back?"

"Come back for dinner."

"That sounds great." He kissed one of the hands he was holding, then stood up and smiled down at her. "See you later, 'teacher's pet.'"

Aggie watched him walk out of the room, noticing, as she had before, his manly grace, though it no longer stirred her as it had.

# Chapter Thirty-Two

Aggie found Mae, Doris and Amy in the kitchen starting lunch, Aggie explained she'd like to eat later, that she needed to rest for a little while. Now, alone upstairs in her bedroom, Aggie curled up in a chair and tried to figure out why she felt blocked in her feelings toward Luke.

Suddenly, the old tiredness, that had plagued her in Dallas, came over her. Getting up from the chair, she pulled down the spread, kicked off her sandals and lay down on the bed falling immediately into a deep exhausted sleep. Soon, she began tossing, dreaming. Case after case swirled, in a confusing parade, through her brain—the defendants each turning into her father or Uncle Chester. She awoke with a start, perspiring and shaken.

Sitting up, she looked at her watch. She had only been asleep for an hour! Leaning against the headboard, she hugged her knees and breathed deeply until she felt calmer.

What caused her to dream like this? she wondered. Hadn't she gone over it enough to put it behind her? In a flash it came to her—also giving her an answer to the numb feeling she was experiencing toward Luke. Relief came with understanding—but what she should or could do about it, she had no idea.

She got up, quickly freshened up in the bathroom and ran down stairs. When she entered the kitchen, she found Mae reading the paper. She looked up and smiled. "Did you have a nice rest, Aggie?"

"I fell asleep and even dreamed...which I never do in the daytime."

Noticing Aggie's troubled brow, she asked, "Would you like to tell me about your dream?"

Aggie sat down at the table and sighed. "Yes, I would." Surprising herself, she told her everything—her inability to feel anything toward Luke, then her dream. "Mrs. Barnes, I don't know why I can tell you so much. I haven't even been able to be this open with Doris, whom I consider my dearest friend." She searched the face of the woman before her as if she could explain it.

"I don't know either, Aggie. No one in my own family has ever confided in me as you have. I...I consider it a compliment," she added tentatively, not wanting to let on just how heart satisfying it was to *her*. "Why do you feel you dreamed that today?"

"I was puzzled, but as I thought about it the answer came. My mother's ability to forgive was a wonderful example to me. Miss Marks...Ann, helped me to forgive enough to take away a pain I was having in my chest.

"I watched my sister literally die of a broken heart, and I watched my gentle mother shoulder the roll of my errant father, wearing out her heart. In the years that followed, the anger and resentment began to build inside me again.

"During my career taking on cases of abused and battered women and children, I saw cruelty in many forms. I witnessed so much contention, so much hate and anger. All this, combined with my own baggage, my health, as I told you before, began to suffer. I finally had to come to grips with it and try to forgive as my mother had done, as Miss Marks taught me, and as the Bible teaches. But you know, Mrs. Barnes, this has been so *recent*, I feel vulnerable. I can't deal with Luke's anger and resentment. I've had enough of it to last a lifetime. After you, Amy and Doris left the room this morning, Luke told me he loved me, but...but there is no chance for us unless he can rid himself of what he's carrying around inside."

Mae's heart was heavy—knowing that these feelings of Luke were directed at her; she should be able to do something about it to save her grandson. But what? Facing her part in it all was too painful—so she asked, "Are you going to explain this to him, Aggie?"

Aggie's troubled face was thoughtful for so long, Mae felt uneasy. At last Aggie smiled and shook her head. "I can't believe my first impulse, especially after what I've learned through the years."

"What have you learned, Aggie?" Mae asked, relieved to see Aggie smiling.

"That a woman can't change a man. Almost all the women I represented knew or saw signs of problems in the men before they married them, but each thought she could change him. *My* first impulse was that I could explain to Luke and *help him* or to be more accurate, *change him.* To answer your question—no! I am not going to explain anything to Luke. He will have to come to it on his own."

The sound of a car door slamming, relieved Mae of any further painful introspection.

Luke broadsided the kitchen door, stepping in. "Hi," he grinned.

"Hello, Luke," his grandmother replied.

Aggie couldn't say anything, for the 'old heart trouble' had returned. She was both relieved and uneasy over its recurrence. Luke was so darned good looking standing there in his green T shirt, jeans and boots, smiling that infectious smile of his, that her heart was simply out of control. She realized her new insight had freed her, allowing her feelings to return.

"Where are Amy and Doris?" he asked.

"They are both resting. The three of us had a salad for lunch. Would you both like some lunch?" Mae asked, looking first at Luke then Aggie.

"I would, how about you, Aggie?" he asked, sitting down at the table.

"I would also."

"Why haven't you eaten, Aggie?" Luke asked studying her.

"I had a nap."

Mae placed a bowl of salad on the table and a plate of corn bread. Luke watched as his grandmother placed ice water, bowls, utensils and dressings on the table.

"I would like to take all of you out to dinner tonight, Grandmother."

"That sounds nice. Thank you, Luke," Mae replied.

"How about you, Aggie?" Luke asked.

"Sounds like a vacation from cooking to me. And I'm sure Doris and Amy will think so too. Since you only brought your truck we can use my van."

~~~~~~~~~~

As Aggie and Luke finished cleaning up and putting things away, Luke asked, "Aggie, would you like to see my ranch before we go out to dinner tonight?"

Aggie stalled, wondering if she had the willpower to resist Luke's charms until he realized what he needed to do. What if he never realizes? This thought unsettled her.

"Aggie? I know you mentioned something about tonight, but to tell the truth, I couldn't wait until then. I had to see you this afternoon."

"Yes, I would like to see your ranch, Luke. Mrs. Barnes, would you like to come with us?"

Mae smiled at her grandson's apprehensive glance. "No, thank you. You two go on and enjoy yourselves."

"Let's plan on leaving to go into Austin about 5:30," Luke suggested. "And why don't we all go just as we are. That way I can keep Aggie a little longer." He grinned.

"Sounds fine," Mae said, smiling. "See you later."

Riding next to Luke in his truck, Aggie felt both excitement and unease. Before long they passed through the entrance of the King Barnes Ranch. Instead of following the winding road to the house, Luke took a left on a side road away from it.

"This is the most beautiful ranch I've ever seen, Luke," Aggie murmured.

"I'm glad you like it," he said, pleased.

They left the stand of trees, driving over the gently rolling range. Cattle were grazing here and there on the green range grass. Some were standing under the shade of several trees, escaping the hot Texas sun.

"What kind of cattle are those, Luke?"

"Hereford, but we're raising more and more Black Angus because the finer restaurants and barbeque places throughout the country feel they make better meat. We've sold some of each in the auction barns and right now the Angus are bringing top dollar."

The road led them over another knoll. On the right, round bundles of hay dotted the field. "We raise a little coastal hay for winter," Luke explained.

After driving some time, they came to another crest with a thicker cluster of trees. Luke pulled off the road close to a magnificent old cottonwood tree. He got out and opened the door for Aggie.

"Come and I'll show you our Black Angus." They walked through the trees, looked out over the range and saw the cattle grazing.

"Why aren't you ranching full time, Luke?"

"It's hard to make money raising cattle—between drought and unpredictable cattle prices. My father made money ranching because he owned so much land. Besides this ranch, he owned ranch land south and southeast of Bastrop. They struck oil on his property southeast of Bastrop and he ended up making more money from the oil than the cattle, so he sold the oil land, keeping the mineral rights and, of course, kept this ranch.

"My sister and I divide the profit from the cattle when there is any. Mostly it supports my foreman and his family and it's a tax write-off for us. The oil leases bring in a lot of money for both of us. This is why I have organized an investment company. One of the most profitable investments I've made is in a large computer company in Austin. However, my dad loved the land and instilled it in me, so I want to keep this ranch. Bob Burke and I have decided to put in a commercial tree farm on several hundred acres. This should help make the ranch profitable again. My foreman also manages grandmother's ranch."

"When did your grandfather die?"

"When I was three years old."

"Your grandmother has been alone a long time," Aggie said quietly as she started walking back through the trees, studying them. "Look, Luke, there is a beautiful old live oak."

"Yeah, and it looks like a good climbing tree, my little wood nymph," he said, his eyes twinkling.

"It does doesn't it? Want to climb it with me?" she asked, grinning.

"No. I'd rather watch you. You are a feast to my eyes, Aggie, especially today in that shirt the color of your eyes."

Her breath caught. "Thank you." Turning quickly, she walked on through the trees. "That looks something like the old red oak I used to climb in McKinney. I think that's a juniper," she pointed at another one "and that one over there looks like..."

"Aggie?"

"Yes?"

"Are you running from me?"

"Yes."

"Why?"

"It's warm, Luke. Let's go back."

"Come on," he said grabbing her hand, "I've got a jug of cold water in the truck."

When they reached the truck, he opened the door on the driver's side. "Here, Aggie, take these," he said reaching behind the seat of the truck and handing her the jug and two cups. Next, he pulled out a blanket and spread it under the old cottonwood, sat down and poured Aggie a cup of cold water and then one for himself. Leaning against the wide trunk, he sighed. "I've always thought this was a good place for a picnic."

Aggie smiled. "I agree," she said, seating herself a couple of feet from Luke. This is a wonderful spot for a picnic. We have such beautiful glimpses of the range all around us."

"Come on over, Aggie," he coaxed, patting a place beside him, "sit a little closer. You can rest your back against the trunk like I'm doing." Aggie shook her head.

"Please, Aggie, there is something I need to tell you and it will take some time, so you need to rest your back here beside me."

She smiled at his irresistible plea and gave in. She leaned against the wide trunk.

"Thanks." he grinned. "That's better."

A small breeze came up from the south and blew through the trees, cooling them off. A peaceful feeling came over them as they listened to the birds, and the soothing rustle of leaves. When the breeze died down, even the buzzing of the insects was a comforting sound of summer.

"Do you remember when a man came to see me?" Luke finally asked.

"Yes," she said, holding her breath.

"The man's name was Barry Slocum," he began, staring straight ahead. "He brought me some startling news. I didn't believe him at first because it was so private. I couldn't figure how he could possibly know. At first, I was suspicious for several reasons, but he was a man I couldn't help trusting. Remember that evening I left for the ranch for a couple of days?" She nodded. "I had to get away and think, so the next morning early, I saddled up ol' Savage and rode and rode. On the way back, I stopped, got off the horse and rested my back against this very tree and went over it all again. You see, Aggie, it was wonderful news—news that eased my aching heart. It was here I poured out my gratitude to God for that information, and for the friend who arranged for and paid Barry Slocum to find it out and bring it to me. I decided then and there that I couldn't rest until I found out who that friend was."

He paused, then his head and shoulders slowly turned toward Aggie, his eyes burning with gratitude, he said, "Thank you, Aggie."

She gasped in surprise. "You know!"

"I know....and 'thank you' seems so inadequate at the moment." He reached for Aggie, wrapping her in his arms, soothing somewhat his fear of losing this 'little Aggie McBride,' once lost to his mother, but who so miraculously reappeared *in his* life. "Because of you, Aggie," he spoke softly into her ear, "my heart was relieved of a crushing and unnecessary grief."

"I'm happy that it's gone, Luke," she murmured, wondering how she was going to be able to pull away from this man whose arms felt as safe and joyous as heaven itself.

"I love you, Aggie. Will you marry me?" He felt her body become still. Slowly he pulled back to look into her face.

Looking down, she fought the desire to cry out, *yes!* It was only a short time ago she thought she would never hear those words from Luke.

"Aggie?" he asked anxiously.

Fighting for control, the silence lengthened. At last she looked up into Luke's penetrating eyes. "Oh, Luke...I don't know if I can...I wish I could say yes...but..."

"Aggie," he pleaded, sounding a little desperate, give me some time...give *us* some time together. I don't expect you to care for me as I care for you, but in time maybe...maybe you can."

"I...I can give us some time, Luke, but I can't promise you anything. I'm too vulnerable."

"Vulnerable? Vulnerable to what?"

"You'll have to figure that out yourself, Luke."

"I what?!" he exploded, his arms dropping from around her.

Aggie remained silent, refusing to repeat it.

He shot to his feet and moved away, his back to her. She stood up also.

He turned and in a sudden rush of hope, he asked, "Are you vulnerable to *me*?"

She smiled at him and at herself for using that term, but what else could she have said?

"Yes, I'm vulnerable to you, but that isn't what I meant. I'm vulnerable to something else."

He let out a sharp breath. "Well, at least I'm glad you're vulnerable to me," he stated, grinning, "that gives me hope."

Aggie didn't respond and in frustration, Luke blurted out, "Is this going to be a guessing game?"

"No, because I'm not going to tell you. You are an intelligent man, Luke. If you try and think about it carefully—and maybe pray about it, you'll figure it out."

"I hardly think I have enough facts to go on, Aggie."

She thought a moment. "Maybe you don't. I guess I had better give you a few more." Looking at her watch, she said, "We had better start back, It's almost time to leave for dinner."

Luke glanced at his watch. "Yes, we better. You can tell me on the way back to Grandmother's."

As Aggie fastened her seat belt, she said, "Thank you, Luke. I have loved seeing the ranch."

"You're welcome, I've enjoyed showing it to you—and I've enjoyed your company. You know, Aggie, I feel such peace when I'm with you. I've felt this from almost the moment I was around you. In fact, I can't imagine life without you, so go ahead with those facts."

Aggie wanted to tell Luke she couldn't imagine life without *him*, but instead released a pent up breath. She paused, trying to decide just how much to tell Luke. She started by telling him about her health.

"After going to several doctors and haunting all of the health food stores, I realized my declining health was the result of something else."

He glanced over at her. "Go on, Aggie, what was it?"

"How do you feel about feminists, Luke?"

He stiffened slightly. "Doris brought me a folder full of newspaper articles about you, Aggie...I guess you..." He stopped.

"Yes. I joined a feminist group when I was in college. Luke, many women who have been terribly wounded by men are drawn to that group. I was one of them."

"I didn't know you actually joined. The newspapers call you a feminist...but you're different, Aggie."

"If you knew some of the other women as you do me, you might say that about them. You can't judge women who join the feminist movement as a *group*. Many are so wounded and confused they join in order to have support from other women who understand what they've gone through. However, as Barry Slocum put it, 'Some feminists are out to destroy the family,' and sadly enough—for the contemporary feminist leaders and many in their group—that is true."

"What does all this have to do with us?"

"It does in a round about way. I got caught up in 'the cause' of women, but it turned out to be *my own cause*. In every case, down deep inside, I was prosecuting my father and Uncle Chester. Because of this, I kept the bitterness, distrust and yes, hate alive in my heart. It nearly destroyed me, Luke. That abortion case shook me up and awakened me to what I was doing."

"How is your health now, Aggie," he asked concerned.

"Thanks to Doris, she told me of an 'old man named, Lucas' who needed a cook."

Luke chuckled. "He needs more than that! But how are you feeling?"

"I stopped the vicious cycle just in time, Luke. I got things straightened out in my life so that the minute I came to work for you, my exhaustion left."

"Hey! Is that good to hear! Go on with your story," he said, turning into his grandmother's driveway.

"That's it, Luke. Those are the facts you need. The ball's in *your* court now."

# Chapter Thirty-Three

On the way home from the restaurant, Aggie thought about the evening. The food was good and everyone had been in a relaxed mood. During the meal Doris, Luke and Amy had reminisced and teased each other. Aggie found out the names of Amy's children, their ages and something about each. They even got Mae to tell stories about herself when she was a little girl.

Doris and Amy informed them that they were returning to Dallas in the morning. Amy planned to visit with Bob, Doris and the boys for a day then return to Pennsylvania. This left Aggie feeling a little sad; as with Doris, she felt a kinship with Amy and wished she lived closer.

When Luke drove into his grandmother's driveway around back and stopped, he whispered to Aggie. "Can I talk to you, Aggie?" She nodded.

"Goodnight, Grandmother, Amy, Doris...I'm going to keep Aggie for a little while."

"Come over and eat breakfast with us, Luke," Amy said.

"I'll do that, sis. Goodnight all."

When the three had gone inside, Luke, rolled down the windows and a pleasantly cool breeze blew in. Luke turned toward Aggie and smiled. "So the ball is in my court. Good. I feel more comfortable with it in my court than if it were in yours. How about a date tomorrow night for dinner. There is something interesting I want to show you."

"Do you want to invite your grandmother?"

"We can get to know each other better if we're alone."

"All right, Luke. What time?"

"I'm going home tomorrow morning and go to work. I think I can pick you up about 6:00."

"All right," she said opening her door.

"Don't go in yet, Aggie...please. I'm not through. I'm going to delegate some things at work so I can take you horse back riding day after tomorrow, that is, if you still want to go."

She smiled. "I'd like that, but I warn you, I'm a novice."

Luke put his arm around her and pulled her as close as the separate seats permitted. "I'll teach you," he said kissing her forehead.

"I need to go in, Luke."

"Why?"

"Because...because I want to visit with Amy and Doris a while before they go to bed."

"All right, I'll let you go in, but first..." he leaned over and kissed her lips. The thought of her dilemma was only fleeting—the sensation of his lips on hers sent her into a state of reckless joy. Her free hand reached up, lacing fingers through the hair on the back of his head, holding him fast as she returned his kiss with passionate abandon.

When they finally pulled apart, Luke held her close, muttering, "Aggie...Aggie, how I love you."

"Luke, dear Luke..." She kissed him on the cheek. "I had better go in."

"Let me come around for you," he whispered, still holding her fast. Reluctantly, he let her go, got out, moved around the van, opened the door and walked her to the back steps.

"Here are your keys. Thanks for the use of your van."

"You're welcome. See you in the morning, Luke. Goodnight." She turned, ran up the steps and went in. Inside, she stood a minute, allowing her heart to resume its softer beat, then headed upstairs.

She was about to step into her room when she heard laughter. Down the hall, light streamed from an open door. Curious, she walked toward it, stopped and peeked in. Mae, in her nightgown was in bed, and Amy and Doris in their nightgowns were curled up on the bed with her.

"Hi," Aggie said.

Their faces lit up when they saw her. "Hey, Aggie, throw on your nightgown and come join the pow wow," Amy said.

"Okay! I'll be right back."

Hurriedly, Aggie disrobed, threw on her nightgown and was soon seated on the big bed with the others. "What's going on here?"

"Girl talk," Doris said. "We didn't expect to see you for a while. How did you manage to leave the presence of my handsome cousin?"

"It was hard, believe me."

"How do you feel about him, Aggie?" Doris asked eagerly.

Aggie, impulsively hugged her. "Thank you, dear friend, for conniving and pushing me to work for Luke."

Doris beamed with happiness. "I guess you know how that makes me feel, don't you?" Aggie nodded, smiling. "Bob is going to get the surprise of his life. He was so skeptical of my match making."

"Ah ha! So it *was* match making!" Aggie exclaimed. "Luke and I suspected it, but didn't know for sure."

"But...how is my match making going?" Doris asked. "I know you are grateful, but I don't feel too secure about it yet."

"I would like to know that too," interjected Amy, still feeling a little anxious for her brother.

Aggie and Mae exchanged glances. "I've told your grandmother my dilemma. I will tell you if you both promise not to tell Luke."

"We promise," they each said.

Aggie, as briefly as possible, told them, then waited a little uneasily for their separate reactions.

With the insight they had gained from Ann's journal they both silently thought it through—and understood.

"Before I comment on this, Aggie, would you tell us about your mother and Beth? What has happened to them?" Amy asked.

When Aggie finished answering Amy's question, a somber mood pervaded the small group. Amy let out heavy sigh. "I'm sorry, Aggie. I can see why it's so important to you that Luke rid himself of his destructive emotions."

Mae, the uncomfortable recipient of Luke's resentments, was silent.

"Doris you know your cousin and Amy you know your brother. Do you think he will realize? And if he does, will he..."

Doris interrupted with, "I don't know. You are brave to leave it up to him, Aggie, men are so obtuse at times."

"I agree with Doris, Aggie, but—this will be good for Luke. He needs to be shaken up a little—and I think Mother would agree."

"I don't know if I *am* brave. It's all I can do to stick with this decision. I love Luke so much."

Doris clapped her hands. "Oh, Aggie, I'm so happy!"

"Why do you love Luke, Aggie," Amy asked pointedly.

Aggie smiled. "I think the first thing I was impressed with was his kindness. Of course he's a difficult man and at times seems to have a short fuse, but I know that's not his basic nature."

"Has he hurt you other than that night when Joy Marshall maliciously informed him of a few things, Aggie?" Amy asked.

"No. He's thought so several times and apologized, but for some reason, I can see through his bluster. He's a very vulnerable man. I love him because he's the most protective man I've ever known. I love him because he's a moral man with strong values and...."

Thank you, Aggie. You needn't go on. I'm grateful you appreciate my brother. I will be praying that things will work out for you both. You are perfect for him, Aggie."

"Ditto," Doris was happy to add.

Feeling deeply grateful for their confidence in her, she replied, "Thank you both." Looking at Mae, she asked, "Do you think I'm right for Luke?"

Mae's heart swelled with joy at being part of this, having the three clustered around her. "I most certainly do," she said, smiling.

"It was down in your parlor, Mrs. Barnes, that Luke told me he loved me for the first time...so your parlor has become a special place for me."

"Have you told Luke you love him, Aggie?" Amy asked.

"No."

"Good. He's had females after him all his life," remarked Amy. "He hasn't had to lift a finger to win any of them."

# Chapter Thirty-Four

After breakfast the next morning, everyone was gathered at Doris' car to say goodbye. Tears were close as Aggie hugged Amy. "Thank you for coming out to help your brother. I don't know what Luke and I would have done if you hadn't come and read your mother's diary. It has made such a difference in our lives."

"In mine, too, Aggie. I hope it won't be long before we see you again."

Luke hugged his sister. "Amy, when are you and Ron going to move west? Pennsylvania is too far away."

"We're hoping to one day."

Luke gave Doris such an exuberant hug, she squealed. "That's a thank you for sending Aggie to me."

"You're welcome, cuz," she grinned. "Remember, you owe me one."

"And I thank you," Aggie whispered, as she hugged her friend.

Amy and Doris hugged and thanked Mae, got into the car and waved goodbye.

When the car was out of sight, Luke turned to Aggie. "I've got to get back to work, but I'll see you at 6:00."

"All right, Luke."

"Bye, Grandmother, thanks for breakfast," he said, getting into his pickup. Soon he, too, turned the bend of the back driveway and was out of sight.

Aggie looked over at Mae. "It feels a little lonely."

"It does. I always feel that way when company leaves. What would you like to do now, Aggie?"

"I'd like to go in and help you clean up the kitchen for starters."

~~~~~~~~~

Aggie hummed as she slipped on a short half slip since her mid-calf skirt had two slits to the knee. She pulled on the flowing skirt of yellow with its large and small dots of white. Next, she slipped over her head the square-necked pullover of yellow cotton knit with side slits, adjusting it to hang evenly over the skirt. The three inches of small cut-out details at the top of the tunic and on the edge of the long sleeves added distinction. She was glad that in her hurry to leave the cottage, she'd grabbed this outfit.

"Aggie!" Mae's voice echoed up the stairs.

Sticking her head out the door she answered, "Yes?"

"Luke's here."

"Thank you. I'll be down shortly."

Aggie, looking at her watch, saw that Luke was ten minutes early. Dashing to the dresser with its large mirror, she put on the finishing touches: square earrings, yellow opal-like with a dangling dew drop of white, then slipped white sandals onto her bare tanned feet. In the mirror, she checked her hair and dabbed on some perfume, took a deep breath to calm her fluttering heart and walked to the stairs. Luke was standing at the bottom watching for her.

"Well, if you don't look like a beautiful butterfly just emerged from her cocoon."

Taken back a moment by the familiar simile, she stood a moment then slowly walked down to him. "Thank you, Luke." She grinned. "You look like pretty cool yourself. I like your olive chinos and ivory shirt."

"Thank *you*," he grinned back, leading her by the arm to the back door of the kitchen.

Aggie, stopped and went over to the table where Mae was sitting and gave her a kiss on the cheek. "Take care, Mrs. Barnes, and we'll see you."

"Aggie, 'Mrs. Barnes' sounds too formal, call me Mae."

Aggie smiled and hugged her. "Thank you, Mae."

Luke's heart softened a little toward the family matriarch. "Goodnight, Grandmother."

"Have a good time you two," she said as they opened the door and stepped out.

Luke opened the car door for Aggie, quickly went around and got in. "Ah, I have you to myself once more." He turned the key and rolled down the windows. "Do you mind, Aggie? It's a warm evening, but not as humid."

"No, I love the windows down."

"You don't mind the wind blowing your hair?"

"No, it easily goes back in place because of a slight natural curl."

"I love your hair, Aggie," he said, reaching over and fingering it. "I love the color, the texture of it—and the style."

She beamed. "Your mother would be pleased that you like it—this is the style she gave me after that horrible haircut I had the barber give me long ago."

He gaped at her, "You don't mean it!"

"I do." She laughed.

"I'm touched that you'd keep it that way."

"Well, you see," she began, a twinkle in her eye, "I decided that it must be a wonderful hair style when Woody, my best friend and baseball buddy, all of a sudden got this goofy expression on his face and asked to walk me to the next class, putting Gayle Harrington into a snit." Luke laughed.

A pleasant interlude of silence fell over them, as they enjoyed the smooth ride of the Lexus and the pleasant smell of the air. They were heading for Austin.

"Did you ever wear that outfit in the courtroom?"

The question was so unexpected, Aggie didn't answer.

"You are the most silent girl I know, Aggie. Are you going to answer my question?"

"Why would you ask that?"

"You know what?"

"What?"

"You sound like a lawyer!"

Aggie smiled. "When you said that before, it made me very nervous since you weren't supposed to know that I was. As I said, why did you ask that?"

"Remember, Doris gave me a bunch of newspaper articles about you and I read something about you looking glamourous in the courtroom."

That's why he said I looked like a butterfly, she thought. "As a matter of fact, I did wear this in the courtroom."

Luke threw back his head and laughed. "How I wish I could have been in the courtroom that day or any day and watched everyone's reaction. I would love to see you in action, too. I bet you won every case—how could anyone resist you?!"

She was so tickled at Luke's wonderful contagious laugh and his total prejudice, she almost got the giggles.

Luke smiled at her, his hand tenderly caressing her neck. "It's good to hear you laugh like that, Aggie. You are far too serious."

"I know. It really isn't my basic nature. Before Beth was hurt, I was extremely carefree and fun loving, so much so, Mama scolded me quite frequently for not taking my schoolwork seriously or for not doing my chores."

Reaching Austin, Luke drove downtown to Congress Street and into the parking lot of the Raddison Hotel, located a mile south of the Texas State Capitol.

When the restaurant hostess greeted them, Luke said, "I have a reservation for two...Barnes."

"Oh yes. I see you've reserved one on the deck outside facing the Congress street bridge." She led them out and Luke seated Aggie.

"This is nice, Luke. I love eating outside."

After they had ordered, Luke settled back in his chair and asked, "What did you do today, Aggie?"

"I had a wonderful day, Luke. How was yours?"

"Busy. What did you *do*?"

"I asked your grandmother if she would show me some albums of her when she was small." Aggie's face turned contemplative. "She looked like a sad child, Luke."

"Remember, Aggie, back then the custom was *not* to smile in pictures."

"I know, but it was her eyes. I asked her about it, but she was evasive, and told me what good people her parents were."

"That's what she's always told us."

"As an attorney, I've learned how to get information out of people so I was a little persistent. Eventually, she told me that her parents were very austere and strict, that they never showed emotion or affection. She said they were very proud of their status in life and in the community and drummed this into her, giving her the feeling that she should be undeviatingly proud of them. She told me it wasn't until your mother left your father for a while that she began to think more objectively about her home life before she married."

"Does that give her an excuse to be dominating and cold with her own family?"

"No, Luke. We are all responsible for our own actions. Believe me, that is certainly one lesson I learned well in my profession, but I ask you, do you think that perhaps your grandmother was emotionally abused?"

The waitress brought their food and they began to eat. After a few moments, Luke said, "To answer your question, I guess it does. I'm sorry to hear that about Grandmother, but she is still responsible for her actions."

"Are you responsible for yours, Luke?"

He looked up from his plate, frowning. "What do you mean by that, Aggie?"

"I meant only what I asked you."

"Of course I'm responsible for my actions. Why would you ask that?"

Already, Luke's attitude toward his grandmother had deflated her happy mood. She'd made no progress by telling Luke about his grandmother's life as a child. "If you think about it carefully you can answer that yourself."

"I'm sure you're referring to my feeling toward Grandmother aren't you?" Taking her annoying silence as an affirmative, he continued, "Grandmother's dominating ways began the day she was married. She dominated her husband. When he died, she dominated and controlled her only child, my father. My father, as a result, became a controlling man. In addition to that she tried to dominate my mother, Amy and me. Her interfering ways caused my mother to leave. Maybe we could have handled it better if she'd shown some affection toward all of us."

"Luke, as I said before and as you yourself agreed, it wasn't your grandmother, it was your father who caused her to leave. But then, if she hadn't, Luke, I never would have known your mother. In fact, I don't know what kind of a person I'd be if I hadn't had her added influence in my life at that time."

Luke's face softened. "I'm glad there is a silver lining to it...and I'm glad to have shared my mother with you. I can't even express how grateful I am to know," his eyes riveted on hers, "that she loved the girl I'm going to—*marry*."

Ignoring Luke's intent, she questioned. "Would we have met, Luke?"

"It's possible that we would have anyway because of the Biedermans. I have to think that somehow I would have found you, Aggie."

They ate in silence for some time and then the waitress came to take their orders for dessert, and cleaned off the plates.

Luke looked at his watch and saw that it was 8:00. "It's almost time, Aggie. Time for what I wanted to show you."

"Oh. That's right, you did want to show me something."

The dessert came and they ate for a while and then Luke said, "There, Aggie look over at the bridge. It is the beginning of the emergence of the Mexican Free-Tailed bats. They reside in the vertical crevices beneath the bridge roadway. The crevices provide ideal temperature and humidity conditions for their maternity colony in which mother bats raise their young. Each mother gives birth to one 'pup.'"

Aggie's eyes were wide with amazement as she watched multiple columns of bats fanning out from under the bridge. "There are so many of them!"

"It is the largest urban bat colony in North America. Nearly 1.5 million."

"This is a wonderful sight, Luke. Thank you for bringing me here."

"The bats provide a valuable environmental service to central Texas by consuming 10 to 15 tons of insects nightly—including mosquitoes and many crop pests such as corn-borer moths."

Aggie laughed. "I can't imagine 10 to 15 tons of insects, can you?"

"I can't."

They continued to watch. When the emergence was over, Aggie said, "Bats are intriguing creatures with such cute faces."

Luke chuckled. "Most women I know wouldn't say that, but then you are one of a kind, Aggie. Shall we go?" She nodded.

In the car on the way home, Luke smiled at Aggie. "Are you ready for horse back riding tomorrow afternoon?"

"I am. Do you have a very tame one for me?"

"Yeah, so tame and old you can hardly get her to move."

"Good."

They rode in silence for some time. Aggie glanced at Luke, longing to tell him she loved him, longing to tell him what he had to do so they could be together.

He looked over at her and touched her cheek with the back of his fingers. "What are you thinking, Aggie?"

"How good looking you are."

"That's nice to hear—anything else you want to tell me?"

"Yes."

"What?"

"That you've passed your grandmother's place."

"I know."

He turned and drove through the gate of his ranch, drove to the house and stopped. Turning off the engine, he got out and went around and opened the door for Aggie. "I thought it would be nice to be alone here for awhile," he said, leading her to the porch and into the house.

Aggie looked around the room and smiled. "I like this room. It's so nice, big and comfortable."

"I like it, too."

Walking over to the grand piano, Aggie rubbed her fingers over it. "Who played this?"

"My mother. She was an accomplished pianist."

"She didn't tell me she played," Aggie said almost to herself. "I've always wanted to play the piano, but we were too poor to have one, let alone pay for lessons. Do you play, Luke?"

"No, Mother tried to interest me in it and gave me lessons, but I wasn't interested, I'm sorry to say. Amy didn't have my stubbornness, so she plays well. This belongs to Amy when she has room for it. Come and have a seat, Aggie."

She walked over to the couch and sat down. Luke promptly sat beside her and gathered her into his arms. "Aggie...Aggie, I can't get enough of you." He leaned down and kissed her hungrily. She returned his kiss with such feeling, Luke pulled away, searching her face. His voice low and ragged, he managed to ask, "Aggie, what are you telling me?"

She pulled out of his arms, stood up and walked away, battling her desire to tell him how she felt.

Luke got up, his jaw rippling with determination, picked her up in his arms and stood her on the large ottoman. "There! It will be easier to kiss you now."

Aggie laughed. Instantly making the decision, she threw her arms around his neck and kissed him so hard and long her heart was almost pounding in her ears. Breathless, she gazed into his surprised face, "Luke Barnes, I love you so fiercely, I don't know what I'm going to do!"

"You...you do?"

"I do."

He laughed, a jubilant, resounding joy-filled sound. He picked her up and exuberantly swung her about, then set her back on the ottoman, his eyes shining with happiness and excitement. "When did you realize you loved me?"

Smiling and thrilled over Luke's reaction, Aggie had to catch her breath. "I've never loved a man, Luke. I didn't know what it *felt* like to love. I don't know when I unconsciously knew, but it suddenly slipped out of my mouth that I loved you when I was talking to Mary the Friday night after I discovered that your mother was my Miss Marks."

Astounded, Luke blurted out, "Back then you realized?"

"Yes."

Remorse replaced his excitement. "And I sent you away by my actions."

"Don't flog yourself over that anymore, Luke. Let's take care of the present."

"All right," he said slowly. "If you remember, before we were interrupted, we were going to spend more time together, so let's take care of the present and begin where we left off."

"I think we have begun tonight, haven't we?" she said, smiling, feeling relieved that she had finally confessed her love. "So...tell me about each of those pictures on the mantle."

# Chapter Thirty-Five

Thursday morning, at Aggie's request, she and Mae continued to look through albums. Aggie found Mae beautiful as a child and as a young woman. On their wedding day, she and her nice looking young husband, Isaac, though unsmiling, looked hopeful for the future. Already Isaac, who was ten years older than Mae, had worked hard and acquired land through the years so when they married, they built a small home on the ranch and began their life together with some financial security.

"How long had you been married when King was born?"

"Six years. I couldn't get pregnant for some reason. Isaac was so thrilled when his son was born. We built this bigger house, hoping for more children. We wanted another child right away, but again I couldn't get pregnant. Little did I know that in three years I would lose my husband."

"How have you managed alone all these years?"

Mae smiled at Aggie. "Just the way you managed alone. At least I had a son—you were totally alone, Aggie."

"But what a responsibility for you to raise a child and run a ranch at the same time."

"It was hard—and very lonely, but I made it. When King got old enough, he took over. He loved ranching."

They finally got to the albums with pictures of Ann and King and their children. Aggie had only one picture of her teacher so she was thrilled with the number Mae had. She almost cried when she saw the first picture of Ann...then Luke as a baby. Aggie felt such tenderness toward Luke as she saw his winsome face grow from babyhood on into childhood—becoming an adorable little boy, then a good looking, but at times morose looking teenager.

After lunch, Aggie slipped into her jeans, ready for horseback riding with Luke. While waiting for him to arrive, she and Mae continued to look through albums. Then they came to Luke's wedding pictures. She saw Lila, a beautiful blonde woman who was totally photogenic, and seemed to pose as if she'd been a professional model. Jealously crept into her heart when she saw Luke's happy, smiling face standing beside his bride, his arm around her.

"I've toyed with the idea of throwing away these pictures," Mae said.

"They disturb me, Mae."

"Lila can't even begin to compare to you, Aggie. If Luke manages to win you, he'll be a very fortunate man."

Aggie leaned her head on Mae's shoulder and wiped away a tear from sundry emotions: gratitude to Mae, worry over Luke's attitude, and fear of losing him. Why does life have to be so complex? she asked herself.

~~~~~~~~~

After Luke picked Aggie up in his truck, and had turned into the gate of his ranch, he drove only a short way when he pulled over and stopped. His arms encircling Aggie, he kissed her. The world seemed to stop; a world of their own enveloped them gloriously—a place where no problems existed. Only their love was a reality.

As they pulled apart, they gazed into each other's eyes. Aggie was first to speak. "I wish I had grown up with you and had known you as a little boy. I know I would have loved you then, too. You would have been my first and only love—as you are now."

Luke's brows rose in surprise. "I am? Where did all this come from?"

"We looked through more albums this morning. You were an adorable little boy, Luke, with the same wonderful smile you have today."

"Really?" he questioned, thoroughly pleased.

"Really."

"You know, that is the way I felt when we were listening to Mother's diary. I found myself wishing I could have known you when you were twelve. I would have given Woody a run for his money, in fact, I would have said—get that goofy expression off your face, she's my girl!" Aggie laughed. "Did he ever get over you, Aggie?"

"After about a week of walking me to classes, I couldn't stand it any longer. I had to break it to him that I only liked him for a baseball buddy."

"Poor guy," Luke said, smiling, giving her a hug just before he pulled back onto the road. Arriving at the ranch house, he drove around back until he reached a corral. Switching off the engine, he turned to Aggie. "There she is, old Sadie, just waiting to take you on your first horseback ride."

She studied the old gray horse as Luke went around to open the door for her. "She looks harmless enough, Luke."

"Go talk to her while I get the saddle out of the shed," he said, grinning.

Aggie did just that, but received no response from the blank looking horse. Luke came back with a saddle and bridle. Throwing the saddle and blanket over the fence, he opened the gate and went in. He patted the horse and put the bridle on. "There you go ol' Sadie, you have a special rider today." Luke threw the blanket on, then the saddle, buckling and cinching it. Aggie watched, fascinated. Leading the horse out of the corral, he grinned. "Now come the lessons. This is the way you get on. You stand with your left side to the horse, grip the saddle horn, put your left foot in the stirrup and swing up like this." He demonstrated. Once up he gave Sadie a kick and as the horse ambled around, Luke showed Aggie how to handle the reins to turn her left, right and to stop.

Aggie was so mesmerized by the way Luke looked in his jeans and boots, his manly movements, his skill, the way he looked on the horse, she could hardly keep her mind on what he was instructing her to do. She was certain she'd never seen a cowboy in the movies that was as irresistibly attractive as Luke.

Luke broke into her thoughts. "Come on, you try it now."

Aggie did as Luke had instructed, but her foot slipped out of the stirrup. She tried again and was surprised how easy it was.

"You're in good condition, Aggie. That's the best mount I've ever seen from a new rider."

Pleased, Aggie smiled. "I hope I do as well trying to guide this horse."

Luke shortened the stirrups for Aggie and explained how to stand in them when the horse trotted.

"All right, give her a kick with both heels."

Aggie kicked, but Sadie didn't move.

"Kick her harder."

"I don't want to hurt her, Luke."

He laughed. "Her hide is so thick, I doubt if you kicked her as hard as you can that you could hurt her."

"Well, I'm not going to kick hard, Luke," she said with finality. Aggie kicked her again and old Sadie began to walk. Successful in getting her to turn left and right, Aggie turned her toward Luke and successfully stopped her.

"Good job, Aggie," he said grinning. "Now practice some more while I saddle Savage."

Aggie watched Luke go to a gate leading to a pasture. He whistled. Savage came trotting up to him, following him to the corral where he waited patiently for Luke to go get the bridle and saddle. When Luke had finished saddling and bridling his horse he got on and came over to her. "I thought you were going to practice, Aggie."

"Oh. I forgot, I was so intrigued with the way Savage came to you and followed you. He acts as though he really likes you, Luke."

Luke laughed. "As much as a horse can like a person—which isn't much. You can never trust a horse."

"You can't?" Aggie asked, surprised. "Well, Savage acts trustworthy and Sadie certainly seems benign."

Luke chuckled. "You've seen too many old cowboy movies. Let's go."

Luke led them to a dirt road around the shed and they rode side by side. "This is so much fun, Luke."

"I'm glad you like it so far. I like to ride because I can get away and be alone and think, and I can go places where a car can't go."

After only a short time, Sadie found something she wanted to eat and stopped, munching on it. Aggie kicked her. She didn't budge.

"Pull her head up with the reins, Aggie."

Aggie pulled, jerked and begged, but to no avail. Luke shook his head. "She knows she has an inexperienced rider on her back and she's taking advantage of you." He eased his horse close to old Sadie and hit her rump with one of his reins. She started trotting. Aggie, startled, grabbed on to the saddle horn, then tried to stand up in the stirrups as Luke had shown her while trying to keep hold of both reins. Finally, Sadie slowed to a walk.

Aggie looked over at Luke, who was smiling. "It's hard to do everything at once," she said breathlessly.

"You're doing great for the first time."

The road led to a cluster of trees giving them some relief from the hot sun. All of a sudden Sadie veered off the road toward a tree, walking so close to it, it scrubbed Aggie's leg, then headed for another tree. No matter how hard Aggie tried to turn her away, she seemed intent on doing it again. This time Aggie lifted her leg up so as not to get scraped.

"Why that old nag is trying to scrub you off!" Luke exclaimed. "Duck, Aggie!"

Aggie ducked just in time to avoid a low limb on the third tree. "Pull on the reins, Aggie. Stop her!" Aggie did as she was told and Sadie stopped, but immediately started to kneel. Luke jumped off his horse like a flash, ran to Aggie and pulled her off the horse just before Sadie lay down completely on her side.

Traumatized, Aggie asked, "Why...why did she do that, Luke?"

"She wanted you off her back." Looking down at the prone horse, he yelled, "You worthless bag of bones!"

Aggie, still a little shaken over the incident, giggled nervously, then laughed. Luke stared at her a moment then started to laugh, too—their laughter escalating until their sides hurt.

"Well so much for my first horseback ride," Aggie said after they had calmed down.

"Yeah! Sorry about this, Aggie. I've never seen her do this. You'll have to practice more but on a different horse next time."

"So what are we going to do now?" Aggie asked, giggling again.

"This," stated Luke as he stepped over to Sadie and slapped her on the backside. The old horse laboriously got up and Luke took her reins. "Hold these, Aggie, while I get on Savage, then hand them to me and you climb on behind me." After Luke mounted, he held out his free hand to Aggie. "Here put your foot in the stirrup and swing your leg over." When she was on, she wrapped her arms around Luke and he headed back home. "Hey," Luke said, "I kinda like it this way."

"Me too," she muttered to his back.

When they got back to the corral, unsaddled the horses and sent them into the pasture, Luke said, "How about going to Bastrop and see some of the historic old homes, then we'll eat at the Mexican restaurant there."

"Sounds fun to me, Luke, and—a little less dangerous," she stated, laughing.

# Chapter Thirty-Six

"When are you coming back home, Aggie?" Luke asked as they were driving back from the afternoon and evening in Bastrop.

"You mean to the cottage?"

"Yes. We can see each other more often that way."

"Wouldn't that be a little awkward to come back and resume cooking for you as I was before?"

Luke smiled at her tenderly. "It wouldn't if you came back as my *wife*."

Aggie looked out the window, thinking how wonderful it had been the last few days with Luke. She couldn't bear to have them end, so she held her breath a moment before she asked the question.

"Would it be all right with you if I stay a while longer with your grandmother?"

Luke was silent, thinking. "You know, Aggie, I felt such gratitude over the news Barry Slocum brought me, I vowed right then not to neglect grandmother as I had and I intend to keep that vow—but it's still hard to be around her. There are too many things in our past to get over quickly, so I would rather you wouldn't stay there any longer."

Aggie's heart sank. This was the answer she dreaded to hear. Doris was right—men are obtuse! A decision already formulating, she asked, "How is Mary, Luke?"

"She's been lonesome with you gone. She left to visit her other son and family this morning. In fact, her son, who lives in El Paso, wants to build a connecting apartment to his home for her and when I told her everything that has transpired since you left, she informed me that she felt this was the time for her to go. Luke looked at Aggie and smiled. "I think she's feeling hopeful for me."

Feeling close to tears, Aggie said, "I'm glad she's been there for you for as long as she has, Luke."

"Me too. I know that with her gone, it may seem even more awkward to come back to the cottage, but hopefully it won't be too long before we..."

"I'll think about it and let you know tomorrow night."

"Let's go to dinner in Austin. Hopefully you'll have your bags packed so we can both drive back home tomorrow night."

Luke turned into his grandmother's driveway and parked in the back as usual. Aggie said quickly, "I see that your grandmother is still up. Since I may be leaving, I need to go in and visit with her a little while before she goes to bed."

"All right," Luke conceded.

On the porch, he leaned down and kissed her. "Goodnight, my little wood nymph. I love you."

"I love you, Luke, so much—it hurts. Thank you for a wonderful day and evening."

"I can hardly wait until tomorrow night, Aggie." He kissed her again and Aggie clung to him tightly a moment, then turned and went in.

Mae looked up from her reading to see a troubled expression on Aggie's face. "You're home early. Is anything wrong?"

"I wanted to visit with you a little tonight before you went to bed. I'll be leaving tomorrow."

Surprise and disappointment flickered over Mae's face. "So soon?"

"How kind of you to say that, Mae. I came to you a total stranger and what do you do? You invite me to stay indefinitely! Thank you." Aggie sat at the table. The troubled look appeared again. "I wish I could stay, but I can't." Quickly putting on a brighter face, Aggie told her of the disastrous horseback ride she had. They both had a good laugh over it. Ending on this happy note, Aggie said, "I guess I had better get to bed because I would like to leave right after breakfast."

"All right, Aggie. Have a good nights sleep."

"You too, Mae." Aggie bent down, kissed her and went upstairs.

~~~~~~~~~~

Aggie prepared for bed, hardly daring to think about her half-hearted decision, a decision not yet fully formed. Turning on the lamp next to the bed, Aggie turned off the overhead light and climbed into bed. She lay there staring at the ceiling, not wanting to think. In spite of it, tears flowed over and down her temples. Knowing this would come, she'd grabbed a handful of tissues, but soon silent sobs choked her, forcing her to a sitting position. Palpable fear shook her body because she knew she'd already made the decision. She couldn't live with Luke's unbending resentment toward his grandmother. Until this moment, she didn't realize just *how* emotionally fragile she was; her own resentments, so recently let go through prayer, had taken their toll.

She had to move out of the cottage tomorrow and go back to Dallas, relieve Sally so she could get another job, then close her law office permanently. Next, she would apply at Southern Methodist University and start on her goal of getting a teaching certificate. The thought of this goal, made so long ago at 12 years of age, which felt so right then, now only depressed her. Anything without Luke in her life, sounded devastatingly empty. "Will Luke figure out what he needs to do before the semester begins? Or will he be so hurt he'll turn bitter and angry, making it impossible for us to ever get together?" she asked aloud. "Luke is so stubborn and unpredictable!" Her heart felt as if it had a hundred pound weight on it.

Aggie got up and moved around the room restlessly. How did Ann Barnes have the courage to do what she did? she asked herself silently. Ann took a chance that her children would not understand and become so hurt they'd become bitter toward their mother—especially Luke. However, Ann did know her husband well. Did she, herself, know Luke that well? The tears began to flow again. She didn't—and the thought of losing him was almost too much to bear. This much she knew—she had to proceed as if it were going to be permanent because Luke's reaction to her leaving so abruptly and without warning was so uncertain.

She asked herself again if leaving Luke was really necessary. She went over it all again in her mind. Why couldn't she come right out and tell him that she couldn't live with his resentments toward his grandmother? If she did, maybe he would change. Hope rose in her heart, and she knelt beside her bed and prayed for this.

The longer she prayed, the stronger she felt about leaving Luke, allowing him to work it out on his own. "Dear God, please give me the strength." Sobs choked her. "Please..."

"I'll keep in touch, Mae and I'll come and see you," Aggie said, as she hugged Mae goodbye the next morning.

"I hope you will, Aggie. It will be lonely without you."

"Thank you for everything, Mae. Being here was healing to my soul," she said, blinking back tears. Aggie really wanted to say, 'you feel like the grandmother I never had,' but she didn't. She just got in the car and waved goodbye.

She felt badly about not telling Mae what she was really planning, but she knew it was best for Mae to be surprised when Luke showed up tonight. She wasn't quite sure why she felt this way, but she did.

On her way to Austin, she dreaded what lay ahead of her—packing and moving out of the cottage—knowing that her heart would break while doing so. She was grateful Mary wasn't there. It would be easier on Mary as well as herself not to have to say goodbye under these circumstances.

~~~~~~~~~

Finally through packing and cleaning the cottage, she drove out of Luke's driveway, feeling numb with grief. She left the keys and a note on the couch in the cottage saying: "Dearest Luke, Leaving like this is the most difficult thing I've ever done in my life. I have to leave because, as I said, the ball is in your court and you haven't picked it up. Until you do, we can't be together. Please, Luke, don't get angry or bitter...just pray for answers. I love you more than I can say." Aggie. "P.S. Your house was locked, so I couldn't get my cooking pans and utensils. I'll have to come back sometime and get them."

The drive back to Dallas was long and lonely. When she drove into the underground parking of the condominium complex, she could hardly keep herself from turning around and heading right back to Austin.

~~~~~~~~~

Luke pulled up the Lexus behind his grandmother's house and ran up the steps, knocked and stepped in. No one was around.

"Grandmother?" he called out as he walked through the dining room to the stairs.

"I'm in here, Luke," he heard his grandmother's voice in the front room.

Luke found her seated on the couch looking through albums. "Hi. Aggie said you both looked through those."

"We did. What are you doing here, Luke?"

Surprised at the question, he said, "I'm here to pick up Aggie."

Mae got up and came toward him. She looked puzzled. "She left early this morning, Luke."

"She left? Where...where was she going?"

"You know, she wasn't clear about that, I assumed that she was going back to your place."

Luke frowned. "She knew I was coming to talk about her returning to the cottage. She said she'd let me know tonight. Why would she leave like that without letting me know?"

"I don't know, Luke. Maybe she wanted to surprise you."

"Maybe that's it," he mumbled distractedly. "I guess I'll go home and see." He turned and walked toward the back door and Mae followed him.

"See you later, Grandmother," he muttered as he went out.

Luke frowned as he drove toward Austin. This wasn't like Aggie, he thought. Maybe she tried to reach me at the office and someone forgot to give me the message. This thought lifted his spirits somewhat, but the uneasiness persisted.

As he turned into his driveway and turned the bend to his garage, he could see that Aggie's van was not under the carport of the cottage. His heart filled with fear. What if something's happened to her? Unlocking the kitchen door from the garage, he stepped over to the key hook, pulled off the one to the cottage, ran back out and on up to Aggie's door. He unlocked it, threw the door open wide and looked around. Aggie's books and computer were gone; she had come and moved out! His heart hammering against his chest in anxiety and confusion, he noticed the note on the couch. Stepping over quickly, he grabbed it and read it, then read it several more times, hoping to find a clue he'd missed.

He sat down heavily, trying to think. Why would she do this? She said she'd let me know tonight if she was coming back here to stay! Was this the answer she intended to give him—move out without an explanation?! What was this business about the ball being in his court? Didn't that mean he was to continue on his campaign arranging things to do together? Suddenly angry, he blurted out, "What in the heck could it mean other than that? What does she expect me to be—a mind reader?!" He got up and went into the small kitchen and into the bedroom. Opening up the closet door, he found it empty. "Damn!"

Walking quickly out of the cottage, he ran back to his house and picked up the kitchen phone. He dialed his grandmother's number.

"Hello," Mae's strong voice came over the wire.

"Grandmother, this is Luke. Aggie has packed up all her things and has gone!"

Mae's heart plummeted clear to her toes. She'd been hoping that she and Luke would come to an understanding that would ease Aggie's fears, but it was clear they hadn't. "Do you think she's gone back to Dallas, Luke?"

"How in the heck would I know? I take it you didn't know she was going to do this then?"

"No, I didn't. Did she leave you a note?"

"Yes. I'll read it to you and see if you can understand it." When he finished reading it, he asked, "Does that make sense to you?"

"Had she ever said that to you before?" Mae hedged.

"Yes, but I thought it meant I had to go on with what I had planned before."

"And what is that, Luke?"

"Court her, as you might say, Grandmother, which means spend more time together—get to know each other."

"What are you going to do, Luke?"

"I don't know...I don't know....I've got to think. Talk to you later. Goodbye."

After Luke's call, Mae sat down at the kitchen table. Placing her elbows on the table, she covered her face. Why hadn't Aggie told her what she was going to do? she wondered miserably. She'd confided everything else, why not this? It would seem she'd given up on Luke—

or was she trying to wake him up as Ann had King? "Oh, Ann and King, if only you were here now. You'd know what to do...how to help Luke."

Mae sat there until dark thinking. She knew she was in the middle of this problem between Luke and Aggie—but what could *she* do? Slowly, she got up and started upstairs deciding that there was *nothing* she could do. Her legs felt heavy and she was winded by the time she'd reached the landing. Breathing heavily for a few moments, she walked on slowly toward her bedroom. The old feelings of loneliness and despondency were back. Gone was the happiness she'd felt when Amy, Aggie and Doris were here.

~~~~~~~~~~

How could Aggie do this to him? Luke wondered. He sank into a chair in the family room. Surely she knew what he must have suffered when his mother left and now *she* leaves him—and without a real explanation—and after telling him she loved him! It didn't make sense! Why? Why?! He'd been certain that Aggie was one woman he could trust, but apparently not, he thought bitterly. His anger sustained him for some time, but that night in the loneliness of his bedroom his anger gave way to grief. The grief he'd felt over Lila was a drop in the bucket compared to the grief he felt over Aggie. How could he live without her?

Several hours later, he got into bed and fell into a deep and exhausted sleep. He awoke early the next morning depressed—not wanting to face the day. Impulsively, he called information for Aggie's phone number in Dallas only to find out it was unlisted.

He dialed Doris. She answered in her usual cheerful voice.

"Doris, this is Luke."

"Oh hi, Luke...what's up?" she asked eagerly.

Trying to sound casual, he asked, "Aggie has returned to Dallas and I was wondering if you could give me her unlisted phone number."

"I can, but why did she return so soon?"

"I don't know, Doris. She left without telling me she was leaving and without an explanation except for a short ambiguous note."

Doris frowned, thinking. "Would you mind reading it to me, Luke?"

He did and waited for Doris' reaction. She understood the note, but had promised Aggie she wouldn't say anything to Luke. Instead she said, "That is ambiguous, Luke. You have no idea what it means?"

"Not a clue."

"Are you all right, Luke?" she asked, concerned by the tone of his voice.

"No. I'm not all right, Doris. I can't live without Aggie."

Doris gave him Aggie's office number and home phone. "Her secretary, Sally, is there taking her calls Monday through Friday until Aggie decides what to do about her law practice. Call both numbers and I'll try also, then let's get back in touch."

"Okay, Doris, thanks. Talk to you later."

The minute he hung up from Doris, Luke called Aggie's home phone. A recorded voice from an operator said, "This number has been temporarily disconnected."

It was Saturday; he couldn't call Aggie's office until Monday! What was he going to do with himself until then? The phone rang and he quickly picked it up.

"Luke, this is Doris. I tried Aggie's home phone and it's still disconnected."

"That's what I found out, also. And I can't call the office until Monday. Do you think you could run over to Aggie's apartment to see if she's there?"

"I would do that in a minute, Luke, but Bob's father had to be taken to the emergency room and his mother is frantic. She wants us to come over immediately and stay the weekend if needed."

"Oh." Luke was so disappointed he had a hard time feeling concern for Bob, but managed to say. "Tell Bob I'm sorry. I hope his father recovers soon. I'll talk to you later."

"All right, Luke. The minute I get back, I'll go over to Aggie's condominium. Try not to worry, Luke, I'm sure she's all right. And I have to believe things will work out for you two."

"I just want to know if she's all right—but as far as things working out between us, I don't know. It was a low blow for her to walk out like that without any explanation!"

"I understand, Luke, but still..."

"I'll talk to you later, Doris," he interrupted. "You and Bob better get over to Fort Worth. Goodbye."

# Chapter Thirty-Seven

Relieved to be going to work Monday morning after suffering through the weekend, Luke dove into his work at a feverish pitch. At 10:00, he picked up the phone and called Aggie's office in Dallas.

"Law office of Agnes McBride, Sally speaking."

"Sally, has Miss McBride returned to her office yet?"

"No sir. She is on a leave of absence."

"Sally, this is Luke Barnes. She's been in Austin working for me and she left last Friday to return to Dallas. Has she contacted you?"

"Oh. Hello, Mr. Barnes. Miss McBride called about an hour ago. She'll be here in about a half hour. Shall I have her call you?"

"No, thank you, Sally. I just wanted to know if she had returned safely." Luke hung up the phone with mixed feelings: relief that she was all right, and hurt that she hadn't let him know she was leaving, let alone that she'd arrived safely!

He stared unseeing at the work on his desk. The confusion and hurt were so intense, he couldn't think. Slowly, he came to a decision. Somehow he was going to have to put Aggie and her actions out of his mind for awhile. He needed time and space so he could look at it a little more objectively—if that was possible.

A clap of thunder startled him, then the rain started. He got up and looked out the window at the rain. Jagged lightning split the black clouds then another thunderclap shook the windowpane. The thunderstorm took his mind away from Aggie momentarily and he was able to accomplish a little work.

~~~~~~~~~~

When Aggie walked into her office, Sally greeted her exuberantly.

"It's good see you, too, Sally."

"Boy, it's good to have another person in this office, Aggie! It's a little lonely working alone."

"I'm sure it is, Sally, but it won't be for long."

"Mr. Barnes called to see if you had arrived. I asked him if he wanted you to call him and he said no that he just wanted to know if you had arrived safely."

Aggie closed her eyes briefly to get hold of herself, then forced a smile. "That's just like him. He's a very caring employer."

"Are you back to open your office, Aggie?"

"No...not yet at least." At the moment she wasn't emotionally prepared to discuss it further. "I came in to tell you that I'm in town, but I have some things to do. I'll let you know if and when I decide for sure what I'm going to do so you can interview for another job."

"All right, Aggie, but potential clients keep calling."

"Are you referring them as I told you to?"

"Yes, Aggie, but many of them are waiting for you to return. We've got to give them an answer one way or another."

"I know, but I *did* leave Mr. Barnes' employ sooner than I'd intended, so I have some time. I have to leave now as I have some things to do. By the way, Sally, if my friend Doris Biederman calls, tell her that I can't talk with her yet—that I'll call her when I can. Tell her that I think she'll understand why."

Sally wrote it down. "All right, Aggie."

Heading out to the parking lot to get her van, she had the urge to go talk to Barry. She resisted it and headed toward the University to check on everything she needed to know in order to enroll at the beginning of the next semester.

It felt like deja vu for Aggie as she determined to go on with her life. She had steeled herself to go on after Beth died and again when Mama died. Now it was much more difficult, but somehow she managed to dispassionately go about starting the day, benumbed—afraid of feeling. She had learned how to keep her fears bottled up quite well through the years. How long she could keep this up she didn't know, but felt any moment the damn would burst irreparably. She'd have to take life hour by hour, hoping she could endure without Luke—if it came to that.

It had taken Doris most of the morning to monitor her boys with their chores and see that they were content in their playing. Finally at 11:00 A.M. she seated herself at the kitchen table, dialed Aggie's condo and found it still disconnected. Next she dialed her office. Sally told her Aggie was in town and then gave her Aggie's message.

After hanging up the phone, Doris remained sitting—thinking. She understood the message. Apparently, Luke had expressed his resentment toward his Grandmother in a way that had discouraged Aggie to the point of taking the action she did. Doris' brows knit in concern. "What is going to happen with these two? They just have to get together! They have to," she whispered to herself.

She realized she needed to call Luke. She wished that Aggie hadn't asked her not to tell Luke what the problem was, but then, hadn't she herself asked Aggie to keep a secret from Luke? Hesitantly, she picked up the phone and dialed Luke's office.

A curt "hello" came over the wire.

"Luke, did you reach Aggie?"

"Oh, hello, Doris. I called her office and found out she was going to be there in a half hour."

"Did you leave a message to have her call?"

"Of course not!" he exclaimed a little too vehemently. "She wouldn't call me back if I had. She doesn't want to talk to me or she wouldn't have gone off as she did."

"I guess you're right, Luke. I called her office and she left a message with Sally for me. The message was that she couldn't talk to me yet, that she'll call me when she could."

"Why in the heck is she being so damn mysterious?!"

"Luke," Doris began softly, "didn't her note tell you she loved you and suggested that you pray for answers?"

"Pray for answers?!" he exploded. "I don't know what answers I'm praying for!"

Doris was silent. She knew Luke so well. She knew it was useless to discuss it when he was is this kind of a mood. Also, she knew Luke needed time to get hold of himself so he could think more rationally.

"Doris?"

"I guess I'll just have to wait until she calls me, Luke. I'm sorry that this has happened, that you are hurting. I wish I could help."

"Thanks for calling, Doris. How is Bob's father?"

"He's fine. They thought it was a heart attack, but it only turned out to be a mild attack of angina."

"I'm glad to hear that. Well, I've got to get back to work, Doris. Talk to you another time."

Doris hung up the phone and covered her face, muttering, "Maybe Bob was right when he said matchmaking was risky business."

Just as Luke had hung up the phone, it rang again. Irritated he answered it.

"Luke, this is your grandmother. Have you heard from Aggie?"

"No." He told her of his call to Aggie's office and then of his conversation with Doris.

"Will you call me, Luke, if you hear from her?"

"I will...but don't hold your breath. After the way she left, I don't know if I want to hear from her."

"You don't mean that, Luke."

"At the moment, I do."

# Chapter Thirty-Eight

Sunday afternoon, August 1st, Luke restlessly walked up to the cottage and into the woods behind it, remembering when he went hunting for Aggie that first Sunday she was here. He couldn't believe that it had been only a little over three weeks since Aggie left. It felt like three months! He'd run the gamut of emotions during these weeks: first, anger and bitterness, next deep hurt and confusion. Then he had made a rash decision to go to Dallas and confront her, but stubbornness came to his rescue—today he was suffering the most intense loneliness he'd ever experienced.

His Grandmother had called him at least three times a week checking on him and asking him if he'd called Aggie or if she'd called him. He'd never known her to be so solicitous of his welfare and so upset over what he was going through.

~~~~~~~~~~

Aggie walked the path along Turtle Creek Sunday afternoon. It was hot and humid and the trees were filled with the deafening songs of cicadas. Her heart was so heavy with sadness and loneliness she felt as though it was literally weighing her down physically. Her feet felt like lead. She'd asked herself over and over why she should expect Luke to come after her—a changed man. Nevertheless, try as she would to plan life without Luke, she couldn't squelch her hope, her longing.

She had registered for the Fall semester at the University. The first day of school would start soon. She dreaded it. She dreaded getting up each morning. To keep busy, and earn some money, she had offered her services to the two attorneys to whom Bob had recommended she turn over her cases. They both were grateful to get her as a consultant for several of their abuse cases and they were paying well for her advice. She hadn't formally closed down her practice as yet. Sally was still there, so she had soon to make a firm decision. For the first time in her life, she was indecisive about everything. She vacillated over the decision to apply at the University and the decision to be a consultant to the attorneys. Luke had made her life worth living, without him it wasn't. It was as simple as that. How tempted she was to get in the car and go to Luke and beg his forgiveness for leaving like she had! When she'd thought about it seriously, she prayed about it, and again the strong feeling came to her that she had done the right thing—painful as it was.

~~~~~~~~

Mae walked slowly, restlessly, through her large lonely house, wondering how Luke was, how Aggie was. She hadn't dreamed their separation would go on this long. They loved each other very much and if any two people were meant to be together, it was Aggie and Luke! Each day her agony increased because she was in the middle of it—no, to be totally honest, she was the *cause* of it.

Something was nagging at her, something pressing...something urgent. What was it? she asked herself. She hadn't prayed very often in her life. Her father wore religion like a fine cloak to be admired, yet he was an unloving, an unfeeling father to her—turning her away from religion and all the empty prayers which were uttered from his lips.

When King and Ann were killed, her grief had turned to anger toward God. Bitterly, she felt he was truly the harsh, punitive God her father taught her about and had warned her she should obey. However, a few times through the lonely, hard years, she had in desperation knelt in supplication to the God she didn't really know and had miraculously found solace. Maybe she needed to pray now for Luke and Aggie—and herself. Now, in the front room, she knelt at the chair and prayed for the first time in several years. As soon as she stood up, she knew what was nagging at her. It was something she'd forgotten all about. Why this felt important now, she didn't know.

She walked to the stairs and took the steps with more energy than she'd had for weeks. Entering the bedroom, she went over to the big cedar chest at the foot of the bed. She lifted the lid and gazed at the old crochet-edged pillow cases her grandmother had given her as a new bride. They had turned yellow with age, but she couldn't bear to part with them. She loved her grandmother. Her visits were infrequent because of the distance she had to travel and because, Mae felt, her father disliked his mother-in-law.

She carefully lifted the pillow cases exposing the crocheted table-cloth beneath, also made by her grandmother. Lifting layer by layer, she found *it*—buried deep in the treasured linens. She picked it up and stared at it, wondering why she felt such urgency to find it—to retrieve it from the place she'd put it over five years ago.

With it in her hand, she walked back down stairs and went into the front room to her comfortable chair by the window. She sat looking at the book, remembering when she first found it.

*When she had answered the doorbell and found a neighbor with the sheriff on her front doorstep, her heart sank with a sudden foreboding. She invited them inside and they broke the news of the plane crash. She was in such a state of shock and grief, the neighbor offered to have his wife come and be with her. She refused and thanked him. After they left all she could think about was getting over to Ann and King's house almost believing she would find them there—finding that it was just a horrible mistake. She got in her car and drove over. Entering the unlocked kitchen door she called out to them. Wandering through the house, the terrible truth began to sink in. She realized she had to break the news to Amy, married and living in Pennsylvania and to Luke, living in a condo in Austin.*

*Finding herself in the big front room of the ranch house, she was drawn to Ann's piano. Absently her fingers trailed across the keys. It was then she saw the book sitting on one corner of the piano top. Picking it up she saw a note sticking out of the pages. Removing the note she read: 'Appointment at Sandra's home—2:00 P.M. Friday.' Ann had spoken of Sandra, but she didn't know her last name. Mae remembered thinking in her benumbed state, today is Wednesday, the appointment must be this Friday. Ann will miss that appointment. She was amazed at how practical and mechanical her mind was working at a time like this.*

*Without thinking, she walked out of her son's home with the book in her hand and drove back to her own home. In the kitchen, she sat down at the table, trying to get her thoughts together enough to make the calls to Amy and Luke...and to Ann's sister Edie in Fort Worth.*

*She stared at the book in her hand and opened it. It looked like some kind of religious book. She knew that Ann read the Bible on a regular basis, so what was this book? Suddenly the thought of the Bible turned her angry. God had just dealt her a terrible blow. She didn't want to have anything to do with this book! Getting up, she turned to throw it in the garbage, but stopped short, realizing it wasn't her right. It was Amy and Luke's prerogative to do whatever they chose with the book. For now, she wanted it out of mind, out of sight!*

*She quickly left the kitchen and went upstairs to her bedroom. Opening the cedar chest, she buried it deep. Later, when she could think more clearly, she would give it to Amy or Luke.*

*The funeral had been a private one attended only by the immediate family: Amy with her husband and children, Doris with her family, Edie, Jim, and their boys, Luke, Mae and Mary with her children.*

*Afterward Mae cut herself off from everyone, rebuffing attempts by various individuals and groups. One, she recalled, had been particularly persistent—a man accompanied by a woman and two young men in dark suits—who had tried to explain that they were from the church... She had cut them off, shutting the door in their faces. In her bitterness, the last thing she wanted was platitudes from a pastor or minister or whoever they were.*

MAE marveled that she'd forgotten all about the book. Why she needed to get it out now, she had no idea. The book fell open to page 20. Randomly, she began reading:

> "And the angel said unto me: Behold the Lamb of God, yea, even the Son of the Eternal Father! Knowest thou the meaning of the tree which thy father saw?
>
> And I answered him, saying: Yea, it is the love of God, which sheddeth itself abroad in the hearts of the children of men; wherefore, it is the most desirable above all things.
>
> And he spake unto me, saying: Yea, and the most joyous to the soul.
>
> And after he had said these words, he said unto me: Look! And I looked, and I beheld the Son of God going forth

among the children of men; and I saw many fall down at his feet and worship him.

And it came to pass that I beheld that the rod of iron, which my father had seen, was the word of God, which led to the fountain of living waters, or to the tree of life; which waters are a representation of the love of God; and I also beheld that the tree of life was a representation of the love of God."

Mae stopped reading. She didn't understand it completely because she hadn't started at the beginning of the text—but somehow, she understood enough to whisper, "Could God be the *loving* God this seems to indicate?" She wanted to believe it—she wanted to believe that God loved her in spite of the mistakes she'd made—especially with Luke. Slowly, a warmth filled her breast until it became a burning within. Mae, a woman who had allowed only a few tears in her adult life, now let them flow freely because she knew without a doubt—that *God was a loving God* and that He loved *her*!

She had no idea how long she sat there savoring the feeling of peace—peace she had never felt before. What was it about this book that had drawn her to it—a book she knew nothing about, whose cover and pages were not, in themselves, remarkable?

Why then her reaction to it? Could it be this simple? Could a few short verses really have this effect upon her? If so...why?

At last she glanced down at the book in her lap and noted that the corner of one page, near the center of the book, had been turned down. Opening to that page her eyes fell on verses which had been under-lined:

"And now, my brethren, I wish from the inmost part of my heart, yea, with great anxiety even unto pain, that ye would hearken unto my words, and cast off your sins, and not procrastinate the day of your repentance;

But that ye would humble yourselves before the Lord, and call on his holy name and watch and pray continually, that ye may not be tempted above that which ye can bear, and thus be led by the Holy Spirit, becoming humble, meek, submissive, patient, full of love and all long-suffering.

Having faith on the Lord; having a hope that ye shall receive eternal life; having the love of God always within your hearts, that ye may be lifted up at the last day and enter into his rest."

The last line of the first verse, burned into her heart ...*not procrastinate the day of your repentance*. Gone was the revulsion she'd felt growing up as her cruel father constantly railed on her to repent of sins she didn't know she'd committed. Pondering this for some moments, she felt a stirring need to...to *repent* of her actions which had caused so much pain to her family.

Stiffly she knelt again beside the chair. Filled with emotion, she began hesitantly. "Dear God in Heaven, please forgive me—forgive me!" She couldn't go on, for sobs of Godly sorrow racked her body.

It was sometime before her sobs of remorse subsided, but as they did, a feeling of peace and joy filled her heart and soul. "Thank you. Dear God...thank you."

Pulling herself up and seated once more in the chair, she clutched the book to her bosom knowing that she had to read it from cover to cover. And when she had, she would tell Amy and Luke about it.

Closing her eyes, she smiled. Suddenly, Luke's grief-stricken face appeared in her mind, and she knew—knew with a certainty she needed to ask *Luke's* forgiveness also! Standing up, she walked as quickly she could to the phone in the kitchen and dialed Luke's number.

His hello was hopeful, but when he heard his grandmother's voice, she could hear the disappointment.

"Luke, I need to see you tonight."

"Tonight? It's after 8:00. Can't it wait?"

"No, Luke, it can't. It's very important."

"What do you want to see me about?"

"I can't tell you on the phone, Luke. I have to have you here in person."

Luke felt irritated—but there was something in his grandmother's voice that caught his attention. "All right, Grandmother, I'll be there as soon as I can."

Mae felt restless and anxious while waiting for Luke. What was she going to say to him exactly? How? Walking around in the kitchen, she repeatedly looked through the back door for him. Finally, she sat down at the table, closed her eyes and prayed for help, knowing how much she needed His help if she were ever going to bridge the gulf between herself and her grandson.

When Luke opened the back door of his grandmother's kitchen, he saw that she was sitting there calmly, a serene expression on her face. Surprised to find her like this, he said, "You certainly don't look like you need any help, Grandmother."

"Oh, but I do, Luke, and I need it from you. Let's go into the front room to talk. It's more conducive to what I have to say."

Luke followed his grandmother. When they had seated themselves, his grandmother on the couch, he on the overstuffed chair next to the couch, he said, "Okay, shoot."

She smiled at him, then her face became serious. "Would you please tell me, Luke, why you harbor resentments toward me?"

Luke, surprised by the question, was speechless for a moment. "What makes you think I have resentments?"

"Luke, let's be honest with each other. I've known how you've felt ever since you were a teenager. I just need to hear 'the why' from your own lips."

"Well," he began hesitantly, not wanting to hurt her, "it seems you know why."

"I think I know, but as I said, I need to hear it from *you*."

"Why? I really would rather not get into it."

"Luke, I can't even express how important it is to me right now."

"Why now? Why after all these years?"

"I will say this much. I've just had a special experience this afternoon—something I want to share with you, but not now...later."

He studied his grandmother, very curious about this experience, noting that her demeanor had changed—in someway *she* had changed. He took a deep breath and began, "I imagine it was hard on you to have to take over raising my father and running the ranch after Grandfather died. I guess that's why you became..."

"Luke, don't soften it for me. Just say it right out."

"All right. I resented you dominating my father, I resented you dominating me. I resented you interfering in Mother and Father's lives."

"Is that past tense I'm hearing, Luke?"

Luke, his arms leaning on his thighs, fingers laced together, stared at the floor. "No. It's present tense." He looked up at her. "Mother kept telling me to love you and to forgive you, but every time I did, you'd do it again." He looked down and muttered, "It just went on too long, it's too deep. I can't seem to let go of it."

"I'm sorry, Luke." Mae watched him. The apology didn't seem to affect him. "Luke, look at me."

He sat back in the chair and looked at her, his face troubled.

"Luke," Mae's chin quivered, tears blurred her eyes, "I know I've hurt you and caused your mother and father pain. I can't tell you how much I've suffered over it, but for some reason I couldn't express my remorse over it—until now." She fought for control and finally gaining some semblance of it, she continued. "It took Aggie coming into my life and watching you both together and seeing your happiness—and then seeing your grief..." She couldn't go on.

Luke was shocked and disbelieving at what his grandmother was saying; at her very real emotion. He'd never heard her express remorse nor had he ever seen her express much emotion and, now all he could do was sit there immobilized, unable to respond or to comfort her. He only stared at her—waiting for her to get control of herself.

Wiping her tears away, Mae looked deep into the troubled eyes of her grandson. "Please, Luke, please forgive me." The dam broke. All the tears she'd held back for years came out in a flood. She covered her face and sobbed.

His grandmother had just said the three most healing words in the English language—*please forgive me,* breaking down his wall of pride and resentment. He went over to his grandmother and took her in his arms. Her sobs touching his heart, he cried with her. At last he was able to say, "Thank you, Gram, thank you." In a sudden rush, like a cleansing fire, the past was gone. "I...I do forgive you. Please forgive *me* for my resentment of you."

# Chapter Thirty-Nine

Mae and her grandson had hugged a tearful goodbye with a promise to see each other soon. The catharsis of repenting and receiving forgiveness was so great that Mae could only sit at the kitchen table and thank the God she was beginning to know. She thanked Him for his kindness and mercy—and for His love.

She finally realized she needed to do the same thing with Amy as she had done with Luke. She looked at the kitchen clock and saw that it was too late tonight. Getting up, she turned off the kitchen light and walked toward the stairs, her feet lighter—the burden gone. Tomorrow, she would call Amy.

Driving home, Luke spoke to the unhearing ears of his mother. "You would be proud of me and Gram tonight, Mother." He blinked back the tears that momentarily blinded his view. The heavy burden he'd been carrying for years had been lifted by the actions of his grandmother, and himself—but mostly by divine help, he knew. He whispered a prayer of thanks.

Once home, preparing for bed, his thoughts turned to Aggie. Gone, also, was the stubbornness he felt about going to see her, gone was the hurt and bitterness. All he could feel now was intense love for her and a determination to go after her and never let her get away from him—ever again. He would, somehow, find out why she left and what she meant by the ball being in his court. But, he decided, it would have to be with God's help, for he knew it was only with His help that he and his grandmother were able to mend fences.

With this decision in mind, he knelt and prayed. Afterward, he turned off the light and got into bed and lay there planning. He had to go to Dallas tomorrow no matter how much he had to do at work. He had to see Aggie tomorrow! The first thing in the morning, he would call Doris to get Aggie's office and home addresses—and bum a room for at least one night—maybe more.

~~~~~~~~~~~

At 2:00 Monday afternoon, Aggie drove into the underground parking of the condominium complex, feeling exhausted. It had been a grueling morning as she consulted with one of the attorneys on a tragic abuse case. Lunch had been sent up, the meeting continuing on through the lunch hour, ending only twenty minutes ago.

Luke, having parked in the guest parking, saw Aggie's van drive in. The guard had already been alerted by Doris that Luke, her cousin would be arriving, and to let him walk into the underground parking area.

Aggie pushed the elevator button and waited. A man stepping beside her, asked, "May I ride up with you, Ma'am?"

Startled, she looked over at him. It was Luke! Her heart lurched with both shock and joy. "Luke! Wh...what are you doing here?"

"I came to get you and never let you go again," he stated firmly, his eyes burning into hers.

Aggie sucked in her breath. Oh, if only that were true, she thought. She just stared at him. Words wouldn't come. The elevator opened and they got on. They ascended in silence; getting off at the fourth floor, he walked with Aggie to her door, waiting while she unlocked it. Luke held it open for her to enter and followed her in.

Still silent, Aggie led him into the front room. He looked around and smiled. "This looks like you, Aggie, feminine and charming."

"Thank you, Luke," she mumbled. "Have you had lunch?"

"Yes, thank you. Have you?"

She nodded. "Please have a seat, Luke."

They both sat down, Aggie in the chair, Luke on the couch. They faced each other. "How are you, Aggie?"

"I'm fine. How are you, Luke?"

Luke chuckled. "This is some stimulating conversation we're having, Aggie. But...to answer your question—I'm great! In fact I'm better than great. I'm marvelously happy because I'm here with you."

Aggie felt off balance, tentative. She couldn't say anything for a moment. "I...I can't believe you are sitting here, let alone saying that after I...I..."

"After you left me like you did without an explanation?"

"Yes and since it's been over three weeks..."

"Three weeks and two days, to be exact," he finished.

"Do you know why I left?" she asked hopefully.

"I don't have a clue, Aggie."

"You don't?" she asked, disappointed.

"How could I?"

"I thought I gave you a broad enough hint, Luke."

"Hint?" He laughed. "You gave me a hint?"

"I did, but I see that Doris is right; men *are* obtuse!" She smiled grimly. "I can see that I have a lot to learn about men."

"I'll give you a lifetime to learn—on *me*," he said, grinning.

Aggie smiled at his charming remark, resisting the overwhelming urge to go throw her arms around him and never let go. "You really didn't get the hint?"

"No. Let me educate you, Aggie. Men don't catch hints. You need to be more direct with a man. We *are* an obtuse bunch."

"Then...then why are you here?"

"Because I love you too much to let you get away."

Aggie got up and walked to the window, looked out, then turned to face him. "But Luke, if you didn't get my message, the problem still exists."

"What problem?"

"The one that made me leave," she stated in exasperation.

"Aggie, my darling," he said standing up and taking her hand and leading her to the couch and gently pushing her down, "sit here beside me." He sat down and took her in his arms and held her tightly. "Oh, Aggie, Aggie, how I've missed you. How good it feels to have you in my arms again."

"Me too," she muttered, "but..."

He covered her mouth with his lips not wanting to hear any 'buts.' She melted into his arms unable to do anything but return his kiss, releasing all the love she'd painfully suppressed. They parted. Luke's chest heaved as he gazed into her eyes.

Something was different about Luke, she thought, feeling out of breath. She had expected an angry, bitter Luke, but he was far from that.

"Aggie," he began, his voice husky with emotion, "I need to tell you some things—important things, so open your heart and listen carefully." He took hold of her hand and held it with both his. "During these long three weeks and two days I've been away from you, I have been going over all those newspaper articles that Doris gave me. I've read them over many times hoping I'd find a clue telling me why you left. I didn't find one, but as I reread them last night, a sentence stood out, like a neon light, giving me profound personal insight I didn't have before."

Aggie, eyes anxious, asked, "What, Luke?"

"It was only last night late that the realization came to me. In one of the articles it described how you dressed in the court room. Then it said: 'Agnes McBride looked as out of place as an innocent and colorful butterfly fluttering around in a gray, winter garden.' Last night, I realized that *you* were a *butterfly* in the '*winter*' of my mother's heart. When she was alone and away from her family you gave her joy. You inspired her with added courage to go back to her family and do the things she needed to do for them. You entered the '*winter*' of my grandmother's heart, succoring her, giving her the love and warmth that *I* had denied her. And last, but far from least, you were the innocent, beautiful *butterfly* that fluttered so gently into the *winter* of *my* heart, renewing my hope that I could at last have a marriage and family as I have always dreamed of having."

Aggie swallowed past the lump in her throat. "How beautiful, Luke. Thank you," she said softly. After a moment of silence, she asked. "You mentioned your grandmother. How is she?"

"Something amazing happened last night, Aggie. Grandmother called me about 8:00 telling me that she had to see me...that it was very important. Because of the hour, I really didn't want to go, but there was something in Gram's voice that...well...I knew it was important to go see her." Luke related everything that had transpired between them. Aggie's questions stimulating his memory, he recalled every detail of one of the most memorable evenings of his life. He ended with, "It was because of this...this humbling experience, that I realized that all my stubborn pride, anger and bitterness were gone... even the hurt over you leaving. All I could feel was my deep and ardent love for you, Aggie and my determination not to let you out of my life."

Aggie clutched her chest and laughed. She stood up and walked a few feet away and turned back to him, now alternately crying and laughing. "Don't you see, Luke," she said stepping over to him and kneeling in front of him, taking his hands in hers, "the problem is solved! My beloved, Luke, it's solved!" She kissed his hands, leaving tears on both. Though his face mirrored her happiness, it also reflected bewilderment.

Aggie laughed, got up and sat beside him, explaining what the problem had been—why she had left—all the while studying his face until she saw some signs of understanding.

In spite of this enlightenment, he shook his head. "I see that you did *hint*, Aggie, but please, in the future be very direct with me," he pleaded, smiling. Then, a grave expression came over his face as he said, "I can relate a little now, Aggie, to the struggles that you have gone through to reach the point where you could let the hate go...the feelings toward your father and your uncle. Grandmother taught me a great deal last night. I hope I'll always remember the lessons I learned—for your sake, for both our sakes." After a moments pause, "What I want to know now, Aggie, is where are *we?*"

"I have enrolled at the University to become a grade school teacher, Luke."

"You have?" Luke asked, shocked.

"Yes. And I have to make a decision about whether or not to close down my law office."

Luke's heart sank. He got up and began pacing the floor. Could it be that Aggie couldn't be happy just being a homemaker? He stopped and exhaled sharply. "What about *us*, Aggie?"

"I had to plan as if we weren't going to get together, Luke—I didn't know."

Luke's brow furrowed in apprehension. "You know now, Aggie. Will you marry me?"

Aggie gazed at his anxious face a moment then suddenly jumped up onto the couch and stood there, holding her arms out wide, laughing with joy. She shouted, "YES!"

Momentarily startled by her actions and exuberance, in one long stride he reached her—wrapping his arms around her, almost squeezing the breath out of her. Suddenly, he leaned back, his eyes piercing hers. "Really?"

"Really!" For the second time, Aggie initiated a kiss full on the lips.

And what a kiss it was! Luke thought, as he returned it with all the bursting happiness of his soul. When they pulled apart, Luke exclaimed. "Wow! What am I getting myself into?!"

"More than you know, Luke Barnes, more than you know. So— look out!"

He laughed that deep, resounding joyous laugh. Picking her up, he swung her around and around until they were both so dizzy they fell onto the couch laughing and clinging to each other, remaining that way for many moments before he whispered in her ear. "What about your enrollment at the University, Aggie?"

"What enrollment?"

He laughed in relief. "You scared me, Aggie. Now what about your law firm?"

"Come with me to my law office tomorrow and see," she said, smiling.

"I will!" he grinned, his anxious heart finally at rest. "You know what, my little wood nymph?"

"What?"

"I'm starved. Let's go out to dinner."

# Chapter Forty

Tuesday morning, Luke drove into the guest parking of Aggie's condo and waited. They had agreed to meet there at 10:00 A.M. so they could go to her office. He'd stayed at Doris and Bob's the night before, and noticing how upbeat he was, Doris fired question after question at him. Since Luke refused to tell them anything until Aggie could be with him, Doris eagerly invited them both for dinner.

He smiled, remembering the events of the previous evening. Just as he was wondering if it was possible to be any happier than he was right this minute, Aggie opened the passenger door of his Lexus and got in. "Yes it is!" he exclaimed, grinning at her.

"She grinned back. "What is?"

"It *is* possible to be happier than I was a moment ago. In fact, seeing you this morning just sent my happiness thermometer soaring to such a degree, that I'm afraid it will burst any minute."

Aggie laughed and leaned over and kissed him.

"Wow! I think it just did!"

"You'll just have to arrange for a much bigger thermometer then, my darling, because you haven't seen anything yet."

Luke let out a happy sigh, smiling at what she had just called him. This wasn't the reserved Aggie he'd known. "I can hardly wait." he said, looking at her like a man with an enormous sweet tooth. He started the car. "Show me the way to your office."

When Luke arrived at the parking lot of the office building, Aggie said, "Barry Slocum's office is also in this same building. As soon as possible, we'll have to go tell him our news. He's a good friend of mine. For over five years I've hired him to help me out with many of my cases."

"I can see why. He seems like an honest and capable man, and I feel that he is my friend also," Luke said. He walked around and opened the door for her.

Together they walked up the steps of the old brick building and down the hall to the door of Aggie's office. When they entered, the surprised face of Sally greeted them.

"Hi, Sally, I want you to meet my former employer, Luke Barnes."

"Oh, how do you do, Mr. Barnes. It's nice to meet you."

"Nice to meet you too, Sally."

"Please have a seat, Luke, while I cover some things with Sally."

"Any messages from yesterday, or this morning, Sally?"

"Bunches!" she sighed. "There were more than usual yesterday and several this morning. Aggie you just have to keep your law firm open! These women are begging me to convince you to take their cases."

"Are there new ones or the same ones calling?"

"There are new ones, but the same five keep calling. I keep referring them to the two attorneys Mr. Biederman recommended, but all five said they didn't want to go to a man."

"I'll call them and talk to them as soon as I can, but I've made my decision, I *am* going to close the office."

"Oh Aggie! You should hear their cases. They are so sad, so tragic. I know you are the only one who can help them. Somehow, they've managed to find out that you have only lost one case."

Aggie glanced over at Luke noting the concern on his face. She smiled at him. "I've never known Sally to be so evangelistic over prospective cases."

"That's because," Sally began in her own defense, "I've been here fending off case after case ever since you left, Aggie and it's getting harder and harder on me to turn them away."

"Well, we'll just have to take care of that, Sally." She turned to Luke, "Come and see the rest of my office."

He followed her and Aggie closed the door. "This is my office. I'll sell the furniture and..."

"Aggie," he interrupted, taking her face in his hands, he gazed down at her, his eyes full of anxiety, "I can't ask you give up your work helping women."

"I don't remember you asking me to. This was my decision."

"Can you just leave these women in the lurch?"

"Do you want me to continue my work after we're married, Luke?"

"No...but I feel so rotten...so selfish..."

"Luke, let's go. I want to show you a special place where we can go for a walk and talk about this."

As they left the office, Aggie said, "I'll get back with you in a couple of days, Sally. I promise I'm not going to let you go through this anymore."

"All right, Aggie," she said with relief.

In the car, Aggie instructed Luke where to go. Passing her condominium complex, she told him to turn right a couple of times and then park. They got out and she took his hand and led him to a path. "The path follows this creek which is called Turtle Creek. I've always thought this would be romantic to walk along this path with the man I loved." She looked up at him with radiant eyes and smiled.

"It's a beautiful place, Aggie," he replied, still looking troubled.

They walked together, hardly aware of the already sweltering heat of the August morning. After a short time they came to a bench near the path that was shaded by a large tree. "Let's sit down, here, Luke." When they were seated, Aggie continued, "You said once you would have liked to watch me in the court room."

"Yes," he said warily, uncertain where this was leading.

"Well, you are going to see me in action—right now."

Luke looked askance at her.

Ignoring it, she went on. "You are going to play the defendant and I will be the prosecutor."

Luke laughed. "What are you doing, Aggie?"

Aggie's face turned serious. "This is important, Luke, please go along with it. I want you to present the case for me to continue practicing after we're married, with the major portion of my practice transferred to Austin and a small portion here in Dallas. I want you to be as convincing as you possibly can, and I'll be just as determined, as I cross-examine you, to prove otherwise."

He smiled, shaking his head. "Aggie, you are such an unpredictable woman—but okay, I'll do my best." He looked around. "It's a good thing it's hot today because no one wants to be outside, but us. We're quite alone in this park."

"Yes we are, with the exception of the cicadas. Their loud chorus will be cheering us on," she said, her eyes dancing with enjoyment.

Luke watched her pace up and down on the path in front of him—a wisp of a figure in the long narrow, sage colored jumper with its buttoned straps over the white T shirt. How could she possibly be a courtroom lawyer? She looked so young, so vulnerable.

Stopping in front of him she began, "Now, Mr. Barnes, you said you felt you couldn't ask your fiancé to close her law firm because there are so many women out there who need her. Is that correct?"

"Yes."

"Why do you feel that way?"

"Well, I feel a little guilty...a little selfish taking her away when she is so needed."

"Do you think there might be other attorneys out there who could help these women?"

"Yes, but I don't feel there is another one out there who is as empathetic as she is, and as well qualified to help these women."

"Do you feel you are able to be objective about this, Mr. Barnes?"

The defendant smiled. "No, but I'm not prejudiced. I have experienced her empathy, understanding and wisdom and I'm not the easiest person to understand and put up with."

"Does she love you, Mr. Barnes?"

A broad grin spread across his face. "Yes."

"Then she would naturally be more understanding and empathetic, wouldn't she?"

The defendant smiled, a confident expression on his face. "She wasn't in love with me at the time I'm talking about. I'm afraid I...uh...showed my difficult nature the first day I interviewed her, and for the next several days my actions were less than pleasant, and yet she seemed able to see through me and understand."

The prosecutor smiled. "How astute of you to see this, Mr. Barnes. So you think she's competent to do this with her clients because she's able to do this with you?"

"I do."

"Do you need her to stay home and be a full time homemaker?"

"I do."

"Is this need great?"

"Very great. My mother was a full time homemaker and I saw how nurturing it was to my father, how successful he was because she was there for him as a full time wife, counselor and companion."

"If your wife works out of the home and comes home physically and emotionally exhausted, will she be able to fill your needs?"

"There may be times she can."

"So, Mr. Barnes, your wife will be out in the work force filling the needs of abused women who need her. Who will fill your needs when she can't?"

"No one."

"When you have children, the women will still need her. Will her children need her also?"

"Yes."

"Who will fill your children's needs—needs only their mother can fill—when you are at work and your wife is out in the world filling other peoples needs?"

"No one."

"What is your wife's number one duty or responsibility?"

"Please make that more clear, Miss McBride."

"When you marry, who *belongs* to your wife, you or the women she defends in the courtroom?"

"Me."

"Then, her obligation is *to you*, is that right?"

"Right."

"Who belongs to your wife, your future children or the women who pay her to help them?"

"The children."

"Then secondly, the children are her responsibility. Right?"

"Right."

"Will the women she helps come and take care of you or the children?"

"No."

"Then who will, when your wife is tied up taking care of other peoples needs?"

"No one, or some one I hire."

"If I'm correct then, Mr. Barnes, you are willing to go without your needs being fulfilled and your children's needs not taken care of so your wife can take care of the needs of strangers who are paying her to do so?"

"The defendant was mute.

"Now, Mr. Barnes, when God gives a woman a trust...a husband and children, do you think He'll ask for an accounting of that trust someday?"

The defendant's throat constricted with emotion. "I hadn't thought about that, but it makes sense that He would."

"Are you still feeling guilty or selfish about wanting your fiancé to be a full time wife and mother when you marry?"

The defendant's eyes were moist with gratitude and happiness. "No...but when the children are raised, maybe she could go back and help those unfortunate women."

"Will her number one responsibility—*you*—be neglected and feel neglected, and feel lonely, less important?"

"Yes, but maybe I should sacrifice..."

"Mr. Barnes, have you asked your wife to be if *she* would be unhappy neglecting the one person who is more important to her than anyone else in the world?"

"No."

"Why?"

"I haven't had time. Do you think that I could have a moment to do that now, Miss McBride?"

"You may take a moment."

"Aggie, sit down here beside me." She obliged him. He took her hand in his, "Would you be unhappy neglecting me?"

"I would, Luke, more than you know. I do want to serve people, *we* both need to do that, but working as an attorney for women is so demanding, it would take my thoughts, emotions and my mind from you. You see, women tend to carry their problems and concerns of their job home. Ninety-five percent of women are not able to leave the problems at work. Whatever their job, they bring their problems home with them. So when they're at home, mentally and emotionally they aren't there one hundred percent. I've seen this problem come to the fore in case after case. This has been the complaint of many wounded, abusive husbands. Even though the way they've handled their feelings of inadequacy and their feelings of being less important, isn't always the right way, their complaints need to be taken seriously. In the broken marriages of several of my friends, this has very often been cited as a major cause by the husbands. I've learned a lot during my years as an attorney."

Aggie stood up and resumed her role. "Now that you've had a moment to ask your fiancé what her feelings are, Mr. Barnes, do you still feel guilty or selfish wanting her to stay at home and be a full time homemaker?"

"No," he stated with a broad confident smile.

"What if, Mr. Barnes, you had some financial reversals. Would you want your wife to go out into the work place?"

"No."

"Why?"

"For the same reasons you have brought out so eloquently this morning, Miss McBride."

The prosecutor knelt down in front of the defendant, took his hands in hers and gazed lovingly into his eyes. "I rest my case, Mr. Barnes."

# Chapter Forty-One

The joy and peace Luke felt, as he and Aggie walked hand in hand back to the car, was something he had begun to despair of ever feeling. He smiled, thinking of Aggie's unique way of revealing her total commitment to him and their upcoming marriage. Some tough courtroom lawyer she'd turned out to be—in the park!

Back in the condo, Aggie started preparing lunch. "So many of the things I cook with are at your house, Luke."

"*My* house? It could be *Your* house, Aggie, which brings me to several important questions. Where do you want to live? When can we be married? And all that good stuff."

Aggie stopped her preparations and sighed. "I'd rather discuss our plans before we eat lunch."

"Then, my beautiful fiancé—who doesn't even have an engagement ring yet—let's go sit down on the couch and plan."

Sitting down beside Luke on the couch, she gazed at his ruggedly good-looking face and smiled. "I can't believe that we really are engaged, but since we are, the big question is when are we going to get married?"

"Tomorrow?" he asked eagerly.

"I wish. It will take time to call some of those who have kept calling for me to take their cases, arrange to sell my office furniture and hand my lease over to a realtor to find someone else to take it over. I also have to put my condo up for sale."

"How long will that all take?"

"A couple of weeks at least."

"Is it possible to get married in a little over three weeks, Aggie? Say August 26th? That will let Amy and Ron and other family members get plane reservations ahead of time, yet it isn't so far in the future I can't stand it."

Aggie contemplated this. A slow but radiant smile spread across her face, her eyes warm with happiness. "I think I can get everything done. August 26th sounds wonderful. We need to get busy, Luke; don't we want to have as many children as time will permit?"

"Oh, Aggie...Aggie, thank you!" he exclaimed, hugging her. "I don't deserve you, but—I'm going to spend my life trying my best to do so." Presently, he leaned back against the couch, the joy on his countenance fading, knowing the next logical question was the one he dreaded asking. "What kind of a wedding do you want, Aggie?"

"I hear you and Lila had a very elaborate wedding," she said, casting him a sideways glance.

"Who told you that?"

"Mary."

"Is that what you want, Aggie?" he asked, dreading the thought.

"What if I do?" she asked, amused at the flicker of panic in his eyes.

"Then we'll have one."

Aggie laughed. "Thank you, Luke, but no thank you."

"You mean that?" he asked in relief.

"I do! I've gone to enough elaborate weddings and wedding receptions to know that is not what I want."

Luke hugged Aggie so hard she squealed, then promptly kissed her. "Okay," he grinned, "after scaring me to death, what kind of a wedding *do* you want?"

"I do want a white wedding dress."

He smiled tenderly at her and nodded. "Of course, what else?"

"Believe it or not, I have given this a lot of thought while going about my plans to try and live without you."

Gratified, Luke grinned. "In your heart, you knew you couldn't live without me, so back to the question—what kind of a wedding do you want?"

"If this isn't all right with you, Luke, we'll do something else, but this is what I would like to have. I would like to have a small wedding out on your wonderful deck—but in the early evening because of the August heat. I only want our family there and a few friends like Barry Slocum. We could cater a dinner, have a good visit and afterward leave on our honeymoon."

"Every time I think what an exceptional woman you are, Aggie, you do something else that makes you even more wonderful. I love the idea. In fact, I'm so relieved, I could jump up and click my heels."

She smiled. "I'm glad you like the idea." At length she said, "Just think, Luke, I'll have a family! Most importantly I'll have *you*, and, just imagine, my beloved Miss Marks, will be my mother-in-law! I'll have a sister, Amy, and a brother-in-law, Ron. I'll have cousins, Doris and Bob, an Aunt Edie and Uncle Jim. I'll have a grandmother and nieces and nephews!" Her deep blue eyes pooling with tears—was a stunning contrast to the rapturous smile rising from deep within. "I've been alone so long, Luke, it's hard to believe. I can hardly internalize it. Oh how I wish your parents and Mama and Beth could be here to share our happiness with us."

Luke wrapped her in his arms and held her tightly, touched at the thought of Aggie being alone for so many years without any family. "You'll never be alone again, my mother's precious little Aggie McBride."

# Chapter Forty-Two

As Doris prepared for bed, she thought of the dinner and evening with Luke and Aggie. The boys were thrilled to see Luke and jumped on him, wrestling with him. They were also happy to see Aggie.

Bob had shaken Luke's hand vigorously, chiding him about taking so long to visit, then hugged Aggie. The two of them, Aggie and Bob, threw their usual jibes at each other, but this time it was pure teasing. Doris wasn't concerned about them hurting each other as she had before. Things were different now. Almost immediately, Luke excitedly announced his and Aggie's engagement. Needless to say, this brought an uproar of shouts from the boys and more excited hugs all around.

The meal was spent mostly talking with the boys and then after dinner, Aggie and Luke played a game with them while Doris and Bob did the dishes, after which the boys were sent to bed.

Doris had kept Amy informed about Luke and Aggie, but had suggested that she not call either one—instead pray that they would be able to work out their problems. When the boys had gone to bed, Doris immediately called Amy and Ron. Turning on the speaker phone, Aggie and Luke announced to them their engagement. There was silence for a moment then they heard a squeal from Amy and an "All right!" from Ron. Luke told them the date of the wedding and explained to Amy and Doris that they would be able to relax this time, that he and Aggie would take care of all the arrangements for a outdoor wedding and dinner.

Now in her nightgown, Doris sat down beside Bob on the small couch in their bedroom. This was their nightly ritual: watch the news together, then visit awhile before going to bed. This evening they didn't turn on the news; instead, they discussed the happy events of the evening.

"Well, my lovely," Bob said, putting his arm around her, "I'll have to hand it to you. Despite my skepticism, your matchmaking worked.

Not only that, I think you may have been an instrument in the strange workings of fate."

She smiled at him. "I kind of think so myself—but I don't think 'fate' can take its course without prayer, do you?"

He thought a moment, then said, "No, Doris Ann, I guess not. I like to think that anyway. I suppose that gives us freedom of choice rather than being pawns of fate."

~~~~~~~~~~

On the way home from the Biederman's, it turned out that Aggie and Luke both wanted to tell his grandmother in person about their engagement; both were equally eager—much to Aggie's joy. Luke insisted on driving Aggie down to Austin and back. Aggie argued, explaining that it was needless driving on his part.

Luke stated firmly, "I want to make sure you get there and back safely."

"But, Luke..." Aggie began, feeling a little choked up. "I've driven myself for years. I'll be perfectly safe." Never had she felt so loved and nurtured.

"That was before you were engaged to me, my daring little tree climber."

Aggie laughed. "I promise that though I may be a daring tree climber, I'm not a daring driver."

"I'm sure you're not, my beautiful," he said, driving into Aggie's guest parking. He went around and opened the door for her. "But, I would feel much better if I could drive you down and back."

They rode the elevator silently because a couple of people got on with them. At her door, Aggie said, "Come in and let's finish the conversation."

"Finish? I thought it was finished," he replied firmly, brooking no more discussion of said subject.

"Oh, I'm totally happy with you driving me down and back. I look forward to any time I can spend with you. You see, I am starved for your company."

"You are? Me too! I mean, I'm starved for your company, too," he corrected. Closing the door behind them, he lifted her up by the waist and kissed her. Mischief flickered in the depths of his eyes. "Maybe we could find some stilts for you."

Aggie smiled as he put her down. "Come on in and sit beside me on the couch, I want to finish the conversation."

"I thought we were through with..."

"You'll have to learn about women, Luke. Conversation hardly ever ends with us because we have so much more in our minds to talk about than men can ever imagine."

"You? You're a woman of few words, Aggie and the most irritatingly silent woman I've ever known."

"I've cultivated that, Luke. Just you wait," she said with an impish grin on her face. When they seated themselves on the couch, Luke placed his arm around her and she snuggled against him. "Now to the unfinished conversation. Tell me about your father."

"Well, that's a surprise question. That's part of the conversation?"

"Of course. I know your mother, now I want to know your father."

"As I've said before, we are very much alike...both reactive so we butted heads all our lives."

"Did you admire him?"

"Very much."

"Why?"

A considerable time passed before Luke answered. "You know, since that experience with Grandmother, I'm able to concentrate more on his good points." He shook his head. "Amazing. My father was a leader. He was at one time the president of the Texas State Fair Board. He was a brilliant business man and knew how to turn a profit better than any man I ever knew.

"Amy adored him and he her. He was a good father to her—and to me actually. In spite of our run-ins, I learned a lot from him. I learned the value of hard work and I learned to have pride in workmanship. I learned to work and save money for what I wanted and needed. He didn't just hand out material things to me, I had to earn it. I found that most of my friend's fathers did just the opposite and I saw later on what that indulgence did to them. They became selfish. I would say that over half of them are divorced now."

"How did he feel about your mother?"

"I think you already know that, but I have often thought it was best that they died together. My father cherished my mother and I don't think he could have lived without her."

"He was protective of her wasn't he, Luke?"

"He was. I've never seen a man so protective of a woman as was my father of my mother—even though he let my grandmother influence him for those years before she left. Because of this quality, I can imagine, now that I'm older, how terribly he must have suffered without her those nine months. How did you know that about him? Did Gram tell you?

"No. I knew because *you* are the most protective man *I've* ever known. I knew you must have had a good role model."

Luke studied her curiously, then gazed into her intense, beautiful eyes, "Thank you for me, and for my dad."

"Did you know, Luke, that *protectiveness* is the most manly and attractive quality a man can possess?"

"It is?" he asked, straightening his shoulders slightly, expanding his chest, thoroughly pleased.

"It is. This wonderful quality began to show up in you almost immediately, therefore almost immediately, I think, I began to love you." Aggie noted the effect of her words on Luke.

"My dear Luke, as I'm sure you know, it is so rare that a man values a woman's virtue *today*—as well as his own. You are a rare man, Luke. In my line of work I've come to realize how powerful the sex drive is in a man. Few men know how desirable it makes a man, in a woman's eyes, when he's able to harness that drive."

"Thank you, Aggie, that means more to me than you could possibly know. Not many girls or women, for that matter, realize how difficult it can be for a man."

Aggie nodded. "Yes, and most girls and women, today, don't try to help a boy or man in that way."

"Thank you for helping *me* in this area, Aggie," he said, gratefully.

"You're welcome." She smiled, then continued with the thoughts she needed to express. "Luke, one of the reasons many women are drawn to the feminist movement is because the men they've known were blatantly unprotective, abusive, and selfish. I've noticed something else. I know that most women today want a career for many different reasons. However, in my practice, I found many women who truly wanted to stay home and nurture and raise their children rather than sending them to day-care. In these particular cases, the husbands demanded they go out into the work place to help provide more material things. I've been in a man's world, even though feminists insist it's a woman's world, too. I know what the marketplace is, Luke. It makes a woman *hard* because she's trying to be as tough as a man.

"Do you remember reading in those newspaper clippings when they called me 'the *Iron* Butterfly'?" He nodded in rapt attention. "Well, I was becoming hard, and I didn't like what I was becoming.

"There are many areas in which a man can be a caretaker to a woman, not just with his superior physical strength, or as a provider, but by treating her as an equal, respecting her opinion and treating her always with tenderness. Luke, my love, as far as I know, you most certainly qualify in every area."

"But, Aggie," he rebutted, his face pained, "I've been reactive with you, angry and unkind...I don't know how you can say that."

Aggie smiled. "Luke, I'm not saying we won't have some rocky times because of *both* our weaknesses, but I'm talking about your *basic nature*, my dear one."

Luke gathered Aggie up in his arms. His heart full, he murmured, "No other woman has seen these things in me. I love you, Agnes McBride."

# Chapter Forty-Three

Aggie and Luke left the next morning at 8:00, Wednesday, August 4th. It was when they were almost to Austin that Luke said, "Aggie, I had the house built for Lila and if you want to live elsewhere, we will. We'll build our own home anywhere you want, just as long as it isn't too far to drive to work."

Aggie had already given this a lot of thought. "I never felt it was Lila's home, Luke, even when Mary told me you had built it for her. I love that home and the woods around it. It's a wonderful place to raise children and if it's all right with you, I would like us to live there. Besides," she smiled at him lovingly, "it is the place I met you, got to know you and love you."

Luke, so touched he couldn't reply, could only tenderly stroke her cheek with the back of his fingers. They rode in silent contentment through Austin and on out 71 to the big old home of Grandmother Barnes. She wasn't expecting them and they smiled at each other as they drove around back and got out.

Hand in hand, they stepped up onto the porch and opened the back door. Not finding his grandmother in the kitchen, Luke put his fingers to his lips and closed the door quietly. "Gram?" he called out. No answer. They walked into the dining room and again Luke called out, "Grandmother?"

"I'm in here, Luke."

They walked on through the foyer and into the front room. Mae looked up from her reading to see Luke and Aggie standing before her hand in hand. She blinked, not believing her eyes, then murmured, "Luke...Aggie?"

"Yes, Gram, it's us," Luke said softly.

Mae closed the Bible and placed it on top of the *other book* and stood up, taking a step toward them. "You are...together?"

"Yes, Grandmother, and not only that, we are engaged to be married—thanks to *you*."

Mae, tried to swallow past the lump in her throat, still not used to letting anyone see her emotions, but it was no use. Her chin quivered, her eyes filled with tears, blurring the view of her loved ones. She smiled through the tears and held out her arms to both. They went into them, and the three of them clung together for several moments.

When they parted, Mae gazed at each of them. Her voice broke as she said, "I'm so happy...so happy," then the tears turned to sobs of joy. Luke took his Grandmother into his arms and held her, tears in his own eyes.

Aggie watched while tears slid down her own cheeks. There was something different about Mae, she thought. Not just her new found ability to show emotion and affection, but something far deeper. Her prayers for Luke and his grandmother had been answered more fully than she dared hope.

Finally, Mae looked up at her grandson and smiled, wiping her eyes and nose with her handkerchief. "Please both of you have a seat and tell me when you are going to be married."

Aggie and Luke seated themselves on the couch. Holding Aggie's hand, Luke told her their plans and the date.

Mae clapped her hands. "So soon! How wonderful. I was afraid it would be a couple of months at least."

Luke cleared his throat. "Now, Gram, what I'm going to ask of you I haven't even discussed with Aggie." Aggie looked over at him surprised, curious. "But, I know Aggie will approve wholeheartedly."

Mae looked concerned. "Oh, but, Luke, you must discuss it with Aggie first—whatever it is."

"Don't worry, Mae," Aggie assured her, "Luke knows me well enough so I'm not concerned."

"Grandmother," Luke began, "I want you to sell this big house and come and live at the cottage. I know it's small, but we can remodel it for you—make it a little larger."

Mae gasped in surprise. Aggie squealed in delight. "Oh, yes! Will you, Mae? We would love having you that close. This house is much too large for you now."

Mae's chin quivered again. "I...I don't know what is the matter with me, I just can't seem to turn off the tears lately. I...I've never done this in my life."

"I know, Gram," Luke said, smiling tenderly, "but I'm glad to see it."

With her handkerchief, Mae dabbed at her eyes. "I don't know...I don't want you to feel you have to take care of me—I don't want to be a bother."

Aggie went over, knelt down and hugged her tenderly. "A bother?" Aggie asked. "You realize I've never had a grandmother and now that I do I would like her closer to me."

Mae smiled at the young woman before her. "Aggie, I've always been independent. Maybe too much so..."

"You can still be independent, Mae."

"If I'm going to be your grandmother, Aggie," Mae began, smiling affectionately at her, "I would prefer you call me that—unless you aren't comfortable with it."

Her eyes shining, Aggie took Mae's hands in hers. "Oh, thank you, Grandmother, thank you!"

Luke was thrilled. Nothing could have pleased him more. Only God could have brought all this about, he thought, glancing at the Bible on the table that he'd noticed his Grandmother reading when they walked in.

Aggie got up and returned to her seat beside Luke. "Well, Gram?" she asked.

"Thank you, Aggie. Thank you both for that wonderful invitation. I will think about it. But let's get you two married first before any decision is made."

"All right, Gram," Luke agreed. "But again, thank you for what you were able to do for me. You opened my heart, helping me overcome my weakness and hard heart. If you hadn't—Aggie would not have even considered marrying me."

"Luke, it wasn't me. After you two are married, I have something to *show* you and *tell* you. I hid something away for years and felt impressed to go get it. When I did, I had a very special experience, a spiritual experience—one that made it possible for me to repent and ask your forgiveness."

A strange expression flickered over Luke's face, "Really?" he asked finally, intensely curious. "I...we'll be looking forward to it, Gram."

Aggie and Luke, deeply touched over what had transpired with 'their' grandmother, were silent, contemplative on the way to Luke's house. When they drove into his driveway, Aggie was surprised that he parked in the carport of the cottage. Opening the door for Aggie, he took her hand and silently led her behind the house to the old oak tree where he'd found her crying that first Sunday afternoon.

"Let's sit down, Aggie, I have something to tell you."

Surprised, Aggie looked up him and saw a serious expression on his face. "All right."

After they had seated themselves upon the ground next to the tree, Luke put his arm around Aggie. "I don't know quite how to say this or explain it. At first I thought it was only my imagination or wishful thinking, but..."

He hesitated so long, Aggie asked, "What are you talking about, Luke?"

"Well, I don't know how you feel about these kinds of things, Aggie, but Amy claims that she has *felt* Mother's presence twice. I was envious when I heard that, wishing I could feel the same thing. When I found you crying here that day and I sat down beside you and put my arm around you and told you to cry, *I* felt my mother's presence. I was so engrossed with what you were suffering it was almost unconscious.

"Later, as I thought about it, I consciously realized that I felt two things—one, that she was smiling, as if happy that I was comforting you, and the second thing, I felt she was wanting something from me." Luke had been looking straight ahead, but now turned to Aggie, noting the expression of awe on her face. "I didn't want to say anything to anyone, not even to Amy—it sounded too far fetched. But today when Grandmother said she had something to show us and tell us—that she'd had a spiritual experience, I felt my mother's presence in the exact same way. I know she was there, Aggie. I felt that what she wants—has something to do with what Grandmother wants to tell us. I don't know how I know this, but I do." He studied Aggie's face for any doubt or incredulity, but saw none. "What do you think about this, Aggie?"

Aggie's eyes, deep and thoughtful, seemed to look past him as she pondered. At last, her eyes focused on his. "I believe you. How I wish I could have felt her presence, too."

Luke held her tightly, deeply grateful that Aggie believed so wholeheartedly. "Thank you, Aggie."

"I can hardly wait to find out what your... 'our' grandmother has to tell us."

# Chapter Forty-Four

SEPTEMBER 7TH, HAWAII, ISLAND OF OAHU: Drying off in the sun after a dip in the ocean, Aggie and Luke sat on the warm golden sand, listening to the gentle lap of the water. Aggie leaned against Luke, and smiled contentedly. "Only one more day before we go back, Luke."

"Yes. These last 12 days have been wonderful. I feel as though I'd never been married before. I didn't know...didn't realize what love really was."

"Oh, my precious husband, thank you!" She smiled. "Me too!"

He put his arm around her and held her close. "Our time before we were married was so rocky, I needed this intimate—gentle, even time together."

"It has been heaven being with you night and day, Luke. I'm also looking forward to unpacking and making a real home for you," she murmured dreamily, "with family pictures on the walls, with flowers and plants in the planters." Immediately, the latter brought back the memory of their wedding day out on the large redwood deck.

She sighed with happiness, remembering all who were there. Amy, Ron and their delightful children, Doris and Bob and theirs. Barry came with two of his daughters. Aunt Edie and Uncle Jim, their two married sons and their families attended, and warmly welcomed her into the family. Bob's parents came, wishing them well. Mary was there, with a big smile on her face, happy for her and Luke. Her two sons, who grew up with Luke, attended with their families. And most important of all, Grandmother Barnes, looking lovely and happy; her radiant spirit pervading the afternoon and evening, unified and drew the family together.

The tables and umbrellas, and the delicious meal were catered so that everyone was able to relax and get acquainted.

His arms still around her, Aggie lay her face against Luke's warm, bare chest, thinking about the marriage ceremony, performed by the minister of the church Luke attended—still feeling the thrill when he said those wonderful words: "I pronounce you husband and wife." Her heart swelling with love for Luke, she pulled his head down and kissed him. Her heart expanded even more over his affectionate response. No matter how small a gesture, just a squeeze of a hand, Luke responded, gratifying Aggie's natural affectionate nature.

Luke looked at his watch. He and Aggie had planned on minimal sight seeing, only wanting each other's company, but this afternoon they had scheduled a trip to the Polynesian Cultural Center. They had been told by several people that this was a must.

"I guess it's time to go, he said, squeezing her. "I love you, Mother's little Aggie McBride...Barnes!"

~~~~~~~~~~

They walked hand in hand at the Polynesian Cultural Center. Stopping and watching each performance: boating, dance, music and drums, all participants dressed in colorful native costumes. They had already enjoyed fresh coconut and sun-ripened pineapple, now they tasted poi, and learned about the different traditions and foods of the several Polynesian cultures represented by native students attending college in Hawaii.

As they neared the end, a free bus tour to see the LDS temple was again announced. Luke looked questioningly at Aggie. "Do you want to go?"

"I would like to see it."

"I would, too," he replied, "but I would rather go in our own car. I'm still a little selfish about sharing you with the public just yet."

~~~~~~~~~~

Parking the car, Aggie and Luke walked toward the Hawaii Temple of the Church of Jesus Christ of Latter-day Saints. A feeling of awe came over both of them as they looked at the magnificent edifice, framed by two rows of stately palms, built in the style that fit the cultures they had just seen. They walked the beautiful grounds in silence, then found a place to sit down.

"This is the first Mormon temple I've ever seen, Luke," she said almost in a whisper. "I've heard there is one in Dallas, but I've never seen it."

"I've seen the Washington D.C. temple. It's totally different than this one, and just as awe inspiring. What are you feeling, Aggie?"

"The word that comes to mind is 'sacred.' Somehow that word describes how I feel about these grounds and this temple."

"Interesting. That's close to the word that came to my mind— 'holy,' that we are on holy ground—yet I know nothing about the Mormon Church or its beliefs."

"I don't know anything about it either, other than the famed Mormon Tabernacle choir. But there is a—special feeling here, Luke."

Luke shook his head, puzzled. "I don't know if I'm imagining it, but what I'm experiencing here is the same warm feeling I had when we were talking with Grandmother the day we went to see her to announce our engagement. Do you think it's my imagination, Aggie?"

The strange expression on her face told Luke the answer before she spoke. "If it is, Luke, I must be imagining the same thing."

They got up and slowly walked back to the parking area to the car, glad that they had one more day together before returning to the mainland.

# Chapter Forty-Five

OCTOBER 7TH, AUSTIN, TEXAS: Letting the warm October sun bathe her face and arms, Aggie relaxed in one of the new, comfortable deck chairs. She smiled as she looked around at the Fall flowers she'd planted in the once barren planters. They were a lovely contrast to the stand of pristine woodland behind them. The leaves on all the trees, with the exception of the evergreens like the live oak and juniper, would be turning yellow, orange and red in several weeks. "It's so beautiful here," she murmured, feeling like the luckiest woman in the world.

Soon, Luke would be home. They were driving out to Grandmother's for dinner. They hadn't seen her since returning from their honeymoon. However they had talked to her at least three times a week. She and Luke had had so much to do—packing and moving all her belongings from Dallas to Austin—along with all the unpacking, hanging pictures, planting flowers and many other sundry things.

Mary was returning tomorrow. She had spent these last six weeks with her son in El Paso, overseeing the building of the addition to her son's home—her new living quarters. It will be good having Mary back, Aggie thought. As soon as everything is completed, she would be moving to El Paso permanently, but with the promise she'd visit as often as she could.

Excitement welled up inside her again, propelling her from the chair to go watch for Luke. Two things caused this excitement—first, hearing what Grandmother was going to tell them. She and Luke had been burning up with curiosity ever since they had returned. The second and most exciting was the wonderful news she had for Luke—news she'd been suspecting, but until this morning didn't know for sure.

Just as she entered the kitchen, Luke walked in. "Luke!" She almost leaped into his arms, she was so happy to see him. "I'm so glad you're home!" she exclaimed.

He laughed, returning her hug. His heart rejoiced every time he came home; this was the kind of greeting he always got. Almost, that is. There seemed to be a little more excitement in his wife tonight. "What's up, my little wood nymph?"

Aggie smiled, her eyes radiant. "You can see it?"

"I can. Come over here to the couch and tell me about it."

Aggie sat beside him and snuggled against him and said, "We have a lot to do."

"All I can think of at the moment is buying furniture for the front room. That was next on the agenda, anyway, wasn't it?"

"The agenda has been changed."

"Oh? What's next then?"

"We have to buy a baby bed."

Luke's silence lasted only a moment. An expression of incredulity on his face he exclaimed, "You're pregnant!"

"I am! I went to the doctor this morning and the test came out positive."

He cradled her gently in his arms, his eyes misty. "Oh Aggie, Aggie! I never thought I could feel this happy."

"Me too, Luke. What do you want, a boy or a girl?"

"I've waited so long for this, Aggie, I don't care. I just want a healthy baby—I just want 'our' baby."

"I love you, Luke. You've made me so happy these few short weeks, and now I get to bear your child—a crowning moment for me, my beloved husband."

"Thank you," was all he could manage right then. They clung together many moments, savoring their joy, then Luke smiled. "Grandmother says she has something to tell *us*—well, we have something to tell *her*!"

"Let's go, Luke, I can hardly wait."

~~~~~~~~~

Mae found it difficult waiting until Luke and Aggie got settled, but she knew that it was best. They needed to have time to adjust to their new life together before she told them. Everything was ready except for seasoning the vegetables, which she did just as Luke and Aggie walked into the kitchen.

"Luke! Aggie!" Mae exclaimed, noting their radiant faces. "It certainly looks like marriage is agreeing with both of you," she said hugging each one.

"Well, something is agreeing with *you*, Gram," Luke said, "I think you look at least five years younger."

"If happiness makes a person look younger, then I'll believe that compliment, Luke. Are you hungry?"

"We're starved!" Aggie stated with enthusiasm as she peeked into a pan and saw mashed potatoes. "Mmm, is there gravy to go with these?"

"There is. I have a roast in the oven. Will you get it out for me, Luke?"

"I would be more than glad to do that, Gram." Opening the oven, Luke lifted the pan out and set it on the stove.

"Luke," Aggie said, "I can't wait."

"Okay, tell her then, Aggie."

"Tell me what?" Mae asked, stopping in mid-movement.

"We're going to have a baby."

"Oh! Oh my." Mae hugged her new granddaughter exuberantly. "I'm so happy for you both...and for myself. How are you feeling, Aggie?"

"I didn't even think to ask her that, Gram. Yes, how *are* you feeling, Aggie," Luke asked concerned.

"I'm feeling wonderful. I'm starting to want a nap in the afternoon, but so far I don't have morning sickness."

"I'm so glad, my dear," Mae said. "A few women are lucky that way. No wonder you're starved. Please be seated, everything is ready."

During the meal, between Aggie's enthusiastic compliments over the food, Luke told his grandmother what they had done to the interior of the house and the exterior such as planting flowers, then he asked her when she wanted to look at remodeling plans for the cottage.

"I think in about three months," she said.

"You are going to come then?" Aggie asked eagerly.

"Yes, my dear, I want to live by my new granddaughter as well as my grandson."

Aggie and Luke both got up and went over and hugged her. "Thank you, Gram," Luke said.

"Thank *you*," my dear children.

~~~~~~~~~~

The dinner over and the dishes done, the three of them settled comfortably in the front room.

"Now, Gram," Luke began, "Aggie and I have been anxious to hear what you have to tell us."

"And I have been just as anxious." She cleared her throat. "First, I have to apologize to you and Amy, Luke. I took something from your mother's piano the day of the plane crash. I was in such a state of grief and shock, I brought it home to look at it. But before I go any further, I need to tell you about your great grandfather, Luke—my father." Mae told of his fanatic piousness and his cruelty and coldness, and of her mother's aloofness. "I'm wondering if this aloofness stemmed from fear of my father. I don't know what caused my father to be like that, Luke. Maybe his father..." She left the thought unfinished.

"Why didn't you tell us about this before, Gram? We could have understood you better."

"I didn't think about it, Luke. I thought that was the way parents should be with children such as I. I need to tell you about it now because what I picked up from the piano was a book. When I got home, I sat down at the table, looked at the book and saw that it was some kind of religious book. I saw your mother read the Bible often, Luke, so I wasn't surprised, but the more I looked at it, the more bitter I felt toward God who had just taken my children from me. In my mind he was the punitive God that my father had taught me about. I couldn't look at the book a minute longer, so I took it upstairs and put it in the bottom of my cedar chest under the linens so it would be out of my sight, intending to give it to you and Amy later. Well—I forgot about it.

"When I was worrying about you and Aggie and suffering because I felt it was my fault, I became so desperate I decided to kneel down and pray to God in spite of my fear of Him. When I got up from praying, I suddenly remembered the book. I went upstairs retrieved it and brought it down here to look at it." She lifted her Bible and picked up the book from underneath. "This is the book. As you can see it is a *Book of Mormon.*"

Aggie and Luke were startled. They looked at each other in wonder then back to their grandmother.

Mae noticed their reaction. "What is it?"

"We'll tell you later, Gram. Please go on," Luke said.

When I opened this book, I read the first thing that caught my eye. If you don't mind I would like to read it to you now. Mae read, and again felt as she had the first time. She gazed at Aggie and Luke with tears in her eyes. "When I read this, I wondered if He could really be the loving God it seemed to indicate. If He was, I wondered if He could love *me* in spite of my mistakes, mistakes that had caused so much suffering to your parents, to you, Luke, and to Amy.

"As I was wondering this, a warm feeling came over me bringing with it a peace I had never felt before. It was then I knew that God was a *loving* God, and that He did indeed love *me* and..." Mae stopped and looked down, fingering the lace on her handkerchief, trying to quell the tears, "and—that He *knew* me." She looked up, noting the rapt attention of her small audience. "I sat there savoring this wonderful sensation then read another couple of verses." Mae read these aloud, then gazed at Luke and Aggie. "The sentence that forced its attention on me was: "'...cast off your sins and not procrastinate the day of your repentance.'

"Growing up, I had a feeling of revulsion at the word 'repent' because of my father's constant denunciation of everyone, but himself, that everyone was depraved and wicked needing to repent of their sins...especially me. Though this made me feel terribly guilty, I didn't know what sins I had committed. But, after what I had just experienced, the word *repent* took on a new meaning—the correct meaning. I knew, Luke, in order to help *you*, I had to repent of the actions that had caused you and your family such pain. So...I knelt down once more, and this time begged His forgiveness...." Mae's struggle to gain control was unsuccessful.

Aggie jumped up and put her arm around her. Luke followed, crouching down on the other side, tenderly patting her knee. Regaining her composure, Mae gazed at each of her grandchildren and smiled.

"Don't feel stressed over my tears, they are good tears, tears of joy. Please be seated. I have something else to tell you."

"It's just that I'm not used to seeing you show emotion, Grandmother," Luke said, sitting down and taking Aggie's hand.

"I know. As you might guess, I began reading this Book of Mormon and...well, there is a special spirit about this book so I decided I wanted to know more about the Mormon Church. After making a few calls I was given a number to call here in the Bastrop area. It was only a day before the missionaries came to my home. I have been taking 'the lessons' as they call them. The next lesson will be number five and I have already committed to baptism."

"What do you mean, Grandmother?" Luke asked.

"I'm going to be baptized into the Church of Jesus Christ of Latter-day Saints."

"Why?" Luke asked abruptly.

"Because I know it is the true Church of Jesus Christ."

"How do you know that?"

"Luke, did you feel anything when I read those verses from the Book of Mormon?"

Aggie looked over at Luke, waiting for his answer which was a long time coming.

"Did you, Luke?" she asked.

"Yes, I did, but..."

"That was the Spirit, Luke," informed his grandmother.

"The what?"

"I didn't understand at first, either, Luke, but the missionaries explained it to me."

"Feeling something and taking a big step such as joining a strange church at your age, Grandmother, are two different things."

"I'm not asking your permission, Luke, I'm asking if you and Aggie will attend my baptism."

He frowned, "I don't know."

"What about you, Aggie, will you attend?"

"I would like to, Gram, but not without Luke."

Luke stood up to leave. "If that's what you want to do, go ahead, Gram, but I don't approve of it."

"Why?" Mae asked, more disappointed than she dare let on. Luke was silent.

"Here, I have a Book of Mormon for each of you. I would like you both to read it."

"No thank you. Let's go, Aggie. Thanks for the dinner, Grandmother."

Aggie walked out with Luke leaving a stunned and unhappy Mae.

When they were outside, Aggie said, "Luke, have you forgotten what you told me?"

"What do you mean?"

"You said that Gram held the key to what your mother wanted you to do."

"I know, but..."

"And remember how we felt at the Mormon temple in Oahu?"

He nodded.

"There must be something special about that book, Luke, to cause Grandmother to change like she has. When I first came here, she was rigid, unbending with a protective shell around herself. Now—there's a soft, mellow spirit about her—a spirit of serenity. She's flexible enough to leave the familiar surrounding and friends of so many years just to come and live at the cottage near us."

Luke pondered on this, and exhaled a heavy breath. "Thank you, Aggie, for reminding me. Let's go back."

"Thank *you*, Luke," she said, smiling up at him, her heart bursting with love for him. Taking his hand, they returned.

Mae looked up, surprised and greatly relieved.

"I'm sorry, Grandmother," Luke said. "I don't know what got into me. We want the books after all—and we will attend your baptism."

Mae clapped her hands with joy. "Oh, thank you, Luke, thank you Aggie! You walked out so abruptly I didn't get to tell you the rest of the story."

"There's more?" Luke asked as he and Aggie returned to their place on the couch. "If it wasn't for Aggie, we'd be on our way to Austin right now. Please...tell us the rest, Gram."

"There was a note inside the Book of Mormon when I found it. It said: 'Appointment at Sandra's—2:00 P.M. Friday.' I didn't know who

Sandra was, but as I read the book, I knew I had to find someone to tell me more about the Mormon Church. I decided to ask Cherie Burke if she knew who Sandra was. She said that Sandra was a close friend of your mother's and that she lived in Austin and that her last name was Bowles. She didn't know her husband's name or her phone number. I came home and called all the Bowles in the phone book until I found her. Sandra told me something quite startling." She smiled at Luke.

"She did? Go on Gram," he said, intensely curious once more.

"Sandra told me that your mother had been meeting with the Mormon missionaries at Sandra's home. She had taken all the lessons and wanted to get baptized, all this without telling King. She didn't dare tell him, but finally decided to confess. He was angry at first, but through gentle persuasion she convinced him to read the Book of Mormon. Well, apparently," Mae was eager to add, "the book touched his heart, so he agreed to take the lessons also."

"You're not serious!" Luke exclaimed in disbelief.

"I am, Luke. I was just as surprised as you. He only had four lessons before deciding *he* wanted to be baptized. They had set the date tentatively for three weeks later, depending on yours and Amy's schedule, Luke. They were going to ask all of us to attend their baptism."

"They were?" he asked, still trying to internalize what he was hearing. "What happened?"

"You know what happened, Luke."

"You mean...you mean, they were killed before they could be baptized?"

"Yes, Luke."

Tears stung his eyes. "What a rotten deal! I wish they could have at least been baptized..."

"They still can, Luke," Mae interrupted quickly.

"What are you talking about?"

"I expressed the same disappointment to the missionaries and they told me about the work that is done in the temples. They do vicarious work for the dead...like baptism."

Luke frowned. "What do you mean vicarious baptism?"

Mae explained. "The Christian churches of the world believe that if you don't accept Christ, and some include baptism, in this world you are lost forever. Does it seem to you that a just and loving God would condemn the millions who never heard of Christ to eternal punishment?"

"I've never really thought about it," Luke said, "but now that you mention it, it doesn't seem right. I know Mother always said that God would judge everyone fairly."

"Of course," said Mae. "So if everyone is to be judged fairly they should all have the same opportunity to accept or reject Christ. And, since baptism is, according to the Bible, necessary for all who accept Christ, those who have died without this opportunity can have the baptism performed for them vicariously, by those who have the authority. This is done in the temples."

Luke and Aggie looked at each other for several moments. "Are you feeling what I am, Aggie?" Luke asked.

She smiled and nodded her head in wonder. "I think I am, Luke."

"This is what Mother wanted, Aggie!"

Aggie's eyes were shining with tears and excitement. "It must be, Luke."

"What are you two talking about?" Mae asked.

Luke related everything—about feeling his mother's presence twice, his understanding of it and what he felt Mae's role was in it. Next, he told her of the experience he and Aggie had at the Mormon temple in Hawaii.

Mae closed her eyes a moment and uttered a silent prayer of thanks. She smiled at her grandchildren and exclaimed, "This is a direct answer to my prayers! I prayed that He would prepare you both so you would accept what I had to tell you—and He did!"

~~~~~~~~~~

On the way home, Aggie and Luke silently pondered everything they had learned. Aggie held the Books of Mormon on her lap. A feeling of reverence came over her as she rubbed her hand over the moonlit sub-title: *Another Testament of Jesus Christ.* Her 'Miss Marks' believed this to be true! She remembered the commitment she and Luke had made to his grandmother—that they would each read it, and she could hardly wait to open its pages.

As they drove into their garage, Aggie asked, "How could so much of an important nature happen in one day, Luke?"

He smiled and shook his head. "Between the news of the baby and what we learned tonight, I find it all hard to absorb." He got out, went around and opened the door for his wife. Hand in hand they entered the kitchen. Luke looked down at Aggie, who was hugging the Books of Mormon, feeling such overwhelming love for her he couldn't speak. Instead, he wrapped his arms around her and held her close for a few moments, then taking her hand walked down the hall, ascended the staircase and entered their bedroom.

He led her to the picture on the chest of drawers, still amazed at what he'd learned about his parents. Together they studied the picture of King and Ann Barnes, poignantly aware of their continuing influence on their lives.

He turned to Aggie. "When you told me about the baby, I was so hopeful for our future. But something tells me that because of our visit to Grandmother tonight and our commitment to attend her baptism plus read the Book of Mormon, our future is going to far surpass our expectations."

Looking up at the man she loved more than life, she replied with a question, "It is?"

He nodded and smiled. "Let's get ready for bed, Aggie, then let's read a little out of those books you have clutched next to your heart."

Happiness flooded through her. He was as anxious as she was! "Let's do!"

Sitting up in bed with only the lamp lights on, Aggie and Luke each took a book and opened it. Silently they read the introduction, the testimony of the three witnesses, the testimony of the eight witnesses and the testimony of the Prophet Joseph Smith. Glancing at Luke, Aggie could tell by the expression on his face he was as deeply moved as she was.

As Luke finished reading the brief explanation about the Book of Mormon, he exclaimed, "This book is a history! A compilation of records—and my parents believed that it is what it claims to be. Let's read the first chapter out loud together, Aggie."

"I would like that very much, Luke. You read."

"All right." He began: *I Nephi, having been born of goodly parents....* " He stopped and gazed at his wife. "You know, Aggie, your sweet mother—my parents—"

"Yes! *We*, too, have been born of '*goodly parents.*'"

He wrapped his arms around Aggie and breathed out a heartfelt utterance, "And I'm feeling an overwhelming gratitude to them—and to the *loving* God Grandmother has discovered."

Tears rolled down Aggie's cheeks. "Me, too, my beloved, me too."